The Apparition Phase

Originally from the Wirral, Will Maclean has been fascinated by ghost stories since he was a child, and has been writing them almost as long as he can remember. He's written for television professionally since 2006, during which time he's worked as a scriptwriter for people as varied as Alexander Armstrong, Al Murray and Tracey Ullman. He is the writer and creator of the Audible Original paranormal comedy drama series 'High Strangeness'. He's written extensively for children's television, and has been part of writing teams that have picked up two BAFTAs and an International Emmy. He lives in London with his wife and young daughter.

Will Maclean

The Apparition Phase

WILLIAM HEINEMANN: LONDON

1 3 5 7 9 10 8 6 4 2

William Heinemann
20 Vauxhall Bridge Road
London SW1V 2SA

William Heinemann is part of the Penguin Random House group of companies
whose addresses can be found at global.penguinrandomhouse.com.

Penguin
Random House
UK

First published by William Heinemann in 2020

www.penguin.co.uk

A CIP catalogue record for this book is available from the British Library.

ISBN 9781785152375 (Hardback)
ISBN 9781785152382 (Trade Paperback)

Typeset in 13/15 pt Perpetua Std by Jouve (UK), Milton Keynes
Printed and bound in Great Britain by Clays Ltd, Elcograf S.p.A.

For Vic

She didn't mean to cause a haunting. She was, however, well aware of how the haunting came to be. Some words that define that particular time: "malignant", "lost", or, in more paranoid times, "premeditated".

High Static, Dead Lines, Kristen Gallerneaux

I

1

And so the first thing my twin sister and I did, when we finally got access to a camera of our own, was fake a ghost photograph.

It was the kind of plan that seemed entirely natural and logical to us, and like so much else that passed between us, the plan was unspoken. I remember both of us being in the attic, in that initial frenzy of creativity, using white chalk to draw on the brown-painted plaster. Almost everything in our house was dark brown, or dark orange, or at least that's how I remember it now. As children, we used to draw with chalk on that wall all the time, but we were almost fourteen years of age now, and our pursuits were more macabre, if not yet more grown-up. And the attic was ours, it belonged to us, and we could do as we pleased there. Mum never came up, not even to tidy, and Dad only ventured up to tell us to come downstairs, raising a bemused eyebrow at whatever bizarre project we were involved in (and there were usually several on the go at once). And so, up there, our works surrounded us.

Just as the plan to fake a ghost photograph had been decided between us on some pre-linguistic level, so too was the execution of the drawing itself – the *design* of our ghost. We spent enough time reading, writing and thinking about ghosts to know precisely what the rules were in this department. Abigail and I were connoisseurs of ghost photographs and ghosts in general, and were very discerning about what was scary and disturbing, and what wasn't. We had many books on the subject, and although our parents didn't actively indulge our fascinations, they tolerated them. And if we wanted to read about ghosts and spirits, well, so be it, as long as it meant we were reading.

Not that our interests were limited to ghosts. We were also interested in standing stones, witches, curses, the British countryside, the ancient Egyptians (with particular emphasis on their burial rites), the Vikings, voodoo, vampires, the mythical giant squid, real-life accounts of people being attacked (and even better, devoured) by large wild animals, Dracula, *Doctor Who*, space exploration, the futuristic domed cities that people would one day live in on the ocean floor, pond life, medieval history, medieval weaponry, medieval siege warfare, eclipses, coral reefs, escapology, how to start fires, UFOs, card tricks, astronomy, astrology, secret codes and alphabets, invisible ink . . . and so on. Despite all this, I still think that we were not unusual children. Not for then.

Ghosts were, however, a perennial fascination for us, and there was nothing we didn't know about the Drummer of Tedworth, or The Screaming Skull of Bettiscombe Manor, or the Poltergeist of Borley Rectory, and a hundred other strange and peculiar stories. We kept scrapbooks. We swapped opinions, and we wrote earnest monographs on scrap paper. We were experts.

Abigail and I were in mutual agreement as to the best ghost photographs ever taken. There were many good ones, and we had scrapbooks full of such pictures, but three truly extraordinary ones were in a class of their own. We both knew

4

exactly which books or magazines or newspaper clippings these nightmares were hidden in, and we always proceeded with caution when looking at them, as if the images themselves might leak into our world: into our house, our attic, our very lives.

Our all-time top three ghost photos were as follows, in reverse order of scariness. They will be instantly familiar, I imagine, to anyone of a certain age:

3. The Tulip Staircase Ghost

In 1966, a retired clergyman from British Columbia took a picture of the empty Tulip Staircase in the Queen's House at Greenwich. And – of course – upon getting the negatives developed, he discovered an image of a spectral figure, ascending the stairs. The figure itself is eerie and sad rather than frightening; there's something about its pose that has a desperation to it, a palpable fatigue, as it hurls itself once again up the staircase it presumably must hurl itself up for all eternity.

2. The Chinnery Photograph (aka 'Dead mother in back of car')

The so-called 'Chinnery photograph' depicts a man sitting in what first appears to be a hackney cab but is in fact just an old-fashioned car. He wears the perfunctory smile of someone enduring being photographed. Everything about the photo appears banal, apart from the fact that the man's dead mother-in-law can clearly be seen behind him, on the back seat. Her face is expressionless, but – most terrifying of all – her eyes (or possibly her glasses) are glowing white, without pupils. It is a shocking, unpleasant image. If these patches are indeed her eyes, what has happened to her? What unimaginable things has she seen, to do that to her eyes?

1. The Ghost Monk of Newby

The Church of Christ the Consoler, Skelton-cum-Newby, Yorkshire: a black-and-white image of a church altar. Standing on the right-hand side of the image is a figure, brazen and almost defiant, dressed in a long black monk's cowl. It is tall, this figure, and very *long*. Everything about it implies *length*, as if it's been stretched somehow. It is transparent, and the altar steps and the rear of the church are visible through the figure's outline. But those are things you only notice later, if you dare, because the first thing that strikes you is the face. The face – such as it is – is a piece of white cloth with ragged eyeholes, like thumbholes in rough clay, with nothing human to refer to at all. Just that horrible, faceless gaze.

As children, Abigail and I found this image almost transcendentally terrifying, and neither of us were ever able to look at it for long. I had vivid nightmares about that faceless face, and used to hide under the hot cavern of my bedclothes on sleepless summer nights, terrified that this tall spectre might be towering over me. The Monk of Newby looks like it intends to cause harm, and offers nothing but malevolence to anyone unlucky enough to cross its path. It was the closest to how we imagined a real ghost might appear.

So, given our expertise in this area, we were painstaking in the execution of our fake ghost. We were good at drawing, so we worked together, Abigail standing on a chair to do the finer detail of the face – not that there was much detail, or much face – and me working beneath her on the general outline. Our first rule was that it should look roughly human, in shape and size. As tall as possible, without scraping the ceiling. Secondly, we shouldn't include any specific facial features. Neither of us was good enough an artist to draw a face that would pass as 'real' anyway, so the more nebulous it was, the more convincing it would be. We agreed that our ghost would be a creature of smoke, of cobwebs, of moonlight, made of insubstantial mist that faded as soon as it was perceived. Even then, we overdid the face with heavy strokes of chalk, and might have given up entirely had Abigail not spat on the flat edge of her palm and ground the face out in angry slashing strokes. After that happy accident, the face was perfect – a clashing patch of light and shade, like bad weather, with angry, empty eyes. It looked less like a face than several faces competing for the same space. We were pleased, and astute enough to know perfection when we saw it, leaving it untouched thereafter. We filled in the rest of the outline with the same spit-and-shine *sfumato* that Abigail had brought to the face. When we were done, we took the chair away and examined our work.

Upon assessing the entire thing, Abi had second thoughts. She argued that it was static, cardboard, not possessed of any kind of animus at all. An observer would suspect they were looking at something inert, something that may not be instantly familiar, but was clearly made, somehow, of familiar things.

'It needs to *live*,' she said.

'It can't,' I said. 'It's dead.'

'I don't mean that. We need an invocation, Tim. To invite it to exist.'

We had already spent ages on the drawing, and I just wanted to take the pictures. 'You do it, then.'

'I will,' said Abi. She went off to her room and returned five minutes later to present me with a sheet of paper, on which she had written a poem:

I am not here
I am not real
I do not fear
I do not feel

I do not eat
I do not drink
I do not breathe
I do not think

I do not know
I do not care
I cast no shadow
Anywhere —

I cannot give
I cannot lie
I cannot live
I cannot die

I am no woman
Nor a man
I don't exist;
Yet here I am.

'Perfect,' I said. And it was, somehow. We read it out loud; solemnly, a verse each, a strange little ceremony that made me uneasy, and then we set up the camera.

We took a whole roll of pictures, which seemed a monstrous extravagance at the time. As we were, when all was said and done, thirteen years old, we didn't think to take pictures from any other angle than face-on, dead centre, so our images would all be identical. We didn't tell our parents that we'd made these pictures, of course, and were careful to erase all traces of our ghost with a wet sponge. After we'd done that, I discovered we somehow still had one exposure left, so I took one of Abi, smiling back at me, in front of the now-clean wall.

We were equally careful when we went to collect the pictures from Boots a fortnight later. Abi distracted Mum by discussing shampoo whilst I paid for the photos and tucked them into the waistband of my trousers, where the glossy packet stuck to my stomach. When we got home, we contrived an excuse to scramble up to the attic as soon as we could, and examine the pictures.

The photo of Abi had, for some reason, ended up at the top of the stack, despite being the last one taken. Something about her smile made her look much older, much more serious than she was, as if her adult self were staring through at us from some unspecified future point. We both found this hilarious.

The images of our ghost, too, were different to our expectation of them, but they were not disappointing. What was good about the pictures was that they were *strange,* they did not immediately make visual sense. You weren't quite sure what you were seeing. One of them – the one we judged to be the best – was properly creepy, the smudges of chalk suggesting a damaged, furious face in which two awful eyes glared.

Of course, as the artists and perpetrators of this hoax, we had little perspective on our work, and our opinion was irrelevant. We would need to test it.

At first we considered taking it into school and showing a teacher, but as there were so many ways in which this could backfire, we quickly rejected it.

'What about showing the whole class?' I asked, as we sat with our dinners on our laps that night, watching *Ace of Wands* on television.

'Showing the whole class what?' said Mum, as she entered the living room with a bottle of ketchup.

'Nothing,' I said guiltily, but Mum didn't hear as Abigail talked over me. 'The sea urchin,' she said loudly, covering my voice entirely.

'Oh *that*,' said Mum, and walked out again. A while back, my sister had bought a large red sea urchin shell from a jumble shop for a halfpenny. It had been furred with grey dust when Abigail had picked it up, but after careful scrubbing had come up bright red, and my sister was proud of it. She kept it in her room, on her dresser, next to the three whelk shells she'd picked up off the beach in Dorset and the ram's horn from a field in Cornwall. I had a similar cache of semi-legal natural treasures in my own room, including the entire sloughed skin of an adder, itself a kind of ghostly after-image of the entire animal.

'I said, what about showing the whole class?'

'We're not talking about this now,' said Abigail, without turning her gaze away from the television. She was sometimes capable of an incredibly adult tone of voice and turn of phrase; it always stopped me dead. We didn't discuss the photo again until we were in the attic.

'I could show it to Malcolm Carpenter?' I said.

My sister made a face. Malcolm Carpenter was a gigantic, placid boy in our year, too large to do anything but stand out, too enormous to be bullied, and too benignly stupid to do much of anything else except eat, which he seemed to do constantly. I judged him to be particularly credulous: I had once seen Michael Shayler convince him that his dad was Evel

Knievel, despite there being no way on earth that Malcolm Carpenter couldn't know that Michael Shayler's dad worked in the carpet shop on the high street. I had watched in wonder as Malcolm Carpenter rearranged his universe to accommodate this new information, to make this contradictory and ludicrous lie make sense.

'*Malcolm Carpenter*,' muttered my sister contemptuously. 'An endorsement from Malcolm Carpenter carries no *weight*.' She was talking like an adult again, which meant she was thinking.

'How about Chris Bennett?' I said. Chris Bennett was the only black kid in our school, the eldest son of the only black family in our town. As such, he probably had more than enough to deal with. My sister waved her hand dismissively at me, and I fell silent. She was gazing at the empty wall, where our ghost had once been.

'Janice Tupp,' she said at last. 'Of course.'

Of course. Janice Tupp. She was perfect. Forever on the periphery, a melodramatic and sickly-looking girl whose hair was always in two long pigtails. She had a nervous, hunted look to her, as if she expected the universe to be consistently unkind to her, which, to be fair, it consistently was. The only other impression I had of her was her nasal laugh, which would make itself jarringly conspicuous during assemblies. She was perfect.

'Yes,' I said.

2

All the next morning at school, Abigail pretended to be secretly troubled, nursing some terrible agony, playing up this private crisis as much as she could in the vicinity of Janice Tupp. Finally, at lunchtime, she took Janice to one side in the playground, and they sat with their backs to the tall brick wall with the wonky cricket stumps painted on it as Abigail told of the Secret Horror of Our Attic. I watched from across the playground, full of admiration for my sister.

We had agreed beforehand to keep the story as simple as we could, but resisting the chance to embellish on our ghost's story had proved impossible. As it stood, the story was this: Abigail had been having a strange recurring dream for some weeks now. In the dream, she would be asleep in her bed when she became aware of strange noises in the attic above her bedroom. It was always the same sequence: a scrape, followed by a thud, repeating over and over again, scrape, thud, scrape, thud, scrape, thud. This would stop with a final, definite thud, and then a horrible silence would descend, which, if anything, was worse than the scrapes and the thuds.

Then would come a truly horrible sound, a wet scream that gargled away to nothingness, and then only a terrible squeaking, ticking sound, as of a tense, taut rope swinging, with a heavy deadweight at the end of it.

Our faith in the deductive powers of Janice Tupp were not great, however, so in the dream, we had Abigail get out of bed, go up the ladder and see a young, beautiful woman, in a wedding dress, swinging from a noose, beneath her the heavy wooden chest she'd dragged across the attic floor for the purpose.

The wedding dress was my idea.

We were right to spell it out, as it was only at the end that the story really came together for Janice Tupp, and her hand went involuntarily to her mouth. The implication was clear, Abigail told Janice, in case it wasn't. On her wedding day, a young bride, who had lived in our house, discovered that her husband-to-be was cheating on her – with her sister, we decided, though we'd only address that if it came up – and as the bridal carriage waited outside, she went up to the attic to do the only thing that now made sense to her. And there she is still, doomed to repeat the last few minutes of her life for ever. I wanted to add the creepy detail that Abigail and I had both been having the exact same dream, but Abigail said that just made things overly complicated, and so left it out.

Abigail would then go on to tell how she was alone in the house one afternoon, and heard the scrapes and thuds in the attic for real, not in a dream. Terrified, she ran up the ladder to see if there was anyone up there. And there, scared out of her mind, she saw the terrible bride, with her rotting face and her black, bottomless eyes.

The weakest part of our story was the last bit. How had Abigail managed to take a picture, whilst being absolutely terrified? We never succeeded in making this sound anything but contrived, like something from the adventure stories we had grown up reading with a relentlessly critical eye, where plucky eleven-year-olds somehow have the presence of mind and physical strength to grab a gun from an armed robber. We settled on the following: the terrible bride began to fade away, but Abigail grabbed her camera and took one single snap before it faded away completely. It stank, but it would have to do. Somehow, I didn't imagine Janice Tupp would dig too deeply into the logic of it all.

Most of the conversation between Abigail and Janice was too far away to read, but the moment when Abigail revealed the photo was unmistakeable. Janice started suddenly and tried to stand, her back sliding up the wall as she pushed away from the ground. Her eyes never left the picture. She tensed up and, to the surprise of both myself and Abigail, ran away, as fast as she could, zig-zagging this way and that through the various games of football and tag taking place across the playground, until she was out of sight.

I judged from this that our photo was a success.

Half the playground away, Abigail grinned at me with evident pride. We had achieved something amazing. Maybe we could now even send the picture to the local paper and get it published, fooling the world like the two girls who took the Cottingley Fairy photographs in 1917, although an audience of sceptical grown-ups would be a lot harder to convince than Janice Tupp. Abigail and I had agreed not to speak at school about the photo. We would decide on what course of action was best at the end of the day. I was feverishly excited.

The next lesson after lunch was Comprehension, presided over by Mr Crutton, a fearsome man in his late fifties who wore an ancient green suit and had luxuriant white hair spilling from ears that supported the arms of his tortoiseshell-framed glasses. Mr Crutton insisted on absolute silence in his classes and, after setting us a series of tedious exercises that would last the exact duration of the lesson, would invariably spend the next hour reading the *Daily Telegraph*. He always smelled of pipe tobacco and Murray Mints, and thinking about him now, as an adult, I suspect he was probably hungover for much of the time.

Abigail and I sat apart, as we always did, me at the back of the class and her at the front. Incredibly close though we were at home, we barely spent any time together at school. Halfway between us sat Janice Tupp. I thought she looked nervous and even more hunted than usual, if that was possible, but after a few seconds I stopped thinking about her altogether.

Experience had taught me that the only way through this lesson was to immerse yourself in the boring exercises without resisting, until you could hear the sound of your own thoughts. This was the method I was employing that day. As such, it was some time before I became aware that Janice Tupp was standing up.

Mr Crutton could fly into a violent rage at even the most minor disturbance to his lessons. In the past, these disturbances had included pupils shuffling papers, sharpening pencils and sighing too loudly, and he was not averse to physically expelling the offenders from his classroom. Janice's behaviour was absolutely unheard of. What was she thinking? I looked at Abigail, and discovered she was already looking back at me. Our looks to each other wordlessly communicated our thoughts – we both suspected this had something to do with us.

'*WHAT* do you think you are doing, Tupp?' Mr Crutton's voice boomed around the classroom walls. Normally it would strike fear into even the most brazen of us, but Janice Tupp didn't look afraid. If anything, she looked disappointed, and sad, and terribly pale. For the first time, I became worried that we might have gone too far.

'I need to go home,' she said quietly.

'*WHAT* did you say?' Mr Crutton was incredulous. His eyes were so wide with furious disbelief I wondered if one or both of them would pop out of their sockets, to press wetly against the lenses of his bifocals.

'I need to go home,' repeated Janice, as if the conversation bored her.

'What are you talking about? Are you ill, girl?'

'*I need to go home,*' she said.

Crutton was still struggling to put his fury into words when Janice twisted to the floor in a dead faint.

As if to counter any accusations that she might be faking, she struck her head, hard, on the corner of the desk as she fell.

There was a pause of about a second and then the whole classroom rang with the tortured squeal of chairs across the parquet floor. A space magically formed around the supine Janice, with desks being pushed aside and our classmates crowding to get a better look at her. Into the midst of this instant thicket of children crashed Mr Crutton, shouting at us to stand aside and give the girl air. At the edge of all this chaos, Abigail and I stood stock still, staring at each other. My stomach felt like it had lightning in it.

Janice came to soon after. She had a large, ugly cut on the side of her head, and blood trickled down her left cheek. Iron-ically, it was Abigail – regarded by the teachers in our school as responsible and grown-up – who was given the task of escorting her to the nurse's office. Janice was still very pale and put her arm around Abigail as they hobbled out of the classroom together. I imagined I was pretty pale too.

Abigail did not return to the lesson until five minutes before the end, and even when she did, she simply returned to her seat without looking at me, as if nothing out of the ordinary had happened, leaving me to stew in my own private agony. What now? If Janice told a teacher that we had shown her a photograph of a ghost, there would be all kinds of uncomfortable questions. No one would be in any doubt that we'd faked a ghost photograph; it sounded like exactly the kind of project that people imagined my sister and I did all the time. I ran the situation through my head again and again, but there was no likely scenario that I could see where we were in anything but a huge amount of trouble. It was all I could do not to get up, to walk out, to run away.

When the bell rang and the class packed up to go to the next lesson, I threw everything into my schoolbag and pelted over to where Abigail sat, slowly and calmly packing up her books.

'Well?' I said. 'What happened?'

'It's fine,' said Abigail, not really looking at me.

'What? How can it be fine?'

'I don't really want to talk about this now,' she said curtly, before turning and walking away. I watched her leave, stunned.

In the corridor, I caught up with her. 'I think we have to talk about this now, Abi.' I still had flashes like hot and cold daggers in my stomach. 'I really don't see how we can't.'

'It's fine,' she said simply. 'Janice is fine. She just has a cut on her head.'

'I know that, *Abi*.' Being as close as we were, I never really used my sister's name unless there was an emergency. It felt strange to hear it now. 'I mean—' I lowered my voice 'Us. If the teachers find out that—'

'It's fine,' said Abi. 'I'm telling you, it's *fine*.'

And with that, she walked away.

3

Miss Nail took us for art. She wore a kaftan and had a lisp and was always encouraging us to do screen printing, an activity she seemed mildly obsessed by. I usually looked forward to art classes, as they were the complete opposite to Mr Crutton's stern Victorian lessons, often breaking out into agreeable chaos or moments of actual creativity. That day, however, I couldn't find joy in anything. Abi had recently given up art, as she said she found it bourgeois, and did religious studies instead, where she took great delight in arguing theological contradictions with the teacher, a pale, putty-coloured man whose name I cannot now recall. Miserably, I worked on a watercolour of a gargoyle until the bell rang.

Abigail had chess club immediately after school, so there was yet more agonising waiting to be endured before she got home. And even when she was home, there was still dinner to get through before we could be alone in the attic and I could hear her plan for how we were going to avoid getting expelled. Dinner was – as it tended to be – a family affair, around the big table in the dining room.

'How was school?' my father asked abstractedly, as he always did. *The Times* was folded in quarters in front of him, crossword up. He did *The Times* crossword every day, always over dinner. I never saw him complete one.

'Great,' said Abigail. 'Janice Tupp fainted.' I stared at her in horror, but Abi ignored me in favour of looking up at Mum, who was shovelling shepherd's pie onto her plate from the Pyrex casserole dish.

'Did she?' said my father. 'Well, well.' I was absolutely certain he had no idea who Janice Tupp was. He barely knew who we were.

'Why did she faint?' said Mum, who definitely knew who Janice Tupp was. Both our mum and Mrs Tupp were on the PTA. 'Was she unwell?'

'Something like that,' said Abigail. I couldn't fathom what she was up to. She clearly had a plan – she wouldn't have addressed the incident if she hadn't. 'Are there any more green beans?'

'Poor girl,' said my mother. 'It has been very cold of late, I wonder if that's what brought it on. I shall phone Gwynn later and see how she is.'

Abigail nodded and started work on her shepherd's pie.

After dinner, Abi and I did the washing-up. It was part of a list of weekly chores from which we earned pocket money, and usually we conducted this ritual in good-natured silence, or discussing some topic of mutual interest. This time, how-ever, we were neither silent nor good-natured. As soon as we were out of earshot of our parents in the living room, I imme-diately hissed at Abigail.

'What are you *doing*?'

'I'm sorting it out.'

'It doesn't look much like it to me. You've already told Mum about it and now she's going to ring Janice's mum. We should just tell her.'

'No! What happens if we do that? We'll lose the attic. Use your head.'

'You should use *your* head! Thanks to you, we're going to lose the attic for good. If we just tell the truth now, we'll be banned from using it for a month, and Dad will mumble about turning it into a games room and getting a slate-bed snooker table, like he always does. The camera will get confiscated and we'll lose some books. But, eventually, we'll get everything back. We have to tell her.'

'No.'

'I'm going to tell her.'

Abigail grabbed my arm. I winced. Her grip was always surprisingly strong. 'Don't you dare!'

'I don't hear much dishwashing in there,' said Dad from the living room.

'Yeah, sorry, we're just deciding who washes and who dries,' said Abigail, with a casual intonation I wouldn't have been able to muster. My dad harrumphed and was silent, probably returning to his crossword.

She looked directly at me. Her hair was so deeply black it gathered a dull blueness in the curls, and her eyes were slate grey. She looked very striking – we both did – and we had learned to use this to good effect when required.

'Trust me,' she said.

'But—'

'Trust me,' she repeated. 'I'm not going to tell Mum what we did. Or Dad, or Janice's mum. I'm going to tell Janice.'

I was stunned for a second. It was a daring tactic, and it simply hadn't occurred to me. I couldn't see the sense in it.

'What possible good will that do?'

'Janice might be gullible, but she's also proud. We tell her what we did, and she'll be too embarrassed at being taken in by it to tell anyone. We say sorry, she learns a valuable lesson about not believing everything you see, and we get to keep the camera, the attic and our books, and everything goes back to the way it was.'

I couldn't decide whether this was brilliant or stupid. Either way, it was risky.

'What if she's too angry with us for fooling her, and she tells on us anyway?'

Abigail shrugged. 'Well then, we're back to where we are now. But I think it will work. I just have to get to Janice before she talks to anyone else about it.'

'She's probably talked to someone else about it already. She does have brothers and sisters.'

Abigail chewed a fingernail. 'I'm not so sure. They're all either a lot older than her or a lot younger. And she doesn't really get on with them. I know for a fact her mother is exasperated by her too. I actually saw her call Janice a "silly girl" one parents' evening, after she told her that stupid story about a girl falling off the big slide in the park and dying.'

The slide story was routinely used by bigger children to scare the little ones in the local park. There was a lurid splatter of red house paint at the bottom of the big slide (so-called because there was a smaller slide in the same park), and it was common practice to tell children graduating to the big slide that a girl had fallen off it and died, and that the paint was – gasp! – her blood. Abigail and I had both been told this by bigger kids when we were small.

'Well,' said Abi. 'What do you say?'

I thought about her plan. It didn't seem likely Janice would tell her younger sister, and the other two Tupp children were much older, as Abi said, and very aloof. The older girl had the buck teeth common to all of the Tupp clan, and wore make-up that she couldn't quite carry off; the oldest, a boy, had a leather jacket and a car and a not-quite moustache and smoked, and always seemed to be carrying an LP with a fantastically self-important band name on it – King Crimson, Pentangle, Jethro Tull – as if it were some indecipherably adult statement about his entire being. Both the two elder Tupps were too self-consciously grown-up to associate with their middle sister.

'What about her dad?'

'Her dad's dead, you moron. You know that.'

Two winters ago, when Mr Tupp had been cutting across the waste ground at the back of the cinema, he'd come across a small boy thrashing around in panic in the crust of thin ice and slush that sat on the rank black water of the pond that festered there. He had dived in to recover the boy but they had become entangled in the wreckage of a submerged mattress that had been fly-tipped years ago, and both had drowned. I had somehow forgotten all about this. I wondered if I would have been so keen to show Janice Tupp our ghost photo if I'd remembered this fact. And then I realised with a start that Abigail had not forgotten it, and had shown Janice the picture anyway.

'Well?' said Abigail.

'OK,' I sighed. 'What have we got to lose?'

I was very restless that night and couldn't sleep, and not merely from contemplating, from all conceivable angles, Abi's high-risk strategy. Our ghost photograph had proved a resounding success. Janice Tupp would probably always have a scar on her forehead because of it. And yet, it was impossible now to extract any satisfaction from this. For the very first time, I was forced to look at the things my sister and I got up to, our macabre experiments and reading habits, the gleeful bleakness of the imaginary world we shared, and wonder – *is this right?* Is this normal? And later that night, in my pyjamas, my bedside light burning brightly, I forced myself to look again at the photo of the Ghost Monk of Newby, considering for the first time the possibility that it was a fake, a double exposure rendered by some process I was ignorant of. That meant that someone had had to plan and stage the photograph, just as we had done with ours. It meant that someone would have put together the costume that the ghost wore, cloth mask and all, and someone would have had to wear it. The idea that a person would do this, would design this terrifying thing with no purpose other than scaring people, was in some ways more troubling than the idea that it might be a picture of a real ghost. If the Ghost Monk of Newby was a prank, it was not an amusing or enjoyable one. It was malevolent and unpleasant, a manifestation of someone's darker thoughts and feelings, feelings that couldn't be expressed any other way.

And if that were the case – what, then, was our ghost?

4

Janice was not in school the next day. It was a Thursday, a day crammed full of lessons I didn't like. Music, which meant singing until one's head ached; PE, which meant running around the hard, cold football pitch being shouted at; and Maths, which meant maths. Thursday was usually a day to be endured, but the events of the previous day gave it an edge I was fearful of, as if all the circumstances and things contained within the day held the potential for catastrophe. The smooth red brick of the changing room block, where somebody had written COULOREDS OUT NF in magnolia gloss paint; the boarded-up doorway of the rotting lodge next door to it, a hangover from when the playing field was part of the estate of a stately home, unimaginable though that was now; the unsettled sky that drowned the silver sun in drenching waves of black cloud over the football field where we played out our inconsequential battle – all of this spoke of some hard-edged cataclysm in my future, assembling itself from the world around me, curving towards me in a knight move, unstoppable.

Despite all this, my team won 3–1.

That evening, neither Abi nor I had any extra-curricular activities, so Abi moved that we take the initiative and call

Janice in person. As it was Thursday, Mum was out at her pot-
tery class, and Dad wouldn't have cared if we'd called the
Kremlin as long as we reversed the charges and didn't make
too much noise. So whilst Dad sat in the living room watching
television, Abigail sat in the hallway and called Janice Tupp's
house. We'd decided that, as Abi had shown Janice the picture,
she would be the one to conduct the phone call.

Abi wouldn't let me sit with her whilst she made the call,
as it would be a subtle act of performance, delicate and easily
spoiled. So I waited in the attic, wondering. What little I
knew of Janice left me with the impression that she was an
unpredictable creature of many depths and shallows. When
she learned that she had been fooled, her reaction could go
any way. It was simply impossible to tell. The absolute worst-
case scenario – the one that kept playing itself out in my
mind – was that Janice would explode with petulant anger,
and soon her mum would be talking to our mum, and within
weeks our lovely dark attic would be repainted into a bland,
boring space where nothing would ever happen again. To pass
the time, I looked at our bookshelves, and was forced, for the
second time since we'd shown Janice the photo, to examine
our preoccupations through different eyes.

All our reading material, I saw now, was macabre. Most
of the top shelf was older books, many from the 1940s and
'50s, most of it dealing with folklore or the paranormal. Back
then, books on strange topics had to be searched for, sought
out, retrieved and rescued, and our cache of books had been
sourced from jumble sales, bring-and-buy fairs in church
halls, and second-hand bookshops visited on holidays in
obscure English towns and villages, where we would emerge
blinking into the sunlight from some book-lined cave that
reeked of pipe tobacco and mould, clutching our treasure.

Books by Lewis Spence and Alfred Watkins. Books by Elliott O'Donnell and Sacheverell Sitwell. Books by Catherine Crowe and Dion Fortune. Delightful books. Strange and eerie books. Macabre books. Wonderful, wonderful books.

At that point, our top three books were as follows:

1. *The End of Borley Rectory* by Harry Price
2. *Haunted England* by Christina Hole
3. *Here are Ghosts and Witches* by J. Wentworth Day.

Here are Ghosts and Witches was illustrated with incredible line drawings of various terrifying phenomena – a demented owl-thing labelled 'Bird Elemental', a hooded figure holding up a severed Hand of Glory, the white-eyed ghost of a Viking. *Haunted England* was no less lavishly illustrated, but in a completely different style, a sort of jazzy modernism-lite, which must have been state-of-the-art for 1940, when the book was published. Here, the ghosts were rendered as restless, energetic shapes that seemed almost to vibrate off the page. These pictures, by the wood engraver John Farleigh, were fascinating to me, and though Abigail didn't care for them, I thought they summed up the state of being haunted better than any traditional depiction could. Everything in Farleigh's drawings was haunted, it seemed – buildings, walls and doors were depicted as sharp, angry, and almost aggressively nonsensical, with further shapes and shadows concealed within them. Some of the drawings were comical, but some were so uniquely eerie that I can still recall them now.

Fascinating though both of these books were, they paled when compared to our all-time number one, *The End of Borley Rectory* by Harry Price. My sister and I knew all about Price – he had been Britain's most famous ghost hunter a generation earlier – and Borley was his most famous case. An oppressive Victorian warehouse of a place (Price called it 'a two-storeyed monstrosity in red brick'), the Rectory looked every inch the archetypal haunted house. It was reputedly haunted from the day it was built, in 1863, to the day it burned down in mysterious circumstances in 1939 (and, it was rumoured, long afterward). *The End of Borley Rectory* was a sensational account of Price's investigations, illustrated throughout by black-and-white photos that made Borley look even more unwelcoming than Price made it sound. Best of all, there were stories of recovering *human remains* – part of a skull and a jawbone – from the cellar, and transcriptions of séances held in the Rectory itself. The flyleaf informed us that Price had written an earlier book about Borley, but we were never able to find it.

We begged our parents to take us to Borley, where we were sure to see a ghost, either on the patch of land where the rectory had stood, or in the local church, but both Mum and Dad, in their different but equally emphatic ways, refused, and so we had to be content with our one volume on the subject. Which was, in a way, more than enough; even the word *Borley* was terrifying to us, with its suggestions of *borstal* and *ordeal*, *abhor,* even *abortion*. The very sound of the word seemed to imply something endlessly anti-social and untameable. In a similar way, that phrase, *human remains*, I always found extraordinarily disturbing and unsettling. It implied something more intimate and terrible than mere bones: the ruins of a person. Skin and hair, fingernails. Mouldering clothes, jewellery dulling as it tarnished. A belt buckle, the belt rotted away. Playing hide and seek with Abigail, years earlier, I was always terrified of stumbling across something I would for ever regret seeing, stuffed into the bottom of a hedgerow like so much rubbish, the litter of some murder or other, long forgotten. What could be worse than that?

I looked at the spines of these books now. How would all this look to anyone else? I took *Haunted England* from the shelf and sat staring at one of the modernist ghosts until I heard footsteps jounce on the ladder and saw Abigail's head appear through the trapdoor.

'Well?' I could see from her face that whatever had transpired had not been as straightforward as she'd hoped.

'Erm,' said Abigail thoughtfully, hoisting herself up into the attic. 'So I tried to tell her that it was all pretend, that we faked it.'

'Tried to?'

'Yeah.' Abigail looked exhausted. She slumped into her favoured armchair and I saw something on her face I couldn't quite read.

'And?'

'She didn't believe me.'

I stared at her in disbelief. 'Sorry?'

'I told her we faked the picture, in our attic. She didn't believe me.'

I couldn't absorb this information at all. 'Did you tell her how we did it?'

'Of course.'

'That it's just chalk and low light?'

'I told her, Tim.'

'And not drawing specific features so that the observer—'

'Yes! Bloody hell, Tim. I told her all of that. She said she didn't believe me.'

'Why would we lie?'

She shrugged. 'Why would we fake a ghost photograph?'

I had no answer to this. We sat for a long moment, thinking, looking through each other.

'Has she told her mum?' I said at last.

'No.'

'Oh.' That was something. 'So what do we do now?'

'Well,' said Abigail, 'that's just it. She wants to come over and see it for herself.'

'See what?'

'The attic. She says that it's haunted and we took a real ghost photograph whether we know it or not.'

I pinched the bridge of my nose as – I realised in later life – I often do when something makes no sense to me.

'So what do we do now?' I repeated.

Abigail shrugged. 'She comes over and sees.'

'You're not serious?'

'I am. Mum and Dad won't mind. In fact, they'll be relieved that we finally want to have a friend over.'

'But there's no ghost here!'

'But don't you see, Tim? This is the best thing that can possibly happen, from our point of view. We have Janice over, she sees there's no ghost and that we faked it, and that's the end of the matter.'

'How can that be the end of the matter? She'll tell her mum, her mum will tell our mum . . .'

'By that point it will be next week. Everyone will have forgotten about Janice fainting and if she starts talking about ghosts and photos, people will ask why she didn't bring it up sooner. She'll just make herself look bonkers.'

I considered this. 'I still think it's asking for trouble.'

Very often in conversations between us I would offer the emotional, instinctive side of a given issue, and this would force

Abi to respond analytically. She was conscious of this and would play up to it, as she was doing now. She steepled her fingers like Basil Rathbone as Sherlock Holmes.

'Trust me. It's the best course of action.'

I looked about me at our attic – the library, the horrible bits of Victorian taxidermy we'd picked up from junk shops, the dust-furred oil paintings of bleak landscapes, the interesting and peculiar objects that inevitably gathered on any horizontal surface in the vicinity of either of us. The only significant thing we hadn't added to the place was a large home-made doll's house, which we had discovered in the attic the first time we ever went up there, and had deemed both creepy enough to keep and too heavy to move.

'We'll have to tidy up a bit.'

'Yes. Get some extra lights, hide the books, that sort of thing. Make it look respectable.'

Abigail must have read some element of doubt in my face. She leaned forward in her armchair and fixed me with her dark eyes.

'All we have to do is make out that it's all fine. We take her up here, she sees how absolutely un-haunted our attic and indeed our entire house is, and that's that.' Abi touched her fingertips to her lips. 'All we have to do is be *normal* for a while.'

And so it was agreed between us that Janice Tupp would come over to our house after school next Thursday, in order to not see a ghost.

5

We spent all of the following Wednesday night preparing the attic for our visitor. Abigail even skipped chess club to make sure we had enough time to do the job properly. It would have been easier to transform the attic at the weekend, but we didn't want Mum becoming accustomed to the way it looked and insisting we keep it that way. It would be ironic indeed to save our attic from one line of attack only to have it succumb to another. After dinner, we set about removing and boxing away anything that could be construed as eerie, disquieting or unsettling.

It was a long evening.

One thing that became obvious as the work of sanitising the attic progressed was that my sister and I had very little idea of the sort of things 'normal' almost-fourteen-year-olds liked. My sister had a record player, but used it primarily to play BBC sound-effects records and Vaughan Williams' *The Lark Ascending*, which she seemed never to tire of. Similarly, I liked painting, but mostly enjoyed painting historical methods of execution. We both enjoyed watching television, but I could tell that the sort of things we liked to watch would not be in Janice Tupp's cultural orbit. Books were completely out. We had some board games, but most of them had been customised by us in some way to make them more interesting, which of course meant it was best they stayed in their boxes. The only other distraction in the attic was the Edwardian doll's house, which, whilst possessed of a certain desolate charm, was not enough to occupy the mind of a thirteen-year-old, even one as immature as Janice Tupp seemed to be, for longer than five minutes.

What did other people our age *do*? We had no idea. Their behaviour had always been incomprehensible and uninteresting to us. And now, like some Dante-esque punishment, we were being forced to emulate that behaviour in order to preserve our way of life.

It was decided, eventually, that we'd drink coffee, and talk. Coffee was Abigail's idea – it was the most adult non-alcoholic drink we could get our hands on, and it projected (we hoped) an air of bohemian sophistication. The three of us would drink instant coffee and chat, and Abigail and I would do our best to have a grown-up conversation with Janice, discussing current affairs and pressing issues of the day, as if we were Malcolm Muggeridge and Germaine Greer on some late-night cultural analysis programme on BBC 2. It was a lousy plan, and threatened to be an extremely dreary evening, but we had absolutely nothing in the way of better ideas. It was vital that we kept the evening as dry and sensible and boring as possible, as far away from talk of the supernatural as we could (we agreed beforehand that, when the topic came up, we were to be sceptical and dismissive, and would move the conversation on as quickly as possible). We were confident that we could, between us, create an atmosphere whereby anything ghostly would shrivel and flee.

And so, all of our strange paraphernalia – two small lifetimes' worth of trophies of the extraordinary – were packed away into empty fabric softener boxes I had scrounged up from the local Co-op, and the boxes stacked into a corner and covered with an orange sheet. We then rolled up the dark carpet and stashed it in a corner behind the boxes, replacing it with a rush mat from Abi's bedroom, which seemed more grown-up, somehow. We put a tablecloth over the coffee table and on top of that we placed a vase stuffed with lavender cut from the garden. The severe dark brown walls were still a problem, but after we taped up a map of the world and a few other boring educational posters, which had previously been gathering dust under my bed, the attic looked almost light. The wall where we'd chalked the ghost we left as it was, so we could show Janice exactly what we'd done, and how.

Finally, Abigail and I stood, gazing upon what we had wrought. There was something extremely unsettling about the temporary room we had made. It was a room where two versions of us I didn't like or trust lived. Our attic had been an entirely unselfconscious expression of who we were, individually and as a pair. Peculiar it may have been, but there was nothing in the way of pretension or artifice in it. The room now was a deception, at odds with itself, the fixed grin of the guilty. In seeking to exorcise it we had made it somehow untrustworthy, strange to ourselves. We knew without saying it out loud that we wouldn't tolerate the place like this for a minute longer than the duration of Janice's visit.

Thursday at school passed slowly, as it always did for me, subjecting me to the familiar barrage of subjects I neither liked nor enjoyed, nor could see any use for. None of us would ever make our living singing or playing an instrument, so why teach us music? None of us had the skill to be a professional footballer, so why teach us PE? Thursday was to be ground through, hacked through, with no short cuts, a day where time was hard as granite and the clock gave grudgingly.

At the final bell, I went straight home, and straight upstairs when I got there, hollering a hello to Mum, who was clattering about in the kitchen. My intention was to go to the attic and spend an hour preparing for the ordeal of entertaining Janice, and I was halfway up there before I remembered that it didn't currently exist. My head poked through the trapdoor into unfamiliarity, a bland, tidy zone where creativity was banished and ideas couldn't survive. I was reminded of the room that Dave Bowman finds himself in at the end of *2001: A Space Odyssey*, built for humans but not by them, where all the books and furnishings are fake, an attempt to comfort that misses by a mile and ends up simply being eerie. It smelled pungently of lavender now; I hoped the smell wasn't permanent. I shivered and retreated to my room, there to await the visitation of Janice Tupp.

I fell asleep on my bed. When I awoke, Mum was calling me and Janice was already downstairs with Abigail. I splashed cold water on my face at the bathroom sink and set about trying to look serious. Part of me had forgotten what the advantage was of even doing any of this, and I headed downstairs in a bad mood.

Abigail was in the kitchen, chatting animatedly to Janice Tupp, who sat at the table drinking orange squash. Janice wore her school uniform, almost lost inside a gigantic grey jumper, which I guessed was a cast-off from the older Tupp sister. There was a large pink fabric plaster on her left temple, where her head had struck the desk. She gave me a sour, efficient smile when I came in, and I gave her as warm a smile as I could in return. Janice's mean smile was enough to jolt me out of my complacency and remind me what was at stake. I could live with our sterile attic, and Janice as a guest in it, for one night, if it meant keeping things as they were.

As Mum came back in, I realised what my sister was doing

with her incessant chatter. She was controlling Janice's presence in the house, herding Janice's conversation like a vigilant
sheepdog. As Abigail turned away, to pile custard creams onto
a plate and stir three mugs of instant coffee, she signalled with
her eyes that it was now my turn to keep watch. And so I dutifully monitored the interaction between Janice and my mum,
as Mum asked Janice the kind of questions parents always ask
visiting children – *how's your mum, how are your siblings, did I see
your Gary in the shopping arcade? I thought he was away at college* –
interjecting only when I thought the conversation might veer
towards the one topic we had no real answer for: *Janice, what
are you doing here?*

Only once did we almost come unstuck. Mum began to take
grapefruit and canned spaghetti and other groceries out of a
bag, and, as she turned, she said, 'Well, I must say, it's very
nice of you to come round, Janice.'

Janice smiled the unpleasant smile again. 'It's not like they
left me any choice, Mrs Smith.'

Mum half-turned, looking briefly puzzled, and was about to
ask a question when I, in a voice that sounded terribly fake to
me, said, 'Yes, we certainly wouldn't take no for an answer!'
Janice said something else, but Abigail and I both talked over
her. Shortly afterwards, we ascended the stairs. I went first,
Janice Tupp second, and Abigail, carrying the coffee and biscuits
on a tray, brought up the rear. Janice ascended the ladder every
bit as gingerly and wetly as I had imagined she might do. Abigail
passed the tray to me whilst Janice looked around our bowdler-
ized attic.

'Is this your room?' she said, looking about her.

'Tim and I both have our own rooms, but, yes, this place is
ours,' said Abigail. 'We can do whatever we like here, really.
Mum and Dad pretty much leave us alone.'

'I don't much like it,' said Janice, running a finger down one of the dark walls. 'It's very hot, for a start.'

'The tops of houses often are.' Abigail was smiling. I knew how little capacity she had for suffering fools, and I suddenly realised just how much of an effort she was making.

'Hmm.' Janice wrinkled her nose. 'Well, I have to say, it's not what I was expecting.'

'And what were you expecting, Janice?' A confrontational edge crept into Abigail's voice. I tried and failed to catch her eye.

'I dunno.' Janice sniffed again. 'More books. You two are meant to be really brainy, aren't you? You're always coming top in stuff. I expected more books.'

'All our books are over there.' I pointed to the orange bulk of the stack of boxes with the sheet over it. 'We're going to paint it up here, make full use of the light, so all our books are stacked away.' This just came to me, as I said it, and I was as surprised to hear it as Abigail was. I found myself thinking it was actually quite a good idea.

'Anyway, look,' said Abigail. 'We can pretty well do what we like here without anyone interrupting. Which is why . . .' She took an almost imperceptible inward breath. '. . . we faked that terrible photograph.'

Janice said nothing and simply glared at us, arms folded.

'It's true, Janice,' I said, in as soothing a tone as I could. 'We shouldn't have done it, but we did.' I had sat down on the arm of the chair, but stood up now, hands open in a gesture I hoped she saw as conciliatory.

'We just wanted to see if we could. I said we couldn't, that it would never work—'

'And I said it would,' Abigail interjected. 'So we made up a story – the creepiest story we could –and chalked a figure on the wall. We rubbed the chalk outline so that it was all blurry and vague, made it as convincing as we could.'

'But I still didn't think it would convince anyone,' I said, smiling a contrite smile. 'So Abi and I had a bet.' We were rattling through our prepared story without a hitch. 'I bet Abi she couldn't convince someone we'd taken a photo of a real ghost. She said she could, and, well, you know the rest.'

Abi and I were now both looking as contrite as we could manage, smiling pleasantly. I wondered if Abi's face was hurting as much as mine.

'We're sorry, Janice,' said my sister. 'Really.'

Janice Tupp looked sad. For a long time, nobody said anything. Janice looked up and I saw that her eyes were wet. For the first time since this whole thing began, I felt sorry for her, rather than sorry for myself and Abi.

She walked slowly over to the wall, the one we'd chalked our ghost on, the one we'd deliberately left bare in order that Janice could see for herself what we'd done. She stood with her back to us, looking up at the large brown wall that loomed above her. I shot Abigail a glance – *should we approach her? Comfort her?* Abigail read my look and shook her head, and I stayed where I was.

Janice turned round. She wiped her eyes swiftly and precisely with the back of her right hand, then stared at us both. There was something in her expression I had never seen before. Something almost imperious.

'Why me?'

'We just . . . your name came up at random.' Abigail wasn't smiling now. She looked impatient, as she always did when a matter she considered concluded continued to be discussed.

'*Liar.*' Janice all but spat the word. I felt the situation was slipping out of our grasp but could do nothing about it.

'It's the truth, Janice,' said Abigail. My sister never had any qualms about lying if she believed the ends justified the means. I – a lesser person in all respects – very much did have qualms about lying, and when Janice looked to me for confirmation, I found that I automatically looked at the floor. And that was all Janice needed.

'You two,' she said caustically. 'You think you're so bloody *special*, don't you?'

'Now Janice—' began Abigail.

'Cleverer than everyone else. *Better* than everyone else.'

'We don't, Janice. We really don't.'

'Well, you certainly think you're cleverer than *me*, don't you?'

It was my sister's turn to look at the floor.

'No wonder everyone at school hates you,' said Janice, matter-of-factly.

'Don't be stupid.'

'Oh, isn't this what you wanted? You chose me to look at that picture because you think *I'm* stupid. But *you're* the stupid ones. You don't know anything.'

Janice skewered both of us with a stare that was like a slow, painful ache. I had entered that strange hyper-clarity of fear, and Janice seemed to have become more solid, more real, than the room around her.

'You showed me that photograph thinking you could scare me. Well, you did. But not the way you think.'

'I don't understand,' said Abigail.

'No, you don't. Neither of you. You drew a shape on a wall, thinking it was clever, thinking it was funny. But it's not. And now it's here. And you live here.'

'I'm really lost here, Janice,' said Abigail.

'You *woke something up*,' continued Janice, almost to herself. 'You *let it in*.'

'I don't think—'

'Some things need a shape. To be. Some things wait, in the darkness. For a shape.' Janice looked directly at me, then at Abigail. 'There's something here. In this house. In this attic. It was waiting, for someone to name it, to make it real.'

Despite myself, the hairs on the back of my neck stood up. If this was an act, it was an incredible one.

'You gave it a shape, and you gave it a face. That's what I saw when you showed me that picture. Not all that stupid stuff about a bridesmaid. I saw its *face*.'

'*What?*'

'Horrible, sneering face it is too. Cruel.'

'Janice—'

'I see a lot of things like that. No one else sees. But *I* do. The day Dad died, I knew he wasn't coming back. I could see it on him.'

'I've had just about enough of this,' said Abigail. 'We came clean with you, Janice, and we apologised. And now you're just trying to throw it back at us. It's childish.'

Janice Tupp smiled widely. In that second she seemed anything but childish, anything but immature. She seemed very old, almost ancient. I wondered then if she was genuinely mad.

'But you *did* photograph a real ghost, despite everything. Or you will have done, soon.'

'That's enough.'

'Would you like to see? To see what I see?' Janice put her hands to her eyes. 'I think it's what you two deserve.'

And then, before either of us could answer, Janice collapsed, just as she had in the classroom.

Abigail and I stood, open-mouthed, rooted to the spot, looking at Janice, at each other, at Janice again.

Janice sat up, kneeling. Her posture was strange, as if she were being dragged off the floor by a hook under each arm. Without warning she slapped herself across the face, with incredible force. The slap echoed around the attic.

'Jesus!' said Abigail. Janice Tupp looked up at her with an expression devoid of all thought, as if her head was empty.

She turned to look at me, and pointed. Her voice was subtly different. Thick and grating. Old.

'You. I see you. I see the broken house, with all the broken people in it. I see it coming back for you. I see four halves and two quarters. I see it returning, and it will never let you go. It will always be with you. Twenty grins all grinning back at you, salt in the wound, and you break.'

She swung round awkwardly. The finger was now pointing at Abigail.

'I see you too. I see you there, but you can't see me. Grinning away again, showing your teeth, saying nothing but sand. And you can't stop it now. What else is there to do? What good is being clever now? Here? And you can't stop this. He's coming for you. He has eyes but no face. He's near.'

'Do something,' I said flatly.

'He's near!' screamed Janice. *'He can't be stopped!'*

'Who?' I shouted.

'Essssssss,' hissed Janice. *'ESSSSSSSSSSSSSSS. ESSSSSSSSSSSSSSS.'* She blared the syllable at us aggressively, like a warning.

'Sod this,' said Abigail. She marched over to the vase, tore out the lavender and threw the cold water in Janice's face.

Janice took a very sharp intake of breath, and seemed to suddenly become conscious of where she was. She was just about to sob when Abigail, tears streaming down her face, smashed her to the floor with a sudden slap of her own.

6

'I didn't see Janice leave,' said Mum brightly, as we sat around the dinner table, eating casserole.

Abigail shot me a brief look, which indicated that she'd be leaving the talking to me.

'Janice didn't stay very long. She wasn't feeling very well,' I said. This, at least, was true. She had seemed distracted and disoriented after Abigail had slapped her, and we had sat her in one of the armchairs to recover. I had gone to fetch a glass of water, leaving Abi and Janice alone, which I only began to fear was an unwise move when I was downstairs running the tap. I had expected Janice to be fuming, to be cursing the pair of us, but when I returned with the water, she was merely slumped in the armchair like a doll. She was polite but extremely withdrawn, and strangely distant. None of us was sure how to continue, how to pick up the pieces after what had just happened, and in the end we simply escorted Janice downstairs, where she said she'd walk herself home. She was so bewildered she forgot her coat, and we waited patiently in the hall whilst she staggered back upstairs to fetch it. Then we both watched her leave, striding away as if in a daze, not looking back.

'Well, she's always struck me as a very sickly child,' said Mum. 'Her arms and legs are like pipe cleaners. If you looked hard enough at her she'd probably snap.'

'She's tougher than you think,' Abigail muttered into her plate.

'Well, she certainly doesn't look it,' said Mum. 'Oh, I was going to mention, I had to go up into the attic earlier to bring the tray down. I really like what you've done up there. It's about time you got rid of some of that old junk.'

'Well, it's nice to have a change, Mum. But I don't think we'll leave it like that.'

'Oh. Well, anyway, I like being able to see the floorboards. Maybe you should paint them before you put everything back.'

'Oh, we're painting floorboards now, are we?' said Dad, without looking up from his crossword. 'You're not at art college now, Alice.'

'Oh, really. It would just be the attic, I wasn't suggesting we do the whole house.'

'To be honest, Mum,' said Abi, seizing the opportunity, 'we were thinking of repainting the whole place. Can we?'

Mum looked at Abigail as if she'd just suggested we buy a yacht. 'I'm not made of money, Abigail. I only suggested painting the floorboards because it's the kind of thing you two could do yourselves.'

'What colour were you thinking of painting it, anyway?' said Dad, filling in a crossword answer.

'If you say black, Abigail, this discussion is over,' Mum said sharply.

'No,' said my sister, lying. 'We were thinking about white, *actually*.' She scowled and sat back, checkmated.

After dinner, Abi and I climbed the stairs together, deep in conversation. As in all matters involving Janice Tupp, it seemed,

we had not had a chance to properly discuss what had transpired until an agonising period of time had passed.

'What do we do now?' I said.

Abigail shrugged. 'What can we do? I think it's over, though.'

'You slapped her in the face!'

'She also slapped herself in the face.'

Our footsteps thumped onto the first landing.

'Do you think she was joking?'

'Of course she was joking. She was trying to scare us, to
get her own back for scaring *her*. She did a bloody good job of
it too.'

'Yeah. It was a great performance. Who knew she had that
in her? And the stuff she was saying . . .' I realised I was
sounding a bit like Mum. For the life of me, though, I couldn't
find an appropriate reaction to what we'd witnessed. It was
just so far out of any frame of reference I had in real life.

'Have you read *The Crucible* by Arthur Miller?' said Abigail.

I scowled. Abigail knew I hadn't. She liked to keep her
reading habits just one step ahead of mine, so that she could
have moments like this, where she knew more than I did, and
could lecture me as if she were ten years older than me,
instead of ten minutes.

'Enlighten me,' I said.

'It's set during the Salem witch trials. A group of girls –
powerless in every other respect – make up a story about
witchcraft, and the whole town believes them. That's what's
happening here. Janice wanted to get her own back on us, so
she made up that whole routine.'

I thought about this. We had reached the second landing
now, where the attic ladder was.

'OK, but if she wanted to get her own back on us, why
didn't she just tell her mum?'

'Her mum thinks she's an idiot, just like everyone else does.' Abigail started to climb the ladder. 'No one respects her. She has no authority, so she did something very creative in order to assume some. She's a good actress, I'll give you that, but she did have a week to prepare. She's probably been prac-tising every—'

Abigail stopped mid-sentence, a rare enough thing in itself. She had stopped climbing the ladder too. All I could see were her jeans and plimsolls, entirely motionless.

'What?' I called up. 'What is it?'

Abigail climbed the rest of the ladder without uttering a word. I scrambled up after her, asking what the matter was, until I saw it too, and fell silent.

7

Neither of us had heard the doll's house fall. Both of us were certain that it had been in the middle of the table, nowhere near the edge. The doll's house was very heavy, and difficult to move at the best of times. Now it lay upended on the floor-boards.

'It . . . must have blown off the table?' I said thinly.

My sister shook her head. 'I think Janice did this.'

'When?'

'When she came back to get her coat. She pushed it off the table!'

'We would have heard it, surely? Plus she was only up here for about ten seconds.'

Abigail shrugged. 'When you have eliminated the impossible . . .'

I was about to argue that this was beyond Janice's capabilities, but if today had proved anything, it was that we had both miscalculated in that department. We stood looking down at the upturned doll's house, which seemed half-buried in the bare floorboards, like a meteor in a desert.

'Here,' I said. 'Give me a hand putting it back.' Abigail nodded and we both grabbed one of the gable ends.

'Flip it over first,' said Abigail.

'Right you are.' With some effort, we managed to put the house the right way up.

'No!' yelled Abi, as we did so.

'What?'

'That rotten witch has broken the front of it!'

The facade of the house, the dark bricks which were hand-painted, not well, but with rigour, had cracked from the eaves to the foundation, a lightning slash of old wood, the colour of the honeycomb in a Crunchie bar. Abigail swore and, brushing the hair from her eyes, ran her hands over the front panelling.

'That rotten cow,' she said, not taking her eyes from the damaged house.

'It's not so bad,' I said, trying to sound as calm as I could. My fear was that Abigail would take this up with Janice at school, when, to my mind, tonight had been the end of the matter. 'Look, it's just the front panel. A spot of glue and some panel pins will fix it. We'll just prise it off and mend it. Like so.'

The panel, though held in place by several lethal-looking rusted tacks, had been loosened by the fall and came off easily in my hands, exposing the innards of the house.

It was my turn to swear.

Removing the panel had revealed a compartment, long and thin, like a chimney, running through all three floors of the front of the house, where the main stairwell would be if it was a real house. Jammed in that space, to the point where there was no room for anything else save the fluff of ancient cobwebs, were lots of little wooden bodies. A family of tiny wooden people.

Painstakingly, we laid out the inhabitants of the house on a cloth, like tiny casualties in the world's smallest house fire. Each was comprised of a wooden head and body, each one carved from the same piece of wood, with arms and legs held on by wooden pins. They were a family, certainly, and the house had almost certainly been built by some enterprising father or grandfather to accommodate them. There was a mother and a father, two boys of differing heights, twin girls, and a strangely unformed baby, which fitted into a tiny wooden crib. Their clothes were still present – frayed and ancient miniature outfits in strange colours, saturated with the dust of almost a century.

Though some had an arm or a leg missing, each family member had been further damaged – vandalised was the word that sprang to mind – in a very specific way. Each of their painted faces had been scratched out. There was no mistaking it for an accident or a coincidence. Someone had deliberately and thoroughly obliterated their faces.

Abi and I stared down at the little wooden people for a long while.

'I don't know,' said Abi at last. 'I'm stumped.'

'About what?'

'How she did it,' Abi said.

'I'm sorry? I don't follow you.'

'How Janice did this.'

'She just shoved it off the table! You're right. It's funny we didn't hear it crash, but she did it alright. She had to have done. Once you have eliminated the impossible—'

She turned to look at me. Her face was pale and her eyes were bright, and for a second I thought there were tears in them.

'Tim, don't you remember? What she said?'

'Who?'

'Janice, of course. When she had her . . . episode.'

'When she was going off her head, you mean! No, I don't remember exactly what she said. Do you?'

'I wrote it all down,' said Abi. 'Straight afterwards.'

'Why?' I virtually spat the question at her.

'I wasn't going to let something like that get away from us. Wait a sec.'

Abi got up and descended the ladder. I discovered fairly quickly I did not like being alone with the little wooden family and their ruined faces, so I took the cloth napkin that Abi had placed under the vase of lavender and wrapped them all up in it. I then stuffed the bundle back inside the doll's house and did my best to secure the broken panel back on the front. I must have been reasonably engrossed in this task, because when Abi suddenly appeared at my shoulder, I started in shock.

'Where are the people?' It was funny how neither of us used the word *dolls*.

'Back in their mansion,' I said. 'And they can stay there for ever for all I care.' Abigail, to my surprise, didn't object or mock me, or call me melodramatic. There was something unwholesome about the little family. We had both felt it.

Abi opened her notebook, the one with the owls on the cover. This notebook was where she wrote thoughts even more private than those committed to a diary – ambitions, hopes, fears, dreams both good and bad that she wanted to preserve; sayings and quotations she felt were pertinent to her own life. It was where she'd also written her poetic invocation to our ghost, tearing the page out so she could share it with me. As ever, Abi was careful not to show me any other pages as she laid the book flat on the fresh new page on which she had recorded Janice Tupp's weird outburst. It was strange that Janice's ramblings were now a part of this book too, alongside the words of Keats, Blake and Milton, of equal importance and weight.

'Why did you write all of this down?'

'I told you.'

'That wasn't an answer.'

She stared at me. I understood by her expression the answer was obvious to her and she was baffled as to why it shouldn't be so to me. 'What poured out of Janice earlier was her *innermost self,* a communication directly from how she sees herself. Do you know how rare something like that is? I absolutely had to write it down, and fresh, too. I didn't want to corrupt it with my own syntax.'

We read again what Janice had said.

I see the broken house, with all the broken people in it. I see it coming back for you. I see four halves and two quarters. I see it returning, and it will never let you go.

'*The broken house,*' I whispered. A chill shuddered through me. '*With the broken people in it.*' Panic bubbled up in me. 'Jesus, Abi. How could she know?'

'I don't know,' Abi said tensely.

'How could she know?' I felt cold. 'About the people?'

'Tim——'

'How could she know, Abi? They were sealed into the house!' I was on my feet now, shouting. The world seemed suddenly terrifying, a place where all of our unthinkable and macabre fascinations had leaked out and were free to caper and play. 'She predicted this! She made a prediction and it came true!' I raked a hand down my face. Fear gave me an excess of energy and I ran to the window to look out at the street, the world, to reassure myself it was still there.

Abi came over to me. To my supreme annoyance and incalculable relief, she was smiling. I looked out of the window again. A million miles below, in the twilight, Dad was putting the bins out.

'She wanted you to be scared,' said Abi softly. 'And you are.'
'You're *not*?'

'No.' She sniffed contemptuously. 'She's just a silly girl, play-acting.'

I carried on looking out of the window. Somewhere, a distant ice cream van was improbably plying its trade at nightfall, in February, and a demented, nerve-jangling rendition of 'Greensleeves' hung in the air, like a manifestation of some psychotic illness.

'So what does that leave us with?' said Abi. 'A melodramatic, gullible girl is humiliated by a fake ghost photograph, and instead of admitting she's been fooled, she concocts a plan to get us back. She does a fake psychic act and we fall for it, at least in the short term.'

'The *people*, though, Abi. The broken people in the doll's house. How could she possibly know about that? They've been trapped inside there for decades. She couldn't have set that up.'

Abi smiled. 'She didn't. She just noticed we had a battered old doll's house and made a guess it would have battered old dolls in it. It's a reasonable guess that an old doll's house would have old dolls inside it. She just got lucky, that's all.'

I thought about this. It made sense. Abi shoved the doll's house experimentally across the tabletop.

'Then she just pushes the doll's house off the table, when we're downstairs. The only bit I don't get is how we didn't hear anything. It must have made a heck of a noise.'

'We *were* downstairs at that point,' I said. 'We might well not have heard it at all.'

'There you are, you see?' My sister grinned. 'Turns out she's not clairvoyant after all. She's just really good at pretending to be.' She sank into an armchair. After a couple of seconds, I sank into the other armchair.

We sat facing each other for a minute or so, silent as bookends.

'We really did pick the wrong person to show that photograph to,' said Abi eventually.

'What about all the other stuff she said? All that stuff about giving something a shape?'

'She was just throwing her own fear back at us. Trying to ruin this place for us.'

I thought about this too. It also made sense.

'Anyway, don't worry,' said Abi, 'I won't tell anyone.'

'Tell anyone what?'

'That you got all scared and upset *like a ickle baby*.' She did a baby voice for the last four words, and stuck her lower lip out.

'Sod off!' I laughed.

'You sod off!'

I returned to the table, where Abi's owl notebook was. It was still open on the page with Janice's rantings on it. I sank back into the armchair and re-read them, whilst Abi hovered anxiously to ensure I didn't look at any other pages. I removed the pen from the book's spine and wrote *'The Compleyte Prophecies of Janys Tuppe of Thisse Parishe'* at the top of the page. I thought Abi would be annoyed at me for writing in her book, but she smirked.

'I see you too. I see you, but you can't see me. Grinning away, showing your teeth, saying nothing but sand. You can't stop it now. What else is there to do? What good is being clever now? And you can't stop this. He's coming. He has eyes but no face. He's near.'

'I wonder where all this nonsense came from?'

'Who knows? It's good, though, I'll give her that. You get off lightly, with the broken people. I, meanwhile, end up in whatever unique hell this is, courtesy of person or persons unknown. I suppose I should be flattered that she reserved the worst of it for me.'

'I think she thinks it was all your idea.'

'Probably.'

We both fell into silence for a while, meditating on the day's events. Eventually, I was the one to break it.

'Abi? Do people at school really hate us?'

Abi shrugged.

'Do you care?'

8

And so neither of us spoke to Janice Tupp for the rest of the school year. Janice avoided us, and we avoided her. We had barely spoken to her before the incident of the ghost photograph, so to everyone else in class it looked as if nothing had changed. However, I was careful always to give her a wide berth, almost as if she were unlucky. Something about the power of her weird little performance unsettled me whenever I recalled it. Also, I didn't like the way she looked at us.

The day after Janice came to see us, Abigail and I set about rebuilding our attic, much to our mother's chagrin. The proposed redecoration never got underway. Pretty soon it was back to the way it had always been, and soon after that, even more so, as my sister and I brought back a never-ending supply of treasure from junk shops, jumble sales, second-hand bookshops and other places where the flotsam and jetsam of other people's lives collected.

In the subsequent weeks, we studied the family from the ruined doll's house very carefully. In many ways, they were the eerie artefact we had been searching for all of our lives, but because of the circumstances under which they had been discovered, we found it impossible to enjoy them in the way we would have liked. Had we discovered them ourselves, we would have been free to mythologise them, to pronounce them proof of a murder, or a haunting, or the playthings of a malformed offspring kept in a secret room. Janice Tupp and her ravings had destroyed any chance we had of regarding them in this way, and our explanations for the mutilated figures were all rooted firmly in the rational. A spoilt child became our considered guess – a pudgy Edwardian boy, with a cruel and horrible streak, who exacted revenge upon his sister for some petty transgression by destroying her treasured dolls. And in time, although we never forgot Janice Tupp's strange performance, we learned not to think about it.

Time passed. For the last five months of middle school, Janice Tupp became just another person of our own age who wouldn't talk to us; one of the massed ranks of those who found us too obtuse, too weird, too clever by half. We didn't care. We had each other.

The ghost photograph debacle, far from ending our fascination with strange projects, seemed instead to bolster it, and we subsequently did numerous experiments in all things paranormal. We tried automatic writing. We tried table-turning. We made our own Zener cards and attempted to read each other's minds, concentrating on the symbols until our eyes were hot and our heads tingled.

We also devised what could be called a long-term project. We read somewhere that Aldous Huxley had said that, in the event of his death, he would contact the living by making a book fall off a shelf, and open on a certain page. That page would have a quotation on it which would communicate what the afterlife was like. Apparently, after Huxley died, his widow received exactly such a communication, and a book did indeed fall off a shelf, but the quotation her attention was drawn to was disappointingly generic. I cannot now for the life of me recall where we heard this story, and I have failed to find it since. It may not even have been Aldous Huxley, and could just as easily have been J.W. Dunne or G.K. Chesterton – or anybody, frankly. However, the specifics of the story didn't matter. What really mattered to us was the idea of communicating from beyond the grave.

And so, we resolved that if one of us died, they would do their utmost, wherever they found themselves, to communicate with the other. However, we judged the method of opening books to be too random, too impersonal, too open to misinterpretation, and so we devised something that we thought better.

Abi and I bought a hardback notebook from John Menzies on the high street and took it in turns to write messages we thought might be useful to our dead selves on alternating pages. As with everything Abi and I undertook, there were strict rules to writing in the Book of Fates. We weren't allowed to write anything ambiguous. We had to really think about what would be useful information to impart to the living. We had to write legibly and clearly. Abi wrote in black ink, I in blue. She wrote on the verso pages, I on the recto:

- *I am in Heaven.*
- *I am in Hell.*
- *I am in limbo*
- *I am with other dead people I know*
- *I can see you*
- *There is nothing*

And so on. When we were done, Abi placed it on our bookshelf, between *Witchcraft in England* and *The Mummy of Birchen Bower*, and there it remained, another thing only we knew about.

In this way, summer passed. In the last week of July, we climbed into Dad's ancient Morris Minor and drove down to Dorset for a week, staying in a whitewashed cottage at the end of a private road of yellow gravel. Both of us found the countryside intoxicating and freeing; I still remember the depressing feeling of getting home and seeing the suburban town where we lived as if for the first time, all clashing colours and noise. Nobody, I remember thinking, would voluntarily live in a town or city.

The summer holidays went on, seemingly for ever. When we all sat down for dinner a week or so later, I knew that something was up, because Dad didn't bring a crossword to the dinner table. Supremely uncomfortable he looked too, having to interact with the rest of his family. Halfway through dinner, he found the courage to say what he wanted to say.

'You two. I've been meaning to talk to you for a while now.'

'Uh oh,' said Abi, not looking up from her plate. 'Serious voice.'

'Like he's going to read the news!' I said.

'You two,' said Mum. 'Listen to your father.'

'Thank you, Alice. As I was saying. I had a talk with your former headmaster at parents' day last year. And whilst he was very effusive about your intellectual achievements . . .'

'As he should be,' said Abi.

'Abi, please. Whilst he was very enthusiastic about your marks, he was less than enthusiastic about your attitudes.'

'Oh,' said Abi, looking at Dad for the first time. 'And what did old Rogers have to say about that, then?'

'He felt the two of you were aloof, you only really respected each other's intellect, and in some subjects this made you pretty much unteachable.'

I smiled. *'Owl, you and I have brains.'*

My sister smiled back. '. . . *The others have fluff.*'

'This,' said Dad. 'This is exactly what I'm talking about. This private little world the two of you share. It allows you to develop . . . airs and graces.'

Abi was incredulous. 'What airs and graces, exactly?'

'Well, the idea you're cleverer than everyone else.'

'Well, we are,' Abi shot back, without so much as a pause. 'That's just a fact.' Her voice was entirely free of boastfulness or vanity.

'I can't believe my own children have become this arrogant!' said Dad, with genuine anger.

'It's not arrogance if it's true.' I said this audibly, but not loudly. I sensed we were on thin ice.

'We're not hurting anyone, Dad!'

'That's as maybe, but . . .' Dad regarded us with a cautious, wary expression that threatened to undermine his authority somewhat. 'You're both fourteen now. Long past time you stopped leaning on each other. That's why your teachers and I have taken the decision to send you to separate schools in September.'

'What? Why?'

'So you learn to interact with kids your own age, that's why.'

'We do interact with kids our own age, Dad!'

'Oh, that Tupp girl? Well, she never came round again, did she?'

'Janice Tupp is a moron,' said Abi.

'And there it is again,' said Dad triumphantly. 'You both need to learn to stand on your own two feet, and not look down on people.'

'How eloquent,' said Abi. 'No cliché left unturned.'

'Abigail,' Dad said quietly, 'I swear to God, I have had it with your supercilious attitude. Do you understand me?'

Abi looked at her plate in truculent silence.

'I said, do you understand me?' Dad seldom lost his temper, but when he did, he went all in. He was close to that moment now.

'I understand,' said Abi coldly.

'Well then,' said Dad. 'That's settled. In September, instead of you both going to Northwood, Abi goes to Meadowlands, and Tim, you'll go to Gorston Park.'

'All girls?' said Abi sourly.

'All boys?' I echoed, equally sourly.

'Absolutely,' said Dad. 'Then you'll have no choice but to make friends your own age. It's all been arranged.'

I shoved my plate aside and folded my arms, but I was going through the motions. One school was, to me, pretty much the same as any other, and Abi and I barely spoke to each other during school anyway. It was hard to see what difference any of it would make.

Abi, meanwhile, was furious.

Accordingly, in September, we went to different schools. My sister, dressed in a pencil skirt, white shirt, and red-and-blue striped tie, walked a mile to Meadowlands girls' school, and I, dressed in a dark green blazer with a green-and-yellow tie, caught the bus to Gorston Park.

Annoyingly for our parents, attending different schools made Abi and me closer than ever, at least in the short term. To be fair, I think either one of us would have been relieved to make a friend outside of our house and family, who answered or even exceeded our exacting standards, and wouldn't stare blankly if we mentioned Michel de Montaigne, for instance, or the surgeon's photograph of the Loch Ness Monster, or remarked that something was a 'three pipe problem'. But we didn't find anyone. And so, our separate experiences at different schools became something we tolerated, to return home to the attic and share with the other. Being at different schools gave us a wider variety of idiots to compare and mock in the evenings.

Nonetheless, a shift occurred. At first, it made little or no difference to our lives, but over the following year, there was no way of ignoring what was happening, even to someone as emotionally obtuse as my teenage self. Our frames of reference began to diverge, in a million small ways. Abi began to be interested in pop music, something that had never happened before. She started to experiment with make-up; I got the impression one day that she'd been smoking, though the suspicion only came upon me afterwards and by then it was too late to ask. I suspected there were boys too. I, also, had become interested in other things – vehicles, for instance, and machines, how they fitted together. Part of me toyed with the idea of becoming an engineer, a private surrender to the forces of conventionality that my sister would have been horrified by. I kept this to myself.

We were beginning to become our own people, slowly but surely. Like two tribes that were once joined and were now drifting apart; the further away we drifted, the less we would have in common, until, one day, we wouldn't speak the same language any more. I can see now that this was right and proper, and is the natural way of things. Siblings, twins especially, must go out and forge their own identities, no matter how close their bond. They have to become their own people in order to remain people, in any meaningful sense. I see that now.

In our case, however, this drifting away from each other would never be allowed to run its natural course.

Autumn came and went; the seasons passed. A year and a half went by.

9

Winter 1972 was an exciting time in the world that Abi and I had built between us, woven from my mind to hers and back again in a trillion complex strands. That Christmas, it seemed as if the world had finally caught up with our obsessions, and the TV schedules seemed crammed with supernatural dramas and general oddness that Abi and I dutifully circled with a red biro in the Christmas *Radio Times*, and looked forward to every bit as much as presents, or Christmas dinner.

Firstly, there was *Dead of Night*, a half-hour spooky anthology series, the first episode of which told the story of a middle-class dinner party going terribly wrong after the guests discovered their converted farmhouse was, centuries ago, the site of an awful tragedy. This series concluded just before Christmas, and whetted our appetites.

Secondly, the BBC's annual Ghost Story for Christmas was an adaptation of M.R. James's 'A Warning to The Curious', which was, of course, one of our favourites. The tale of an unfortunate who seeks one of the lost Anglo-Saxon crowns of East Anglia and is visited by its terrible guardian, the adaptation exceeded our expectations, containing lots of terrifying images and one ambiguous moment of pure nightmare that Abi and I discussed and dissected endlessly afterwards.

Better even than this, however, was Nigel Kneale's play *The Stone Tape*, starring Jane Asher, broadcast on BBC 2 on Christmas Day. This managed to be not only absolutely terrifying but also bring to vivid life an idea we had only previously encountered in books. In *The Stone Tape*, a group of audio researchers stay in a haunted house, and begin working on the hypothesis that ghosts are recordings of traumatic events, somehow impressed into the fabric of the building. I don't think either Abi or I spoke during the entire ninety minutes it was on. It fell exactly into line with our thinking on the subject of ghosts – that science might, one day very soon, explain them, understand them, and in so doing open up a whole new way of thinking about the world. This was a perfectly reasonable expectation, back then. We were not alone in believing it.

December rolled into a cold, hard January. *The Stone Tape* had proved to be a shot in the arm to mine and Abi's obsessions, and had temporarily slowed our inevitable drift away from each other. We were making an earnest attempt to persuade our parents to buy us a tape recorder, which they were resisting – not on the grounds that we would use it to make Raudive recordings, the tape recordings of spirit voices first captured in the 1960s by the Latvian scientist Konstantin Raudive (although that was, admittedly, exactly what we planned to do) – but on the grounds that it was expensive. Meanwhile, we talked endlessly about *The Stone Tape*, and tried to devise ways in which the central theory could be proved or disproved, that we could reasonably organise within our means. The programme appeared to justify what we had always believed; that an answer was just around the corner.

Ghosts would be explained, just like everything else in the universe. Maybe we might even be the people to do it.

I was thinking about this, and many other things, one afternoon in January, as I took the long route home from the bus stop along Everson Road.

I was taking this circuitous route to avoid Tony Finch and his gang, who, over the last two weeks, had taken to picking on me on the way home from school. Tony Finch was both nasty and clever, a terrible combination in a bully, and I was properly and unashamedly scared of him. Rumour had it he once threw a kid off the flyover onto the motorway and broke his hip, after hunting him through the woods for an hour beforehand, and I could quite believe this was true. His gang consisted of Cliff Lang, a sneering, sandy-haired creep who agreed with everything Tony said, and Gary Fisher, a gigantic boy whose nickname was 'Frankenstein'. Gary Fisher had all the propensity for cruelty that Tony Finch possessed, with none of the imagination, and so his principle role was as enforcer. They were delinquent and dangerous, and seemed to attend school only when they felt like it, preferring to horse around on railway lines and by the canal. I was by no means their principal target, but I knew I could easily become so if I didn't handle the situation well. I had decided that the best way to prevent this from happening was to avoid them as much as possible, until they either lost interest or fried themselves on the railway line that seemed to exert such a fascination for them.

That afternoon, however, I was so absorbed in thinking about *The Stone Tape*, and the possible implications of it, that I didn't notice Cliff Lang lurking around the trunk of one of the leafless trees on Everson Road, smiling his trademark unpleasant smile. And now it was too late, and he was standing in front of me, blocking my way. Behind him, I could see Tony Finch himself, all glossy black hair and a brown leather jacket with an elasticated waistband and an enormous, chunky zipper. Behind Tony, I spied the colossal bulk of Gary Fisher, bringing up the rear like a bear on a chain.

Having no better plan, I tried to walk past this grinning obstacle as if he weren't there. Cliff, still smiling, stepped sideways to block my path. I tried to go round him the other way, and he once again sidestepped to block my path. He was the same height as me, and our eyes locked. His were large and blue, with nothing but low cunning in them.

'Tim Smith?'

I nodded cautiously. He grinned.

'Tim *Shit* more like! Eh? Eh?'

Gary Fisher hooted with laughter, but Tony Finch remained impassive, observing, his hands stuffed into his jacket pockets. I could extrapolate nothing useful from his expression. My heart thumped unevenly, as if it were pumping porridge rather than blood.

'Wow,' I heard myself say. 'Were you working on that one all morning?'

I was as surprised as anyone to hear myself say these words. Having said them, I began to observe myself objectively, as if I were someone else; close by, but out of harm's way. *Wow*, I thought. *What else am I capable of?* I was genuinely fascinated to see what I would do next.

Cliff Lang looked furious, and confused, and – after he saw that Tony Finch was quietly laughing – laughing *at* him – murderous. 'Ooh!' said Gary Fisher, in a way that said *Well, you've just signed your own death warrant.*

You spend your life at school, if you're a quiet, bookish child, avoiding physical violence at all costs. I think now – as

I thought then – that this stems more from a fear of unpredictability and chaos than a fear of pain itself. A fight amongst two teenagers is a zone without rules, and anything can happen. It was that savage space, I think – that space of no rules and no help, where you are utterly on your own – that I feared the most. I think most of us do, deep down, and quite rightly.

I was almost relieved when Cliff Lang just punched me in the side of the head, as hard as he could.

I spun around but just about managed to keep my balance. Lang shoved past me, and as he did so, he spat onto the lapel of my blazer. I was just coming to terms with this when Gary Fisher shoved past. As Gary Fisher was essentially a Clydesdale forced into an ill-fitting school uniform, this time I did lose my balance, and went flying onto the pavement.

When I looked up, Tony Finch was looking down at me. I expected a punch or a kick, but he just smiled. Something about his smile made me realise he wasn't laughing at me: he was still laughing at the joke I'd made, at Cliff Lang's expense. Unexpectedly, Tony Finch was amused by me.

'Better luck next time,' he said. 'Say hello to that sister of yours for me.'

After they had gone, I picked myself up, gathered my belongings together and walked soberly down a long tarmac alleyway that was always a minefield of dog mess. Halfway along its length, when I knew that I would be able to see anyone approaching with a two-minute head start from either direction, I broke into a series of short, violent, angry sobs. I was not physically injured, of course, but my opinion of myself had been unacceptably defaced. After five minutes, however, my tears had subsided, and after ten, were gone altogether.

*

Even before I got home, I had resolved not to tell Abi about the bullying.

It was odd to even think that that's what it had been – *bullying*. I had been *bullied*. I had, somehow, turned into the kind of person that that happened to, largely by not paying attention. If I told Abi about it, she would insist on interceding somehow, and that might well make things worse. Besides, I thought, I might be able to keep such incidents as rare as possible, or avoid them altogether, if I was vigilant. As far as masculine pride went, I would just have to lick my wounds in private.

Instead, I decided, I would share my thoughts on the tape recorder project with Abi. My plan was to make recordings in the attic, and then to try and make recordings in places where the atmosphere was more likely to be saturated with echoes of the past. I was already wondering whether the vicar would let us record in the local church.

That, I recall clearly, was my general plan for the evening. Instead, something else happened. It becomes difficult to remember the sequence of it with any real clarity; linear time appears to break down entirely, becoming instead a series of bright, painful memories that, even now, refuse to fit together into anything as streamlined as a neat narrative, or a smooth progression. They are bright, sharp shards, orbiting an ines-capable darkness.

10

It started slowly.

Abi wasn't due home from school at the usual time that day, as she had chess club. She had kept up playing chess at her new school, and I think she found the higher ability level of her new opponents invigorating. Despite the competition, Abigail was, naturally, ranked Board One, the best player on her team. That night, they were playing the nearby Catholic girls' school, St Peter-in-Chains, and Abigail was itching to play their Board One, who had won the regional chess congress the previous year (I learned later that Abi had indeed played their Board One that evening and had won). Afterwards, Abi elected to walk home rather than get a lift in the school minibus with Mr Benson, her teacher, and the rest of the team. It was not out of the ordinary for the supervising teacher to let this happen, even on a cold January evening when it got dark at about five to four.

I think it was sometime around 6.30 p.m. that my mum first remarked that Abi was late, and should be home soon. By 7 p.m. Dad was mentioning this too. I kept quiet; my sister was beginning to have secrets of her own that I was not privy to, and I did not wish to get her into trouble. Besides, 7 p.m.

was not impossibly late, although it was unlike Abi not to phone. Maybe she didn't have change, I thought.

By 8 p.m., we were all worried. My heart was beating very fast indeed, and it seemed as if an awful possibility was gathering strength and sickening speed around us, willing itself into reality, into concrete being. I was shaking with fear by 9 p.m., when my mum phoned Mr Benson, and by the time she called the police half an hour later, I was practically hyperventilating. They promised to send someone over as soon as they could.

At 9.45, the doorbell rang, and Mum, Dad and I scrambled to answer it. I hoped, hoped, hoped it would be Abi. She would be covered in mud, having got lost on the way home. Her face would be tear-streaked. She'd have lost her keys, which would be why she'd rung the doorbell. We'd all hug her gratefully and cry and laugh and tell her off in an affectionate way for worrying us half to death. My dad threw the front door open.

Two police officers stood there, a man and a woman. Their faces were devoid of expression. They looked like the Autons, the evil race of shop-window dummies from *Doctor Who,* only much more real than anything I had ever seen on television. That was their principal terror, I decided, their very solidity and undeniable reality. I watched them, hypnotised by the actuality of them, unable to speak.

'Mrs Smith?' said the WPC.

'That's me, officer,' said my mum.

'You called to say your daughter Abigail hadn't returned from school.'

'That's right, officer. Has she been found?'

'Well,' said the male officer, 'why don't we come inside and you can tell us all about it?'

'Just tell me where she is,' said Mum.

'Alice!' said Dad. 'I'm sorry, she's a bit hysterical. She's very worried. Please come in. Alice, be so good as to make our guests some tea.'

The two police officers shuffled into the living room, with a wordless awkwardness. Again, they seemed more real than the house around them, more real than anything I had ever seen. Whilst Mum made tea, Dad and I told them about Abi.

'Has she ever done anything like this before?' asked the WPC, not looking up from her notebook.

'Never,' said Dad.

'And it's not like her to go wandering off?'

'No,' I said. 'She has very little interest in what she calls "the tedium of suburbia".'

Dad shot me a look. The male officer looked at me curiously, but decided to let whatever was bothering him about this statement go. 'And you say she had . . . chess club?'

'That's right,' said Dad. 'Every Tuesday. Even if it's an away match, it's never more than two or three miles away. So she's normally home by six-thirty at the absolute latest.'

The WPC wrote something in her notebook.

'How would you describe her emotional state?'

My dad looked baffled by the question. He shrugged. 'Normal?'

'What I mean by that is, do you have any reason to suspect she might have run away from home?'

'She wouldn't do that,' I said.

'Timothy, please.' My Dad shot me another look. 'As far as we know, Abigail had no reason to run away.'

'As far as you know.'

'As far as we know.'

'She wouldn't have run away,' said Mum, coming back in with a tray laden with mugs of tea and a plate of Bourbon biscuits. I felt pleased that she echoed my opinion on the matter so exactly.

'Not to see friends? Or a boyfriend?'

My mum shook her head. 'She keeps herself to herself, really.'

'Well, I'm sure she'll be home before you know it,' said the male policeman, winking at me as if we were drinking companions. 'Do you have a photo of her we might have?'

There were several recent school photos of Abi on top of the television, but they were all in glass frames, and too large to take. However, stuck into the frame of one of them were several other photos of Abi, including the photo I had taken two years ago, to use up the last exposure on the end of our roll of ghost film. She had been almost fourteen when the picture was taken; now she was almost sixteen, but the photo had always made her look older, and it was a good likeness. Plus, she was smiling in it, which was rare. Dad tugged it loose from the frame and handed it, and two others, over.

'We'd like those back, if that's possible,' said my mum.

'Right you are.' The male policeman placed the photographs in his notebook, took a gulp of tea, and my dad walked both him and the WPC to the front door.

After they'd left the room, my mum turned to me.

'Where do you think she is?'

'I don't know, Mum. I honestly don't know.'

'Right.'

My dad returned, and the three of us sat in silence for a very long time, until I could stand it no longer and went up to my room.

*

I awoke the next morning, still in my school uniform. There was a tantalising split-second of normality before I remembered the situation, and ran downstairs.

Mum was sitting at the kitchen table, staring out of the window. I felt a huge and terrible kick of desolation.

'She hasn't come back?' It seemed impossible.

Mum shook her head. I pulled up a chair next to her and took her hand, and we both stared out of the window. Neither of us said anything for what must have been half an hour.

Eventually, it was Mum who broke the silence. Standing up, she walked over to the sink and gripped the edge of the metal draining board, with movements that were economical and precise, like those of an automaton.

'Would you like some breakfast?' she said.

'I'm fine, Mum.'

'You need to eat.'

'Really. I'm fine.'

Before the horrible silence could fall again, I decided to speak. *Say something*, I thought. *Anything.*

'What are we going to do, Mum?'

'We're going to wait,' said Mum simply. 'I can put some toast on for you.'

'Mum?'

'I heard what you said, Tim. You need to eat.'

'I'm not hungry.'

'If I make it, you'll eat it.'

'Mum . . .'

'If I make it, you'll eat it. You will, won't you?'

I sighed. 'Yes, Mum.'

Later that day, the police returned, the same two officers who had called round previously (which, I recalled with a shock, was less than twenty-four hours ago). They intended, they said, to circulate the pictures so that they could begin an appeal for more information. And with that, I felt the awful narrative gather strength around us, forcing itself into the world.

After the police left, I tried to fight this new narrative in the only way I could, by acts of small magic and superstition. If I could count ten birds from the attic window in under five minutes, Abi would be home safe. If I wrote all the names of our enemies on a piece of paper and burned it in a glass ashtray, Abi would be safe. If I could throw a screwed-up ball of paper into the bin on the first go, Abi would be home safe. Best of three. Best of five. Best of seven.

Incredibly, the situation continued into the next day. How? How was this possible? I awoke, went downstairs, had a more or less identical conversation with my mother to the one we had had the previous day, and waited. Dad was out at the police station, and returned after breakfast, with no news whatsoever, which, upon pressing him, turned into the news that police were searching fields and woods, waste ground and rubbish dumps. There was talk of *dragging the canal*. My mother and I listened to this in cold silence, a tear slowly wandering down my mother's clenched cheek. I felt terrible for her. For myself, I felt very little. A vast and silent blackness seemed to have opened up beneath me – within me – and I was being drawn into it, moment by moment, now, like a black hole, and I was powerless to resist.

On the third day, Abi's disappearance was all over the news, which I first became aware of when Dad put the radio on in the morning. It was intolerable to hear the newsreader describe her, hearing her full name, hearing her called *local schoolgirl* and so on and so forth. Family members called, some of them tearful, some gripped by a purposeful anger towards some nebulous force or other they considered the culprit. The new role thrust upon Dad — somewhere between publicist and grief counsellor — was exhausting him, as he replaced the phone in its cradle only to have it spring into hateful life again immediately. I went up to the attic.

The attic itself was too much to look at, so filled with Abi's presence I expected her to poke her head through the trap-door at any moment, and so I looked down at the garden, attempting not to think.

At the bottom of the garden, a magpie and a crow fought some vitally important territorial struggle over the stone bird bath. The birds fought silently, and as I watched, the battle became more serious, more loaded with intention. They danced around the rim of the bird bath like boxers, jabbing occasionally with their beaks. The magpie started to make a series of aggressive staccato cries, and the crow responded with a single, supremely threatening sound, a mirthless dead laugh that caused the magpie to jump backwards and take off. The crow seemed to find not even the merest sliver of satisfaction in this victory, and instead paced the border of the sandstone bath with an affectedly serious air, like a respectful undertaker. I became aware that someone was standing behind me.

Watching the birds as they fought. Watching me, too. Close enough for me to feel their breath, or the warmth of their body, to hear any words they might speak. I turned, instantly and absolutely afraid, instantly and absolutely hopeful.

The attic was empty.

I was alone.

Of course I was. Who else would have been up there? And yet, I had felt, with the certainty that bypasses the mind and belongs to the memory of muscle and bone and gut, that there had been someone with me. Standing deliberately behind me, deliberately close. To see me turn. To see me gasp. No, I told myself, beating my head with a useless half-fist that fear had made for me, no. There was no way it could be anything. What you felt, you didn't feel. Something that isn't allowed to be grief, but desperately wants to be, is seeking release. I had felt – nothing.

And yet I had. The creeping discomfort of being looked at, scrutinised, assessed, *evaluated* – a feeling so central to the human experience. To discern a gaze, and recognise the intent behind that gaze.

And now, somebody was calling my name, over and over. In tones of rising annoyance. Dad's voice.

Quietly and calmly I walked towards the trapdoor and swung myself onto the ladder, taking one last look at the attic, which seemed to seethe with scheming emptiness.

Downstairs, Dad was on the phone again. 'Yes,' he was saying, over and over. 'Yes. Yes.' I stood and waited as he listened to things I couldn't hear.

'Yes. One second, Richard.' He placed a hand over the receiver. 'Could you go down to the shops for me, Tim? Get the papers?'

'Which ones?'

He fished in his trouser pocket with his free hand and produced a crumpled pound note.

'All of them.'

11

Retrospectively, we give our lives shape, regardless of the chaos they seem to be at the time.

Here, then, begins the story of how I ended up having what I can now see was some kind of nervous breakdown. It all feels neat and tidy, expressed in this way, as if I understood at the time what was happening to me, and could clearly see a direction to events, but I would only realise it many years later.

It was the first time I had left the house in three days, since I had come home from school and Abi had not. Outside, the world seemed mockingly ordinary. Cars were still parked along the street, lampposts hung like question marks against a featureless sky of white wax. The houses on our street – large and Victorian and, for the most part, crumbling and time-beaten – ignored me, as they always did, haughty as duchesses. It was all familiar, but in no way comforting.

At the end of the road, a choice: go to the newsagent in the small shopping arcade by the council houses, or the one on the high street? Both were roughly equidistant, but I decided on the high street as there was a strong chance that Tony Finch and his two lieutenants would be hanging around the arcade, and meeting them was the last thing I needed that day. The streets seemed strangely empty, as if everyone had disappeared, following Abi's example, and it took me a while to remember that today was Friday, and therefore still a school day. My parents had taken the unprecedented step of not insisting I go to school, which I had previously imagined nothing short of a full-blown world war could precipitate. Upon this realisation, I stopped, momentarily, in my tracks, reminded again that life as I had always understood it was transforming.

Everson Road, which eventually connected our road with the bottom of the high street, was empty, with the white sky pressing down so tightly upon it that it felt as if the road itself was struggling to breathe. Slug-shaped blobs of dirty, unmelted snow perched on garden walls and fences, on kerbs and car bonnets.

And then, with a shock, I saw Abi. Staring back at me.

MISSING: HAVE YOU SEEN THIS GIRL? Her face, on a poster, pinned to a tree. I stood and stared, as if I had seen Abi herself. She smiled out of the past, looking through me to something I couldn't identify. It was the photo I had taken in the attic. I felt hot tears come, and chose instead to run on, run away.

The newsagent's shop was oppressively dark. Behind the counter was Mr Edgar, a man who seemed to exist in a permanent state of apoplexy, and hated the schoolchildren whose patronage was the cornerstone of his business. For some reason – probably for the same reason that grown-ups always liked Abi and myself, because we seemed responsible and mature – he was always pleasant to me. In many ways this was worse than his dislike, as he harboured a staggering array of extremely right-wing views I always felt compelled to nod along to, out of some sense of misplaced deference and respect for my elders, and I was always terrified lest someone from school heard me agreeing with him. Today, though, he only greeted me with a watery, cowardly smile and found something urgent to do behind the counter. I soon saw why.

The same picture of Abi – my picture – was on the front page of every single paper. The same picture, over and over. Abi, taken by me, grinning with satisfaction at the thought of our fake ghost photograph, and the sheer delight at completing another strange and macabre project. Only I would ever know, ever completely understand, what that smile was for. I scooped up a copy each of all of the newspapers as best I could and placed them on the counter, now fighting back tears in earnest.

Mr Edgar didn't return my gaze as he gathered up the newspapers, didn't see the thin smile I had scraped together for him out of some semblance of basic courtesy. He also wouldn't accept the pound note, and pushed it gently but firmly back into my hand.

As I walked home, laden with newspapers, folded over so I wouldn't have to look at the picture of Abi, deliberately walking down the opposite side of Everson Road from the tree with the poster on it for the same reason, I remembered something. I remembered what Janice had said that day she came over, when she had fallen to her knees and started shouting at us with a voice that wasn't quite hers. Most of it I recalled only vaguely – and I had the distinct impression it had been the kind of things myself or Abi might have said, if we had found ourselves attempting to achieve what Janice was attempting – but some parts had been too powerful and strange to forget.

She had said something I had never quite been able to satisfactorily quantify or accommodate, and it had marked the point at which Janice's strange performance had genuinely started to scare me.

But you did photograph a real ghost, despite everything. Or you will have done, soon.

We had taken twenty-three pictures of our ghost, and I had taken one of Abi, the one where she looked far older than her nearly-fourteen years. I had taken it almost as an afterthought, to use up the roll of film. And now it was displayed everywhere – on trees and in newspapers, the icon at the centre of her disappearance. The image that people would think of when they heard her name.

But you did photograph a real ghost, despite everything. Or you will have done, soon.

I was so absorbed in thinking about this and the possible implications of it that I didn't notice Cliff Lang appear from around the trunk of one of the leafless trees, smiling his unpleasant smile, where a crowd of too many teeth jostled for position. I inhaled sharply. He saw the shock and fear in my eyes and drank it in. I looked down the road, but there was no sign of Tony Finch or Gary Fisher. Again, I tried to walk past him; again he blocked my path.

'Going somewhere?'

'Leave me alone,' I said. I was surprised at how tired I sounded. I tried to walk round him, but Cliff Lang wasn't going to let me go, that day. He turned me round and slammed me up against the tree.

'What do you want?' I said, exasperated.

'What do you want?' he repeated, in a baby voice. 'Listen to you. You sound like a girl.'

'Is this about the other day?' I said. I noticed something for the first time. I was very slightly taller than Cliff Lang. Broader.

'No, not a girl. You sound like a *queer*.' Cliff Lang jabbed my face with a finger as he said these words. I wished he'd just get on with whatever he was doing and stop wasting my time. I looked down at the newspapers over my arm and sighed. Cliff Lang followed my gaze.

'Oh yeah, your sister's gone, hasn't she? That's right. Probably run away from *you*, you little prick. It's a shame, she looked right dirty.'

Cliff Lang might have had other things he wanted to say on this theme, but my fist came up faster than both he and I could think. He must have bit his tongue, as he squealed, and blood burst from his mouth. He staggered back, in momentary shock, and I hit him again, inexpertly, the flat palm of my outstretched hand slamming into his nose, which also bled. He recovered enough from this to land one really excellent punch on my left eye, but then the situation became something he hadn't anticipated and couldn't control; I leapt on him with the full force of my anger, kicking, slapping, biting, scratching, grabbing hold of his face and tearing it. I was operating from pure fury, drawing on a vast subterranean reservoir of resentment and bile that I was unaware of, a white light that flowed through me. My animal howls rang up and down empty Everson Road. I was barely present for any of it.

I remember being pulled away from Cliff Lang, first by one pair of hands and then by another, far stronger, pair.

'Easy there, psycho.' It was Tony Finch. To my surprise, he was not talking to Cliff Lang. He was talking to me.

Cliff Lang got shakily to his feet. There was mud all over his clothes, and his face was a mess of blood and snot. And tears.

'He's crying,' I said, sneering. 'God, he's crying!' And I went for him again, but Gary Fisher anticipated this and held me back.

'Don't you dare talk about my sister!' I said. 'Not now! Not ever!'

'Did you say something about his sister?' said Tony Finch, in a quiet voice of pure flint. Cliff Lang looked absolutely terrified.

'I didn't mean it, Tony! I was just joking! It was a joke!'

Tony Finch looked almost sad. A line had been crossed. And nobody knew that more than Cliff Lang, who, having got his tears under control, looked as if he would start crying again.

'Tony—'

Tony Finch ran his hand through his hair, a very deliberate, almost delicate gesture. It seemed to take a long time. Then, he punched Cliff Lang in the stomach, and, as he went down, kicked him twice more, in the stomach and the head. He stopped at that; justice had been served, and no more effort need be expended. With surprising grace, he picked up the sheaf of newspapers I had dropped and handed them to me.

'See you around, *psycho*,' said Tony Finch. Gary Fisher smiled a lopsided smile at me, and the two of them turned and made their way along Everson Road.

Cliff Lang gasped and sobbed at my feet.

I gave him a final kick in the stomach.

Dad was still on the phone when I got home. The way he raised his eyebrows in greeting when I came in was so redolent of normal times, of business as usual, that I felt as if I might weep. He paused when he saw my eye, but I was gone before he could properly register it. My mother bustled in soon after,

79

having been to the doctor's for stress and insomnia, both of which had manifested themselves since Abi's disappearance. I waved hello but she barely saw me, instead removing a box of tablets from her bag and taking two in rapid succession.

I headed upstairs. I remembered I had been thinking about what Janice had said, and something about how it might fit together in a way I hadn't considered before, but I was too weary and full of adrenalin to pursue it.

12

A week later, Abi had still not returned. Daily life in our own home became a thing of unbelievable pressure and strain, where carrying on as normal was simply impossible, but was nonetheless the only available course of action. None of us were sleeping well, and the sleep I did manage to attain was filled with bad dreams that were less nightmares than insoluble problems from which I would awake in darkness, a frustrated scream echoing round the room. If my parents heard me scream, they didn't mention it. And why would they? It would not have seemed unusual or incongruous. Waking hours were the mirror image of these unsettled and tormented nights, long, featureless days punctuated by the shrill ring of the telephone and my heart leaping, only for the situation to reassert itself, the atmosphere of the house instantly and totally returning to cloying claustrophobia. We were all losing weight, and none of us now ate at the same time. We only spoke to each other when we needed to. My parents did not seek me out for comfort, nor I them. And every day, Abi remained stubbornly, intractably, hatefully absent.

Over the ten days since Abi had vanished, various people had come forward to say they'd seen her, all of them utterly unreliable and useless as witnesses in their various ways. An old woman, Mrs Penrose, who lived two streets away and had always had great difficulty telling me and my sister apart, said that she had seen 'Amanda' accepting a ride from a young man on a motorbike, the day she vanished, or possibly the day before. Harry Belt, the locally tolerated 'Gentleman of the Road', who drank methylated spirits and lived on the benches outside the Town Hall, stopped my mum to say he'd seen Abi a week previously, in the park, getting followed around by a 'gang of coloured lads', declaring that he 'wouldn't be surprised if they'd kidnapped her', because 'you know what they're like'. My mother, unfailingly polite at the best of times, had thanked him for this valuable information and promised to pass it on to the relevant authorities. She had smiled a smile so tight and contained I thought her teeth might crack, and I wanted to punch Harry Belt in his red, drunken face for making her pretend like that. One local busybody insisted in letters to the local paper that Abi had run away with the gypsies, or possibly joined a cult, and the correspondents of national newspapers were no less shy in advancing their own theories, always in a high-handed tone that implied they were experts on the matter.

On it went, people with no connection whatsoever to Abi or my family, voicing their idiot opinions and half-baked theories as to what might have befallen her, in pubs and shops and periodicals, local and national. I could not be expected to go to school under these circumstances, so I didn't, instead wandering the streets, or taking trains and buses the full length of their route, disembarking at whatever far-flung terminus I found myself on and getting straight back on the same train or bus in the opposite direction. It seemed as good a use of my time as any.

And then, a week later, an apparently reliable witness came forward, and everything changed again.

The police told us about this lead before it was in the papers, thankfully. Mrs Lacey worked in the Co-op on the high street, which would definitely have been on Abigail's route home from chess club that fateful night. She worked the afternoon shift, before the shop closed at 6 p.m. She knew Abi by sight, and had seen her that night.

Abi had come in to buy a can of lemonade, and had been followed around the shop by a man, who was chatting to her so animatedly that Mrs Lacey had assumed that Abi knew him, even though she said very little in return. He had moved around the shelves talking to her, whilst Abi had smiled respectfully and kept her distance. Eventually, the man had bought twenty John Player Special and a box of matches, a copy of the *Daily Mirror* and a packet of sweets, and had chatted a little to Mrs Lacey, whose attention was focused on ringing the items up on the till. The man had left and Mrs Lacey watched him through the plate-glass window at the front of the shop, as he leaned against a large brown van and smoked. He seemed to be waiting for something, and it was logical to presume that something might be Abi.

Mrs Lacey couldn't recall anything else, apart from one detail. On the side of the brown van he drove was a name – his name, she assumed – which was also the name of his business. Mrs Lacey couldn't remember the name, or what line of work the man was in, but she did remember one thing: the name started with an S. In fact, a day later, when the story found its way into the newspapers, they were already describing the man as 'Mister S'.

In the attic, I read all of these details in a one-page spread in the *Daily Express*. As well as a photo of Mrs Lacey, and one of the Co-op, and the ubiquitous photo of Abi, there was an illustration accompanying the piece, an artist's impression of the man in the shop, drawn from Mrs Lacey's description. It sat alongside the photo of Abi, and was exactly the same size.

I looked at the illustration, and it seemed to telescope away from me, downwards, into a place where there was only blackness.

I recalled now my train of thought before I had been interrupted by my fight with Cliff Lang. I remained motionless, staring down into the depths of the illustration, and considered the unthinkable.

A perfunctory police search notwithstanding, Abi's room was almost as she'd left it the morning she'd gone out and not returned. Her schoolbooks were on her desk; an olive-coloured cardigan hung on the brass bedstead. Abi would have found comparisons with the *Mary Celeste* trite, so I considered instead that I was entering her room in the service of an investigation, like a detective, a scenario she would definitely have approved of. Nevertheless, I felt very much like an intruder, as I always did in Abi's room. I was suddenly worried about how I would justify being in here when Abi found out, and this thought made me laugh, cheered me, and – worse still – gave me hope. We would laugh about this one day. We would.

Her desk drawer was locked, but the key hung on a ribbon round the neck of a porcelain Siamese cat that had sat on her desk for as long as I could remember. There, inside the drawer, amongst other things – letters, a diary, some photos – was her owl notebook. I locked the drawer again and replaced the key.

Crossing the landing, it suddenly hit me. The last person to lock that drawer had been Abi. She had locked it, and I had opened it. It was odd, but that fact upset me considerably, and made the unthinkable feel suddenly very real. Children and teenagers went missing all the time, the papers were always full of such stories, and the narratives, as far as I knew, always went the same way, without exception. A child went missing. A family was distraught. There was a space of time – a week, two weeks, a month – where the hope that they might turn up alive burned and guttered like a candle. After a time, and usually not very much time, a body would turn up. And that would be the end.

I had done my best not to think about the situation that we were all – my mother, father and myself – trapped in. However, suppressing it only made it stronger, and now it broke over me like a vast black wave. A living hand had opened the drawer, but in all likelihood the hand that had locked it was now dead. And in that second of absolute isolation, of the utter undeniable truth that we now inhabited – I knew. I knew that Abi was dead. To deny it would be to deny all the things that Abi held dear – pragmatism, method, the necessity – the duty of facing facts in life, no matter how unpleasant they may be or how we might wish things were otherwise. I would never see my sister again.

I went to the attic and sank numbly into an armchair. I didn't have a desk, but it hadn't felt right to stay in Abi's room and sit at hers. I stared at the owl notebook in front of me. I realised I would never have opened it if I thought Abi was still alive. In its own way, this was a test. I opened the book.

Much of the book was beautiful. She had written poems, a great many of them, and she had illustrated each one with a large illuminated letter, or a floral border, or a one-page illustration. I flicked through the titles. *Mercy Me. I am the Owl. A Test of Faith.* Other pages had sketches, some of them simple – the Uffington White Horse, with which she had covered two pages – and some very complex, such as a series of geometric solids that she'd drawn in order to understand how light and shade fell on such things, until the maths of it eluded her and mistakes overwhelmed order like flames leaping from a burning building.

Eventually, I found what I was looking for. My own handwriting, looking undisciplined and childish next to Abi's: '*The Compleyte Prophecies of Janys Tuppe of Thisse Parishe*'. It seemed a lot less amusing now than it had then. Janice's words came back to me, with unexpected force: *You two think you're clever, but you're not.*

I read over Janice's words from that afternoon, beginning with those she'd spoken whilst pointing at me.

I see you. I see the broken house, with all the broken people in it. I see it coming back for you. I see four halves and two quarters. I see it returning, and it will never let you go. It will always be with you.

Apart from the bit about the broken doll's house – which actually seemed more like a lucky guess now than ever – this all seemed reassuringly gibberish. Delivered cold on the page, in Abi's still-comforting handwriting rather than Janice Tupp's hissing rasp, it seemed risible, foolish even.

I read the next line. A cold, tight panic gripped me.

Twenty grins all grinning back at you, salt in the wound, and you break.

I was out of the armchair now, standing up – totally and completely afraid. For this line was entirely, chillingly precise, and had come to pass. An image in my mind, terribly vivid, of the rows and rows of newspapers before me, and from each one, the same face grinning back at me, the picture of Abigail that had become the symbol and icon of her vanishing. Twenty versions of the same picture, grinning up at me from the newsagent's rack.

If this was right, what else was right?

Trembling, I read the part Janice had directed at Abigail.

I see you too. I see you there but you can't see me. Grinning away again, showing your teeth, saying nothing but sand. And you can't stop it now. What else is there to do? What good is being clever now? Here? And you can't stop this.

He's coming for you. He has eyes but no face. He's near.

Any observer who chose to watch me in the attic at that moment would see a boy, almost sixteen, behaving with virtually preternatural calm: sitting down very precisely, smoothing out the thighs of his corduroy trousers, inhaling and exhaling very deliberately, before holding the book up to eye level and reading the words carefully, over and over.

I see you but you can't see me.

Abi was dead.

What else is there to do?

Nothing.

What good is being clever now?

No good. No good at all.

He's coming for you. He has eyes but no face.

I had construed this as a reference to our fake ghost that had scared her so much, whose chalk eyes burned out of his formless face like a threat. At the time, I had thought it was pathetic. Now, however, I held up the newspaper where the police sketch of Mister S – from the scant details given by Mrs Lacey – was printed.

Long, lank hair framed an empty space. There was no mouth, no nose. But there were eyes. Two dark eyes, with a defiant, amused look, their glare burning out of the sketch.

Eyes. But no face.

And then the words that Janice had practically screamed at us: *He's near! He can't be stopped!*

My sister's transcript ended there, but I knew it was incomplete. After informing us that *he can't be stopped,* but before Abigail had doused her with water and slapped her into submission, Janice had said something else. The same word, twice. Elongated into a thin hiss. As if she were about to utter a name but couldn't quite bring herself to do so. Abigail, whose memory was even better than mine, would no doubt have recalled this, but had clearly deemed it irrelevant and not written it down. I was surprised that I recalled it at all. But, now, I found that I remembered it very clearly.

'*Esssssss . . .*' Janice had hissed. '*Esssss . . .*'

I discovered I was crying again. I forced myself to stop, and the attic fell silent.

My mother was ironing, mechanically pressing and folding sheets and napkins. My father was simply sitting, and either thinking or daydreaming, staring at the pattern on the wallpaper as if it were a scrying glass, and might tell him secrets. They both, in their separate ways, looked defeated and reduced, eaten away by the corrosive, inescapable now, the unendurable situation that nonetheless had to be endured.

I stood with my back to the mantelpiece, until I had both of their attention. My mum set the iron on its base and looked at me searchingly.

'What is it?'

I cleared my throat. There was no point in trying to dress this up.

'Abi is dead.'

II

13

On the first anniversary of Abi's disappearance, I sat in Mr Henshaw's room, the one with the large bay window, and talked, for the hundredth time, about my feelings.

Although I didn't like talking to him very much, I quite liked Mr Henshaw. 'You can call me Neville, if you want to,' he had said, during our first ever appointment. I had not wanted to, so Mr Henshaw he had remained. This call-me-by-my-first-name business was typical of Mr Henshaw, who was at pains, always, to appear sympathetic to me, *on my side*, just as baffled by the big old crazy world as I, a person twelve or thirteen years his junior. Mr Henshaw's consulting room was the front parlour of his large Victorian house. Apart from the chairs we sat in, there was only one piece of furniture, a bookshelf filled with psychology books called things like *You – Me – We*, and *The Path of Progress* and *The Listening Cure*. An acoustic guitar lurked ominously in a corner; I was perpetually afraid that Mr Henshaw would one day be moved to strap it on and express himself in song, but he never did. Mr Henshaw himself – with his shoulder-length brown hair, tidy beard and bead necklace – had undoubtedly been 'in a band' at some point: folk-rock, most likely. The songs would be called things like 'The Ballad of Pippin Took' and 'Vinegar Tom'. The second side of their one and only LP would conclude with a cover of a folk standard: 'The Lincolnshire Poacher', perhaps, or 'The Barley Grain for Me'. Mr Henshaw had probably always been too serious to be anything as strident or frivolous as lead singer, though he'd probably written the songs. My guess was he'd been rhythm guitarist, whilst his more charismatic friend, who had a hairy chest and an Eye of Horus pendant, was lead singer, and got all the girls, who he naturally called *birds,* including the blonde keyboard player, who Mr Henshaw secretly—

'Tim?' I became aware of Mr Henshaw's face, creased in a frown, staring at me. 'Are you all right? I asked you a question.'

'I'm sorry,' I said. 'I was just thinking about something.'

Mr Henshaw's face looked even more laden with concern than usual. 'What were you thinking about, Tim?'

It was, as always, easier to lie. 'I was thinking about how *unfair* the world is,' I said. In this place, with this audience, I found I could play the petulant teenager indefinitely, railing at gigantic, nebulous issues – society, violence, man's inhumanity to man – all day, to absolutely no avail, moving the therapeutic process on not one jot. Indeed, this was what I had been doing for six months.

Mr Henshaw leaned back in his wicker chair, hands clasped around one thin knee, in a way that looked incredibly uncomfortable. However, once settled, he did not move.

'Well now,' he said. 'Is there any reason you can think of that you might be thinking that?'

'I don't know,' I said, taking a deep breath. 'The abduction and murder of my sister, perhaps?'

Something flashed in poor Mr Henshaw's eyes, something intimately connected to kindness and empathy, and I felt very, very bad for hurling this rock at him so brutally. Whatever else Mr Henshaw was, he was genuine in his concern for me. He cared. I was immediately gripped by a small passion of adolescent embarrassment, replaying my last spoken sentence over and over again in my head, listening to how spiteful and juvenile it sounded. My face became hot.

'I'm sorry,' I said, eventually.

Mr Henshaw smiled a brave smile.

'That's fine, Tim. If I were in your position, I expect I would be very angry. Very angry and upset.'

'Yes.'

'A terrible thing happened, to someone close to you. It's only right you should feel anger sometimes.'

'Yes.'

'There are no wrong feelings, Tim. Just feelings.'

'Yes.'

'You have a right to be angry, Tim. A perfect right.'

'Yes.'

'But,' said Mr Henshaw, his voice soft, 'you have to remember that the world is, at its root, a *good* place. A place where good people live, and good things happen. I mean, yes, bad things too, but those are the exception, rather than the rule. The basic law of the world – I believe – is love. Wouldn't you agree, Tim?'

I looked out of the bay window. The pathway to the house was edged with large stones, all covered with green moss, apart from one. This one was dusted with large and small fragments of the same material, patterned brown on one side, pearl-white on the other. I had half-noticed it this morning, although it was only now I realised what it was. Every so often, a song-thrush would come to that stone with a live snail it had caught, which had retreated into its shell. The thrush would then batter the snail against the stone. When the shell had collapsed to the thrush's satisfaction, the bird would clutch it with its clawed foot, then extract the ruined mess of the snail with its beak.

'Tim?'

'Yes,' I said.

Outside Mr Henshaw's enormous house, I felt the same numbness I always felt after our sessions together, as the effort of carefully managing an entire hour of conversation in order to avoid discussing anything of consequence came to a close. Part of me wished Mr Henshaw was more aggressive, that he might one day just grab me by the shoulders and shout at me to *pull myself together*. I was aware that I permitted myself this fantasy safe in the knowledge it would never happen.

At the gate, Tony Finch lurked, smoking. He smiled when he saw me.

'How was the shrink, psycho?'

'Great. You'll be glad to know I'm still dangerously insane.'

He grinned sloppily and gave a thumbs-up. 'Nice one.'

There were just the two of us now. We constituted Tony's gang. Cliff Lang avoided us, if he knew what was good for him, and enormous, stupid Gary Fisher had also departed, sloping off in the face of my constant mockery to find something new to do. It was just Tony and me now.

Without talking, we headed off. Words were unnecessary: we knew where we were going. We traversed the posh, dilapidated suburb inhabited by Mr Henshaw, and people like Mr Henshaw, until the enormous, crate-like houses abruptly gave way to the sand-coloured brick and white window frames of the 1960s development, still referred to by everyone in the locality as 'the New Houses', even though their roofs were by now spotted mustard and white with lichen. Skirting the New Houses, we took a path of orange mud into the woods, where fly-tippers had dumped sofas, fridges and car parts. Past the ancient oak where someone had written BARRY IS A SEX MANGANAC on the trunk, in green gloss paint. Down into, and up out of, a ditch which might have been an Iron Age earthwork once, now merely a piddling brook of milky industrial run-off from somewhere. And, finally, to the slatted concrete fence, six feet high, topped with barbed wire, a hole gaping in one of the bottom slats. Tony kept lookout whilst I fetched the car jack from its hiding place in the hollow of a dead tree, and wedged it under the hole.

Ten or so pumps of the jack, and the stack of concrete panels rode high enough in their vertical concrete runners to open up a space of about 18 inches at the bottom, the top slat above us leaning dangerously against the coils of barbed wire, almost falling out of its setting. Tony lowered himself to the ground and scrambled through first; I followed. Once inside, Tony wedged a breezeblock under the concrete panels and retrieved the jack. I pulled the breezeblock carefully towards me, and the stack of panels clapped back down with all their weight, like a great stone guillotine.

And then we were in. And the entire factory was ours.

The factory, as far as we could tell, had made some kind of industrial machinery, and had closed sometime in the mid-60s. It consisted of a large red-brick warehouse, a workshop, and an administrative block with many rooms, most of which were locked. These buildings were clustered round a square courtyard, which was steadily crumbling away, and by spring would be a riot of ragwort and rosebay willowherb. In fact, the factory was overgrown on all sides with thick brambles, and when we'd first arrived last autumn, we had to hack our way through with sticks.

Over the months we'd been coming here we'd gone through many different phases of activity. Initially, we had smashed the windows, but this rapidly became tedious, as there were so many of them that the project stopped feeling transgressive and felt instead like a chore. After that, Tony had brought along his brother's air rifle and we spent a couple of weeks shooting tin cans, oil drums, and, eventually, pigeons, who nested by the hundreds in the iron rafters of the warehouse, streaking the walls with their droppings. We found a sack of clothes pegs and hung our kills by their wings from ropes stretched between the walls, where they dried like smoked herring. The smell was transcendentally appalling, and we were pleased with our work. From there, we graduated to arson, and set a variety of fires inside and out, though we stopped after one of these blazes – in one of the wooden sheds by the warehouse – became almost too large for us to stamp out, coughing and red-eyed.

Currently, our favourite activity was tearing open the locked rooms of the administrative block, a project which took real work. Shortly after the factory had closed, it had become a well-known hangout for what my father called 'dossers and druggies'; in this case, hippies, who had squatted the place. As far as Tony and I could tell, the squatters had inhabited all the rooms in the administrative block, which was why these rooms had since been padlocked shut.

In the three rooms we'd so far managed to open, the traces of the former occupants were everywhere. Like the vanished Neanderthals, we knew our forebears largely by their wall art.

In the first room, vast swathes of green and yellow climbed in waves, engulfing all of the fixtures: architrave, light switches, ancient fire safety notices. The green and yellow waves, far from being tranquil, were troubling in their mindless multiplication. The second room had been painted in pink and turquoise blotches, and in the limited light the room looked as if it were succumbing to some exotic disease, an impression heightened by the stalagmites of fossilised candle wax dripping over desks and chairs.

The third room, a large space that was formerly some sort of boardroom, was dominated by a childlike painting of a tree, which covered one wall like ivy. One corner of the room was blackened from a fire having been set there: the filthy stain reached to the ceiling and warped the corner into a black hole, devouring all light.

The rest of the rooms we had been unable to penetrate, as the double doors guarding them were too securely chained to pry open. But today, as we stood before them, Tony – dogged as always in his pursuit of the forbidden – unshouldered his holdall and produced a pair of bolt cutters. With a matter-of-factness that indicated that this wasn't the first time he'd done something like this, he cut through one of the links of the heavy chain. On the second cut, the link came apart, and the chain and lock thundered to the floor.

Tony smiled at me, and pushed the door open.

We were in a short, dark corridor. The walls were painted cream, the floor covered in grey rubber tile. There was a door on the left-hand side, and one on the right, both unlocked.

We each took a torch from Tony's holdall. Tony took the right-hand room, and I the left.

My room turned out to be a small office, still with a desk in it, although two of the legs were gone, so it looked as if the desk was trying in vain to get up after having sustained an injury. There was a door to another room and I saw that it was heavily padlocked, in the same way the double doors had been. I was about to give this mystery a closer look when Tony called my name.

I left the shattered office and ducked back into the corridor, then the room Tony was exploring. Tony grinned when he saw me.

'Look,' he said. On the desk in front of him, I saw a small stack of faded pornographic magazines.

My stomach tightened involuntarily. I had never seen a photograph of a naked woman before, and I found it almost impossible to believe this situation – desired, dreamed of, wondered about – was happening now, here, in this place, of all places. I picked up the first one and, without ceremony, it fell open, revealing a spread of a smiling, red-haired woman reclining on a yellow divan. And there were her breasts, her upturned, conical nipples brazen and hard. And there, between her legs, surrounded by a mass of red hair, was her vagina. Her actual vagina. In the same picture as her smiling face, so that you, the viewer, had no choice but to consider the two things as part of the same person. There was so much hair. I didn't know women had that much pubic hair. My mouth was dry and I felt I had no clear way to react.

'Wow,' I said, which sounded pathetic even to me. I couldn't think of anything else to say, so repeated myself. 'Wow.'

Tony Finch flipped through one of the other magazines, and the two of us stood for a while, unable to stop looking. I felt cold and hot and exhilarated. I was too stunned to find the situation arousing.

'Wow,' I said again.

Tony sneered, and that broke the spell. 'These are old,' he said, with the practical dismissiveness of the connoisseur. 'I can get newer ones.' Nevertheless, he put the magazines into his holdall, and then held his hand out and grinned, as he saw from my body language that I involuntarily didn't want to hand the magazine to him.

'Don't worry,' he said. 'I'll give it back later.' I gave him the magazine. I felt light-headed, intoxicated. Several questions had been answered, but a million more had sprung up in their place.

'What was in yours?'

'Nothing,' I said. 'Oh – another door, with a chain on it.'

'Great,' said Tony, and hoisted the bolt cutter onto his shoulder, like a rifle.

The chain gave way as easily as the earlier one, slithering to the floor in a heap. Only, this time, the wooden door opened to reveal another door, made of metal, painted dark green. The wheel of a combination lock stood out halfway down. I rapped on the door with my knuckles; the surface returned barely any sound at all, and the bones in my fingers hurt.

'Locked,' Tony said with a shrug, in case I hadn't grasped the fact.

'Yeah.' I rubbed my fingers. 'But why padlock the outer door? What's the point?'

Tony shrugged again. Idly, he turned the dial on the combination lock. It clicked smoothly.

'We'll never open it,' I said. 'There must be a million combinations.'

'Hold up,' said Tony. His torch beam played over the ruined shelves. Then a thought struck him. He reached upwards, to the wooden architrave above the door. Incredibly, his hand came down holding a thin strip of paper.

Tony smiled in triumph. 'Three, oh, oh, seven, six, six. Try that.'

'How did you know it would be up there?'

'My brother worked in a builder's merchant, and they had a safe. No one ever remembers the combination, 'specially if loads of people use it. Go on, open her up.'

I turned the heavy dial. Under my hand, it moved with monstrous certainty. Three. Zero. Zero. Seven. Six. Six. Instantly, cleanly, I felt the colossal bolts release.

I peered around the door. I just had time to glimpse a row of empty, dented shelves before I was shoved inside.

The door closed, and the blackness and silence were absolute. 'Tony,' my voice whimpered, and I knew he couldn't hear me. I heard the bolts slide back into place.

'Tony!' My voice was a scream now, but all noises were small in this place. He would leave me here. He would go home and leave me here, and I would suffocate and rot, and nobody would know.

No grave could be this dark.

My fear became absolute, like the blackness, like the silence. This, I knew, was what had happened to Abi.

The lock clunked heavily, as before. Torchlight flooded in. Tony Finch's face was crumpled with laughter.

'You rotten *prick*!'

'Your *face*!' said Tony.

'I could have died in there!' My voice sounded high-pitched and childish. This statement seemed to amplify Tony's mirth still further. I told him to stop, but found that I was also smirking, despite myself.

'Ah, bollocks,' said Tony at last, wiping his eyes. 'Let's go outside and look at some tits.'

Later, I let myself into the house and started to head upstairs to my bedroom. The hallway smelled of cigarette smoke, as it always did now, and the house echoed dully when there was noise. I was halfway across the hallway when a frail voice called to me from the living room.

I walked to the threshold but did not enter. There she sat, her back to me, staring out of the window at the lifeless tangle of the garden, smoking a cigarette. In front of her on the coffee table were a packet of Player's No. 6, a box of matches and an ashtray, half-filled with ground-out filters.

'Mum.'

She inclined her head very slightly to acknowledge she'd heard me. I sat down next to her.

Once more, I was forced to consider that time might be passing more slowly for my mother than for the rest of us. The almost-grief that was her sole emotional diet was corroding her; her skin was visibly more coarse and wrinkled, and grey strands predominated in hair that had been glossy black just over a year ago. As if to underline this process, she had taken up chain-smoking in earnest, and a soft layer of blue smoke hung just above head height at all times throughout the house. The place smelled like the school staff room.

'Where have you been?' said Mum, not turning to look at me.

'Out,' I said. 'With Tony.'

'He's a bad influence,' said Mum, but this was a mere gesture towards parental responsibility. Tony Finch was one of the few things my mum actually showed any enthusiasm for in her new life, the life that had been forced upon her, grey and featureless as fog. Even as she looked at me I saw her interest in me, and the present moment, wane.

'Where's Dad?' I asked.

'Doing his DIY,' said Mum. 'Not sure where. I heard him banging around earlier.' One hand brushed a strand of grey-black hair behind her ear. Her hand looked terribly frail.

'Have you eaten? Can I get you anything?'

'I'm fine, thanks,' said Mum, without emotion. Her gaze returned to the window.

'You can't just sit here like this,' I said. I got up and turned the television on, punching the button for BBC One. Even the television was better than the awful silence, surely; even banal noise was a reminder that the world carried on, and that out there, somewhere, was a place that glittered and shone, and wasn't macabre and desolate, a place where somebody was having fun.

The set warmed up and the image grew to fill the screen. *Clunk Click* was just starting, with Jimmy Savile.

Mum sank into the sofa and lit a fresh cigarette with the old one.

I climbed the ladder to the attic, as I had done every day since Abi had vanished. As ever, a second of hope gave way instantly to disappointment; our Book of Fates, in which Abi and I had detailed every outcome we could think of after death, was still securely tucked away on the bookshelf, in complete accordance with the laws of everything. I was almost angry; I had expected the first anniversary of Abi's disappearance might yield a concrete result.

A thought occurred, not entirely rational: maybe the attic was the wrong place for the book to be. Maybe it needed to be somewhere more saturated in Abi's presence. I eased the book from the shelf and carried it with solemn ceremony down the ladder.

No one had been in Abi's room for months. The air was cold and stale; everything in there remained just as I remembered it.

I pushed the notebook onto her bookshelf, between *A Study in Scarlet* and *The Sign of The Four*.

I did not glance behind me as I left, but I half-expected to hear the notebook fall.

14

In February, I turned seventeen, alone. No one wanted to celebrate a birthday where someone was so obviously absent, but I did find a card and a postal order from my parents on my bed that day. It was the second birthday Abi had missed. She had vanished three weeks shy of our sixteenth.

Time passed, somehow, until it was, I realised with a strange, charged suddenness, the second spring since Abi had gone. Very soon it would be summer; we were already halfway through May. Whilst for my mother the time since Abi vanished had crawled, for me it had accelerated, a situation that seemed to have worsened since I had been given leave from school. And here I was staring through Mr Henshaw's windows again, and here he was smiling at me with the same benign calm Mr Henshaw extended to all things equally. It was a filthy day, windy and raining, and the trees clashed and writhed in their great and private agonies at the bottom of Mr Henshaw's garden. The sky was so dark and threatening that Mr Henshaw had put the lights on, even though it was only 2.30 p.m.

I had just arrived and was gearing myself up for another afternoon of lying and evasion, when I was all of a sudden conscious of the inescapable fact that I was running from. Abi – to me, the only completely worthwhile person I had ever known, and my twin sister – was gone, and my way of coping with this fact had been to bury it, ignore it, hope it would go away or change. I had taken my energy and put it into breaking and burning things, as if the sadness of all those accumulated acts might somehow equal the unconquerable sadness it was now my fate to dwell in. And what sadness it was, now that I was forced to look at it. I recalled the cube of absolute blackness that had enclosed me when Tony had locked me in the walk-in safe. The sadness was the same, but without limit.

I became conscious that Mr Henshaw was calling my name at the same time I became aware that I was crying. I was hugging my knees, seeking to make myself smaller, subatomic; to vanish entirely, to meet Abi on whatever plane she had been removed to.

Mr Henshaw was offering a tissue. I took it and wiped my eyes.

'Tim,' he said tenderly. 'It's OK.'

'There's just so *much* of it,' I said. My voice was warped by the effort of not breaking down completely.

'I know.'

'She's *dead*, Mr Henshaw.'

Mr Henshaw said nothing.

'I know she's dead,' I whispered. And it was strange, to hear myself say it out loud.

'You can't know that, Tim. No one does. Or rather, only one person does and that's whoever—'

'*I* do.' And there it was. Against all of my stalling, my changing the subject and pretend silences, we were getting to the heart of things.

'How, Tim?'

'Abi and I took a photo,' I said. It sounded stupid immediately, but I pressed on. 'We faked a ghost photograph. Years ago. We drew a figure in chalk on the wall and took pictures of it.'

Mr Henshaw smiled. 'Your parents said you were always doing stuff like that.'

'This was different.' I was back in control of my voice now. 'It was – unpleasant. We took the most convincing one to school and we showed it to one of the other kids. A girl.'

Mr Henshaw said nothing, but listened.

'She was really upset by it, more than we expected. In class later that afternoon, she fainted and had to be taken home.' I paused. It was odd to be telling someone all of this after so long.

'Abi and I thought we'd get into trouble, so we decided to nip the whole thing in the bud. We invited Janice over to our house – that was the girl's name, Janice – and showed her how we'd done it, with just chalk and a camera. And then—'

How to describe what happened next?

'She had some kind of – fit. Not like a proper fit, but . . . she started saying things. Weird things. Like she was . . .'

'Like she was . . .?'

I groped for the word.

'Foretelling.'

Mr Henshaw inhaled, very slowly. Outwardly, he retained his usual air of peaceful equanimity, but something flickered in his eyes, and I couldn't determine what it meant.

'I know how it sounds. We thought she was just being stupid, play-acting. Saying stuff that sounded scary to put the wind up us. Abi actually slapped her, she thought she was being hysterical. Anyway, we wrote down everything she said.'

I sighed. Even if it sounded mad, I had to tell the whole story now. So I did; the smashed doll's house and the broken disfigured dolls, everything.

'Some of the other stuff Janice said to Abi . . . She said someone was coming for her, that she'd end up somewhere grinning away. What does that mean if it doesn't mean she's—' I choked back a sob.

Mr Henshaw's expression was neutral. 'Tim, this is extremely morbid speculation. And very vague.'

'But that's just it. She said *he's coming for you, he has eyes but no face.* And – Abi didn't write this bit down, but I remember clearly – Janice made a hissing sound at the end, *Esssss,* like that, and I thought that was just more play-acting. But—'

Mr Henshaw's brows furrowed underneath the thick lenses of his glasses. I persevered. I wanted to make him understand.

'Later, when Abi had – gone – I saw the article in the paper. There was that woman who saw Abi in the shop, talking to a man. Next to a picture of Abi was the police sketch of this man.'

'Yes,' said Mr Henshaw. 'I recall seeing it.'

'Do you? Do you remember what it looked like? That sketch?'

Mr Henshaw remained silent.

'The woman in the shop couldn't remember anything about him, except his hair and his eyes. So the police sketch was just his hair, the collar of his jacket, and his eyes. *Eyes, but no face.* And the woman said the man's van had a name on the side and she couldn't remember it but knew it began with an "S". "Mr S", they called him, in the paper. So Janice wasn't hissing, she was saying "S, S", over again, do you see?'

Mr Henshaw's expression was unreadable.

'What she said, all of it, it all happened! It's all true! And if it's all true then Abi is dead, somewhere, and pretending she isn't is . . . stupid!'

I was properly crying now. 'She's dead, Mr Henshaw! She's *dead*!' I was standing up. My hands were balled into fists at my side, my fingernails digging into my palms.

Mr Henshaw looked up at me. His face was perfectly calm.

'Tim, you're a very bright young man, with very eclectic interests, so I assume you're familiar with a phenomenon called pareidolia?'

Of course I was.

'Pareidolia is the phenomenon of seeing a pattern in random data,' said Mr Henshaw, before I could answer. 'Faces in tree trunks, figures in wallpaper, stuff like that. Those things aren't really there, but that's how the brain chooses to interpret them.'

'I'd take issue with the word *choose*,' I said. 'Evolution has conditioned us to look for patterns, because they confer a huge survival advantage.'

Mr Henshaw smiled. 'I'm sorry, I forget how bright you are. Yes, you're entirely correct.'

I suddenly felt foolish standing up, and sat down.

'So you think that's what I'm doing?'

'Undoubtedly, Tim. I'm sorry. Your parents already told me this story, but I was waiting to hear it from you. It was the reason they called me in the first place. Your insistence that Abi was dead, and the – manner – in which you arrived at that conclusion, upset them greatly.'

Bitter anger flashed through me. 'Oh, it upset them, did it? I'm her twin brother! No one was closer to her than I was!'

'I'm not sure anyone can be closer to a child than a parent, Tim. And your suspicion that she is . . . dead, terrible and tragic though that is, is something your parents have to face every second of every day.'

I folded my arms tight around myself. Outside, the day was getting darker, the clouds a deeper and more ominous blue.

'So what's the bloody problem, then?' I said. 'If we all agree?'

'Tim.' Mr Henshaw steepled his fingers. 'I know it's hard being a teenager in today's world. There are so many distractions. Pop music. Television. Violent films. Plus your own emotions, which are all over the place.'

'What's your point?'

'My point is – well, it's twofold really. The first thing to mention is that being a teenager is a heightened emotional state. I remember that much. Everything has equal weight, equal importance. Little dramas and big tragedies are of identical value to the adolescent mind, and both are just as wounding.

'The second thing is – don't be so hard on yourself. Or your mum and dad. This attempt to find a pattern is entirely understandable, considering the magnitude of what happened – what's still happening, every day. We often look for logic where logic is absent. It's—I get it. But it's causing your parents a huge amount of pain.'

I thought for a while.

'Even considered objectively,' I said, 'what Janice Tupp said is still an incredibly accurate prediction.'

For the first time in our acquaintance, Mr Henshaw seemed almost annoyed. He set his jaw and frowned, changing the aspect of his face almost entirely.

'It's frustrating to me how you can be so bright on the one hand, Tim, and so . . . *dim* on the other. This girl came to your house and said these things, yes?'

'Yes.'

'And then your sister wrote them down, later.'

'Only a short while later. But yes.'

'Well, that short while is important. It's extremely unlikely – impossible even – that your sister was able to remember verbatim what this girl said.'

'Abi has an excellent memory,' I said, unconsciously using the present tense. 'We both do.'

'I'm sure you have a great memory, Tim, but nobody has a perfect one. So that's one distorting filter these predictions have been through. Next, you say that the doll's house broke, revealing broken dolls, just as Janice had said. But you yourself conceded it might just be a lucky guess.'

'We did consider—'

'I mean, it's hardly surprising an old doll's house would have old dolls in it, is it? I grant you it's interesting that the doll's house broke immediately after her visit, but that's the only out-of-the-ordinary thing I can see in all of this.'

'During,' I said quietly.

'I'm sorry, Tim?'

'During her visit. She was still in the house when it happened.'

'Ah.' Mr Henshaw smiled smugly. 'Really? Where was she?'

I swallowed. 'In the attic. She went back up to there to get her coat.'

'On her own?'

I nodded.

Mr Henshaw looked at me for a long time.

'You weren't there!' I said at last. 'The doll's house is very heavy. It took two of us to lift it back. We didn't hear it fall. Janice *couldn't* have pushed it.' My voice sounded small and weak. I longed for Mr Henshaw to say something.

A long minute passed where the only sound was the fizz-ing of the rain on the path outside. It had rained all day. I imagined even the thrush's anvil would be washed clean by now.

'You think I'm making it up, don't you?' I said, eventually.

'Tim,' said Mr Henshaw. He was smiling again. 'I think you're *coping*. Telling yourself whatever story you need to tell yourself to get through each day. And that's fine, up to a point. But the way you've chosen to do it . . . it's enormously upsetting for your parents.'

I thought about this. Outside the wind had changed direction and the rain was now hurling itself against the window panes. I looked for patterns in the chaos, and could see absolutely noth-ing, just the random play of drops of water on glass.

'For me, this is the root of the problem here, Tim.' Mr Henshaw's face loomed large, his gaze unblinking. 'This insist-ence on a paranormal explanation for Abigail's disappearance . . . I think it's a mask. I think it prevents you from accepting the truth, so you cling to it. It stops you from moving on, from recovering. This thing has attached itself to your life and become part of the story, when in fact it has no real existence.'

I glared at him.

'We need to get beyond a supernormal explanation and focus instead on the facts. Are you ready for that journey, Tim? To accept the facts? To become an adult?'

He looked slightly manic now. He wasn't going to let go of this.

'Can you do that, Tim?'

I smiled and nodded, and resolved with every fibre of my being to retreat back into surly, uncooperative silence next time.

*

I waited in a sandwich bar until the worst of the rain subsided, paying 5p for a revolting cup of tea I left largely untouched. By the time I got home it was dark. To my enormous surprise, when I opened the front door, my mother flung her arms around me. She smelled faintly of sherry, and strongly of cigarettes, and had clearly been crying. She had been worried about me coming home late. I told her over and over again what my movements had been, that I was late because I had to seek shelter. I told her over and over again that I was fine.

15

Last week's 'frank exchange', as he put it, had energised Mr Henshaw's approach to me, and he felt we were close to a break-through. It had become hugely important to him – the key, in fact, to unlocking my grief and enabling me to move forward – that he dissipate the power, in my mind, of the prophecies of Janice Tupp, and my obsession with what he termed 'non-scientific explanations' for Abi's disappearance. I was astonished by the number and range of opinions he suddenly had on the subject of my wellbeing. Even in our initial conversations it became obvious that he had a very clear shape for my immedi-ate future, whereby I recovered fairly quickly from the worst effects of my grief, resumed school in September; and was able, as soon as possible, to go on to university, which was where somebody bright like me belonged anyway.

In order to achieve this goal, Mr Henshaw had a two-part plan.

The first part of his plan was that I find, and talk to, Janice Tupp. Once I saw – in his words – that she was no more than 'a silly girl with a malicious streak', I could progress beyond the idea that she had either foreseen a terrible fate for Abi, or cursed us somehow, or both.

The only problem with this plan was that I was unable to find Janice Tupp, at all. She had left school the previous summer, and drifted off into the netherworld reserved for those determined to neither continue in education nor find a job. I heard a rumour she was 'shacked up with a bloke'; another rumour went so far as to say she was either pregnant or had actually given birth. Either way, she was nowhere to be found.

Mr Henshaw was not deterred by the frustration of this first part of his plan. In addition to confronting Janice, Mr Henshaw had another idea, but he wouldn't tell me what it was. All he insisted was that I keep next Saturday free, and travel with him somewhere. He wouldn't say where.

On Saturday morning, I met Mr Henshaw on the high street outside Woolworths. The day was grey and oppressive, as it always seemed to be whenever I visited the high street, both at the time, and now, years later, in my memory.

Mr Henshaw had a surprisingly sensible car. I was expecting a grimy VW Beetle, with CND and SAVE THE WHALE stickers, tail-lights held together with parcel tape. Instead Mr Henshaw pulled up in a tan-coloured Austin Allegro that looked like it had been washed and possibly even waxed recently, and was entirely free of stickers and tape. Mr Henshaw told me we would be in the car for about two hours, but promised me the destination would make the trip worthwhile. So off we went.

Outside, the suburbs rose and fell in banks of sleepy dilapidation, finally surrendering altogether to blurred walls of corrugated concrete and short, dank tunnels lit sodium orange. The car swooped and dipped like a bird over the concrete bridges and through the underpasses, and by and by, in time marked by the silence between tracks on Mr Henshaw's cassettes of Yes and Wishbone Ash, the houses and streets gave way to greenery, and the motorway was suddenly bordered by fields. After an hour or so, we turned onto an A-road, and after forty minutes the A-road became a B-road, then a confusing proliferation of B-roads. After fifteen minutes of twisting turns on these smaller roads, I couldn't reliably have pointed north.

And the scenery outside became familiar, although I knew I had never been there before. A field of ripening wheat reached to the horizon, where the stub of a Norman church in knapped flint was the tallest point in a landscape so flat it made my head ache. A pine forest gathered gloom about itself, the low trees clustered tightly together as if keeping secrets. Around us, sandy soil sparkled in the shy sunlight that was fighting its way through the clouds, and without reading a single road sign I knew: we were heading into Suffolk. The county where M.R. James had woven his ghosts from half-remembered childhood days and the horrors and heresies that lurked in the masonry and misericords of a hundred parish churches. The sun was fully shining now, matching my rising exhilaration step for step. For the first time in over a year, I was swept by a feeling of freedom, of release. I felt the oppressive weight of being at home fall away.

We passed through one of the larger villages, where I briefly saw a greengrocer's, a war memorial, a second-hand bookshop. We then turned sharply into another B-road.

'What are we doing here?' I said, half-laughing with the wonder of it all.

Mr Henshaw said nothing but pointed ahead, through the windscreen.

And then, glimpsed in flashes through the trees of a small wood, I saw the house.

*

The bulk of it was sixteenth and seventeenth century, certainly. Indeed, the wing nearest to us, as we swept up the gravel road towards it, was a fine example of late Elizabethan or Jacobean design, all grand front windows with stone mullions, clearly modelled on the so-called 'Prodigy houses' – mansions of great opulence and scale – that were popular at the time. However, it was abundantly easy to see why the house would never grace any architectural textbooks. The Jacobean wing must at one point have had a counterpart, but for reasons unknown it was absent, and the wing was now not mirrored but mocked, it seemed, by a Victorian Gothic wing of such extreme ugliness it must surely have been considered tasteless at the time it was built. The transformation from one style to another was gradual; there had been extensive Victorian restorations and additions, and walls of knapped flint nodules were kept standing by buttresses of bright red brick. The overall effect was one of conflict, the original building struggling in the tentacles of the vulgar addition like a whale gripped by a giant squid. The small wood of ash and oak trees approached the house, shading its sides too completely and too willingly, as if attempting to conceal this misbegotten thing from the world. Before the mostly intact Jacobean doorway was a large semi-circular lawn, recently mowed. Mr Henshaw stopped the car in front of the doorway, and we got out.

'Welcome to Yarlings Hall,' said Mr Henshaw, smiling.

On the lawn, two of the most attractive people I had ever seen were playing badminton, wielding curious racquets with long, slender necks and small heads to bat a shuttlecock back and forth. A young woman and a young man, not much older than me, but carrying themselves with a self-assured certainty that made them seem very grown-up indeed; they seemed to own the space they occupied. The young man had sandy-coloured hair that curled magnificently down to his broad shoulders; he wore no shirt, and his upper body was lean and muscular. He looked like a natural athlete, an impression only slightly marred by the cigarette clenched between his teeth. The girl was blandly beautiful, with an edge of studied boredom to her movements, as if she couldn't entirely commit to anything for risk of appearing foolish. They looked like brother and sister, and behaved as if the rest of the world were a boring distraction from each other. I stared at them in wonder. The young woman looked at me.

'Nice day for badminton,' I said.

'Battledore,' said the young woman curtly.

I didn't know what that was, and the woman turned away without explanation, cutting me dead. She and her companion immediately resumed their game, once again sharing their energy only with each other. I had evidently been judged, and found unworthy of further attention. I had been part of a dynamic like this once; it was unsettling to see it from the outside.

Looking again at the racquets the two beautiful youths held, a dark suspicion crossed my mind. This was clearly a refuge for *emotionally disturbed teenagers*. There were obviously sports, but the terrible possibility existed that there might also be campfires, and sing-songs, and group sessions where the participants were invited to express their feelings. The dark-haired girl was probably a recovering drug addict; the athletic young man had probably fallen to pieces on some military training exercise. This was a retreat for the damaged.

My blood froze. No wonder Mr Henshaw hadn't explained where he was taking me. I became aware that I was shaking.

'Just through here,' said Mr Henshaw, blissfully unaware of the battle I was waging to resist punching him in the back of his head. He walked through the open front door. Following him, I blinked for a second in the cool darkness of a long passageway panelled in dark wood, regaining my vision just quickly enough to see Mr Henshaw duck round a corner. I had no choice but to go after him.

16

I followed Mr Henshaw through dark corridors to a large, bright kitchen with a flagstone floor, where the mouth of an enormous black fireplace opened in a wide yawn. Sitting at a table in front of it was a man with shoulder-length light-brown hair, long sideburns and a thin beard. He was roughly the same age as Mr Henshaw; late twenties to early thirties, but seemed to be trying hard to project the demeanour of being somewhere in his middle fifties; what my dad would call a *young fogey*. He was cleaning a pair of large tortoiseshell-rimmed glasses with a cloth when I entered; he squinted at me helplessly and then put the glasses on, blinking.

'Tim, this is Graham Shaw,' said Mr Henshaw. 'Graham, this is Tim Smith. I told you about him on the telephone.'

I smiled, a bit. I was still very unsure about where this was going.

'Hello, Tim,' said Graham, standing up and shaking hands. His manner seemed matter-of-fact, but behind the huge square lenses of his glasses his eyes scrutinised me with a thoroughness I found unnerving. 'Neville has told me a lot about you. I'm sure you'll want to see the equipment!'

'Equipment?' I asked, alarmed. 'I'm sorry?'

'Neville!' laughed Graham, slapping Mr Henshaw on the back. 'You really didn't tell him anything, did you?'

'I thought it best to show rather than tell,' said Mr Henshaw.

What were they talking about? Maybe they were going to give me aversion therapy, to correct my delinquent behaviour, like Alex in *A Clockwork Orange*. Thrust deep in my jacket pockets, my balled fists felt like hot coals. Let them try, I thought.

'Come on then, Tim,' said Graham brightly. 'This way!'

Graham took off at a speed that failed to take into account the darkness of the house's interior and our unfamiliarity with it. The place smelled of mould and dust and ancient bricks, a stale, churchlike smell, fermented over centuries. I felt a sudden flicker of disquiet as we headed deeper into the older part of the house.

Graham opened a door and ushered us into a spacious room, painted pale blue. The huge windows with their solid stone mullions, looking out onto the lawn, told me that we were in the room that took up the entire front of the surviving original wing. At some point it had probably been even larger, but the ill-advised rebuilding that blighted the house had clearly been at work here too, and the room had an oddly truncated feel to it. The windows felt too large for the space now, as did the fireplace, and nothing seemed properly aligned with anything else.

There was no furniture apart from a circular table, around which stood six chairs, and, against one wall, a small sideboard. On the sideboard I could see a reel-to-reel tape recorder, a thermometer, and a large, bulky device with two needle dials, which I guessed was an electromagnetic field detector.

I stared at them in wonder. Together, these items could only have one purpose that I knew of.

'This is ghost-hunting equipment!' I said. 'You're – looking for a ghost!'

'We are indeed,' said Graham, idly flicking a switch on the electromagnetic field detector. Both needles flickered in unison and were still.

'This house is . . . haunted?' I asked.

'Indeed,' said Graham, smiling, almost proudly. 'By one Tobias Salt, no less. From what we can discover, a truly terrible figure who performed his duties as local magistrate-cum-witchfinder with the vicious zeal of the Puritan. People have been encountering his spirit here for years.'

'Encountering – how, exactly?' I asked.

'Well,' Graham pushed his enormous glasses further up his nose as he peered up at the ceiling. 'He's been seen many times, by many people. Usually a black-clad figure, dressed in robes. Witnesses have also spoken of a smell of lavender – lavender is absent from all of the house's gardens – as well as the sound of footsteps, whispering, and, occasionally, the ringing of bells.'

It was curious I hadn't heard of such a haunting before, but Britain, whilst not a big place, is an almost insanely detailed one, rich in superstition and story, and, as such, densely populated by ghosts. There was no way I could ever know them all. Besides, the elements of the haunting described by Graham were so unspectacular, the accompanying phenomena so run-of-the-mill, so precisely the things one heard about ghosts and hauntings with monotonous regularity, that it occurred to me that I may have even read about this place and not actually remembered doing so.

'Have you heard any sounds?'

Graham smiled thinly. 'Not yet, no.'

'What about Raudive voices?' I looked enviously at the tape recorder. 'Have you recorded any?'

'Impressive,' said Graham.

'I told you he knew his stuff!' said Mr Henshaw. 'What on earth are Raudive voices?'

'Disembodied voices picked up as ambient noise in field recordings,' said Graham succinctly. 'And to answer your question, Tim, we've recorded about a dozen hours of audio, but playback has revealed nothing more untoward than the creaking and settling of an old, rambling manor house.'

'What about sudden discrepancies in temperature?'

'Again, nothing that couldn't be explained by the draughty nature of an old place like this.'

'Is there anything else?' I asked. 'Anything more . . . distinctive?'

I couldn't decipher Graham's smile. Part of it was undoubtedly delight at my aptitude for the subject, but there was more to it than that, an edge of almost manic glee. 'Well, there is a more disturbing angle to the story of Tobias Salt than the commonly told tale admits. I was very lucky to discover it. I looked into some old parish records, and those have led me to believe that – well, suffice it to say that far from suppressing witchcraft, Salt was actually intimately involved in it. His campaign of persecution was almost certainly expressly designed to keep his more esoteric interests concealed.'

'Hmm.' Mr Henshaw looked up from inspecting the equipment. 'So, lurid stories aside, this ghost has failed to materialise on tape?'

'Well, so far, yes.'

'And what's this thing?'

'A magnetometer,' said Graham.

'No doubt.' Mr Henshaw smiled.

'An instrument for measuring magnetic fields,' I said.

'Right.' Mr Henshaw tapped the device thoughtfully. 'And have you managed to measure anything with it?'

Graham looked a little awkward. 'Nothing. Yet.'

Mr Henshaw stroked his chin. 'So you've been here a whole week, and you've experienced . . . nothing? Isn't that a little . . . disheartening?'

'Not really, no. These are uncharted waters we're in here. We have no idea what we're dealing with, so we have to keep an open mind.' Graham smiled again, and shifted a little in his seat, slightly embarrassed. 'In fact, lately, we've been considering approaches a little less . . . *scientific* than I would personally prefer.'

'What do you mean?'

'Well, Sally – my co-researcher here – is quite the "white witch", and thinks we should attempt to raise Salt using ritual magic.'

I made a face. I could picture exactly the sort of person who would consider herself to be a white witch, and suggest ritual magic.

'Indeed,' said Graham, in agreement with my undoubtedly sour expression. 'The last thing I wanted was to turn a serious scientific investigation into a pop festival, so I nipped that particular suggestion in the bud. However . . .'

He looked slightly appalled by himself.

'I have agreed to let Sally lead a séance later this afternoon.'

'A séance!' Mr Henshaw's voice was both outraged and concerned. 'You're not serious?'

'Oh, yes,' said Graham. 'The way I see it, if we do it and nothing happens, I get to prove to Sally that it's all a lot of hocus-pocus. However, if we do manage to provoke any supernormal effects, my monitoring equipment will be operational at all times, and I can capture any scientifically relevant data we might produce. Either outcome makes it a worthwhile venture, because, either way, we'll know more than we did before.'

Mr Henshaw snorted. 'The world's first scientific séance? Ludicrous!'

'It wouldn't be the first,' I said. This was true. I had read of dozens of experiments under similar conditions. 'And even if we know séances are a lot of rot, a discarnate entity might not see it like that.'

Graham looked relieved and pleasantly surprised. 'Thank you, Tim. That was my thinking too. If Salt's essence pervades this house, it's worth considering that his beliefs and his worldview might remain unchanged. He wouldn't recognise a tape recorder or any of our other high-tech gear, but he would recognise an old-fashioned spirit-summoning, and want to make his presence felt. It strikes me as an unscientific method of achieving a scientific end.' He paused for a second, regarding me again from the riverbed depths behind his enormous glasses. 'In fact, Tim, would you like to join us later? For the séance?'

'Now, Graham, I'm not sure about that,' Mr Henshaw said abruptly, in a much more teacherly tone than I had ever heard him use before.

'You just said yourself that séances were ludicrous, Mr Henshaw,' I said innocently.

'Yes, a lot of nonsense, but—'

'Well. If they *are* nonsense, you'll have no real objection to me taking part, will you?'

'Tim—'

'I mean, if it is all rubbish, what possible harm can it do?'

Mr Henshaw clamped his jaw shut, as close to irritation

as his studied air of being OK with everything would allow. He was checkmated, and we both knew it. I wasn't about to let anyone stand in the way of my participating in an experiment that managed to incorporate every single thing I found interesting.

17

Graham excused himself to make lunch, so Mr Henshaw and I made our way outside. We sat on white metal garden chairs at a matching garden table and looked out over the front lawn. Mr Henshaw said nothing, but I could feel his annoyance radiating from him in waves as we sat in silence. Over on the lawn, the two good-looking youths had given up playing battledore and were sunbathing, the girl reading a book that I could tell, even from this distance, was *Chariots of the Gods?* by Erich von Däniken. Occasionally, the two of them would play-fight or steal a kiss, or light cigarettes and pass them between each other. They were an entirely self-sufficient unit, it seemed, a blissful island to whom the rest of humanity could only ever be an abstract irritation.

I supposed I should break the silence and strike up a conversation with Mr Henshaw, and was about to do so when a shadow fell across us. I looked up, squinting against the sun, and saw a freckled, red-haired young woman carrying paints, canvas and an easel. She had a cultivated witchy look to her, and wore a long green strapless dress and a yellow headband.

'You must be Sally,' said Mr Henshaw, standing up and offering a hand to shake. 'Neville Henshaw.' Sally put down the fishing tackle box housing her paints and brushes and shook hands demurely, dropping down into the merest hint of a curtsey. 'Charmed. And who is this?'

'Tim,' I said. 'Tim Smith. Hello.' I did not immediately think a great deal of Sally. She looked as if she were trying too hard. Around her neck I could see a silver pentacle on a leather thong, no doubt bought from some hippy shop for an extortionate price. She caught me looking at it and smiled.

'This? Don't worry, I'm not a devil worshipper!' Her voice was silky and confident, the kind of voice that has never had to be self-conscious or awkward, or feel the need to explain itself. If you had a voice like that where I lived, I thought, you'd have to disguise it, coarsen it, keep the vowels sharp and the consonants rough, or simply learn to keep quiet, so as not to stand out.

'The pentagram has many meanings and associations, both good and bad. The symbol is incredibly ancient, going back to the Babylonians,' she explained.

'True,' I said, 'But you're wearing it on your breast, as a lamen. For protection against elemental forces during magical rites.'

Sally grinned broadly, turning the full wattage of her attention on me, allowing me to appreciate for the first time that she was very pretty. 'Excellent! What did you say your name was again?'

'Tim Smith,' I said awkwardly. God, my name was dull. The full impact of the smile had somewhat disarmed me, and I fumbled for something else to say. 'I presume you're wearing it for the séance?'

Sally smiled again, to herself this time, and touched the silver star, running it between her fingertips. 'Yes, I am. You can't be too careful, can you? Will you be joining us?'

'Well, that's still a matter of—' began Mr Henshaw.

'Yes,' I said. We both shot each other sour looks. A moment of tense silence passed, before Mr Henshaw's impeccable manners overrode his irritation with me. He turned back to Sally.

'Can we see your painting?'

'Of course!' Sally removed the canvas from under her arm and held it up for us. It was the house, in three-quarter profile, executed in watercolours on thick paper taped to the canvas. The house had been rendered almost mathematically, with straight lines and diagonals of a ferocious exactness. After successfully capturing the geometry of the place, however, Sally had attempted to get mysterious, and the sky was a labyrinth of sub-Van Gogh swirls and curls, like pale blue ferns. The two styles were entirely antipathetic to one another; the precisely rendered house made the sky look ridiculous and somehow puerile, and the sky robbed the house of its solidity, making it flat and lifeless.

'Wow,' said Mr Henshaw. 'That's great. Really smashing.'

'The house is interesting to paint because of the lack of symmetry,' said Sally. 'One of the original wings still stands, as you can see. The other is a Victorian addition, to replace the wing that's missing.'

I frowned. 'What happened to it?'

Sally smiled. 'The locals came and burned it down. Along with the owner.'

'Tobias Salt?' asked Mr Henshaw.

'Yes. There're a lot of stories about him, though of course I haven't dared ask anyone in the village. They're very stony-faced about our being here, apparently. Graham has warned us to have as little contact with them as possible.'

'Why did you choose to paint the sky like that?' asked Mr Henshaw.

'After a week of being here, we've seen and heard nothing. I wanted to capture that unsettled mood, as we wait.'

'You see, Tim?' said Mr Henshaw. 'Graham and his young assistants are actively looking for proof of the paranormal, and so far haven't turned up a shred of evidence. Not one thing.'

'Why would Tim need to have such a thing shown to him?' said Sally, turning to Mr Henshaw. I could almost hear him wither and crinkle under the same smile she had turned on me earlier, like a sun ray lamp.

'Oh, it's nothing, really.' Mr Henshaw looked hot and embarrassed. 'Tim's had a very . . . rough year and he ended up ascribing certain things that happened to him to, er, paranormal forces.'

It sounded so ridiculous, reduced to its rudiments like that, that I again found myself wanting to punch Henshaw in the head. Sally turned to me, her eyes bright and wide, and it was my turn to wither.

'I— something bad happened and . . .' There was no way to talk about it without it sounding silly, but I had no choice. 'I thought it had been . . . predicted. More than that, in fact, I felt almost like we'd – provoked it.'

'We?'

'My sister and I.'

'Hmm. And what does she think?'

'She, erm— she—' 'I heard my own voice break a little. Mr Henshaw leapt in.

'What Tim is trying to say is that he feels that he brought events on himself, and that simply isn't the case.' He smiled thinly at Sally, who looked perplexed. 'Tim, might I have a word in private for a second? Would you excuse us, Sally?'

'No, please,' said Sally. 'I should help Graham prepare lunch anyway.' She picked up her painting and the wooden fishing tackle box and headed into the house. I watched her leave, although I wasn't sure why.

The second Sally was out of sight, Mr Henshaw turned to me.

'Tim, I think we should go.'

'Why?'

'I am responsible for what happens to you. If I let you partake in this stupid séance, I am failing to protect you from a situation neither of us can control.'

'We've been through this! You said yourself that séances were a load of rubbish. I'm just interested to see one, that's all. For the record, I think they're rubbish too, but I also think it's worth seeing.'

'And with that, you're still going to participate in this? An exercise in pure, unconscious wish fulfilment?'

'I don't follow.'

'You're *grieving*, Tim. You're going to be grieving for a long time. Your twin is missing. She may never return. As you said yourself, she might well be dead. You've already built one explanation whereby her disappearance has a paranormal dimension to it. Given half a chance, I think that part of you will find any way it can to bring her back.'

'What do you mean?'

Mr Henshaw shook his head. 'How will you react if Abi starts to talk to you, through table-rapping or Ouija board or whatever mumbo-jumbo Graham has planned? If she tells you things that only you could know? How do you think your fragile objectivity will hold up then? Scepticism about the world beyond is often the first casualty of grief. Look at Conan Doyle's pursuit of spiritualism after the Great War. Any rationalist can succumb, given enough pressure.'

I fumed, but said nothing. He was right.

Mr Henshaw touched my arm. 'Tim. Don't be ashamed. It's perfectly normal to grieve, and it's perfectly normal to want to speak to a loved one who's been taken from you.'

I nodded. 'Even with that in mind, I'd still like to do it.'

'Well,' Mr Henshaw sighed, 'I can't stop you. But I certainly don't want to participate.' And with that he turned away and walked to the house. He didn't look back.

I saw that the lawn was empty. The day had clouded and the first few drops of rain were falling, pattering on the ironwork of the garden furniture. By the time I made it back to the house, the rain was coming down in a drenching, cancelling curtain, blurring the fields beyond the house into incoherence.

18

It took a moment for my eyes to adjust to the darkness of the house. Sally walked past me, smiling, carrying a cold roast chicken on a very old-looking white-and-blue oval plate. 'Through here,' she said. 'You can meet the others.' I followed her swaying silhouette into an enormous hall, panelled in wood either painted or aged to a deep black. The hideous Victorian renovations had not touched this vast space, and I was able for the first time to consider what the place might have originally looked like. There was an enormous stone fireplace, which the weight of centuries had rendered slightly out of true, and more mullioned windows, looking out onto the woods at the rear of the house. The room was two storeys high, and its beamed ceiling was the roof of the house.

In the middle of the room was an enormous oak dining table, built to seat in excess of twelve, and set for eight. The haughty couple were already seated, occupied solely with each other. The other two guests had their backs to me, and until I sat down, all I could see was the straight dark hair of a girl, and the greasy black hair of a boy.

'Good God, it's tipping down!' said Sally, setting the chicken down in the centre of the table. The rain was now beating against the leaded panes of the old windows, a soft, constant thrum that made me glad to be indoors. 'Everyone, this is Tim. He's come all the way up from London.'

'Just outside London,' I said. 'Home counties.' I didn't want them to think I was a wholly urban creature, completely at sea in the countryside.

'You've already met Sebastian and Juliet, haven't you?'

'Not properly,' said the girl. 'Hello, Tim.' It was the first genuine warmth she'd exhibited towards me since I'd arrived. Sebastian tilted his sandy locks and half-smiled in acknowledgement. 'Hey.'

'Hello, Sebastian.'

'Seb, please. No one calls me Sebastian.'

'OK then,' said Sally. 'That just leaves you two. Polly, Neil, this is Tim.'

'Hello, Tim!' said Polly, and smiled. 'What a lovely day to travel over a hundred miles to have lunch in a depressing old house!' She smoothed her dark hair back from her temples with her fingertips and glanced up at me for a split second, to gauge my reaction to her witticism, and was pleased to see that I was smiling. Her clever eyes glittered as she assessed me, her small, compact face set into a thoughtful expression. I got the impression I was, for her, simply the latest absurdity in an absurd situation. Everyone else was dressed for warm weather, but Polly wore a plaid skirt and a long-sleeved cardigan, as if it were winter.

'Hello, *new person*,' said Neil flatly, with a sardonic curl of his lip. Neil wore thick glasses behind which his large brown eyes flickered nervously back and forth. His black hair, combed self-consciously to one side, was flecked with white dandruff, and his cheeks bore the scars of a long battle with acne, long ago lost. He performed a comically perfunctory wave. 'Will you be joining us for the afternoon's wholesale rejection of the Age of Enlightenment?'

'He means the séance,' said Polly drily.

I nodded. 'Yes.'

'Great,' said Neil. 'I'd hate for you to miss all the things that won't happen, when they fail to happen.'

'Please excuse Neil,' said Polly, pulling her chair in. 'He started off from a position of scepticism and his resolve has only hardened since we've been here.'

'And who can blame me?' Neil picked up his fork and started to examine it as if he'd never seen one before. 'We've spent a week now in what turns out to be Britain's most resolutely un-haunted house, so forgive me if I sound a little jaded.'

'More than a little,' said Polly.

'Who won the match?' said Sally, changing the subject.

'You mean the battledore?' Sebastian's voice was richer and stronger than anyone else's, and it rang around the gigantic room as if that was its natural home. 'Well, keeping score wasn't the important thing. It was just good that we got some exercise. Although I did, of course, win.'

'You!' Juliet slapped him playfully on the arm. 'We agreed it was a draw!'

'Only because you were losing so badly I thought you might kill me.' For the very first time, Sebastian looked at me. 'Terrible loser, this one!' His grin indicated that this was a man's joke, to be enjoyed by men. I smiled thinly in response, and felt uncomfortable.

'Anyway,' his deep voice rumbled on, 'how did the taping go this morning?'

'How do you think?' said Neil. 'An hour and a half of recording, and an hour and a half of playback, which revealed nothing but the frustrated sighs and coughs of two people who found themselves pointlessly recording absolutely nothing.'

'Does Graham know?'

'Yes, we told him. Quite amusing in its own way, that inversion of the usual situation. Someone reacting with frustration to the news that a house *isn't* haunted.' Neil stared at me and sniffed. 'So why are the new people here again?'

'Forgive Neil,' said Sally. 'He doesn't mean to be rude.'

'I wouldn't bet on it,' muttered Seb.

'Tim and Neville came to see what we're doing here and how we're getting on. Graham tells me that Tim here is quite the authority on ghosts.'

'Is he now?' muttered Neil. Juliet whispered something to Sebastian, who smiled smugly.

I was confused. 'But you all are, aren't you? You're all interested in the paranormal, at the very least? That's why you're all here?'

'Yes,' said Polly. 'But that wasn't the only criteria for selection. Graham picked all of us for this study because we're bright, for a start. But as far as spooky phenomena go, we all believe in it to some degree, but have very different ideas as to how it's caused.'

'So at one end of the scale you have people like me,' said Neil, 'who believe hauntings are a mental effect, entirely in the mind, and at the other end you have traditionalists like Juliet, who, despite the last hundred or so years of science and reason, still hold fast to the belief that ghosts are the surviving remnants of the dead.'

'Thank you,' said Juliet brightly.

'You're welcome. However, Juliet's beliefs aren't the most outlandish held by those present. That honour goes to—'

'Oh Lord— 'Sally rolled her eyes.

'—to Sally, with her bespoke mish-mash of superstition, folklore, ghostlore and barely understood concepts from the fringes of current science.'

'Unbelievable,' said Sally. There was a smile in her voice. 'You rotter!'

'I speak as I find,' said Neil. 'Anyway, I think Graham decided that the best way of getting to the bottom of this particular ghost was assembling a group of young people with different opinions on the subject.'

'But all believers,' I said. 'In one way or another.'

Neil wrinkled his nose 'Yes, I suppose you're right. Speaking in the broadest possible sense. Anyway, that's why we're here. To record any paranormal phenomena from differing, yet informed, perspectives. And so far, I think we can all agree, that approach has been a resounding failure.'

'I'm glad you think so, Neil.' Graham stood behind him, holding a jug of lemonade and a wooden bowl filled with salad. Mr Henshaw was with him; I sensed they had been talking. I hadn't heard either of them approach. Clearly, neither had Neil, who flushed and looked down at his plate.

Graham seemed unfazed by Neil's assessment. 'What you're forgetting, of course, Neil, is that a negative result is, nonetheless, a result. The fact that we haven't encountered any ghostly phenomena in a house locally reputed to be extremely haunted – to the point where I can't hire a local cleaner – is itself a tangible outcome.'

Neil's sardonic smile had returned. 'Well, that's very handy, isn't it?'

Graham began to fork salad onto each person's plate in turn, and didn't look up as he replied. 'That's the scientific method, I'm afraid, Neil. Observe, record, but don't influence.'

'Yes,' said Neil. 'And what could be more scientific than a séance?'

'Not this again,' said Seb.

Sally took up the knife. 'Shall I carve?'

'Why ever not?' said Graham. 'What else were you lot talking about?'

'Nothing much. Tim still hasn't quite told us why he's here!' laughed Sally. I blushed slightly, but she smiled at me and I smiled back at her. The knife flashed above her head momentarily as she pushed a strand of her red hair back with her wrist. She really was pretty.

'There's no big mystery,' I said. 'Mr Henshaw is my . . . teacher, and after an – incident – in my own life, he thought coming here would be a good idea.'

'Tim?' said Mr Henshaw, in a tone of voice that said, *is this wise?*

'It's fine, really. Mr Henshaw felt my attempts to explain certain things with paranormal causes weren't healthy. He thought bringing me here would help.'

'Thank you for your honesty, Tim,' said Graham slowly. 'Neville, I'm not clear on something. How did you think bringing Tim here might help him?'

Mr Henshaw stayed calm and chose his words just as carefully as I had. 'I wanted him to see what a real search for something paranormal looked like.'

'Was that all?' Graham's tone remained affable, but he didn't look away from Mr Henshaw, and I felt Mr Henshaw squirm slightly. For the first time, I could hear the sonic signature of the house as an object in space as the rain spattered every inch of it, drumming on the slate roofs and ringing the long, empty corridors with a mindless intensity.

'Chicken's good!' said Seb brightly through a mouthful. Juliet giggled.

'How long have you two young lovebirds been together?' Mr Henshaw asked.

'Nine months?' said Seb, without looking up.

'Ten,' said Juliet definitely.

'So you knew each other before coming here?' I said. 'I thought you'd all met here?'

'Nope,' said Seb. 'Jules, myself and Awful all go to the same school.'

'Very funny,' said Neil. 'As fresh now as it was the first one thousand times I heard it.'

'Awful?' I asked, before I could stop myself.

'It's a stupid nickname,' said Neil. 'My surname is Audle, so I get called Awful.'

'If he's lucky,' said Seb, grinning. Juliet punched him on the shoulder.

'It's not even a successful homonym,' Neil grumbled into his plate, as if this were the major objection anyone would raise to such a thing.

'Which school would that be?'

'Sixth form at Alderston,' said Seb. I was impressed. Even I had heard of Alderston. It was a very posh – and very expensive – Catholic school, somewhere in Wiltshire.

'A friend of mine is a teacher there,' said Graham, 'so that's where I sourced my first lot of volunteers for this project. Polly came to me through a recommendation from friends at the Institute.'

'The Institute?' I asked.

'The Parapsychological Institute of Great Britain,' said Graham. 'They're paying for much of this . . . experiment. And they loaned me most of the equipment. The electromagnetic field detector, and the two tape recorders.' He tilted his head to the far corner of the room, and I saw another large, expensive-looking reel-to-reel tape recorder.

'All mod cons!' said Sebastian. He put on a mocking oriental voice. *'Made by honourable Japanese.'*

'Amazing,' I said. 'We – I – always wanted a tape recorder.'

'Yeah, yeah,' said Neil. 'It's all very exciting. Mind you, you haven't spent all morning with it, recording the sweet sound of absolutely nothing.'

'Oh Neil!' said Polly. 'Really. It wasn't that bad!'

'Oh Lord, it's my turn next,' said Sally. 'Ninety minutes of silence on my own. It is me in the scullery today, isn't it? I haven't looked at the rota.'

Mr Henshaw almost snorted. 'You have a rota? Like house cleaning?'

'You don't change, do you, Neville? Still mocking any approach that doesn't come from a textbook. Just like you did at university.' Graham's tone was, for a second, almost bitter. 'But here, the least you can do is respect my methods. There are over thirty rooms in this house and only two tape recorders. What else would you propose we do?'

'I'm sorry, Graham. I suppose there's no right way of doing these things, is there?' There was the flicker of a smile on Mr Henshaw's lips as he said this.

'What say you, Tim?' Sally smiled. 'After the séance, d'you fancy joining me for an hour and a half of silence followed by an hour and a half of transcribing said silence?'

Such a direct level of female attention was so far out of my experience that I found myself unable to speak, let alone respond. I glanced nervously at Mr Henshaw, and then realised I was looking to a grown-up for help. In an attempt to restore my sense of control, I smiled an awkward, unnatural smile at Sally that I felt sure must have looked almost goblin-like.

'Maybe some other time.'

Sally shrugged and smiled. 'I can hardly say I blame you.' I smiled again, instantly and bitterly regretting the squandered chance to spend time with a bright, pretty young woman, which had flared up and gone out faster than I could properly consider it.

19

After lunch, Juliet and Neil cleared the table and disappeared to do the washing-up. Meanwhile, Mr Henshaw and I went to the blue room, to watch as Sally and Graham prepared it for the séance. Sally removed the tablecloth and folded it, set up candles and partially drew the heavy curtains. An additional dining chair was brought through from the Great Hall to join the six already gathered around the table. Graham was similarly busy, positioning the tape recorder, setting up thermometers on the mantelpiece, and checking the settings on the electromagnetic field detector. I watched both of them with intense fascination.

Outside, the rain battered the window panes relentlessly, and a flicker of lightning lit up the room in a splash of cold white light. This was followed, two or three seconds later, by a clap of thunder, like the noise of a great stone structure collapsing in on itself.

'Certainly the weather for it,' said Mr Henshaw drily, looking up from the *New Musical Express* he had pointedly buried his nose in since preparations for the séance had begun. 'Aren't you worried about the effect of cliché on the experiment, Graham? You do *have* a device for detecting clichés?' He ended this with a little nasal snort of laughter, which I knew, from our time together, indicated that Mr Henshaw believed himself to have just said something enormously clever and amusing. Graham, for his part, shot back a painfully polite smile and carried on checking his instruments. Sebastian, motivated probably by boredom more than curiosity, slunk in through the doorway and flopped into a chair.

'OK,' said Graham, after a few more minutes of staring at jumping needles on dials until they settled, 'I'm ready. Are you ready, Sally?'

Sally was already seated at the table. 'Uh-huh.'

'Well then,' said Graham. 'Shall we summon the others with the servants' bell?'

'We said we weren't going to ring the servants' bell,' said Sally. 'It's a reminder of the obsolete class system that once predominated, and of which this country has no right to be proud.'

'For God's sake,' said Sebastian, getting to his feet. '*I'll* ring the bloody bell.' He leaned past Sally and pulled a faded gold cord. A distant jangling sounded somewhere in the bowels of the house. Seb grinned and started to light a cigarette. Sally grabbed his arm.

'No cigarettes. Not during a session.'

Seb exhaled sharply and slumped into a chair. He caught me looking at him. 'You see what I have to live with? This is the problem with sharing a house with a load of women.'

'And Neil,' said Polly, as she entered the room. She sat down next to Seb.

'Neil doesn't count,' Seb snorted, just as Neil and Juliet appeared at the doorway. 'Oh, hello Neil, we were just talking about you, improbable though that sounds.'

'Most amusing, Sebastian,' said Neil. 'I hope you were finally unburdening yourself of the terrible jealousy you feel towards me.'

Sebastian either couldn't think of an appropriate response or simply couldn't be bothered, choosing instead to shake his head in a dismissive way. 'Let's just get on with this, yeah?'

'Right,' said Graham. 'We're all set up. The equipment is running. Sally, am I all right to leave everything in your capable hands?'

'You are indeed,' said Sally brightly. 'OK everybody. Neville, are you sure you're not going to join us?'

'Quite sure, thank you,' said Mr Henshaw from his chair by the wall, without looking up. He suddenly sounded a great deal older than he was.

'All right then. I suppose it's just the seven of us, which might be a more powerful number anyway.'

'Oh Lord,' said Neil.

'Neil! Please. No cynicism. The time to scoff is afterwards, if we don't produce any tangible effects.'

'I'm just trying to save time,' said Neil, but muttered it quietly, into the table.

'Come down to the end. Graham and I will sit here. Tim and Neil, you sit that side. Polly, Seb, Juliet, that side. There. Like so. Right, are we all ready? Any questions?' Sally's smile was incongruously bright and warm, her manner incongruously keen. We were, after all, attempting to speak with spirits.

Juliet's voice was nervous and thin. 'What do we do if we want to stop?'

'We can stop any time. Just tell us to stop, and we'll do so.'

Juliet nodded. A moment of silence, followed by a distant growl of thunder, pacing heavily round the Suffolk sky like some vast animal. Sally rose and drew the curtains.

'Neville, would you mind turning off the lights, please?'

'Right you are.' Mr Henshaw got up, and after a couple of seconds we were bathed only in the light of the three small candles. Now, instead of faces, six masks stared back at me, all made of a dull, unglazed porcelain the colour of flame.

'OK,' said the mask that was Sally. 'Everybody join hands, please. We're recording, aren't we? Great. This is a séance taking place in Yarlings Hall, at one p.m. on Saturday, the twenty-fifth of May, 1974. Present are Sebastian Stourton, Juliet Fields-Ray, Neil Audle, Polly Rook, Graham Shaw, and Tim . . .?' She glanced at me.

'Smith.'

'. . . Tim Smith. Also present as an observer is Neville Henshaw.'

'Hello,' said Mr Henshaw, from somewhere in the darkness. We all laughed nervously.

'I, Sally Devonshire, will act as operator for this sitting. We have lit candles and extinguished all electric light. As well as the tape recorder, other equipment is in operation, namely an electromagnetic field detector. Now I am going to ask all participants to join hands.'

Sally took my left hand. Her hand was warm and soft, and pleasant to hold. Neil took my right hand. His was clammy and his grip awkward, as if he had never held anyone's hand before. I realised that this was perfectly possible.

'Everybody? Excellent. Let us now invite the spirits to join us.'

The rain pattered incessantly against the great old house, echoing through the dark passageways and the grand rooms. The entire colossal, empty house hummed and sighed with the noise of rain.

'Repeat after me, as we chant in unison. Spirits of this place. We invite you to speak. Make yourselves known.

Spirits of this place. We invite you to speak. Make yourselves known.'

Slowly, at first, but then more confidently, we all joined in.

'Spirits of this place. We invite you to speak. Make yourselves known. Spirits of this place. We invite you to speak. Make yourselves known . . .'

'How long do we do this?' said Neil.

Under all of our hands, the table lurched.

'Shit!' said Juliet, amazed. It was the first time I'd ever heard a woman say that word.

'Which one of you did that?' said Neil, his eyes darting nervously.

'No one did anything,' said Polly, glancing into the darkness around us.

'Are you there?' Sally said calmly.

'I don't like this,' said Juliet. Her voice suddenly sounded childish and small.

'Are you there?' Sally repeated.

The table lurched again.

'Who is that?'

Seb could barely contain the laughter in his voice. 'I'm sorry, I couldn't resist it!'

Polly let out a gasp. 'Oh God. Oh Jesus.'

'Twit,' said Neil.

'You're *such* an idiot sometimes!' said Juliet, a note of real frustration in her voice. '*So* immature!'

'Sor-reeee.' The amusement faded from Seb's voice as he finally realised how seriously other people were taking this.

'All right then.' Sally's voice, not scolding, but infinitely patient. 'For the benefit of the tape recorder, that was Sebastian nudging the table there. Let's start again, shall we? Spirits of this place. We invite you to speak. Make yourselves—'

The table lurched again.

'Very funny, Seb.' Juliet's voice was drained of all patience.

'That wasn't me,' said Seb, very definitely. 'Is that you, Awful?'

'I'm not doing anything,' said Neil. 'And don't call me Aw—'

The table moved again. Under my hands, it almost felt as if it were struggling.

'New boy, whatever your name is. Is that you?'

'No,' I breathed. My mouth was dry.

'Good Lord,' said Graham.

Another movement. One short, angry shove, towards Seb. Seb yelped.

'Ow! That *is* you, Audle! If you do that again, I swear to God—'

'It's – not – me,' hissed Neil.

'Talk to it, Sally!' said Graham.

'Spirit,' said Sally. 'Please rap on the table if you can hear us.'

A sudden and very definite knock. We all jumped. Neil's hand, in my right hand, became a claw, digging into my flesh. Behind him, I saw Mr Henshaw, half on his feet, his mouth open in surprise.

'Please answer our questions. One knock for yes, two for no. Do you understand?'

A single heavy knock. The blood raced round my head, and irrational thoughts came in a flood. *It's all rubbish, of course*, said the mind, during daylight, in company, surrounded by distractions. *It's all nonsense. The ideomotor effect. The unconscious. Trickery. Suggestion. Nonsense.* It was easy to dismiss, because you knew, absolutely and definitely, that it wasn't true. But here in the flickering circle of light, nestled in darkness, enclosed by timber ribs raised centuries ago by hands that were now not even dust, it was all too easy to believe. The rap on the table echoed round the room, like a judge's gavel.

'Do you inhabit this house?' Knock.

'Have you always lived here?' Knock, knock.

A frantic susurration somewhere in the darkness to my left. My skin crackled with gooseflesh upon hearing this; only after a couple of seconds did I realise it was Juliet's voice. She was reciting the Lord's Prayer, as rapidly as she could.

'Did you live in this house?'

Three knocks.

'What the hell does that mean?' said Seb.

'We don't understand,' said Sally. 'Could you repeat your answer, please?'

Silence.

Sally glanced up at the rest of us, uncertain. 'Did you live here when you were alive?'

A very long pause, and then one uncertain knock.

'Are you dead?'

No answer. Even the rain seemed to subside and pause, as if suspended, waiting for a reply. And then, from nowhere, a frantic, repeated thumping on the table, as if something were hammering on the wood with pure, cold fury.

'Whoah!' said Seb.

It was pounding now. It seemed to emanate from somewhere within the table, within the wood itself. It vibrated through the grain, sounding the circular tabletop like a gong. Louder and louder, more furious, more impatient, as if seeking to draw our attention to something so obvious that we would never, ever see it, no matter how hard we looked—

'That's enough!' shouted Mr Henshaw *'Enough!'*

The lights came on. Mr Henshaw stood, white-faced, by the switch. Juliet was on her feet, a hand clamped to her mouth, breathing in rapid, small inhalations. Neil blinked in disbelief, whilst Polly and Seb simply looked stunned.

Sally calmly opened the curtains, and as they screamed along their rusty rails, the miserable grey daylight was restored to the room.

'Bloody hell.' Seb removed a cigarette from behind his ear. He produced a Zippo lighter, lit up and again said 'Bloody hell' as he exhaled a cloud of blue smoke.

Mr Henshaw, meanwhile, was looking through me, at Graham. Graham, alone among us, didn't seem shaken or disturbed. He seemed exultant. He wandered over to his equipment, and slowly and silently switched everything off.

20

Very little was said for the first half-hour of the drive back, as Mr Henshaw navigated the web of B-roads that had brought us to Yarlings. The rain had thankfully subsided a little and was now content with being merely persistent rather than torrential. Eventually, we found the A-road and plunged onto it, but still Mr Henshaw remained silent. Only when we reached the motorway did he finally speak, and only then when we had been on it for ten minutes, listening to the rhythmic squeal of the wipers sliding across the windscreen.

'Look, Tim,' said Mr Henshaw, without taking his eyes from the road, 'I'm sorry.'

'Don't worry about it.'

'I should never have taken you there. Yes, I admit that I intended to show you an unsuccessful attempt to locate something supernatural, which is certainly the impression Graham gave me of his little project, last time we spoke. Turns out that, since then, it's all got out of hand.'

'It was fun. I mean that. How often do you get to be in a real séance?'

'I was just concerned that you might get it into your head that you were – making contact.'

There was a long pause as the wet road unspooled like film beneath us.

'With Abigail, I mean,' said Mr Henshaw, eventually.

'What? No. If Abi wanted to reach out, she'd do it some other way.' I thought of our notebook, our Book of Fates. *If one of us dies, the other one has to find a way to open the book on the page that best describes what they are experiencing after death.*

'Anyway, look,' said Mr Henshaw, oblivious. 'I'm sorry. I was a bit over-zealous in my desire to rid you of what I still consider to be a fanciful and dangerous notion, and a serious barrier to your recovery.'

'Recovery?' I felt the anger come again. 'Do you honestly think one day I'll magically recover from all this? Abi disappeared, and regardless of how I arrived at the conclusion, I honestly think she's dead. Either way, she's not coming back any time soon.'

'My point exactly,' said Mr Henshaw, unruffled by my hostility. 'If she isn't coming back – what then, Tim?'

'I don't follow you.'

'*You're* still here. And you must, *must* look after yourself. It's vital that you come to terms with this situation, that it doesn't spread out and devour your life, taking your future with it. Everyone agrees you're a bright boy with a tonne of prospects, but you seem determined to waste your potential. If it wasn't for your teachers agreeing to you taking a year out, you might already have destroyed any chance of getting on with your exams and going to university. And you may not realise it now, but that would be a terrible shame.'

'Would it?'

'I've seen the way you live, Tim.' There was a sudden hard edge to Mr Henshaw's voice. 'Your parents have more or less collapsed because of all this. Do you want to spend the next ten years in that house? With them? Years when you could be studying or working? Carving out your own life?'

I was silent. None of this had occurred to me. The windscreen wipers squeaked mindlessly back and forth, diligently conjuring up the same slice of the world, only for it to be immediately obscured by the rain.

'It's like they're on autopilot,' Mr Henshaw went on. 'They're not coping, Tim. This thing is eroding them. And I'm certain they don't want the same thing to happen to you. I'm sure of it.'

'How?'

'Because of the one positive, concrete step they've taken since Abigail vanished. To minimise the effects of the devastation on the life of the only person who matters to them.'

'And what would that be?'

'They paid for their son to see a psychologist, so he might somehow find a way out of his grief and salvage the biggest opportunities of his life whilst he still can.'

In a previous age, Mum would want to know every detail of any trip I went on. Did you make any new friends? Meet any nice girls? What did they give you for lunch? However, when I came back into the house at five, my mum merely turned one bloodshot eye over one hunched shoulder as I entered the living room. She was sitting in front of the telly, which was turned down very low. The air, as ever, was grey with cigarette smoke.

I caught her as she stood up. Wordlessly, I hugged her. She had lost a lot of weight; her body felt thin and empty, filled with nothing but dry bird bones that might bend and snap if I held her too long. She neither resisted nor committed, just let me hug her for a while. After a few seconds, I stopped, and she slumped a little. Her lip quivered in what was possibly a smile and her eyes, briefly, held some warmth.

'Do you want a sandwich? A cup of tea?'

'No, love. I'm quite happy here.'

'Can I join you?'

'Of course.'

I sat down beside her on the sofa. Despite it being virtually summer, she wrapped a woollen blanket round herself. She seemed cold all the time these days. We sat watching the news, then *Doctor Who*. The Doctor was trapped on the planet of the spiders. Then there was a programme about rhinoceroses, at which point my head was already tipping onto my chest. I dimly recall waking up intermittently when some kind of Western was on, and then nothing.

Then I was alone in the darkened living room. Next to me on the sofa was an empty blanket, roughly human-shaped, a discarded cocoon. My mouth was dry. On the television was a bleached-out landscape, an impossibly flat, almost lunar beach of brown-and-gold sand, met at the horizon by a cold blue sky. The camera crawled along this blasted emptiness, as an unseen seabird cried. And then a voice:

'Along the coast of Norfolk, there persists an ancient legend . . .'

And then I knew what I was watching. It was a repeat of *A Warning to the Curious*, the M.R. James adaptation from the last Christmas Abi was with us. The last time I had seen it, Abi had been sitting next to me on the sofa, where the empty blanket was, and we had both drunk it in, hearts in mouths, delighting in each and every scare. And now the programme was back, the way all recordings come back, eventually, but Abi wasn't recorded anywhere, neither in the stones of the house nor anywhere clearly enough in my mind, and she was only ever gone now.

I turned the television off, watching the picture as it shrank away to a tiny dot in the blackness behind the screen. Then I went to bed.

21

Over the next few days – partly, no doubt, as a result of the excursion with Mr Henshaw, and our conversation on the return journey – I found myself acutely aware of how direc-tionless my existence had become. I did not have to attend school, but I didn't enjoy being at home. Dad came and went with various things – bits of plywood, plastic pipe collars, sandpaper – and continued his ritualistic quest to perfect abso-lutely everything about the house. His relentless cheeriness, so obviously a mask, was enervating to be around, as was his sheer busyness. His projects spread through the house like the mycelia of some strange fungus, connecting and merging, and I began to feel there were progressively fewer places in my own home where I could be. Withdrawing to the part of the house that was solely mine was no help, as my room had begun to feel oppressively small. It had always been a small room, but now I was seventeen years old, and wherever I sat or even lay in there it seemed I was unable to straighten my legs.

There was another, newer facet to my dissatisfaction. After going away to the house in Suffolk, my own life now seemed small and uninteresting. Somewhere, right now, a group of people I had liked were conducting an exciting experiment in an area I had a real interest in, and I had attended an actual séance during which something, some force, appeared to be active. And now, chances were I would never see any of them again. Whenever I thought of Suffolk, and Yarlings, I found myself thinking of Sally. I pictured her blue-green eyes, her freckled skin, her red hair cascading down her bare shoulders. The adventure in Suffolk and Sally became fused in my mind – possibilities I had glimpsed momentarily, now closed off to me for good. Lying on my bed at home considering these things was like coming to terms with a prison sentence.

It was a relief, then, when Tony Finch called round the following Saturday afternoon. Mum answered the door. Despite the fact that Tony was clearly the kind of person my parents would, only very recently, absolutely not have tolerated, my mum always made him tea and enquired after his mother, who worked at the supermarket. Tony was always polite, although he was not great at small talk and always looked hugely relieved when I came to rescue him.

He was sitting at the kitchen table when I came downstairs, his brown brogue boots and tartan donkey jacket reinforcing his air of chunky solidity. In a house of people who were shadows of their former selves, he was a reassuringly definite presence. He virtually jumped up from his chair when he saw me.

'Where are you two going today?' asked my mum. For a second, she sounded almost like her old self.

'Out and about, Mrs Smith!' said Tony roguishly, in a tone of voice that would charm any mother. 'Out and about!'

'Well, promise me you'll stay out of trouble. And no vandalism.'

'Mum!'

'We'll stay away from them phone boxes, Mrs Smith.

Don't you worry!' Tony was already halfway out of the door, grinning and waving. I smiled at Mum weakly, both of us acutely aware that I had promised nothing.

'Where *are* we going?' I asked Tony, once we were a safe distance from my house. 'What's the plan?'

'What makes you think there's a plan?' He grinned, showing his huge, square teeth.

'Call it intuition,' I said. 'Where are we going?'

Tony looked up at the sky. 'Impossible to say. We could be going anywhere. Up into the sky. Another planet. Who knows?' He grinned again. This was immediately infuriating. One of the things I relied on Tony Finch for was his complete lack of mysticism, his freedom from pretence or artifice. And now he was talking like this. I could get whimsy anywhere; this was not what Tony Finch was for.

'Where are we going?' I repeated.

'Depends. How much money you got on you?'

I dug in my pockets. There was a carefully folded pound note and the large, angular 50p piece I still considered emblematic of The New Money, and which still felt thrillingly futuristic. Tony produced a grimy pound note and a selection of even grimier 5p and 2p pieces.

'Should be enough,' he said, and nodded his head to indicate we should cut through the alleyway at the end of our street. 'Let's go!'

'Where are we going?'

All I got by way of explanation was the square-toothed smile again.

We headed past the shopping arcade, then through the empty patchwork of lawns between the sand-coloured council blocks,

and skirted the woods. After twenty minutes, we found ourselves in a neighbourhood of once-grand houses, three- and
four-storey Victorian dwellings, set in generous gardens, all
now dilapidated. Their windows were invariably occupied by
torn, yellowing net curtains, hung like skins.

The further we went into this once-affluent part of town,
the more decrepit the houses became. Some were boarded up
with corrugated iron; others were halfway towards collapse,
the stucco broken away here and there, revealing bare red
bricks riven with cracks.

Eventually, we stopped outside a large white stucco-fronted
house, screened from the street by an explosion of privet that
reached halfway across the pavement. Through a lopsided gap
in the hedge, a front path of black-and-white tile led to a set of
steps up to a peeling black front door. The garden bordering the
pathway was a Sargasso Sea of chaotic green weeds from which
the sleek lines of a 1950s automobile emerged, like a surfacing
whale. In blood-red house paint, someone had written the word
NEVER on the stone banisters, for reasons unclear. Tony,
unacquainted with foreboding of any kind, clambered up the
steps and, without hesitation, hammered on the door.

'What are we doing here?' I said, despite promising myself
I wouldn't. Tony either didn't hear me or chose not to. I thrust
my fists deep into the pockets of my jacket.

After some thudding around inside – much more than I
would have thought possible for the simple operation of walking down a hallway – the front door opened. A tall, gangly,
bearded man of about twenty, wearing a tatty dressing-gown,
stood looking down his beaky nose at us.

'Hello, Kevin!' said Tony.

'Tony.' Kevin looked at me but decided in a split second I
wasn't worth talking to, and looked back to Tony.

'Have you got it?' said Tony.

'Yeah, man,' said Kevin, in an affected way. 'Do you have the bread?'

Tony held out our money, the majority of which was, I remembered, mine.

'Not here! Jesus. You better come in.' Kevin turned and vanished into the house's dark interior. Tony shrugged and followed him inside, and, after a couple of seconds where I really did consider shutting the door on both of them and walking away, I went inside too.

The house smelled. It was a multi-layered, complex smell, made of many strong odours. There was bad cooking, and burned fat, and stale, sweat-stained clothing, left to dry and stiffen for weeks on banisters and chairs. There was patchouli oil, and incense, and a hint of something I was not experienced enough to positively identify, but suspected was marijuana. Underpinning it all was an ancient smell of earth and water, as if the house were being slowly digested from its foundations up by the relentless English damp. The hallway was lit by one bare bulb, and was lined with clammy orange anaglypta that looked, by this light, peculiarly organic.

We followed Kevin into the front room, which was vast, and had once been a very grand room indeed. Two colossal Chesterfield sofas, their upholstery battered and scarred as rhino hide, formed an L-shape in front of a magnificent bay window and a white marble fireplace, both of which were val-iantly attempting to maintain their Victorian dignity amongst the squalor. The mantelpiece was crammed with clutter: lighters, rolling papers, a statue of the laughing Buddha, a lava lamp. A coffee table in the middle of the room was covered with similar mess, plus several overflowing ashtrays, a pack of

Tarot cards and six mugs, all of which held various amounts of cold tea, or things that had formerly been cold tea. On a sideboard, a record player ticked and crackled, an LP turning pointlessly round on it, having long ago reached the end of the side. Apart from a sun-faded poster of The Jimi Hendrix Experience and a mirror, the walls were bare. The filthy carpet was covered in threads of tobacco, drifts of grey fluff and yet more rolling papers. There seemed to be rolling papers everywhere.

Kevin motioned for us to sit down on the sofa facing the fireplace. He took a key from his pocket and unlocked the top drawer of the sideboard. He threw the money we had given him inside, and, as he reached further inside the drawer, I glimpsed more notes. He then pulled out a battered metal strongbox, which he flipped open with both thumbs. He rummaged around and found a small clear plastic envelope. No sooner had he done so than he snapped the strongbox shut and closed the drawer, in one practised motion. He turned the key and I heard the lock click shut.

Kevin sat down on the other sofa and passed the cellophane envelope casually to Tony, before probing through the butts in the ashtray with one long, bony finger.

Tony held the little envelope up so I could see it, and grinned. Inside, I saw two squares of paper, each with a dark black eye printed on them.

'*Drugs?*' I said. Despite all the mounting evidence, I was still surprised. Kevin sniggered derisively and lit half a roll-up, putting his bare, filthy feet up on the coffee table.

'Lysergic acid diethylamide,' he said pompously. 'LSD to you. Trips. Acid.'

I couldn't think how I was supposed to react to this. 'And?'

'It's for us, you 'nana,' said Tony. 'You said you wasn't into glue, and Kevin says this is great. Colours and lights and see-ing stuff that isn't there. Sounds like a laugh.'

'Sounds like paranoid schizophrenia.'

'Where did you find this guy?' said Kevin, wrinkling up his nose in disgust as he picked at a toenail.

'He went to my school. He's all right.'

Kevin chewed on something retrieved from his toenail. 'He sounds like a weirdo.'

'Where shall we do it?' said Tony, to me. As if I might know.

Kevin sniffed. 'Well, you can drop it here, if you like. I gotta go out in a bit, but you're welcome to stick around. But no freak-ing out, OK? If you do freak out, there's a big bottle of vitamin C tablets in the kitchen. Five of those will take you right down.'

'Great,' said Tony, as if Kevin was showing us how the thermostat worked. My heart was beating very fast, as I real-ised I was on the verge of an experience I neither wanted nor felt I could refuse.

'There's tea in the kitchen, too.'

'Great. Any food?'

'You won't want to eat.'

'What if we do?'

'I would strongly recommend you didn't.'

Tony looked sad. He very much enjoyed eating. 'OK. Have you got a telly?'

'No! TV rots your brain, man. Worst drug there is. Record player, though. Don't scratch anything up, and don't nick my records. I know where each one is, and they're worth money, OK? Oh – and if you do put music on, don't play it loud. My woman's sleeping upstairs.'

'There's a lot of conditions attached to taking drugs in your house, aren't there?' I said, and instantly regretted it. Kevin stared down his beaky nose at me.

'Hey, you're welcome to sit in the cemetery if you're more comfortable with that.'

'He's not,' said Tony. 'Shut up, Tim. We're fine here, thanks, Kevin.'

'Good. Cos I wouldn't recommend the cemetery. A mate of mine dropped acid there and saw the Devil. He hasn't been quite right since.'

I resisted the urge to say something sarcastic.

'OK,' said Tony. 'When should we take it?'

'It takes about an hour to come up, so . . . now?'

'Now.' Tony grinned. 'Tim?'

'Come up?' I enquired. Kevin snorted again.

'Take effect. How long it takes to take effect. About an hour.'

'Right,' I said. 'I just have to nip to the loo. Won't be a minute.' *Nip to the loo.* As if travelling to another mental state was like a long coach journey.

Kevin shook his head and sighed, indicating that I was nothing if not a consistent disappointment.

22

I had passed the downstairs toilet on the way in. It was just as grim as I had surmised it to be from my earlier glimpse, with faded wallpaper and a filthy embroidered toilet seat cover depicting a Pierrot gazing in wonder at a butterfly. I locked the door and thought hard.

What was I going to do? I didn't want to take LSD, which from everything I'd ever heard was the last thing anyone dealing with grief should go anywhere near. Dad had always maintained that The Beatles became unlistenable after taking LSD, that it had done something awful to their brains. I did not want anything awful done to my brain. I was very clear about this. What was I going to do?

Next to the toilet, on a white wicker table, was a stack of old magazines. Inexplicably, for a house with no television inhabited by someone who apparently hated television, most of them seemed to be the *TV Times*. An idea formed. Frantically, I began to flick through the uppermost ones, looking for anything that looked remotely similar to the black eye design I'd just seen. Eventually, I found the trademark of a company that made electric razors in a quarter-page advert towards the back. I carefully tore it out, folding and refolding and tearing the area round the trademark so that I eventually had a small square with a design on it which I could substitute for the acid. I was quite pleased with my ingenuity.

Back in the living room, Kevin was shirtless, spraying his armpits with a can of deodorant. 'You took your time,' he said. 'I hope you've left it presentable in there.' The idea that I could make anything in this revolting hole less presentable was preposterous, but I said nothing and slumped onto the sofa. The small square of the *TV Times* was in my hand. I dropped it surreptitiously on the floor.

'Right,' said Tony, cracking his knuckles. 'We gonna do this?'

'We're gonna do it,' I said. 'What do we do, just eat it?'

'That's right,' said Kevin, buttoning up a purple velvet shirt.

Tony shrugged and patted the cellophane envelope. The two conjoined squares fell onto his palm, and he carefully tore them apart and handed one to me. By the time I'd taken it from him, he'd already stuffed his square into his mouth, grinning as he did so. I dropped my square onto the floor.

'Dammit,' I said. I reached down and picked up the square of magazine I'd put there, at the same time placing my foot over the real tab of acid.

And so it came to pass that I sat in a filthy squat, eating a small square of the *Dear Katie . . .* problem page of the *TV Times*, slowly and reverently, as if it were a communion wafer. I wondered if I should comment on the taste. Was acid bitter, as its name suggested? Sour? Sweet? In the end, I elected to say nothing.

'Doesn't taste of anything,' said Tony, and my heart sang.

'Yeah,' said Kevin, combing his hair. 'It's odourless, colourless and tasteless. But nonetheless, it's the most potent hallucinogen known to man. And those' – he pointed to us – 'were very high doses.' He wriggled into a brown suede overcoat several sizes too large for him. 'Right, you two. Gotta see a man about a dog. I'll be back about ten. Remember – don't wake my girlfriend, and don't freak out. And if you do freak out . . .'

'There's vitamin C in the kitchen,' I said.

He pointed a long index finger at me, the only sign of approval he'd granted me in all the time we'd been there. 'Cool. I'm glad someone was listening. See you later.'

Five minutes later, Tony went to the toilet and, whilst he was gone, I picked up the blotter of acid from under my shoe and burned it in the ashtray.

Ten minutes later, Tony and I sat waiting for an experience that I knew for sure in my case would not come. All the while, I worried. At the very least, I was going to have to pretend I was also high, which was going to present its own difficulties, as I didn't know what I was supposed to be pretending. And there were other things to consider. What if Tony did freak out? What form would this freaking out take? If he got out of control, I was doomed – Tony was much stronger than me, and much more determined. He could do both of us a lot of damage if he put his mind to it. I thought it best to take control of the situation now, so that disaster might be averted altogether.

So, whilst Tony went to the horrible toilet yet again, I decided to put some music on. Flicking through Kevin's records for something calming and familiar, it dawned on me how onerous this task might be. Even reading the names of bands and artists from the LP covers told me I was completely out of my depth. *Odin. Dust. Iron Claw. Leaf Hound. Stack Waddy.*

164

Brainticket. Electric Sandwich. Tyburn Tall. Sir Lord Baltimore. Lucifer's Friend. I selected an album at random and put it on, noticing too late that the first track was called 'World of Pain'.

I wandered into the kitchen in search of the vitamin C. I didn't want to go in there, and my suspicion that it would be the worst room in the house proved to be well-founded. It was epically squalid, from the first sticky steps I took onto the linoleum. Unwashed dishes and rotting food covered every surface. The cupboards were filled with faded packets of cereal, soup, custard. Some of them bore the tell-tale tear marks of rodent teeth. I dared not open the refrigerator. Despite my resolve not to spend long in there, the vitamin C proved elusive, and it took me several drum solos and half an organ solo until I eventually found it, in a drawer next to an old clay pipe, a prescription pad and a toy car.

'You feel anything yet?' Tony was back.

'No. Shouldn't we turn the music down? His girlfriend's asleep upstairs, remember?'

Tony sniggered. 'From what I hear, she wouldn't wake up if the house was on fire. She's a junkie.'

I couldn't see the distinction. 'Isn't Kevin a junkie? Aren't we, for that matter, taking this stuff?'

Tony frowned at me, genuinely puzzled. 'Tim, what do you think a junkie is?'

I shrugged. I began to get the sinking feeling common to all teenagers when their naivety regarding an adult subject is exposed. 'I thought it meant . . . just . . . someone who's on drugs?'

Tony shook his head. 'I thought you were meant to be clever? Junkies are people on *hard* drugs.'

'Right.'

'Heroin.'

'Right.'

The organ solo was still going on. Tony inclined his head towards the record player. 'Shall we put something else on?'

Time passed. I was still unsure what I was supposed to be feeling. Meanwhile, something was happening to Tony. He rubbed his face and looked around the room slowly, as if he'd never seen it, or anything like it, before. The only account of the ingestion of hallucinogens I had ever read was Aldous Huxley's *The Doors of Perception*, and my recollection of that was supremely unhelpful. It seemed unlikely that Tony Finch was achieving oneness with the godhead, or seeing the innate is-ness of all things within all things. He just looked confused by the carpet. I made sure I looked confused by it too.

'Are you getting that?' he said.

'What?'

'Shadows.'

'Yeah.' I was taking all my cues from him. I was thirsty, but didn't even want to drink tap water in this place.

Time passed. Tony became engrossed with the wallpaper, and the bi-coloured poster of Jimi Hendrix. Occasionally, he would look at me and smile, and I would look back and do the same, mimicking his smile. Truth be told, I was bored out of my mind.

I suppose we would have sat like that for hours, if the electricity hadn't gone off, plunging us into absolute darkness. The record player slowed and halted, and the singer's voice became a slurred, oily growl, then nothing at all.

'Christ!' howled Tony. 'What's happening?'

'The electricity went off. I think it's a power cut. Or the place is on a meter.'

Silence.

'Do you have any matches?'

Silence.

'Tony! Do you have any matches?'

'No matches,' he said, infinitely sadly.

I ran my hands over the revolting coffee table, feeling the teacups, the rolling papers, the ashtrays, trying to locate the matches I'd used to destroy the acid. Eventually, my hand knocked something onto the floor, and I heard the rattle of a full matchbox. I picked it up and struck a match.

'Whoah!' said Tony, his eyes sparkling. 'Do that again!'

'We have to find some candles.'

'Yeah!' said Tony, very enthusiastic about this plan. 'Where?'

The match burned down to my fingertips and I swore and shook it out. 'I don't know. That's why we have to find them.' I was done with pretending. I lit another match, Tony watching it intently. Investigating the mantelpiece, I discovered two candle stubs stuck in empty, dust-coated bottles of cherry brandy. I lit them both and sat back down on the sofa.

'Wow,' said Tony. 'It looks totally different now it's dark.'

'Yes,' I said flatly. 'Yes, it does.'

'Flick-ering?' said Tony, becoming unsure of the word halfway through saying it. He turned and peered at me. His gaze moved slowly away to the empty half of the sofa next to me. He then caught me looking at him, and looked away. But no sooner had he done so than he started to stare at the empty half of the sofa again.

'What is it?'

He shook his head and looked away again. But only for a few seconds.

'What?' I said, exasperated.

'Why is it with you?'

'What are you talking about?'

'Why is it there?'

'There's nothing there.'

He shook his head. I stood up to stretch my legs, go to the filthy kitchen, or the filthy toilet, anything to not be in this room. Tony gasped.

'*You* get up,' he said, in a sing-song voice, '*it* gets up.'

'For God's sake.'

'Thin,' he said. '*Tall.*'

I felt a cold thrill crawl across my skin. 'Shut up, Tony.'

'Tall and *thin*—'

'Shut UP!' I shouted. Tony flinched as if slapped. I walked out of the room as quickly as I could. The floor was a mass of jumping, dancing shadows. Where could I go? I had fancied that I had no place to be in my own home, but I saw now that that was ludicrous. I had no place to be in this house, none whatsoever. It was without light and heat, drifting rudderless through the night like a shipwreck. The hallway outside was entirely black.

The kitchen door fell open a crack and I saw light inside, flickering candlelight. I stumbled towards the door and pushed it half-open.

A figure in a stained white nightdress was digging around in the refrigerator, by the light of a candle stuck into a whisky bottle. Her hair was lank, her arms skinny and bone-white. Even from here I could see the needle marks. I pushed the door open a little further. Maybe the girlfriend would have change for the electricity meter, but I somehow doubted it.

'Hello?' I said nervously. My voice was loud and precise. 'Erm – I was wondering—'

The figure in the filthy nightdress straightened up awkwardly, like a rusty pair of scissors closing, and, stroking a stray strand of her greasy hair to one side, turned to me and smiled. I saw the thin line of a scar on her forehead.

'Hello, Tim.'

'Janice?' My voice was hoarse. She was almost unrecognisable. There were dark circles under her eyes, and her skin was pale. She had lost weight, and her cheeks were sunken. She was smiling, a crooked, unpleasant smile, her hair the colour of pond mud. Her eyes glittered with malice.

'You haven't seen her yet, then?'

I took a step back, stung. Janice smiled again, and might have said more, but her attention was caught, as if by a sudden movement. Something just beyond and behind me. She stared at it with all of her concentration, as Tony had done, and I turned.

There was nothing to see but the empty hallway.

A surge of fear carried me through the front door and out into the street, where I didn't stop running.

23

I awoke next morning with a feeling of nagging catastrophe.

The full magnitude of abandoning Tony had hit me hard, and I was determined to go looking for him, find out if he was OK. I had a terrible feeling that something appalling had befallen him, entirely due to my absence. Perhaps he had jumped out of a window, believing he could fly. Wasn't that what people who'd taken LSD did? I was heading for the door when Dad stopped me in the hallway, carrying a piece of dowel and a pot of brown paint.

'Tim! You're in a hurry!'

Why does he want to talk now? I thought.

'I am, yes.'

'I thought you were staying out last night?'

'Well, I came home. Dad, I really have to go out—'

'All right. Well, I just wanted to pass a message along. A friend of yours called last night and asked you to call him back. He said it was important.'

I didn't have any friends. What was he talking about? 'Did they leave a name?'

'Yes, Graham someone.'

'Graham?' Good God. 'Did he leave his number?'

'Yes. It's on the little pad by the phone.' Dad gave a perfunctory smile that indicated the conversation was over, and
padded off.

And there it was, Graham's number, with a Suffolk prefix.
Why would he want to speak to me?

I tore off the page, folded it up carefully and slipped it into
my pocket, before setting out to look for Tony.

Where might Tony be? The shopping precinct. The park. The
demented playground of our abandoned factory. I considered
all of these locations, until I at last realised that I was avoiding
the obvious. Tony would almost certainly still be at the one
place I didn't want to go to, the house where I had left him, last
night. I had to go back, just to be certain Tony was all right. The
guilt of leaving him, drugged and vulnerable, had ballooned
from a nagging ache to something close to panic.

I had managed to find my way back home from the strange,
crumbling house last night, in the dark and in a state of distress,
so I was confident I could find my way back in daylight. But
finding the house again was not the problem. Even confronting
Tony was not the problem. What I dreaded most was seeing
Janice again.

I had been stunned by the change in her, and not just the
physical signs of addiction and deterioration. It was as if the
moment that had once possessed her in the attic was now her
whole mode of being, unashamed and brazen. And, of course,
it was also what she had said, which seemed designed simply
to wound. That single sentence, more than anything else, told
me who she was now, and I knew I never wanted to see her
again.

I was slipping through the orange mud of the pathway
through the woods, turning these thoughts over, when I saw

a figure coming towards me. It walked softly, carefully, as if the world were made of porcelain, and to tread too heavily would be to invite disaster. This demeanour was so different from his normal unselfconsciousness and natural carelessness that I barely recognised him.

'Tony!' I said, genuinely relieved. 'Er – are you OK?'

'Hello, Tim,' said Tony peacefully. 'I'm fine.'

'How are you feeling?'

Tony smiled sardonically. 'You tell me.'

'Look—' I began. Tony waved his hand.

'It doesn't matter that you bottled out of taking it, Tim. You just should have told me.'

I was going to protest, then stopped myself. 'How did you know?'

'I knew last night. There's no way you could have gone where I went and acted normal.' He looked sad. I couldn't be anything other than a let-down in this world, it seemed, even to Tony Finch.

'I'm sorry.'

Tony grinned broadly – not his normal grin – and a faraway look came into his eyes. 'You missed out, Tim.'

'I – I just couldn't stay in that house. Not with her there. You know.'

'I didn't know it was her either, Tim,' said Tony. 'But I didn't mind. She's all right.'

'She is not,' I said hotly.

'She *gets* things, Tim. She knows who you are. And me. She knows a lot of things.'

'Does she?' I said flatly.

'She talked me down. Looked after me . . . where were you?'

'I couldn't stay.'

'Right.' Tony ran a hand carefully through his hair. I had seen this gesture before. 'See you around, Tim.'

'Where are you going?'

'See you around.'

And off he went, through the woods. I watched his silhouette slip through the trees, sadness hardening in my stomach, as if I had just returned some untameable beast that had become very dear to me back into the wild.

'Hello, is that Graham Shaw?'

'Speaking. Is that Tim?'

'It is. Hello, Graham.'

'Hi, Tim. How are you?'

'I'm fine, Graham. How are you? How's the ghost hunt?'

'That's what I wanted to talk to you about. Do you remember the séance we held last weekend?'

I sighed. Had it really only been a week? 'Yes, of course. You don't forget something like that.'

'Well, we've tried to repeat it every day since, and the fact is, that first séance constitutes our one tangible result in this whole endeavour – the rapping on the table. And afterwards, when we listened to the recording of the session, we discovered we'd captured some Raudive audio.'

I sat up. 'Really? What did it say?'

'One voice only, I'm afraid. It's not exactly crystal clear, but it appears to say "Never".'

I shuddered. I remembered a detail from last night. The squat that Kevin lived in, where I had left Tony. Painted on the wall of the stone landing at the top of the steps, the word NEVER in red paint. A meaningless coincidence, but an unsettling one.

'The point is, Tim, that since then we've recorded absolutely nothing at all. Our sessions have proved absolutely fruitless. My study is up in two weeks, so I was wondering . . . if you'd like to come up and join us for our final fortnight?'

'I'm sorry?'

'Our only remarkable results happened whilst you were here – the furious banging on the table, and the voice on the tape.'

'Mr Henshaw was there too,' I said.

'Yes, Tim, but he didn't participate. You did.'

I thought of what Mr Henshaw had said, in the car on the way home. *I was concerned you might get it into your head that you were – making contact. With Abigail, I mean.*

'This voice,' I said carefully. 'What did it sound like?'

'Well,' said Graham. 'It's quite hard to describe. But I think it's a male voice, or certainly a deep one.'

Intense disappointment and intense relief is a strange combination of feelings. I slumped against the wall; my head swam a little.

'Sally assures me that these things are very dependent on the different personalities present, and the mix of those personalities,' Graham went on. 'So she thought it would be a good idea to ask you back up here. I mean, I know it's a tall order, Tim. You're probably busy, and—'

'I'll come,' I said instantly. 'What should I tell Mr Henshaw?'

Graham coughed and fumbled with the receiver a little. 'Well, Tim, to be honest, I'd rather you didn't tell him, if that's OK. He'll only object. We had a very long telephone conversation on Sunday where he made his feelings about my experiment perfectly clear.'

'I understand.' I really believed I did, too, at that point.

'How soon can you be here?'

'Tomorrow?'

'Great. If you get the two-thirty from Liverpool Street, then change at Ipswich. I'll come and pick you up at the station.'

*

Mum and Dad raised the requisite token objections.

I think they did this primarily because they vaguely remembered, somewhere deep in the fug of their separate and profound miseries, that parents are supposed to object to things their children want to do, and therefore they should object to me going away, almost as a reflex. They were performing a ritual, having long ago forgotten what the ritual meant. Mum asked questions, but she was playing a role, rather than expressing real concern. Ultimately, she didn't have the energy to object to the fact that I would be taking part in a study so clearly inappropriate for someone who was in the process of recovering from a traumatic event; she merely asked me for an address and a phone number and insisted that I call to let her know I had arrived safely. Dad's disapproval was more overt, and for a few moments I was reminded of that far-off day he fought with Abi and me, in this very living room, challenging us to drop our strange and macabre interests. Then, all of a sudden, he seemed to lose interest in the discussion before it had really started, and bade me goodbye, whereupon I had to remind him that I wasn't leaving immediately, but was heading off the next day.

I packed a bag in my room and, on a whim, decided to take a bottle of whisky with me from my parents' drinks cabinet. I wrapped it in a towel and placed it deep into my rucksack. I wondered why I was even bothering with subterfuge: neither Mum nor Dad would mention it, if by some miracle they even noticed it was missing. I, too, was performing a ritual that circumstances had made obsolete.

That night, I dreamed I was back in the filthy squat, with Tony. Only now it was labyrinthine, never-ending, the same filthy rooms infinitely recursive, a sickness that had infected the whole universe. Music was playing in one of the rooms, but it was impossible to tell which room. 'Can you hear the music?' I asked Tony. 'I can't hear any music. Is he here?' said Tony. 'Already?' And then the power cut and the lights went out, and I was standing in the filthy kitchen. And there was Janice, her head out of sight, poking around in the fridge, but when she stood up, clicking to a standing posture with the inhuman, hydraulic fluidity of a machine, her face was a mass of buzzing flies, swarming over some unseen obscenity.

24

The next day was sunny and bright, conditions which were wasted on our dark and gloomy house.

Mum gave me an awkward hug, where her forehead hit my chin. Dad was fitting skirting board in the front room, his jumper patterned with clinging sawdust. He shook my hand as I left, as if I were an employee whose name he couldn't quite recall.

I travelled into London, and, at Liverpool Street, boarded a blue-and-red InterCity, train, bound for Suffolk. I felt grown-up, charged with purpose, doing perhaps the one thing in the world I was uniquely positioned to do. Only Abi herself might have been more qualified. I thought of Sally, too, more and more; how she might look when I saw her, what she might say, what I might say in return.

One change of train, at a nondescript platform in Ipswich. From the second train, the countryside flattened, as if the sky were stretching, rising, leaving human notions of scale behind. At eye level, bland fields and squat churches were the only features. Something silent and predatory moved across the sun in an effortless arc, searching the fields below. This was Suffolk, seen from the train, not glimpsed from a passing car, and I saw it as if for the first time, and felt its depth and age.

I was the only passenger to disembark at the station, which consisted of nothing more than a pair of narrow platforms and a ticket hall and general waiting room with a large fireplace. Walking out into the bright sunlight, I immediately saw Graham and Sally. They waved enthusiastically, and the idea that anyone was pleased to see me almost took my breath away. Graham wore a dark orange corduroy jacket, and smoked a pipe like a man thirty years his senior. Sally wore a long summer dress, and a thin leather circlet around her head that let a small blue jewel rest in the centre of her forehead. Graham smiling and pointing with his pipe, Sally showing off her beautiful teeth; I almost wept with gratitude. We climbed into Graham's ancient brown Vauxhall, Sally in the passenger seat and me in the back.

'Any breakthrough in the search for Tobias Salt?' I said. I had intended the word 'breakthrough' to be a subtle yet clever allusion to the book by Konstantin Raudive, the discoverer of electronic voice phenomena, but the car was very noisy, and any subtlety I was aiming for was lost under the sound of the engine.

'Not yet,' Graham shouted back. 'Only what I told you.'

'We're hoping your presence will shake things up a bit,' said Sally, smiling back at me. 'New blood and all that! Plus, you're part of the only definite result we've had in this experiment so far.'

There was that curious turn of phrase again. 'Why do you keep calling it an experiment?'

'Oh.' Sally seemed unaware that she had been doing so. 'Well, that's what it is. An experiment to see if we can raise a ghost.'

'Sally,' Graham admonished, 'I don't think it's wise to talk too much about it at this stage, do you?'

'No, I suppose not. I forget sometimes, how unique what we're doing here is.'

I had questions – many questions – but I didn't feel like bawling them over the car's engine. I settled back into the rear passenger seat and watched the hedgerows swell and sink around me.

The village came first, of course, with its war memorial and parish notice board and medieval church, knapped flint walls glistening in the sun like the skin of some colossal reptile. There, too, was the shop, the pub and the tiny, lopsided bookshop, crammed with stacks of volumes. Then there was the B-road, and the long avenue of trees. And there, far too quickly, it seemed, was Yarlings again, crouched behind the vast lawn, ivy spreading to mask the scars between the original house and the Victorian wing. The two almost-halves looked even more mismatched now than when I first saw them, the sunlight emphasising every irreconcilable detail, so that the place seemed less a clash of styles than a clash of philosophies, rendered in stone.

Graham parked his car next to a sky-blue Rover, and a bright red Triumph Stag.

For the first time, I felt a strange thrill of fear, looking at the house, a thrill that had been absent from my first visit. The house and its warring elements were nonetheless unified in purpose by – something. Was that something, even now, waiting? Waiting for me to join the others, for six to become seven? Seven souls, their little human essences glowing dimly in a grey wash of static, like distress beacons, broadcasting their vulnerability to anything that has eyes to see. *There are seven of them now*, I thought, *and the circuit is complete.*

III

25

It seemed that, no matter how bright the day outside, the interior of Yarlings was always dark, always gloomy, always permeated with a troubled air, as if overthinking its presence. My vision greyed momentarily as we plunged from the day's brilliance into the dark hallway. Summer's heat drew the signature churchlike smell of Yarlings from its ancient timbers, of dust and disquiet, and for a second or two, until my eyes adjusted, the aroma was all I was sensible of. I followed Sally's shadow deeper into the house.

'Graham and I have a few things to sort out,' Sally said, as I blinked away the last of the daylight. 'But everyone else is in here.' And with that, she headed off towards the kitchen. 'See you later!'

'Tim!' Polly's smiling face shone warmly in the darkness of the Great Hall. She and Neil had been sitting by the windows, reading, and she immediately got up, came over and gave me a hug, hands bunched in the sleeves of her cardigan, and asked how I had been. Neil, however, looked up with the slow reluctance of a tortoise waking from hibernation, restricting his welcome to a single grunted syllable.

Seb lounged at the table nearby. *'You again,'* he said, and grinned at me. I suddenly saw why girls might find him attractive. There was something roguish, almost *dashing* about him, something usually entirely absent from boys our age. It was certainly entirely absent from me. Although he was about the same size as Tony Finch – that is to say, *big* – Seb carried himself completely differently. Where Tony's demeanour was a kind of furtive insouciance, Seb's was brazen, unapologetic. His feet were up on the glossy black wood of the dining table, boots resting on what was almost certainly a valuable antique. He had also been reading.

'Do you bring news of the outside world? Has President Nixon been impeached, or impounded, or whatever it is they do?'

'I haven't really been following the news,' I said. This sounded immature, and probably was. Part of me, answering the call of impending adulthood, was starting to feel perennially guilty that I didn't engage more with the world, rather than with my own strange and highly specific enthusiasms. I knew everything there was to know about Gef, the talking mongoose of Cashen's Gap that had baffled the nation for two weeks in the 1940s, for instance, but I couldn't tell you the name of the Chancellor of the Exchequer.

'Oh,' said Seb. 'Well, anyway. Take a look at this.' He tossed the book he had been reading onto the table, and I realised what it – and the similar volumes that Polly and Neil were reading – was.

In the time since Abi had vanished, three separate books had come to my attention that aimed to document all the major hauntings of the British Isles. There was Peter Underwood's *Gazetteer of British Ghosts*, a compilation of sightings, investigations and urban folklore. There was Andrew Green's *Our*

Haunted Kingdom, which came in a dark purple jacket, with a picture of the famously haunted house at Montpelier Road in Ealing in wraparound. In the first-floor window at the back, something – Green is careful not to definitively say what – can be seen, either a trick of the light, or, if you prefer, the face of a ghost girl, staring out at our world from the cage of bricks and mortar she presumably cannot leave.

Best of all, though, was Antony D. Hippisley Coxe's *Haunted Britain*, an exhaustive county-by-county guide to the haunted places of the United Kingdom, irresistibly categorised with a system of symbols denoting which type of strangeness abided at a given location. It was the definitive survey, fully indexed with maps and references, rescued from repetition by both the sheer variety of stories and the author's pithy opinions on them. All three books were superb, however. I longed to show them to Abi, and my stomach knotted whenever I remembered the impossibility of this. Seeing them gave me that feeling I had had the Christmas before Abi vanished – that the world was catching up with our interests, and that the mystery of what ghosts actually were might very soon be solved.

Seb sniffed. 'You're familiar with these, I take it?'

'I am.' I had read all of them, but didn't own them. They were expensive – *Haunted Britain* alone was £4, and *Our Haunted Kingdom* was a whopping £4.25 – and I had only been able to order them through the public library. Tony Finch had, of course, offered to shoplift them for me, but I had politely declined. I began to thumb through *Haunted Britain*.

'I got my mum to send them over,' said Seb. 'Thought I'd better do some research, finally. About this place.'

'And?'

'Not in there,' said Neil, from the window.

'Really? What about the other books?'

Seb shrugged. 'Nope. Not a dicky bird.'

'You're kidding?'

'No,' said Polly. 'This place doesn't appear to have troubled any of the standard refs. Weird, isn't it?'

'What's weird?' said Graham. I hadn't heard him come in.

'Your haunted house,' said Seb. 'It isn't in any of the guide-books.'

'Guidebooks? Oh. *These.*' Graham peered down through his thick glasses at *Haunted Britain.* 'Yes, I'm aware of these. Sensationalist claptrap. Scary stories spiced up for a credulous public.'.

'Wow,' said Seb. 'Not your cup of tea, then?'

'No. And it's unsurprising that Yarlings isn't in any of those books – in fact, I would be annoyed if it were. I chose this location precisely for the unknown nature of the haunting. Apart from the locals, no one else really knows about this particular phantom.'

'How did you find out about it?' asked Polly.

'A mixture of hard work and happy accident. I discovered the story of Tobias Salt after many days perusing parish records. I was looking for a haunting that no one could know by reputation, or read about, thus prejudicing their observa-tions. It seems I was wise to do so, Sebastian.' Graham rapped his knuckles on the cover of *Haunted Britain.* 'I warned you about this kind of thing.'

'Sorry, chief!' said Seb, and saluted sloppily. 'Won't do it again!'

'I also desired an environment where scientific research wouldn't be overturned by sightseers, gawkers and the tin-foil hat mob who generally come in search of spooks.' Graham smiled. 'Anyway, if you'll forgive me, Tim, I still have a couple of things to attend to, then I'll take you to your room, and give you the full run-down of what we're doing here.'

'And I'm going outside,' said Polly, slamming *Our Haunted Kingdom* shut. 'Stupidly long time to spend indoors, on a day like this. Anyone else for fresh air?'

'I'll come,' said Neil.

Seb tapped a cigarette out of a soft pack of Lucky Strike, watching them leave. I had never seen a soft pack of cigarettes before. In my world, cigarettes always came in large, robust cartons of twenty, like the blue-and-white boxes of Player's No. 6 that both Tony Finch and my mum smoked.

As he lit up, he smiled a Cheshire Cat smile through a cloud of smoke.

'What's funny?' I asked.

'About this situation? Everything. Particularly Graham lecturing us about scientific impartiality as we attempt to talk to a bloody ghost.'

'You can always leave if you find it ridiculous.'

He sniggered. 'Lighten up, Comprehensive. I'm here for the duration, not because I really want to be, but because it's an easy vacation. Besides which, Jules wants to be here. She's into all this stuff.'

'Really?' I remembered her visible disquiet at the violent rapping on the table at the end of last week's séance. 'She didn't seem to be, last time I was here.'

'Ah, she recovers quickly. And trust me, her curiosity about all this outweighs her fear. In the meantime, I'm quite happy to go along with any old mumbo-jumbo. At least, until I run out of fags.'

'Or booze.'

'Ah, there is no booze, believe me. I checked everybloody-where.'

I let a couple of seconds pass before playing my ace.

'I have booze.'

'You? No!'

'Bottle of whisky in my bag.'

'You are my new best friend, Comprehensive. What's your name again?'

I laughed. 'You genuinely can't remember?'

Seb shrugged shamelessly, as if to say, *Why on earth would I have done?*

'Tim. It's Tim.'

'Pleased to meet you, Tim!' He shook my hand and granted me the first genuine smile I had ever seen him attempt. 'Let's endure another afternoon of this, then get into that whisky.'

Access to my room was via a single grand staircase of ancient black wood, roughly at the centre of the house. Graham led the way, carrying a small leather folder, as I followed with my rucksack.

The upper floor consisted of one long gallery-style hallway, of the same black wood, with a long-faded carpet of pale puce running its full length. Heavy doors of dark brown oak led into what were presumably bedrooms. On the vast landing, a colossal piece of furniture, somewhere between a Welsh dresser and a sideboard, held numerous pieces of dusty Pekin ware.

Graham stood as if looking at all this for the first time. 'The bedrooms run all through the upper floor. At this end of the corridor are a couple of spare rooms, and, well, long story short, you're in one of those, I'm afraid. But fear not – we've scraped together what we can, and, whilst not up to the standards of the other rooms, I think you'll find it pretty comfy!' As we advanced down the hallway, the corridor grew steadily colder. It was a warm day outside, I thought. God only knew what this extremity of the house would be like during winter.

'Here we are!' said Graham, opening a door. The room beyond was dark, even with the curtains of the casement window pulled open. The woodchip wallpaper was painted a sad cornflower blue, the kind of surface that would always be cold and clammy to the touch. There was a large, boxy wardrobe with an oval mirror set in the front, and a small writing desk with a dining-room chair, the latter upholstered in dark green velvet. There was no other furniture, apart from the single bed, an antique thing with a brass frame. I sat down on the bed, stunned by how hard the mattress was.

'I know it's not ideal, Tim.' Graham pulled the chair out from under the desk and sat on it the wrong way round, his corduroy-clad arms folded across the back. 'But I'm afraid it's the best we can do.'

I shrugged. 'It's fine.' I was trying not to be deferential, not to appear desperately grateful for the chance to participate in all of this. I thought again of Abi, and how much she would have enjoyed herself here. I imagined her here now, castigating Graham for his lack of method and rigour.

'Won't it, Tim?' said Graham. I realised he'd been talking to me.

'Of course!' I said. I had no idea what Graham had just said.

'So, if that's OK, I'll talk you through what we're doing here.'

'You're looking for a ghost.'

'Yes, Tim. And, in a very crucial sense, *no*.' He pushed his glasses up the bridge of his nose with a knuckle. 'We are attempting several things. The first is to establish whether a ghost – whatever that may be – is present in this house. Now, I'm pretty confident there is a genuine haunting in this house, and that whatever entity dwells in Yarlings wishes to make contact. We've seen evidence of that last time you were here, and there's also the recording we made.'

'Can I hear the recording?'

'Later, sure. Our second objective is to communicate with that entity, via sittings and séances with a planchette, Ouija board or similar. Now, as we discussed, séances and the like are in no way scientific, but if I'm right, that won't matter. All that matters is that we provide a conduit that our ghost – if he really is Tobias Salt – will recognise as an *interface*. Are you familiar with that word, Tim? It's from computers.'

'Yes.' I wasn't.

'Right. And so, our aim here is to lure our ghost into a place where it can be measured by the instruments of modern science. As well as the tape recorder, and the electromagnetic field detector, I've set up a voltmeter, and a self-registering thermograph. Oh, and before I forget' – Graham unzipped his leather folder and handed me a couple of sheets of Xeroxed paper – 'please be so good as to familiarise yourself with *this*.'

I glanced at the first page:

THE TRUE HISTORY OF TOBIAS SALT (1601–1662)

'Everything we know about the villain who lived here,' said Graham. 'It's vital you read that document before tomorrow, so you're at the same level as everyone else.'

'The same level?'

'Yes. I think much of what we're doing here is about the interaction of consciousness with place and circumstance. It's just a theory, but I'd prefer it if you knew as much about Tobias Salt as everyone else. It also means you won't be asking him stuff we already know.'

'Great,' I said, flipping the pages.

'That's it for the moment,' said Graham. 'Apart from some general house rules, which we can go through later.' Awkwardly, he disentangled his long legs from the chair. 'In the meantime, just settle in, get to know the place. It might be helpful if you walk around, register the emotional "tone", as it were. Dinner is six p.m. sharp.'

He lingered for a second – gangly, awkward, yet somehow still supercilious – before ducking out through the low doorway and into the hall.

26

After unpacking my few belongings, I lay on the lumpy mattress and read the pages that Graham had given me.

THE TRUE HISTORY OF TOBIAS SALT (1601–1662)

The first page was taken up by a portrait of a man in a black jerkin with white lace collars, long, lank hair and a pinched, thin face. His stare, even in a black-and-white copy, burned with a furious intensity, as if he were constantly angry. The rest of the pages were text.

Unlike the infamous Matthew Hopkins, whom history remembers as the most feared of the so-called 'witch finders' of Puritan England, Tobias Salt sought neither recognition nor reputation. Indeed, it was for very good reasons, inexplicably tied up with the story and eventual fate of this morally reprehensible, though undoubtedly complex, man, that Salt worked to keep his deeds under a cloak of obscurity.

A competent captain in the ranks of Cromwell's parliamentarians, Tobias Salt received Yarlings Hall as a gift for his military service in 1651. Salt's life might have meandered along the typical course of men of his era, standing and age, were it not for an incident that altered the trajectory of his existence for good. On 12 December 1652, his teenage son, Abraham, was thrown from his horse, struck his head on a stone drinking-trough and died immediately. The effect of this tragedy on Salt was immediate and profound, and The Historie of the Noble Familys of East Anglia *(Gadsby, 1700) describes Salt as catatonic with grief for a long time afterwards — 'insensitive to the sighte of his beloved wyfe and daughters . . . unmovinge, as a man deprived of his wittes'.*

When Salt did eventually recover, the scant sources available tell us that his demeanour— previously that of a man of mediocre intelligence and ambition — had changed entirely. Indeed, Salt seems to have spent the following year reading as much as possible, and it is during this period that we can safely assert he became exposed to the subjects that would grow to obsess him — the occult, black magic, and the survival of the human being after death. Salt believed he could, under the correct conditions, journey to the 'immortal realms' and somehow recover his son. This belief shaped much of the madness and evil that was to colour the last ten years of his life.

There were four pages of this, written in a style that seemed to get denser as it went on. Salt appointed himself local witch-finder, a duty he performed with fanatical zeal, condemning twenty-nine women and seven men to death. This was the perfect cover for a man who by that point was a fully-fledged warlock, and head of a secret coven of seven witches, men and women, called The Knot. Entry to The Knot was granted only to those who were 'highe adepts', and even then, they had to pass an initiation rite, which involved 'perswading a pious man out of his faithe'. Salt apparently controlled the sect through magical means, by carving wooden 'mommets' of the members, then threatening them with physical pain by means of violence to the effigies. With his acolytes, Salt sought to perform an ancient ritual involving sacrifice to 'overcome death's dominion', effectively making himself immortal. Preparations for this ritual began with the slaughter of sheep and cows. After this, a string of local children went missing.

At the same time, Salt terrorised the local countryside with fanatical fervour. Judicial hangings and drownings became commonplace. At some point, suspicions about the missing children began to centre on Salt himself, and anger amongst the locals reached boiling point.

Salt became convinced his ritual would only work if his wife and two daughters – at this point, prisoners in their own home – were sacrificed. During the ritual, the north wing burned down, killing Salt and, presumably, the other members of The Knot as well. The cause of the fire was never satisfactorily established, with various local legends telling of either an angry mob burning the wing down, or the ritual itself summoning an infernal force that couldn't be contained. Either way, the bodies of Salt's wife and daughters were recovered, with their hearts removed, as were the bodies of Salt's followers.

Salt's body was never found.

The symbol of The Knot was three small triangles connected by a larger circle, and it was inscribed in the wooden lintel of the fireplace in the Great Hall. Since then, the house had apparently had a long history of haunting, with some of the residents moving out because of ghostly activity.

I finished reading and lay back, my head on the cold pillow, and thought. A coven of seven. Weren't we seven, now, in this house? And making oneself immortal, defeating death – was there really a ritual for that? And, most pressingly of all, how had the story of Tobias Salt – although extreme, hardly uncommon in a place like England – never reached my attention before?

I re-read this fantastic, perfect story, until the words came loose from the page and I drifted off into a deep, satisfying sleep, as if I were finally home.

I was awoken by a persistent rapping on the woodwork that grew louder and more insistent.

I almost fell over getting off the bed, steadied myself, then opened the door. It was Juliet. She flashed a brief, friendly smile.

'Hello, Tim. Welcome to the asylum!'

'Thank you.'

'I come with a proposal. Seb says you have whisky, and whilst we don't have any alcohol, we do have three bottles of soda water, so we at least don't have to drink raw whisky like roustabouts on an oil rig.'

'Great!'

'Who knows? I may even be able to rustle up some ice. And – is it OK if I bring Neil? Seb can't bear him, but I worry he's lonely here. We're the only people he knows.'

'Sure. Bring Polly if you like. And . . . Sally?'

Juliet made a face at both of these suggestions. 'Let's just keep it among ourselves for the time being, hmm?'

'Fine.'

'Oh, and would you mind coming to our room? Your room's just a bit . . .' she peered at the gloomy blue walls, the wardrobe, the complete lack of personal effects '. . . bleak?'

'Of course.'

'Great! Come and give us a knock after dinner. Our room's three doors down from yours.'

A little later, I headed back downstairs. The sunshine was mellowing into bronze, the end of a perfect summer's day in the English countryside. Already, the number of dark corners inside the house seemed to have multiplied, and I remembered with a jolt that I would be staying here for the next two weeks. What was the house like at night?

No one else seemed to be about, although I could hear a radio playing upstairs. I looked into the Great Hall, where the windows framed the sunlit woods just beyond the small, unkempt rear lawn. It was empty.

I wandered out again and into the Victorian extension built long after fate decided, one way or another, to scour Tobias Salt from the earth with fire. I realised I was forcing myself to feel something, to experience the weight and significance of the house's dark history, and stopped. I found my way to Graham's office and knocked on the door.

'Who is it?' said Graham imperiously.

'It's me,' I said. 'Tim.' I turned the handle and pushed, but the door wouldn't budge. 'It's locked!'

'Yes,' said Graham, through the door.

'Why?'

Graham embarked on some kind of explanation, but the door was thick, and his voice just sounded like so much bassoon practice.

'I can't hear you,' I shouted, with more exasperation in my voice than I intended.

Graham mumbled something and I heard a chair scrape across the floor, followed by the clatter of a key in the lock. The door opened about a foot, but Graham stood in the gap, struggling both to fill as much of the aperture as possible, and to make this absurd posture look natural.

'Sorry to disturb you,' I said. 'I was wondering if I could hear the Raudive voice?'

'Ah! Of course. Could you give me a couple of minutes? You can wait in the Great Hall. I'd invite you in, but for the purpose of this experiment, it's vital all data is not made available to participants until the end. We don't want to prejudice the results.'

'How would I prejudice the results?'

Graham smiled infuriatingly. 'It would prejudice the results if I told you.'

I wandered back to the Great Hall. Something occurred to me, and I wandered over to the fireplace, where I scanned the great wooden lintel.

And there it was: cut or possibly burned into the wood. Three triangles, pointing downwards, connected by a large circle, with a notch at the bottom. The symbol of The Knot.

I ran my fingertip along the groove of the design: up, down and around, and wondered.

Ten minutes later, I was engrossed in *Our Haunted Kingdom*.

I was re-reading the entry detailing the haunting at 16 Montpelier Road, Ealing, which, no matter how many times I read it, made me feel as if it were a riddle I couldn't decipher. Amongst the usual drama of a haunted house is Green's testimony of his own visit to the property, where, on the roof – a notorious suicide spot – he found himself possessed by the urge to simply walk off the edge into the garden, despite knowing that it was three storeys below. His father, accompanying him, just managed to intervene in time to prevent Green stepping off the roof to his death. I found this tale supremely unsettling, much more so than other, more lurid accounts of hauntings. Who put the idea into Green's head? How did they do it? And, most terrifyingly of all, *why* did they do it? Why would this force, whatever it was, want a man to walk to his death? These questions were untameably strange, and again I discovered the thrill of encountering the genuinely, malevolently inexplicable that reading them always gave me.

I looked up to see Graham standing over me.

'Shall we?' he said.

I followed Graham through the main hallway to the older part of the house, the south wing. We ducked into the blue room where our previous séance had taken place. It was in darkness, the curtains drawn. Graham flicked the light on.

There was the table, and the seven chairs, and the wooden sideboard. On the sideboard sat the tape recorder, as well as the electromagnetic field detector. Next to that was another piece of equipment, which I took to be the self-registering thermograph, alongside a regular thermometer, and a voltmeter. Dials held needles waiting to flicker at any fluctuation of elemental forces, indicator lights waited to glow: all of this was enormously pleasing and exciting to me. Taped to one wall was the same picture of Tobias Salt Graham had given me – a furious-looking man with burning eyes, staring out of history with unbridled disgust. Next to that was another portrait of Salt, executed in oils, and I recognised it as Sally's handiwork. It was the kind of painting that an art teacher would politely describe as 'enthusiastic'. Salt's arms were raised, and above him, between his outstretched fingertips, the moon glowed. Next to these were taped various other images Xeroxed from books – an engraving of the house when it was new and whole, a woodcut of a witch trial, and a sad-eyed woman in seventeenth-century clothing, with two equally sad-faced young girls.

'Salt's wife, Anne, and his daughters, Agnes and Jane,' said Graham. 'From what we can gather, his control of them was absolute.'

'Right until the moment he killed them.'

Graham's teeth shone white through his beard in a patronising smile. 'Well, I'm glad you read the document, Tim. Yes. It's my guess their deaths were a statement of intent. A sign to whatever forces his crazed mind believed it was contacting, that he was utterly committed to his occult aims.' With his thumb, he packed tobacco into the bowl of his pipe. 'And who's to say he didn't succeed?'

I looked at Graham. He arched his eyebrows cryptically as he lit his pipe. Slate-coloured smoke drifted slowly between us, past the mirrors above the fireplace, tangling and untangling in the air like the stuff of thought itself.

'You're saying he might be haunting this place because he succeeded? In his immortality ritual?'

Graham smiled again. 'Intriguing thought, isn't it?'

'Fascinating.' And it was, too – the idea that someone might, at the moment of death, through sheer will, continue as something lighter, swifter; perhaps seeing and knowing more than they ever dreamed possible. Inevitably, I thought of Abi.

Graham, teeth clamped around his pipe, clicked a reel of tape onto the tape recorder and forwarded it to a precise location. He had clearly done this many times. 'You remember the séance, of course. It all got a bit chaotic at the end. The first voice you hear is Seb's, then our Raudive voice.'

He pressed play.

'*Bloody hell.*' Seb's voice. A pause, and some woolly scuffling sounds, then Seb again. 'Bloody hell!'

'*Nuuuhvuuuh,*' slurred a dark, oily voice.

The hairs on my arms stood up.

'Again.'

Graham rewound the tape.

'*Nuuuhvuuuh.*'

Ancient. Like the voice of a riverbed, clogged with decades of mud. Like something without vocal cords, struggling to make sound. Graham had said the voice was male, but that was only because of the depth of it. In truth, it didn't sound like any human voice, male or female, I had ever heard.

'*Nuuuhvuuuh.*'

'Come on,' said Graham, chuckling to himself at the look on my face. 'It's dinner time.'

27

It was Sally and Neil's turn to cook. Together, they made an enormous pot of chilli con carne, and an even larger pan of sticky white rice. I had never eaten chilli con carne before, and it seemed wildly exotic. We ate around the dining table in the Great Hall and, although it was only early evening, I appreciated more and more how isolated the place was, how thorough the silence. If a ghost – a disembodied consciousness – did dwell here, I imagined it would be half-insane through sheer loneliness.

Graham was in good spirits. He seemed to find the house's atmosphere exhilarating, rather than disquieting. He cracked terrible jokes and talked about a wide range of subjects, not letting the conversation flag, and at one point had to be dissuaded by Sally from going to his room and getting his ukulele. It was almost possible to forget why we were here.

I had been added to the household rota already, and discovered it was my turn to wash up – 'In at the deep end!' said Graham, mock-sternly, and we all laughed – and so, after dinner, I spent forty-five minutes in the enormous Victorian kitchen, scrubbing plates and gouging away at two huge pans with a dishwashing brush. Through the window at the sink, I could see the woods, weaving the early evening gloom into darkness. A treecreeper scampered down the trunk of a pine, forcing its beak into fissures in the bark with small, precise movements worthy of a watchmaker. I could smell cigarette smoke, hear the distant sound of a radio.

This morning, I had awoken in the house I had grown up in, the house choked with misery, the house where black lightning had struck, torching the lives of everyone who lived there. And now I was here. An enormous sense of relief flooded through me, an almost physical reaction to the sudden release of pressure.

I went upstairs. I wasn't sure what I was supposed to do with *The True History of Tobias Salt,* so I folded it up and shoved it into my jacket pocket. Then I lay on my bed, staring up at the ceiling, inhaling and exhaling, enjoying the feeling of simply existing; freed, temporarily, from the nightmare of grief, of not knowing. Out here, there was perspective. There was that, at least.

I was halfway between sleep and wakefulness when I heard a knock. I leapt up from the bed, suddenly and entirely awake, and opened the door. There was Seb, and behind him, Juliet and Neil.

'Police!' said Seb. 'This is a raid! We heard this place has illegal booze!'

'Did you fall asleep or something?' said Juliet. 'We were waiting for you!'

'I'm sorry,' I said, rubbing my eyes. 'What time is it?'

'Nine,' said Neil.

'Party time,' said Seb, talking over Neil. 'Where's the grog?'

'Just a sec.' I opened the wardrobe, took out my rucksack and unravelled the towel. A large bottle of Bells whisky rolled out onto the carpet, where Seb snatched it up. He read the label with distaste.

'Blended? Eeurgh! Is this . . . *supermarket whisky*? Still, I suppose beggars can't be choosers. Down the hatch!' He cracked the cap, unscrewed it and took a large slug. Juliet wrenched the bottle from him and recapped it.

'You'll have to forgive Seb,' she sighed. 'He was raised by gorillas.'

'How dare you. I am the scion of one of the oldest and most noble houses in Great Britain!' Seb ended this grandiose state-ment by burping, colossally. Juliet laughed. Neil simply sighed.

'Come on,' said Juliet. 'Let's go to our room.'

'Agreed,' said Seb. 'This room is bloody awful. No offence, Timbo.'

'It can't be that different to yours,' I said. 'Can it?'

Seb and Juliet's room had undoubtedly been the master bedroom. The wallpaper was a rich, warm red, and the ceiling was painted cream. The skirting boards and cornice-work were also painted cream, and a grandiose fireplace of white marble yawned against one wall. The bay window gave a spectacular view of the front lawn, bordered by the woods, falling away gently into the fields beyond. The dark-ening clouds above were seamed with gold as they caught the last light of the day, and a flock of screaming swifts rolled and collected in the airy freedom of the endless sky. It was a view you could wake up to every day of your life, and never tire of.

'Nice, isn't it?' said Neil. 'This is how the country must have looked to the Romans. Woods and heathland and meadow, as far as you could see. It must have been very beautiful.'

'Dangerous, too,' I said. 'Have you read *Red Shift*, by Alan Garner?'

Neil sniffed, clearly annoyed at the existence of a book he hadn't read. 'No.'

'Oh, you should. There's a whole chunk set in Roman Britain, only the language they use is—'

'Come on, ladies!' shouted Seb. 'School's out. Drink up!' Juliet had managed to mix four whisky sodas, in mugs, using a heavy linen chest as a makeshift bar. True to her word, she had even managed to find some ice.

'Cheers,' I said, and we all clinked mugs. I sipped, too deeply. It was hard and sharp and delicious. You could barely taste the alcohol, but you could feel it almost immediately. I sank down into a large bean bag whilst Juliet and Seb stretched out on the bed. Neil sat stiffly in a high-backed chair he brought over from a writing bureau. *Look at me,* I thought. *Drinking whisky with three kids from Alderston, in a stately home.* I tried to look relaxed, as if the situation were not in any way unusual to me.

'This is surprisingly good,' said Seb, matter-of-factly. I had no doubt he'd drunk whisky sodas before.

'Thank you,' said Juliet. 'Bordering on insulting, but thank you.'

'You know what I mean,' said Seb. He drained his mug and mixed himself another, with a generous shot of Dad's whisky. He was about to say something else, when there was a knock at the door.

Everyone froze. After a couple of seconds, Juliet got up, motioning for us to shush. She opened the door, and Polly burst in.

'Here you all are!' she laughed. 'With *booze*! I knew it! Why didn't you let me in on this?' She sounded bemused rather than hurt.

'Oh, lots of reasons,' Seb smiled. 'But fundamentally, we don't have much booze, and Juliet doesn't trust you.'

'Seb!' gasped Juliet. Polly, however, laughed.

'Well, to address your concerns in order. One, my tolerance for alcohol is embarrassingly low, and two, why ever not, Juliet?'

Juliet blushed. 'I just took you for a bit of a swot, that's all. I thought if we had any kind of fun you'd tell teacher.'

Polly wrinkled her nose. 'Graham and Sally? No. Cooped up in here, it's only right we should have a bit of fun. So, please, anything else like this . . . count me in.'

Juliet looked sheepish. 'Sorry.'

'No problem. Can I share yours, Tim?'

'Sure,' I said. I handed Polly my mug, and she sat down on the floor next to the bean bag.

'I propose a toast,' said Seb. 'To Tim.'

'To Tim!' said Juliet. Everyone clinked mugs again.

'Yes,' said Seb. 'Despite obviously hailing from a deprived background, he was the only one among us who had the presence of mind to bring alcohol.'

'Please ignore Seb,' said Juliet. 'He was dropped on his head in infancy.'

'What? Were you not listening, woman? I was *praising* him.'

'In a backhanded way. And don't call me woman. I'm not your property.'

'Oh, here we go with the bloody women's lib!' Seb made a *Women, eh?* face at me, as if I would automatically back him up. Polly passed back the mug.

I turned to where Neil was peering into his mug, suspiciously. 'And Neil, you go to the same school?'

'I do.'

'Hurrah,' said Seb. 'We get to spend time with Neil. Hurrah.'

Neil bridled. I scanned the room for something else to comment on, and blurted out a thought that had occurred to me earlier, but I hadn't felt it was my place to mention.

'There's only one bed in here. Is Graham OK with you two . . .'

'Sharing a bed?' said Juliet.

'Sleeping together?' said Seb. 'Well, to begin with, he allocated us separate rooms, but it seemed stupid for us to sleep apart. I mean, we don't at home, so why here?'

'Wait, your parents are fine with you – with . . . that?' I was aware that I had begun to blush. Seb roared.

'Of course not! My mum hates it, and Juliet's parents aren't exactly over the moon. But they can't very well stop us, can they? They *tolerate* it. Besides, we're both adults, almost. *Completely* old enough to make our own decisions on that score. Not that the old perverts who teach us would see it that way, so we do keep it a secret at school.' Seb tapped a cigarette out of his soft pack and placed it in his mouth. 'So that's us two. Fornicating.' Juliet slapped him on the shoulder again but I saw that, despite herself, she was smiling at his audacity. Seb ignored her. 'And although we're papists born and raised, I'm sure the man upstairs has got bigger things to worry about than what we get up to, frankly. Wars. Kids dying. That sort of thing.'

'What about you, Tim?' said Polly, playing with the sleeve of her cardigan. 'You got a girlfriend?'

'Me?' I almost laughed. 'No. What about you, Neil?'

Neil reddened. 'No.' Out of the tail of my eye I saw Seb smirking. Again, I decided to change the subject.

'Have any of you ever done anything like this before?'

'What, ghost-hunting? Pffff.' Seb took another enormous swig, during which a thought occurred to him. 'Actually, Jules and I stayed with my aunt near Highgate Cemetery last autumn, so we had a dekko to see if we could spot the famous resident vampire.'

Polly smiled. 'And did you?'

'Of course not. Nothing there but smashed-up graves and the odd druggy lurking among the tombstones. I'll be amazed if they don't concrete over the whole bloody place soon.'

Jules smiled. 'The only spooky thing we saw was a giant ghostly head among the trees, but that turned out to be the grave of Karl Marx.'

'What do you make of what's happening here?' I said. The words came too quickly. I was aware that I was drinking too fast, and resolved to slow down.

'No idea, old man,' said Seb. 'The first séance was fun, but all that knocking could just have been a trick.'

'You're the expert, aren't you, Tim?' said Neil, in a sly voice. 'What do you make of it?'

'Well,' I said, taking a deep breath. 'Table-rapping is easy to produce if you know how. And on its own, I'd be inclined to think it was suspicious. But there's also that voice on the tape. That was recorded when we were all there, and we heard nothing.'

'Eurgh!' Juliet shuddered. 'That voice. It's horrible.'

'It's fantastic!' laughed Polly. 'Our first actual result!'

'I don't know,' said Neil. 'I still think there's something we're not being told. Have you seen the way Graham keeps that office of his closed? I would surmise—'

Seb rolled his eyes. 'Oh, you'd *surmise*, would you? Not for

Audle the run-of-the-mill *supposing* that the rest of us have to make do with.'

'Oh dear, Sebastian. Did I lose you? Did I use a big word?'

'Now then, boys—' said Juliet. Seb ignored her.

'We get it, Audle. You're cleverer than us. You don't have to keep hammering it home.'

'I'm merely . . .'

'Oh, here we go.'

'It's funny,' said Neil. 'You don't object to my intellect so much when I help you with all that schoolwork you can't be bothered with.'

I thought Seb might be embarrassed by this, but he simply grinned broadly, showing off his excellent teeth. 'Very true. Audle has twice helped me out when academic work proved so boring it threatened my continued presence at school. And for that, Audle, I am grateful.'

'Thank you,' said Neil, tipping his mug and drinking.

'As I'm sure you're grateful for the magazines I was able to procure for you.' Neil spluttered and coughed, and Seb's grin broadened as he drank in Neil's discomfort. 'I can't remember what it was now. *Fiesta*, I think. Or *Playboy*. Anyway. Plenty there for you to think about, Audle.'

Neil reddened again, and said nothing. He looked furious. A tense silence settled over the room.

'You really are an idiot sometimes,' said Juliet.

Neil stood up. 'Goodnight, Juliet, Polly. Goodnight, Tim.'

'Oh Awful, don't be like that! I was only joking.'

Neil glared at him with hatred. Seb just smiled.

'It's not my fault you're a weird, creepy frog person, Audle. Everyone knows it. It's not like people can think any *less* of you.'

'Shut up, Stourton,' said Neil.

'Seb,' said Juliet quietly. 'Apologise to Neil.'

'What? For what, exactly?'

'You know very well. Now apologise.'

'Don't worry about it, Juliet,' said Neil.

Seb shook his head at the injustice of it all, then looked up at Neil. 'Hey, I'm sorry, Audle. I was just joking, that was all.' I suddenly understood that Seb was drunk.

Neil stared at Seb with a molten, impotent fury. Then he turned and left.

'Well done,' said Juliet coldly, glaring at Seb. 'Well done.'

'I should be going too,' said Polly into the cold silence. 'Tim?'

'Yep,' I said, lurching to my feet. 'Goodnight, you two. See you tomorrow.'

'Oh, come on!' said Seb. 'Stay! Or at least leave the whisky!'

'It's a long day tomorrow,' said Polly. 'Lots more séancing. Goodnight.'

'Goodnight,' I echoed.

Out in the corridor, Polly and I exchanged worried glances before going off to our separate rooms. As I turned to leave, I heard Juliet's voice. Although distorted by the door between us, I could tell she was almost hoarse with anger.

'You only know how to ruin things, don't you?'

My room was cold.

I undressed self-consciously, as if I were being watched, then climbed into the hard bed and waited for the heat of my body to warm the chilly bedclothes. I reached up to the bedside lamp and snapped it off, and there was darkness, and the total silence of the surrounding countryside.

Which part of the house was this room in? I tried to recall

which way Graham and I had come earlier. And yes, I was indeed in the south wing. The seventeenth-century part. It stood to reason that Tobias Salt, or Anne, or their daughters, had been in this room at some point. Were their lives pressed into the stone here? Did they walk this place at night? I closed my eyes, but no quality of the darkness changed.

Around me, the house ticked and creaked as it lost the heat of the day from its bones, and I lay, alert to every sound, half-terrified of what I might hear. At some point very near slumber I remembered the oily, slurring voice captured on the tape, and, before I was aware of what I had done, I pulled the bed-clothes over my head, like I used to do when I was a child.

28

The next day, Graham called a house meeting. The morning was stunning; the sun shone brightly, and the dew rose from the grass in soft waves of steamy vapour, so, after breakfast, we assembled on garden chairs on the front lawn, the house squatting behind us. I felt hot and my head ached a little; Tony Finch had introduced me to alcohol a long while ago, so I knew what this was. Of last night's argument, nothing was said; Seb and Neil simply ignored each other.

Graham arrived last of all. Even though the morning was hot, he wore his usual university lecturer outfit: a bottle-green corduroy jacket, a mustard-coloured jumper, and flared jeans with desert boots. I noted also that Polly wore her ubiquitous cardigan; I wondered how either of them could stand it.

Graham made a short speech, re-introducing me to the rest of the group, then talked us through the scientific equipment, a talk superfluous to all of us, as he made it clear that only he was qualified to operate any of it. Perhaps aware he was losing his audience, he fell silent for a few seconds until he had regained our full attention.

'One more thing,' he said. 'I just wanted to say that as of today, with the arrival of Tim, our approach to what we're

doing here will be changing somewhat. We're going to intensify our search for Tobias Salt, with a slightly different method.

'As such, we might expect a more emotionally exhausting
session. Some of you may feel unaccountably drained, others
might be overcome with sadness, or anger. These are perfectly
normal reactions to what we're doing here. Plus, I know that
some of you are – how can I put this? – already a little troubled
at the moment, whether with issues of depression, or frustration, or the problems of being a young person in today's world.

'In fact, without getting too personal, I know that at least
one of you has already endured an enormous amount of psychic
stress. And I know that one of you is recovering from the
recent loss of a close family member, so that might well make
you vulnerable, emotionally speaking, in this setting.'

I stared down at the lawn, sudden hot tears in my eyes.
Why would he single me out like that? What right did he have?
To declare that Abi was dead? I felt like punching him, in the
same way I'd punched Cliff Lang, wildly and without restraint,
until he sobbed. I immediately decided to confront him about
this after the meeting, whilst at the same time knowing I
never would.

'With that in mind,' Graham went on, 'if anyone wants to
stop the session at any point, just tell me or Sally, and we'll
stop, OK? Juliet?'

Juliet looked up at Graham anxiously. 'Yes?'

'I know you found that first session somewhat . . . trying.'

'Yes, but that was just the – I mean, nothing's happened
since then, has it?'

'No. But I need you to be prepared in case something does.'

Juliet nodded slowly. 'I'll be fine. It just freaked me out the
first time, that's all . . . Really, Graham. I'm fine. I want to
participate.'

'Are you sure?'

Juliet nodded.

'OK then,' said Graham. 'The last thing I want is for any of you to feel uncomfortable.'

And so, my second ever séance took place in the early afternoon, at roughly the same time as my first. Graham made us sit in the same places as before, round the table, only this time we were not to hold hands. Graham had something different in mind. He rummaged in his Gladstone bag and unfolded a large board on which the letters of the alphabet were carefully printed, as well as the words YES and NO. He then produced a heart-shaped piece of wood, on tiny castors, and set it down on top of the board.

'This,' said Graham, 'is a planchette. The idea is, we all place our fingertips on it, and the pointer at the end there will move to letters, spelling out words.'

'Where on earth did you get that?' asked Seb.

'I made it,' said Graham, as if that were the most normal thing in the world.

'Well, shall we?' said Sally. Her thigh, underneath the table, touched mine, and stayed there.

Polly wrinkled her nose. 'It's not a very séance-y day, is it?'

Graham's brows furrowed with the humourless concentration he seemed to bring to everything. 'What do you mean?'

'Weather-wise.' Polly gestured to the tall windows, where the morning sun had matured into a sweltering early June day, and was streaming, in ever-strengthening bars of brilliance, onto the blue carpet.

'*Is* there appropriate weather for a séance?' said Neil.

'Don't worry,' said Sally. 'It doesn't matter. We're going to draw the curtains and light candles, as before. Seb, will you do the honours?'

Seb made a face commensurate to being asked if he would donate a kidney. 'If I *must*.' He rose from his chair petulantly, drew the curtains closed, then lit the candles with his Zippo.

'Anyway,' said Sally, 'strictly speaking this isn't a séance. Just an attempt to see what's out there.'

'What, like . . . fishing?' I said. 'Dangling our lines over the side?'

'Yes. Fishing, for long-dead souls,' Sally said softly, and smiled. I smiled back.

Neil made a face. 'Lord, this gets less scientific with every passing day.'

'Let's just do it,' said Seb. For the first time since I had met them, Neil nodded in agreement. 'What do we do?'

'We're recording, aren't we?' said Sally. Graham nodded. 'OK. It's Tuesday, the fourth of June, 1974. This is a mediumistic session using the planchette, and a printed alphabet. Present are myself, Sally Devonshire, and Graham Shaw. Also present are Tim Smith, Sebastian Stourton, Juliet Fields-Ray, Polly Rook and Neil Audle. Can I ask you all to place a finger onto the planchette?'

We did so. Seven arms reached across the table, like spokes in a wheel. Sally cleared her throat, then continued.

'Can we ask any spirits present to make themselves known? Please excite the planchette if you can hear us.'

Under our fingers, the planchette stayed where it was.

'Please make yourself known to us.'

Nothing.

'What I like most about this,' said Seb, 'is how entirely unfoolish I feel doing it.'

'Seb!' hissed Juliet. 'For God's sake. Concentrate.'

'Yes,' said Seb. 'I'd hate to break our incredible record of communicating with—'

Under our fingertips, the planchette trembled, then juddered across the table, to stop neatly at the word 'YES'.

Even Seb was quiet then.

'Is anyone there?' breathed Sally.

The pointer juddered along the smooth wooden board, stopping at the letter S, then at the A, then the L.

'*Salt*,' breathed Juliet. 'Oh my God! It's him!'

'Oh God!' gasped Polly. The pointer did not move again, did not complete the word.

'Excellent,' said Graham, with rising excitement. 'Excellent!'

Unbidden, the pointer moved, crawling slowly this time, to YES.

'Tobias Salt,' said Sally. 'Is that you?'

The pointer, our hands on top of it, meandered over to the other side of the board, and NO.

'What does he mean, no?' said Seb. The planchette moved smoothly down the board towards the alphabet.

S-A-Y

'Say what? Is there anything we can do for you?'

P-R-A-Y

'Prayers?' said Juliet. Underneath our fingertips, the pointer trembled.

YES

'Say prayers. You want us to say prayers for your soul?'

I-N

'In what? In Latin? Where are you?'

I-N-F-U-R-U-X

We all exchanged baffled glances. With his free hand, Graham wrote the letters down as the pointer moved.

N-O-N-O-P-U-S-I-T

'We don't understand,' said Sally. Undeterred, the plan-chette continued to glide across the table, pointing patiently at individual letters. I remembered the gibberish Latin that the sitters had recorded at the Borley Rectory séances.

S-C-I-S-M-E

'We don't understand.'

V-O-S-N-O-N-S-C-I-T-I-S

'Well, it's not quite Latin,' said Juliet, 'apart from the last bit. Which means—'

S-A-L-T

'Is that who you are? Tobias Salt?'

YES

'He just said he wasn't,' said Seb. 'He should make up his bloody mind.'

In response to this, the planchette jumped as if startled, and moved closer to YES. Seb laughed, although it was a nervous laugh. The planchette now seemed to be grinding its castors against the tabletop, as if it were a living thing, impatient for direction. A slight shiver of revulsion wormed its way up my arm.

'Make yourself known to us!' said Sally. Nothing and nobody moved. 'Make yourself known!' Again, there was silence.

'Hey, Tobias,' said Seb. 'How's it going? Sorry you killed your missus!'

The pointer froze, immovable, as if it were welded to the table. I looked up at everyone's tense faces, the blood drained from them. Even Seb had stopped smirking now. A long moment passed.

'Mr Salt?' said Sally nervously. 'Do you wish to make—'

From upstairs came a great crash, the sound of an enormous piece of furniture being thrown to the floor. It reverberated through the house, like a fist coming down on all the darkest notes of a piano keyboard.

Graham was on his feet first, staring up at the ceiling. 'Good God!'

'Whose room was that?' said Juliet.

'I think it was the landing,' I said.

'My room.' Polly looked up fearfully, gripping her own forearm. 'I think it was my room.'

'Jesus Christ,' said Seb. 'My heart's going like a hammer!'

'That big dresser thing on the landing.' Neil rubbed his glasses. 'The one the size of Blenheim Palace. I bet it was that.'

Polly swallowed, her face pale. 'There's a grandfather clock in my room.'

As a group, all seven of us trod warily up the creaking stairs, led by Graham.

In the colossal hallway, the great Welsh dresser stood undisturbed, all of the Pekin ware cups and saucers in their places, as they no doubt had been for years. I touched one of the teacups; my fingertip came back green with dust. Inside the teacup was a dead fly.

'Well,' said Neil, 'it wasn't the dresser.'

'Nor the grandfather clock,' said Polly, emerging from her room.

'What else could it be?'

We searched our individual rooms. Everything in mine was just as I had left it. I returned to the landing, just as Juliet and Seb were emerging from their room.

'Nothing amiss in our room,' said Juliet.

'Nor mine,' said Neil. Sally shrugged too, and Graham.

Confused, we checked the bathrooms, the airing cupboard – even the wardrobes. Nothing had been disturbed.

'It doesn't make any sense,' said Seb. There was a note of genuine wonder in his voice.

'It makes perfect sense,' said Polly. 'It just doesn't make a sense any of us are used to.'

'What's that supposed to mean?' Seb asked. 'We all heard a crash. We come up here to find nothing's moved. How can that possibly be?'

No one had an answer to that.

We headed back downstairs.

'Maybe it was thunder,' said Neil, leading the way back to the blue room. He pushed the door open. 'Or some sort of atmospheric—'

I was at the rear of the group, and watched as everyone in front of me stopped and stared. And then I saw what they saw, and I stopped and stared too.

The seven chairs we had occupied had all been tipped backwards and were now lying flat on their backs on the floor. They appeared to have been laid out neatly and carefully, like the petals of a flower. There was, I suppose, a tiny chance that this could have happened by accident, and the chairs had somehow all fallen equidistant from each other, in an arrangement so precise, so deliberate, that it looked like the work of a conscious mind.

'Did we . . . leave them like that?' said Seb. His tone betrayed his lack of confidence in this explanation.

'No,' Polly said quietly. 'No, we didn't.'

A long interval passed. All that was audible was the spools of the tape recorder turning, and the ancient timbers of the house, cracking smugly, like knuckles.

29

We had been waiting for something, it seemed, without knowing quite what, and now that thing had finally occurred, there could be no going back. The energy of the house – or us, or both – seemed different, charged with potential.

Immediately afterwards, Graham made all of us go off alone into various parts of the house and write up our individual reports on what had just taken place, without conferring. Once we had submitted these reports, he came to interview us separately. Alone in my room, I found myself glancing around, as though some sly, unpleasant trick might be played on me, if I were not vigilant. It was almost a relief when Graham came to talk to me. I recounted what had occurred as faithfully as I could.

The interviews took the entire afternoon, and by the time we were allowed to speak to each other again, it was 6 p.m., and dinner time. According to the rota, it was my turn to cook, but thankfully Polly volunteered, saying she felt like doing something 'normal', and we were spared whatever horrors I would have cobbled together. After dinner, Graham magnanimously gave us the evening off to do as we pleased, but nobody was willing to be alone, and so we congregated naturally in the large lounge next to the blue room, with its just-about modern furniture. Graham vanished to work up his results, but Sally brought a teapot and mugs from the kitchen and poured strong tea for us all.

There was, inevitably, only one topic of conversation.

'It was so *loud*!' said Juliet. 'And that thing with the chairs is the weirdest thing I've ever seen. Euurgh.'

'It was horrible all right,' said Polly, pouring the tea. 'Like something did it on purpose.'

'It was pretty weird,' Seb agreed. His habitual confidence had temporarily left him, and he seemed genuinely rattled. 'What do you make of it, Timbo?'

Again, I wished Abi were here. She would have a much clearer idea of what to think about all of this. What would she say, if she were here?

'I'm not sure,' I said.

'What are you unsure about?' asked Sally. She sat on the floor with her hand over the arm of my chair, and rested her head on the back of her hand to look at me.

'I don't know,' I said. 'I'm just concerned that in situations like this, it's very easy to drift into a group delusion whereby we're all convincing ourselves that something paranormal is happening. Both the Society for Psychical Research notes on this and Harry Price's instructions to investigators at Borley Rectory bore this fact in mind.' This was very much the kind of thing Abi would say. I felt suddenly almost breathless with sadness.

Sally smiled at me. 'But you have to agree it was impressive. You do agree with that, don't you, Tim?' Her eyes sparkled up at me.

'I do,' I said.

'Well then,' she said, and sank back to the floor. 'We all agree. We've had our first, genuine, psychokinetic event!'

'Hurray,' said Neil from the corner of the room, raising his tea mug. I realised he'd been very quiet all afternoon. Since we had seen the chairs, in fact.

'Hurray!' Seb, immune as ever to disquiet or nuance, raised his mug too. 'To Mr Salt. Finally shaking a leg after all these years, the old bastard! Tobias Salt!'

'Tobias Salt,' we said, in untidy unison.

A peculiar spell of consensual quiet followed, filled with the expectation that the house might find the power to answer back. The house, however, answered with silence, the silence of the long corridors and the black, cavernous hall; the silence of the Victorian rooms as they sat over the scorched stones of the original wing, as they slumbered in the cold red earth. Somehow, this was a more effective, more chilling response than we had bargained for, and nobody spoke for a long time.

'Can someone take me upstairs?' Polly said quietly. 'I don't want to go up there alone.' Strangely, she looked at me when she said this, her expression almost challenging.

'I'll take you, my love,' said Sally. She got to her feet. Polly smiled politely and they headed for the door. 'Goodnight, everyone.'

'I think we're going to turn in too,' said Seb, standing and stretching. 'I mean, what's there to stay up for? You coming, Jules?'

Juliet laughed. 'Rather than follow you upstairs on my own? Course I am.' She padded over to the door. Seb grinned back at us.

'Night, all. Don't let the bedbugs bite. I mean, I'm sure Comprehensive is perfectly used to bed bugs, but the rest of us have higher—'

'Just GO!' snapped Juliet.

'Goodnight, Seb,' I said, smiling. He was very hard to dislike. He clattered into the corridor and up the stairs, Juliet following behind.

'Well,' said Neil, after the noise of Seb's departure had finally ceased to reverberate. 'What do you make of all this?'

I inhaled and exhaled very slowly.

'I have no idea. It was creepy, for sure.'

'I think we're being tricked,' Neil said simply.

I stared at him.

'You probably have two big questions about that assertion,' he said. 'Let me deal with them in reverse order of importance. Question one – how were we tricked?'

'You're that sure that we were?'

'Look at it this way. Either the laws of physics work, and are consistent and predictable in all cases or— Who's that spoon-bending weirdo, the one who's all over the telly? What's his name?'

'Uri Geller.'

'Yes, him. You either believe he has uncanny powers that rip up all we know about the physical world, or you accept he's doing a magic trick. It may be a very good trick, and even he might believe it's real by this point, but it's a trick nonetheless. Now. Which of those two explanations strikes you as the most likely?'

I nodded. Neil smiled.

'And so, our hosts, Graham and Sally, arrange for a loud noise to go off upstairs. It leaves no physical traces, and we can't find any evidence of it. That tells me it was probably made by the second tape recorder. The one we've been using to record the empty rooms.'

'Are you sure? It was a very loud noise.'

'Those things can make a huge racket if you want them to.'

Yes, I thought. *Once you have eliminated the impossible, what remains, no matter how improbable, must be the truth.* I had grown up alongside someone who liked to play Sherlock Holmes. It irked me that, once again, I was to be Dr Watson.

'But still, it sounded like a real noise rather than a recording.'

'I agree. But we were all in a state of heightened awareness, all subconsciously scaring ourselves.' Neil sipped his tea thoughtfully. 'We are neither reliable nor objective witnesses.'

He was right. We were all too ready to turn any noise into something ghastly. But then, this explanation didn't feel correct, as if it were too neat, too tidy. I raised my other objection.

'How did it happen on cue, then?'

Neil snorted derisively. 'Did it? Seb directed one of his trademark tedious needling comments to the planchette. Then there was a silence. Then, the crash, just as Sally was asking for a response.'

'It did happen after she asked, though.'

'Not after. It happened *as* she asked. Like she'd messed up the cue. Also, you'll notice that everyone searched their own room afterwards. We haven't seen inside Graham or Sally's rooms at all. And Graham keeps the second tape recorder in his room.'

I was sad. It was exciting to be at the centre of paranormal phenomena, to be one of the chosen few to have experienced first-hand something otherworldly; something if not numinous, then at least holding the possibility of the numinous. It was not exciting to be duped.

'And the chairs?' I said, almost not wanting to know.

Neil sighed, almost sadly. 'Who came upstairs last?'

'I didn't see.'

'*I* did. It was Sally. She followed us up a little after everyone else. It would have been the work of seconds for her to tip all the chairs over, especially if she'd practised it. It was impressive, I'll give her that. But it was all fake. The more I think about it, the more sure I am.'

It all sounded more than plausible. Conflicting and contradictory thoughts struggled for the upper hand in my mind.

'I can see you're confused,' said Neil. 'And if I'm right, you're confused about the same thing I am. Which brings us to Question Two.'

'Which is?'

'Why would anybody *do* this?' said Neil. 'I mean, what's the point? Graham's clearly spending quite a bit of money on this whole ghost hunt – renting this place, keeping us, and so on. So my question is this – what kind of person fakes a ghost? And why?'

I shrugged awkwardly. I had more experience in this field than I wished to divulge.

'What do we do?' I asked.

'I don't know,' said Neil. 'Keep an eye on things. See how they progress. If we are being tricked, by either Graham or Sally, or both of them, they'll no doubt try it again, and at some point they'll slip up.'

I thought for a moment. This was all very well, but Abi and I always liked to consider the unimaginable in any circumstance; ultimately, it was the only way one really learned anything.

'You said earlier that this boils down to either accepting that the laws of physics are the same everywhere and at all times, or they're not. But what if what we're witnessing here just belongs to a realm we don't currently understand, that contradicts everything we believe we know?'

Neil screwed up his face in confusion. 'Meaning what?'

'I mean, what if it's not Graham or Sally? What if it's real?'

Neil paused. 'I suppose we'll deal with that when it happens,' he said. 'I'm sorry, I don't really know. In the meantime, I think it's best if we keep these suspicions among ourselves, don't you?'

'Of course,' I said. 'Absolutely.'

I was the last to go to bed. I stood for a moment in the hallway, lit by a single bare bulb. For a few minutes, I tried to believe, to fully grasp, that I was standing in a haunted house, but the proposition now seemed so absurd I couldn't make it real. I turned off the passageway light and fumbled my way up the staircase.

Once upstairs, I half expected to see movement in every shadowy corner, but there was nothing. I expected to feel uneasy, but instead I simply undressed, climbed into bed and turned the light off.

The blackness on the stairs and on the landing had been severe enough, but, in my room, the darkness was absolute, like the inside of a coffin.

I expected to be unsettled after the day's events, but the conversation with Neil had banished my earlier disquiet, and I lay in the empty darkness, arms by my sides, eyes open.

Was this what it was like to be dead? I wondered. Not knowing where you began or ended, seeping out into the world like liquid? Was this now Abi's world? If so, was she conscious of it? Again I remembered our notebook, where we had written the various fates we could expect in the afterlife; I hadn't checked up on it in Abi's room in weeks.

Is it more terrifying to believe somewhere is haunted, or to believe that nowhere is? After a while, I crossed my arms across my chest like a knight on a tomb, and lay as still as I could, listening for something, anything, that would unambiguously solve the riddle, prove or disprove, one way or another. The darkness, empty of everything save itself, kept quiet.

30

The next morning, at breakfast, with the initial shock having subsided, it seemed everyone had a theory.

Juliet and Seb were of the opinion that Tobias Salt had been contacted and was now making his presence known. I listened as Seb described the mischievous spirit of a dead man playing with us, moving objects and causing crashes, as we, the living, grew more and more scared. Juliet said we should be seeking a way to lay Salt to rest, once and for all, possibly by employing a priest. I listened to all this, nodding politely, inwardly deriding them for their lack of imagination.

Neil asserted a revised version of the suspicions he'd shared with me last night – namely, that no ghost was involved at all. He ventured that either we were working ourselves up into a state of group delusion, or that we were subconsciously creating the phenomena because the tension of expectation had become too much. He carefully excised from this theory any of the more specific suspicions he had shared with me the night before. I found this cowardly.

'What about you, Pols?' said Juliet.

Polly smiled. 'I honestly don't know. And I don't think any of us *can* know, until we have more data. Sorry to be a bore, it's just all so new to me.'

Sally smiled at me. 'All right. What about you, Tim?'

'I don't know either. It's very hard to explain the crash upstairs, once you rule out . . . trickery of some kind.' I glanced at Neil, who immediately looked down at his cornflakes.

'Tim!' Sally sounded almost offended. 'Surely you don't think this is a hoax?'

I smiled a weak smile. 'I just want to be certain, that's all. We need to be as scientific as we can.'

Sally sounded affronted now. 'You don't think we're being scientific enough?'

'No, of course I do!' I felt my cheeks redden. 'It's just that – Neil's right. The pressure to produce phenomena is huge, and we might be meeting that pressure – subconsciously.'

Sally smiled a tight smile, nodded, and said nothing. Neil played with his spoon, turning it around in his cereal, like a child. Why wouldn't he help me?

Seb's cutlery clattered loudly to his plate and he patted his pockets for his cigarettes. 'What about you, Sally? We've all shared our theories with you. You must have heard one you agree with? One you think is correct?'

Sally smiled again, an enigmatic smile. 'Why can't they all be correct?'

Seb frowned at her for a split second, and then collapsed into a good-natured guffaw at her joke, which effectively ended any further discussion of what Sally had said. However, something about her demeanour suggested to me she was entirely serious. But then again, how could she be?

As if on cue, Graham appeared, his unlit pipe clenched between his teeth, a bundle of books under his arm. He snatched two pieces of cold toast from the silver rack and proceeded to plaster them with half a pot of thick-cut marmalade.

'Well, at least you're in a good mood,' said Polly.

'Hmm?' Graham looked up at her. 'Yes, I suppose I am. Wouldn't you be? We've spent many fruitless days in this house, at great expense, attempting to summon up some sort of poltergeist reaction, and yesterday – bang! – two for one!' He crunched happily into his marmalade-slathered toast.

'You're not . . . afraid?' said Juliet.

Graham looked thoughtful. 'Well, cautious, yes. Curious, absolutely. But not afraid. This isn't the dark ages, Juliet. Whatever arranged those chairs – and caused that crash – can be explained by scientific method. It's our duty to apply that method.'

'That's great,' said Seb, through a cloud of cigarette smoke. 'Only, Tim thinks it's all balls.'

'That's not what I said!' I shot Seb a look of such ferocity that he actually looked chastened. Sally looked at me as if personally wounded.

'Really, Tim?' said Graham. 'What makes you think that?'

Enough was enough, I thought. 'It was Neil's theory. He shared it with me last night.'

'Audle!' said Seb. 'I might have known.'

'All I said was we don't have concrete evidence yet,' Neil said. 'We only have a series of happenings which might – or might not – be connected to our current activities.'

'Pfffff.' Seb would never, I realised, miss an opportunity to belittle Neil. 'It's a bit of a bloody coincidence, though? We ask for a noise. A noise happens. In case we doubt the noise, the chairs are arranged deliberately. I'd say that was pretty conclusive.'

Neil shrugged. 'I'm just saying. I think Polly's right. We need further data.'

'Thank you, Neil.' Polly nodded and smiled.

'Well,' said Graham, pointing at us with his second slice of toast. 'You may get your evidence later today. I suggest we press our advantage and carry straight on. Let's assemble in Tobias's room after lunch, and see what he has for us today.'

And so, that afternoon, we again gathered in the blue room. I drew the curtains, obscuring another glorious day, and Seb lit the candles. Graham was last to join us, setting the tape recorder to record, switching on the equipment and knocking his pipe out in the fireplace.

'All right,' said Sally. 'We're all present. Same personnel as yesterday's session, and we're trying again with the planchette. Only, this time, I want to try automatic writing.'

'Right,' said Graham. 'Are you sure this is a good idea, Sals?'

'I am,' said Sally. 'I think it will speed things up a bit. Does anyone mind?'

No one did. We all sat around the table, in our usual places. I noted with a thrill that Sally's thigh again touched mine, and she didn't move it away. The planchette was duly produced, and we placed our fingertips on the pointer. However, this time, Graham fixed a freshly sharpened pencil into a hole at the front of the planchette, the point of the lead touching a large sheet of blank paper, like the needle in a seismograph.

We waited nervously in the darkened room, sunlight glowing at the edges of the drawn curtains.

'Tobias,' said Sally. 'Tobias Salt.'

Nothing.

'Tobias Salt.'

Nothing.

'Are you there?'

The table lurched. Again – as we had done last time – we all gasped. Sally gasped too. I looked at her closely; she certainly didn't look as if she was faking anything. Graham, too, looked alarmed, taken aback by what was happening. I glanced over at Neil, and saw his eyes dart back and forth, perhaps looking for the reassurance of blatant trickery, so he would know precisely where he stood.

'And just to be sure,' said Sally, almost fearfully. 'No one else is doing that?'

We all turned to Seb. He looked genuinely hurt.

'I'm not doing anything!'

Sally looked around at the rest of us. 'And no one else is doing that?'

Neil's voice sounded embarrassed. 'You don't have to go out of your way to—'

Beneath the planchette, the table lurched again, as if reminding us to include it in the conversation.

'Good God,' said Sally. 'Wow. OK. It seems that – yes. Tobias Salt, is that you? Can you hear us?'

The rapping again; once for yes.

'Good God,' repeated Sally. 'What should we call you? Tobias?'

A knock, and then, after a short pause, another knock.

'No? Too informal, I imagine. In that case, how about Mr Salt?'

I thought of the newspapers, telling of Abi's disappearance. Of the portrait of *Mister S* that accompanied them. Of Janice's voice as she hissed the single syllable, *ESSS,* out from clenched teeth.

'I don't—' I began.

A definite knock this time.

'Ah! Mr Salt it shall be. Are you willing to talk to us today, Mr Salt?'

A pause, then a vague knock.

'We have something different for you today, Mr Salt,' said Sally. 'Do you see the pencil?'

Knock.

'We have paper, too, and we're willing to be a conduit for you. Do you know what I mean by conduit?'

A single, loud knock, almost angry.

'Of course. My apologies. Well then, in that case, guide our hands. Let's see what you can tell us about yourself.'

Graham turned to Sally. 'Are you sure?' Sally nodded, biting her lip.

There was another knock at the table, catching us all off guard, and everyone laughed nervously.

'OK. In that case, Mr Salt, please make yourself known.'

We all watched the pointer on the white expanse of paper, but it did not move. Everyone exchanged glances, but no one spoke.

'Mr Salt,' said Graham, after a minute or so. 'Can you move the pencil?'

An indeterminate scratching sound, like the burrowing of rodents. I wondered if anyone could produce a noise like that on purpose. The pencil did not move.

'Maybe he's thinking,' said Neil.

'Don't be shy, Mr Salt,' said Sally, looking upwards. 'You're among friends. You can tell us anything.'

Knock.

'Are you ready, Mr Salt?'

Knock.

Five seconds went by, then the planchette jerked violently forward, as if pulled by a rope. We all gasped, or swore.

Beneath my fingertip, I felt the pencil scratch feverishly across the paper. I looked down. Words, cut into the page in a jagged, slanting hand, like a length of barbed wire:

tht voys why wont it be quite

'Tell us more,' said Sally. 'We don't understand. You can hear a voice?'

The pencil slashed across the page, awful to watch, awful to feel. Something like nausea crackled across my cheeks as it wrote.

plantic voys of subtil madders

'I'm sorry, I still don't understand. Could you tell us more?'

I an the remiannder when all is subreacted
I am th daxzzling brite

'You are bright? Shining?'

No answer.

'Do you mean your soul? Your soul is bright?'

No answer.

Sally took a deep breath. 'Are you dead?'

NEVER

'That word again,' I said.

'You aren't dead?'

thou arts in one regeim onlie
I am in them
all I am the
sickell the promis

'We can't understand you.' Somewhere behind Sally's voice, I heard Juliet whimper involuntarily.

'Tell us more. You are Tobias Salt?'

Was

'You were? When you were alive?'

Am

'You are now?'

Will be

'What does that—'

I can straedge and
see beyonf all I
can see all

'What does that mean?' implored Graham. The pencil didn't move. 'Do you mean you are in a place beyond time now? In the realm of the dead?'

A collective gasp as Sally's hand jerked violently, dislodging all of our fingers. Sally gave a distressed moan as, under her hand, a slashing storm of cancelling lines grew, like thick black rain. Graham grabbed Sally's arm and shushed and soothed her, and the slashing motions subsided.

'Christ,' said Sally. 'Jesus Christ.' The pencil began to write again – only this time, not the urgent, frantic printing of the earlier messages, but a faint, controlled rhythm; a different hand, grey in contrast to the sharp black barbs of the previous messages.

Egow Sum Non Sum Egoe Sum Non sum

'What does that mean?' said Seb.

'Sally? Are you alright?' I asked. Sally didn't answer. She stared down at her hands on the planchette, in terror.

'We need to stop this,' I said.

'No!' said Graham. 'We need to see where it goes.' Sally lurched forward again.

Ego Sum Non sum

'What's he *saying?*' shouted Seb.

'It means—' began Juliet. But the planchette, under Sally's painted fingernails, answered for her.

I am I am not I am I am not

'What?' said Graham. 'What does that mean? We can't understand you!'

a meting place a meting place I will mete you ther

'You will meet us? You want to meet with us?'

'Please!' Sally's voice was barely a sob. Her face contorted with distress.

'Graham!' I shouted. The pencil jumped into savage life once more, scoring the page with dark black strokes.

Reuntied with wat is gon

You Wil See

I am thruogh now

YU WILL SEE

SILT STREAM

'You're . . .' Graham didn't get any further. The planchette danced madly across the paper, trailing words.

I bring the liek of witch I bring skalld and renned raw you of living lives

Sally was sobbing uncontrollably now. The pencil slashed through the paper and through the pages below as she wrote the same meaningless pattern over and over, a looping shape like a sound wave folded in on itself, again and again, until the pencil lead broke and she was just writing with a blunt stump of wood.

Under the pointer, the pencil snapped in two. Sally screamed and threw her arms up in an unnatural, mechanical movement, overturning the table as she stood. The table crashed onto its side, almost hitting Juliet, who shrieked. Sally clasped her hands to her face and howled, whilst Graham, Seb and I manoeuvred her into a chair.

She didn't stop crying for fifteen minutes.

Graham was elated.

'This,' said Graham, reading from the scrawled notes laid out on the kitchen table, 'this is amazing!'

'I'm not sure Sally would agree with you,' I said.

'Yeah,' said Polly drily. 'We had to give her a sedative.'

Graham ignored us. 'Listen to these sentences. "*I am the sickle, the promise.*" The broken syntax is entirely consistent throughout. It sounds convincingly like the thoughts of an external entity, rather than even the deep subconscious.'

Neil shook his head. 'I think the subconscious may be a lot deeper than you think.'

'You're not still doubting all this, Neil? After what we just witnessed?' Graham's voice was almost annoyed.

'No, I just – it's a lot to think about, that's all.' Again, Neil looked embarrassed.

'What about you, Tim?' said Graham, folding his arms. 'Are you still on the fence about all of this?'

'I think Sally definitely experienced something,' I said carefully. 'I have no doubt that what she felt was real enough to her. It certainly felt real enough in there.'

Graham smiled. 'Qualify it with faint praise as much as you like. I think this represents a breakthrough. Sadly, the audio tapes are clear and there were no anomalous readings on any of the meters, but nonetheless. We must conclude that we are now able to communicate fully with our Mr Salt.'

'Providing that *was* him,' said Juliet. 'He didn't sound too sure. And there *are* two sets of handwriting.'

'A classic sign of automatic writing,' said Graham, knocking his pipe on the edge of the table. 'I'm almost surprised there weren't more. No, this is Mr Salt all right. The genuine article. Who else would it be?'

I looked down at the table, at the scrawled and scratched words, and the unthinkable occurred to me. *This was the kind of thing Abi would have found amusing. To see the look on my face.*

Then I remembered Mr Henshaw's warning, the thing he had been afraid of, and felt ashamed.

That evening after dinner, we all sat once more in the lounge, drinking tea. Even Seb was subdued; the events of the séance were not something any of us could easily shrug off, and, as before, no one really felt like being alone. I felt an urgent need to ask Neil's opinion, but only, I realised, because I wanted him to explain the experience away, to make it safe and controllable, because I found that I couldn't.

After an hour or so, Sally still hadn't reappeared, and Graham went up to check on her. After forty-five minutes, he re-entered the room, looking somewhat subdued.

'How's she doing?' said Juliet.

Graham removed his glasses, polished the lenses on his sleeve. 'Fine. Although, looking back, it was maybe unwise to press ahead so soon after yesterday's . . . results.' He put his glasses back on. 'In fact, for the good of us all, and Sally especially, I suggest we take tomorrow off.'

'Great!' said Seb.

'I also think it might do us good to get out of the house for the day.'

'Even better!' said Seb.

'Maybe on some kind of educational or archaeological excursion.'

'Christ!' said Seb.

Juliet shot him a look. 'Where were you thinking of?' she asked.

'Well, we have the cars, so . . . the sky's the limit, really. Anyone have any ideas?'

'Grime's Graves are the obvious place,' I said. 'They're not too far.'

Graham pointed the stem of his pipe at me. 'Excellent, Tim. And let's not forget Sutton Hoo.'

Polly frowned. 'Or . . . we could go further afield. Make it a real day out.'

'Oh, better and better,' said Seb, into his coffee mug.

'What about Stonehenge?' said Neil. A small thrill went through me. Abi and I had often petitioned our parents to go to Stonehenge, to no avail. Dad had driven past it numerous times – never once thinking to stop – and had decided from these fragmentary glimpses that the world's most famous prehistoric monument was hugely overrated. It was very disappointing, he said. Much smaller than you'd imagine. Half of it had fallen down, for Pete's sake.

'Now, Neil, that really is too far,' said Graham. 'You're looking at an eight-hour round trip, and for what? To see a monument that's lost its original pagan significance long ago. It's no doubt currently full of hippies, readying themselves for what their drug-addled minds think the summer solstice entails.'

'What about the Uffington White Horse?' said Polly. Another delighted thrill went through me. All of the places I'd ever wanted to visit – ancient, mysterious, strange – a million miles from my suburban existence – were now being idly touted as possible destinations.

'Hmm,' said Graham. 'A lovely thing, to be sure, but again, maybe *too* far.'

'Avebury?' I said. I knew it was even further away than Uffington, but I just wanted to join in.

Graham shook his head. 'Again, too far. Which is a real shame, as the Avebury complex is probably my favourite Neolithic monument in the British Isles. Despite the truly stupid

decision to drive a tarmac road through the circle itself, which
to my mind is emblematic of—'

'Right,' said Polly. 'Given that everything we suggest is
halfway across the country, it seems we're out of options.
We might as well head to Grime's Graves. Or Dunwich? Or
maybe—'

'Rollright.'

We all turned. Sally was framed in the doorway. Although
she had dark circles under her eyes, her voice was sure and
certain.

'Sals!' Graham got to his feet and rushed over to her. 'How
are you feeling?' He guided her into a chair as if she were an
invalid.

'I'm fine, thank you. Honestly. It was just a shock, that's
all. The – realness of it.'

'I'm sure. Are you OK to be up and about?'

'Yes. And I want to visit Rollright. If we can.'

'Hmmm,' said Graham. 'It's still a long way. And the original stones have been repositioned many times over the years.
If we wanted to look at an ancient monument that's been
poorly restored, we could just stay in this house.' He laughed
mirthlessly at his own joke, such as it was.

'Nevertheless,' said Sally, 'I've always wanted to go.'

'How far away is it?' Juliet asked. Neil scanned the AA
Road Atlas.

'Er . . . quite a way. Not as far as Stonehenge, though. Still
about a hundred and forty miles? So about two, two and a half
hours.'

There was a silence whilst we waited for a decision.

'It's far away, but . . .' said Graham, '. . . if that's what you
want to do, Sals.'

'It is,' said Sally. 'I've always been fascinated by the Roll-right Stones, but I've never been.'

'How does everyone else feel about a long drive?'

Sebastian sighed heavily. Everyone else looked keen.

'It'll be an adventure!' I said. It really would be. Despite reading about stone circles for my entire life, I had never actually been to one. I felt almost sick with excitement.

'That's the spirit, Tim!' said Graham patronisingly. 'We'll come back refreshed, and take on Tobias Salt with renewed vigour!'

31

After breakfast the next morning, we drew matchsticks to decide who would undertake the boring chore of going into the village and getting supplies for our trip.

I lost.

Everyone bar Polly had something to say about the village. Seb told me it was the most boring place on earth; Juliet said some of the shops looked interesting. Graham told me the church was fourteenth century, and a good example of the period, and Neil chipped in that the church had a rood-screen that had survived the Reformation largely unscathed, apart from the saints' faces being obliterated. Sally simply gave me directions, telling me I could take a short cut through a five-bar gate marked Cobbett's Wood.

The day was a fine one, showing off Cobbett's Wood at what I suspected was its most beautiful. The only woods I knew well were filled with fly-tipped debris; these woods felt primordial and unspoiled, as if I were the first person ever to walk in them. Birdsong rose from the undergrowth, the woods were sweet-smelling, and everything felt resoundingly alive. I realised I had been in Suffolk for four days now and had seen virtually none of it. Inside the house, it was easy to forget we were in one of the most beautiful parts of the country.

After half a mile, the woods stopped abruptly at a wooden gate leading onto the road. Turning left, I came to some houses of red brick and knapped flint, huddled around a tri-angular lawn at a fork in the road; as Sally had instructed, I ignored the left-hand fork and carried on walking. The next twenty or so houses were squat 1930s bungalows, which had long ago congealed into a stale, one-dimensional Englishness, with identical pink and yellow rosebushes in every garden, and smiling concrete gnomes pushing wheelbarrows into nowhere.

These houses were put to shame by the chaos of seventeenth- and eighteenth-century dwellings that made up the village proper. Each one a different size and shape, it was easy to ascribe to every house a distinct personality. Some of them were merely two tipsy, sloping storeys, whilst others stretched to three and even, in one case, four; stiff-backed and tall, the houses of the aspirant middle classes of two or three hundred years ago. The village was a pretty, unpretentious place, neither preserved in the unnatural stasis of heritage, nor allowed to run down into shabbiness. It was clearly a place thought of fondly by the people who lived there.

The single street around which the village clustered was lined with shops – a butcher, a fishmonger, a greengrocer, and, eventually, the small shop that Sally had told me about. Everyone I passed – an old woman with an extremely pale face; a fat, ruddy man in a brown shirt walking a colossal Alsatian; a man with grey sideburns and a comb-over, wear-ing a lemon-yellow jacket – either smiled or acknowledged me with a nod of the head. I wondered how they would react if they knew what I was part of, what I had been brought to Yarlings for.

As I walked round the gloomy interior of the village shop, placing things from the list into a wire basket, I noticed that, staggeringly, they seemed to have a licence to sell alcohol here, in an actual shop. Was this normal, out here in the countryside? Could I get away with purchasing any? I still had some of my own money in my jacket. Sally had mentioned at dinner yesterday that she liked red wine. There was a cluster of bottles of red wine here, and I could easily put one among the other items, and if I was denied, it would not be embarrassing, as no one here knew me. I looked at the shop's selection of dusty bottles. The labels and the names meant nothing to me, some being in French and others Spanish, as if to make the task of assessing their merits doubly impossible. Eventually, rather than risk handing Sally a bottle of something that demonstrated beyond all doubt my lack of worldliness or maturity, I decided not to bother. The red-faced woman at the till smiled at me as she filled two yellow carrier bags with cheese and tomatoes and bread.

'On holiday, are you?' She smiled. The smile seemed fixed.

'Yes.' I smiled back. 'Sort of.' I had an idea. 'I'm staying about a mile away, with a few friends. In a house.'

'Oh?'

'Yes. You might know it . . . Yarlings?' I watched carefully for any reaction on her part as I said the name. If strangers came to the village of Borley, wanting to see the ruins of the rectory, I imagined that the locals knew immediately why they had come, and what they were looking for.

'Lovely!' she said. She smiled at me again. 'That's one pound and five altogether.' I handed her the money. She bashed

away at the noisy till and handed me my change, smiling yet
again for good measure.

The shops in the village all seemed to have their doors propped
open to catch the morning sunlight, apart from one. The front
of this shop was a heavy black Victorian bay window with
small, square panes, the whole thing sagging with age, almost
melting into the street. A hand-painted sign above the door
read 'H. Wells, Bookseller. Modern and Antiquarian'. I never could
resist a bookshop, and certainly not one like this. I pushed the
door open with one of my shopping bags, and a bell jangled.

Like most small second-hand bookshops, the place strad-
dled the line between stocking a range of titles on all subjects,
and the kind of compulsive book-hoarding that, if exhibited
by a close relative, would be enough of a concern for you to
seek professional help on their behalf. There were books
everywhere; in rows two-deep on the cramped black shelves
that ran floor-to-ceiling across every wall; in precarious forma-
tions atop the free-standing bookcases; stacked in piles on the
floor, the desk, the radiator, the window ledges. At the sound
of the bell, a French bulldog emerged from beneath the desk
and regarded me with a weary look before curling up in a
wicker basket. I saw a tall, reedy woman in her thirties standing on a battered kick-stool as she placed books on a high
shelf. She wore a pinstriped jacket with the arms rolled up,
and a black pencil skirt. She turned to look down at me as I
entered, pushing her spectacles up the bridge of her nose.

'Good morning,' she said, now not looking at me. 'Were
you looking for anything in particular?'

I had spent much of my young life learning how to make
suspicious adults trust me, so much so that the routine was
now second nature. You had to speak enthusiastically and

clearly, in a received pronunciation, BBC announcer voice, with no hints of rough edges. You had to declare an interest in something dull and worthy, like model aeroplanes or military headgear, which subconsciously reassured your target adult that you were a morally upright young person and weren't interested in pop music or drugs or Satanism. And above all, you had to be polite.

'Do you have any books about local wildlife?' I asked. I was pleasantly surprised by how bright and eager my voice sounded, even to me. 'Birds, specifically, but any general guide would be good!'

She turned back to me and smiled. I had her full attention now. 'Well, there are several things scattered around, but I fear they're all either rather dry or old, or both. You're welcome to have a dig around, though!' She said this last sentence as a joke, rather than an extremely precise description of what I'd have to do to find anything in this place.

'Great!' I said. 'And . . . do you have anything about local folklore, myths and legends, that sort of thing?'

'You might be rather luckier in that regard,' she said. She pushed her glasses up onto her forehead. 'We had something of a glut of that sort of thing a while back. A prominent local historian popped his clogs and I – as a somewhat less-prominent local historian – inherited most of his library, once the relatives had stripped the carcass, as it were. There's plenty of his bequest still scattered around, if you're willing to rummage. What were you looking for, exactly?'

I stopped myself from shrugging. There is, or was, a certain class of adult – and this woman, with her ferociously bright blue eyes and her excellent, stiff-backed posture, was very definitely a member of that class of adult – that hates shrugging. I was forced to provide a more definite answer.

'Er – well, I'm looking for information about a specific house. Me and my friends are currently staying there. Yarlings? You know it? The large one up the road, about a mile away?'

'I do indeed,' said the woman. 'Early seventeenth century, but since subject to many alterations. I think the only original part of the house left is the dining hall, and some of the reception rooms. It's in Pevsner's, but I think he's rather more damning.' She seemed proud to show off both her knowledge of the place and the speed of her recall of it. 'You're looking for information about the history of the house?'

'Yes,' I said. 'You know. The stories and legends. Especially about its owner around the time of the Civil War.'

She stared down at me with a curious expression on her face. 'Which owner would that be?'

'Tobias Salt?' I hazarded carefully. I felt her gaze intensify. 'I don't know the name.'

Her stare was intolerable. However, if the stories of Tobias Salt were half as lurid and unpleasant as Graham had made out, was it any wonder the locals wished to keep their murderous former resident to themselves? A wife-and-daughter-killing psychopath was hardly the kind of thing that would bring tourists flooding in, at least, not the kind of tourists anybody wanted. Again, I had never been to Borley, but I could understand how tiresome the locals must find the stream of researchers, dowsers and devil-worshippers who made the pilgrimage to their quiet corner of the world.

'As I say, it was just after the Civil War,' I continued, watching her closely. 'A thoroughly bad lot, by all accounts. A Puritan witch-finder with a zeal for burning those he suspected of witchcraft. Apparently, he also did away with his wife and daughter, in some kind of ritual.'

The woman looked extremely alarmed. 'Where did you hear this story?'

'A – friend – of mine uncovered it. Apparently, it's not very widely known.'

'It certainly is not,' said the woman. She stepped down from the kick-stool, smoothed her hands over her skirt, then offered me her right hand to shake. 'Forgive my manners. I'm Hattie Wells, I'm the owner here.'

'Tim Smith,' I said. 'As I say, I'm staying here with friends. At Yarlings.'

'I see.' Again, Hattie Wells peered at me with her uncomfortable, assessing gaze. 'And what else have people told you about . . . Tobias Salt?'

'Not much. Apparently, he was given the place as a reward for his military service with the Parliamentarians. After that, he went bananas, and started to practise witchcraft whilst affecting to suppress it.'

Hattie Wells slipped behind her spectacularly cluttered desk and produced a notepad from a drawer. She immediately began to scribble something down.

'Apparently,' I said, watching her carefully, 'the place is haunted.'

'Oh?' said Hattie Wells, looking up at me, grinning dismissively. 'Where isn't?'

'Yes. There's, um, some talk of people being driven out by ghostly activity. Former owners and tenants.'

'Really? Well, it certainly wasn't the last lot, the Collmeres. They left because the place got too expensive to maintain.' She chewed her pencil thoughtfully, as the possibility of an alternative explanation took hold. 'At least, that's what they said. I have to say, this is all very interesting. The village is largely free of the grotesques one routinely finds in English social history, especially in East Anglia and Essex. Are you sure about all this?'

'You've honestly never heard of Tobias Salt?'

She shook her head. 'But if what you're telling me is correct, I can see why the subsequent owners of the house kept the story to themselves.'

'Yes,' I said. 'This – friend – only discovered it by chance, in the parish records.' I remembered something. Fishing in my jacket pocket, I found the folded foolscap sheets that were *The True History of Tobias Salt*. 'Here. This is everything we know.' Before I could think better of it, I handed it to her.

'May I keep hold of this?'

'Of course!' I said, unsure whether or not I was crossing a line. I didn't want to be expelled from Yarlings.

'Hmmm.' Hattie Wells tapped her teeth with her pencil as she scanned the pages. I wondered what she was thinking. Despite the mess and clutter choking her tiny bookshop, I got the impression she knew exactly where everything was, where it came from, and what it was worth. I imagined she would be a terrible person to get on the wrong side of: she was currently being friendly to me, and that was almost too much to bear. I wondered, with a sudden, stabbing terror, if I had said too much. I wanted to ask for the pages back, but it was too late now.

'Well, thank you for your help!' I said, just as brightly as before. 'I'd best be off.'

Again, she skewered me with her gaze. I saw that her blue eyes were flecked with gold, like those of a bird of prey. 'You sure you don't want to look for anything now? I'm sure it wouldn't take two minutes.'

I held up the carrier bags and smiled ruefully. 'I'm afraid not.' I was going to lie about there being a block of ice cream in one of the bags, but I got the distinct feeling that if I deviated from the truth in any way, Hattie Wells would know. 'I was sent to get supplies, and I'm already running late. But I'm staying for another week or so. I'll be back.'

Hattie Wells sniffed and pushed her glasses up the bridge of her nose again, reaching across the desk to a porcelain frog with several sun-yellowed business cards in its oversized mouth. 'Well, we're closed on Saturdays and Sundays, but apart from that we're open ten a.m. to five-thirty p.m. weekdays, apart from Wednesday, of course, which is half-day closing.'

'Thank you,' I said enthusiastically, taking the card. Wide-eyed cheerfulness was becoming wearisome to maintain, and my face ached from smiling. 'I'll pop in during the week!'

'Please do,' said Hattie Wells. Her attention had been caught by a sheaf of receipts paper-clipped together on the desk. She started to go through them, and I took this to mean I was dismissed.

The French bulldog watched me leave, her large black eyes regarding me mournfully, as the door jangled shut.

32

An hour or so later, we had all been drafted into making component parts of our picnic lunch. Juliet and Neil were charged with putting together cheese-and-tomato sandwiches, Sally and I were making coleslaw, and Polly and Graham were assembling a fruit salad. Several thermos flasks were filled with cold lemonade; there were bottles of ginger beer. Jokes about the Famous Five abounded. And, for the first time since I had been there, the atmosphere in the house felt free and happy. Into this jolly assembly line of food preparation marched Seb, fresh from outside, shirtless and smoking, still with his sunglasses on.

'I'm not going,' he said, instantly. 'Have fun at the Right-old Stones, or whatever they're called.'

'What?' said Juliet. 'Of course you're coming with us!'

'Nope.' Seb grinned round his cigarette. 'I just looked at the road atlas in my car. The place is bloody miles away.'

'That's kind of the point,' said Sally. 'Get away from the house for a bit.'

'I'm sorry,' said Seb, 'but a two-hour drive to see some stones in a field followed by another two-hour drive back here sounds like my idea of total hell.'

'Seb!'

'I've made up my mind. If you lot want to cross Britain to gawp at rocks, that's your lookout. I'm staying here.'

'Fine,' said Neil, perhaps a fraction of a second too soon.

'Unbelievable,' said Juliet coldly. 'Well, you just have a good time without us, yes?'

'I will,' said Seb, eyes twinkling. He tried to grab Juliet round the waist, and she shoved him away.

'Get off.' He tried again, and she shoved him harder this time.

'Ow!' he said, his eyes suddenly ablaze.

'Stop manhandling me, you *pig*!' said Juliet. There was real anger in her voice. The kitchen went quiet. Behind them both, I could see Neil take a step forward, his expression utterly blank, but his eyes wide. I saw him tighten his grip on the knife he'd been using to cut the tomatoes, although he was probably unaware that he still held it.

Even without Seb's Stag, we still had two cars at our disposal, Graham's brown Vauxhall Viva and Sally's Rover. Graham's car would go first, with me navigating from the front passenger seat with the road atlas. Juliet and Neil would travel with us on the back seat. Sally and Polly would follow in Sally's car. This arrangement irked me for two reasons, which could be boiled down simply to spending time with Graham, and not spending time with Sally, but as it was only two hours or so, I felt I could bear it. And the day – already almost unbearably beautiful that morning – had become perhaps the best of the year so far, the blue sky brazenly cloudless, the fields urgently and passionately green, shouting the same secret over and over again.

Upon leaving the clutches of the house, I had the same feeling of absolute ease and liberation I'd had that morning, as the desperate, needy atmosphere that clung to Yarlings fell away.

I couldn't speak for the others, but there seemed to be a pal-pable sense of relief as we headed into the web of B-roads that surrounded the house, and escaped.

Escaped. There seemed to be no other word.

Navigation was not a taxing affair; a straightforward string of A- and B-roads ran across the country almost to our destination. I was able to sit with the atlas covering my knees, my elbow out of the window, feeling the breeze ruffle my hair, and appreciate the sun, the sky and, eventually, even the beautiful bland ribbon of road ahead of us. After the drab interior of the house, the bright colours of the passing cars had an almost carnivalesque air.

'Shall we sing?' said Graham. 'Come on, let's sing.' And so, improbably, we all sang 'Lily the Pink' whilst the motor-way thundered along beneath us.

The Rollright Stones turned out to be not in an isolated field, as I had supposed, but next to a B-road. In fact, the entire complex of monuments, comprising the Whispering Knights, the King Stone, and the King's Men circle itself, was not merely next to a B-road, but cut in half by it, just as Graham said Avebury was. We parked at the roadside, next to another brown Vauxhall Viva, and got out, grateful to stretch our legs.

The day remained glorious, the sky an endless blue vastness, unblemished by even the merest wisp of cloud. The country-side rolled down and away from us in all directions. And there were the stones themselves, weathered and pock-marked, loll-ing and stretching in the grass, frozen in curiously organic attitudes: large and small, squat and monstrously elegant. Indi-vidually, they were as grotesque as mandrake roots; collectively, they resembled a ring of jagged fangs, like the teeth of some primitive river-dwelling fish. They were stunning.

Even Neil was impressed.

'Good Lord,' he said, probably unaware he was doing so. 'Good *Lord*.' Through the tall crescent of pines between the stones and the road, I could see the blue of Sally's car arriving, and felt glad.

Neil stretched out a hand and placed it on the nearest stone. Juliet followed suit, and then I did, too. It was almost impossible not to expect some mystic tingle of energy to flow through me, but instead there was just the sensation of touching ancient rock, older than England, still standing after thousands of years, warmed by the summer sun. And that, somehow, was more than enough.

We spread out blankets and picnicked among the stones. There was a slow dribble of other people there – tourists and sightseers, Graham-like academics trailing bored-looking girlfriends – but by 2 p.m. or so, we had the circle to ourselves, another miracle on a day when miracles seemed commonplace. Adding to the air of a holiday, we all wore summer clothing – even Polly wore a summer dress with yellow flowers on it, although she wore her grey woollen cardigan over it almost defiantly.

'Do you ever take that cardigan off, Pols?' said Graham playfully, as we stretched out on various blankets.

'Mind your own beeswax,' said Polly. She laughed and stuck her tongue out at him. 'I love this cardie.'

'I read about the myths of this place somewhere,' said Juliet, through most of a cheese-and-tomato sandwich. 'How a witch used it to trick a king.'

'*If Long Compton thou canst see, King of England thou shalt be!*' said Graham, smiling.

'Yes, that's it,' said Juliet. 'How did you know?'

'*As Long Compton thou canst not see, Thou and thy men hoar stones shalt be!*' said Sally. Both she and Graham laughed.

'All right,' said Juliet, 'how did you *both* know?'

'We both studied comparative folklore,' said Graham, loading his pipe with tobacco. 'Which, in England, includes the myths and legends of places like this.'

'Aren't the stones supposed to be uncountable?' I said. I knew that this was so, I just wanted both Graham and Sally to know that I was not ignorant of this kind of thing.

'Very good, Tim,' Graham said condescendingly. 'Although the myth of the stones being uncountable applies to many, if not all, stone circles, in both Britain and France.'

Thanks for that, Graham, I thought. 'Didn't there also used to be a barrow here? Associated with the witch?'

'There was,' said Sally. 'The witch turned herself into a tree and grew from the barrow. Both tree and barrow were ploughed away years ago, sadly.'

'Wow,' said Polly. 'Amazing that people could just do that back then. Scour away something ancient, which belonged to everyone.'

'All too common, sadly,' said Sally. 'Even the stones aren't what they were. It used to be customary for travellers to chip off a bit and take it with them. For luck.'

'Good God,' said Neil. 'What's funny, Jules?'

'Oh, nothing,' said Juliet, toying with a blade of grass. 'It's just – the witch turned the king and his men to stone and herself into a tree. And yet, she's long gone, and the king and his men are still here. I mean . . . what a rubbish witch.'

We all laughed. Neil smiled up at Juliet. Away from Yarlings – away, perhaps, from Seb – he seemed to be almost another person. His entire demeanour was different – he was much less stiff and awkward, much more relaxed. I wondered if he was in love with Juliet.

Everyone else had been lulled to sleep, napping on the soft grass. Sally curled a finger at me, beckoning, and silently the two of us went walking in the blue and gold.

'Do you like the stones, Tim?'

'They're . . . amazing,' I said.

'The stones are sacred.'

'To whom?'

'To one who is mighty and all-powerful. To the Goddess. The landscape is a living thing, Tim, and the stones are a gathering point for the power of our mother, the earth.'

We were approaching the Whispering Knights. Even on a perfect summer's day, they leaned together tirelessly to conspire.

'Tell me what's happening,' I said.

She blanched a little. 'What do you mean, what's happening?'

'In the house,' I said. 'Everyone else has a theory about what manner of – thing – we've conjured up.'

'Not quite true. You haven't, and neither has Polly.'

'Touché,' I said. The phrase sounded clumsy and old-fashioned, and I blushed a little.

'So what do you think?'

'Oh, I'm supposed to tell you, but you won't tell me?'

'Oh!' She shrugged and smiled slyly at me, her eyes large. 'Show me yours and I'll show you mine?'

'Pretty much,' I said, slightly surprised I could still speak.

'All right. I think it's a *gestalt*,' she said. 'Do you know what that is?'

Of course I did. 'No,' I said.

'A group entity. A psychic thing composed of all of our energies, rolled together. We have given it life and being, and now we can communicate with it. Although we must be very careful. It's very strong – wilful and undisciplined.'

'What was it like? When you did the automatic writing?'

'Terrifying,' she said earnestly. 'I don't really want to do it again unless I have to. Now, since you don't have a theory to share with me yet, tell me what's going on with you.' Her green eyes held me mischievously.

'Wh-what do you mean?'

'I've seen the way you look at me, Tim. It's fairly obvious that you like me.'

I blushed, hating myself for doing so. 'And if I do?'

'Well, that's fine. But we're at Yarlings for a reason, and I can't let anything get in the way of our experiment.'

'I can wait,' I said. 'I really do like you, you know.'

'I like you, Tim.'

'Can I kiss you?' I couldn't believe I was asking this.

'Yes.'

Polly held a hand over her eyes and squinted up at us. 'Where have you two been all this time?'

'Over to the Whispering Knights,' I said. My heart was still thumping. Neil and Juliet were chatting idly, their backs to one of the taller stones. I heard Juliet laugh. Graham was still asleep, sprawled across a blanket like some gangling, long-limbed dog.

'Did they divulge any secrets?' Polly asked.

'They weren't very talkative,' said Sally. 'If they said anything, we couldn't hear them.'

*

We drove back to Yarlings in a jubilant mood. I made sure I was in Sally's car on the way home, sitting next to her on the passenger seat.

Sometimes, facts that are obvious have to scream at the top of their voice to be heard, to be noticed. We were all young. We were in hundreds of acres of unspoilt countryside. We were embarking upon an endeavour both unique and strange. The sun was shining so hard it might burst and the late afternoon was golden and infinitely pleasing. The mood at Rollright had been different too — everyone looked happy and relieved, not oppressed by each other's company, or the house.

Instead of singing campfire songs, Sally put in a Led Zeppelin cassette. It was the first time I'd ever heard 'Stairway to Heaven', a song now, years later, rendered as meaningless and bland as a brick wall by constant repetition, but then, to me, utterly new. The first part struck me as ridiculous, and still does, but the second part — when the joyful guitar solo rolls in and everything lifts, is, for better or worse, for ever fused with my memory of that journey, that day, that moment of pure, unadulterated bliss. At the start of the journey it was new to me; by the time the journey ended I could bellow every word.

33

I expected everyone to be as energised by the day as I was, but pretty soon everyone succumbed to exhaustion. Even Sally, I was disappointed to note, went to bed early, turning in shortly after Graham did. Soon afterwards, Juliet and Seb went to bed, Seb still trying to coax Juliet to talk to him, and then, some ten or so minutes later, Neil. Eventually, only Polly and I were left, holding mugs of tea and staring into the dead fireplace in the Great Hall. I looked up at the symbol carved into the hearth, the emblem of Tobias Salt's coven, but it seemed no more comprehensible to me now than it had the first time I had seen it.

Without getting out of her armchair, Polly scooted it closer to the empty grate, as if seeking warmth.

'This place,' she said, almost to herself, as she gathered her woollen cardigan around her, 'gives the impression of being cold even when it's warm.'

'I wouldn't like to stay here in the winter,' I said.

A couple of awkward seconds passed. I expected one of us to concoct some further banality about the ambient temperature of Yarlings, but with a level, cool voice, Polly said:

'You and Sally seem to be getting very close.'

I felt myself blushing, I hoped not too spectacularly. 'No!'

'It's all right,' said Polly. 'I mean, it's none of my business.'

'Well, there's nothing going on, so it's everyone's business really, isn't it?' I wondered if I always sounded this unused to speaking in sentences.

Polly shrugged. 'You seemed to spend a lot of time with her today, that's all.'

'She has some interesting theories about this place.'

'I bet she does.' Polly was grinning as she sipped her tea.

'What's that supposed to mean?'

'I don't know.' Polly's voice became practically a whisper, as if she didn't want the house itself to overhear. 'Call it intuition. But I think there's more going on here than meets the eye.'

'Have you spoken to Neil about this?'

'What? No. Why would I?'

'He thinks the same thing you do. That Graham and Sally are under pressure to get results and might be faking things, or encouraging us to act up.'

'Does Neil really think that?'

'He pretty much told me that, yes.'

'Wow.' Polly took another sip of tea. 'Well, it's nice to hear what Neil thinks, but I don't think that at all.'

'You don't?'

'No. I think something genuinely . . . strange is going on here, but I don't quite know what it is. Not yet. You must be able to feel it too. This house. It's a place of . . . weird emotional textures.'

'That's an interesting way of describing it.'

'That's how it feels. You know I'm right.'

She *was* right. Yarlings was a patchwork place, where the tectonic plates of different eras met and ground together unhappily. It wasn't just the Victorian wing, attached to the

Stuart house like a prosthetic limb. It was the sense of stone meeting stone, timber meeting timber, and none of it matching or fitting easily together. It felt like a place that didn't want to be, that had been called into existence from chaos, as we all were, but resented the whole business.

'Anyway,' said Polly, looking into her mug. 'You avoided the question. Do you like Sally?'

'You mean, like a friend?'

Polly made a face. 'You know what I mean, Tim.'

'I – think she's very nice. I mean, I like talking to her. I mean, yes, she's very pretty but that's not *why* I like talking to her. In fact, I'd barely even noticed *that*.' Was I still talking? It felt like I had been talking for a long time. Polly smiled into her cup, holding it with both hands.

'I think you've just answered my question.'

I snorted indignantly. 'Even if I did like her, what's wrong with that?'

'Do you think she likes you?'

My hands quivered. 'What – what's that got to do with you?' My voice sounded wounded and whiny. 'Why would you ask?'

'Well,' said Polly, looking directly at me. She clearly couldn't see in my expression the thing she was looking for; she smiled ruefully and sipped her tea again. 'So, what great theory does Sally have about what's going on here?'

'It's complicated.'

'It's likely to remain that way if you don't tell me.'

I squirmed in my chair. I didn't want to share anything that Sally had told me. Polly smiled at my obvious distress.

'Oh, don't bother if it's that painful. I'm sure you and Sally had a *lovely* time today.'

'You don't like Sally, do you?'

Polly pursed her lips. 'What I feel about Sally is beside the point.'

'Ah!' I was relieved, for the first time in the conversation, not to be on the back foot. 'So you don't like her?'

'It's not that,' said Polly, looking away.

'What is it then?'

'It's . . . it's nothing. Just forget it.'

And then I saw, just for a second. My ignorance and lack of experience with people, and the prism of my own anger, cleared, or coalesced into a solid, comprehensible perspective, and I understood.

'You're . . . jealous!' I said, before I could stop myself.

Polly stared at her cup.

'Do you . . . like . . . *me*? Is that what this is?'

Polly nodded, very slightly. 'Is that so strange?'

'No, it's just . . .'

'You don't like me?'

'I don't really know you.' I was going to say *'I've barely noticed you'*, but even at seventeen years of age I suspected that might not be a prudent thing to say.

'But you don't know Sally!' said Polly.

'I know her better than I know you.'

Polly smiled and shook her head. I shifted uncomfortably in my chair. She shook her head again. 'I'm sorry. I shouldn't have said anything.'

'No,' I said. I was flattered and embarrassed all at once. No girl had ever 'liked' me before, and I had never given the matter much thought. And yet, in the space of one day, all of this had happened. My head was flooded with unfamiliar feelings, large, complex, commingled emotions I could not see the entire shape of all at once. I floundered. 'No, it's . . . you seem a nice girl.'

261

Polly scowled. 'Bloody hell, Tim! *Nice girl* is what you say about someone when you don't care about them.'

There was a long pause. I didn't know how to continue. All the words I had to address this situation were clumsy, bumbling, second-hand, of my dad's generation.

'Is Sally a *nice girl,* Tim? Was she *nice* to you today?'

'Nothing happened today!'

'Well, if nothing happened,' said Polly slyly, '*this* should be OK'.

Putting her hands on my knees, she craned her neck up, and her lips were on mine. I felt the world turn in a strange way. It was a very careful, precise kiss, as if Polly were keeping something hungry dammed up behind it. It was also long and delicious. My mouth hung open as she stood up.

'I'm going to bed now,' said Polly. She got up and walked to the door, and I heard her footsteps pause at the threshold as if she were about to say something else. But then I heard the stairs creak, and the house was silent.

I was exhausted. The day had given me everything, and I was worn out to the ends of my nerves with new and strange things to think about, to feel and consider. It was all too much, and not enough.

The stairs were like an escalator I couldn't stop ascending until I was on the upper landing, where the shadows gathered to blackness, but when I reached for the light switch my hand stroked the fuzz of the ancient wallpaper and I couldn't find it, because it had never been there. I knew I had to make it to my room but I knew that I would not. As I turned the corner I saw, in the corridor — a brazen black shape, like a column of dense black smoke, not really there but there all the same, as if in two places at once, caught in the act of deciding to be. It was the height of a man but not a man, and the more I looked at it, the deeper and blacker it seemed, and the taller and more menacing it appeared to grow. And I knew then that this was him. He was becoming, thirstily sipping at our attention, our imagination, our focus, his long-dead fingers probing, seeking a way in, and it was already too late to stop him because he was already here and always had been, now.

One rotten, charred hand with age-blackened flesh reaches out, almost idly, to touch the wallpaper, to delight in real contact with real things, and it rots under his terrible attention, ages to dust in seconds and drops from the wall.

I woke in my room to the sound of my own rapid breathing, as if I were being pursued. The darkness was no-colour, but seethed with tiny, unseen things, the charged soup of existence itself, quarks and leptons and gluons and electrons; simple, momentous events we are too crude to notice, or even see. A feverish chattering, a roaring chanting that built and fell away in great waves, coming apart and coming together, and I could only hear it and wonder, and its meaning would only ever be opaque to me.

34

The room was blurred, the morning light turning everything to blue chalk. Last night's conversation with Polly and the kiss she had planted on my lips returned to me before the nightmare, the one that had expelled me from sleep into the frantic darkness in the early hours. I wondered if breakfast would be uncomfortable. Not only did Polly *like* me, she also knew that I *liked* Sally, and I felt for the first time in my life that I was completely vulnerable to things I had no understanding of. And then I remembered the dream.

We were, of course, supposed to write down our dreams, and although I had dreamed nothing of note since I had been at Yarlings, I still felt guilty that I hadn't written anything down. Everyone else had: Juliet in particular seemed to dream a lot, and told us that she had almost filled her dream journal. And so, more to avoid heading downstairs than anything else, I wrote up my dream, of the thing that was more a column of black smoke than a man, a vortex of malign intent, breaking through into the house, the fixtures crumbling underneath its awful fingers. When I had finished, I changed into my clothes and, having no more reason to delay, headed out of my room.

I saw that everyone else was gathered on the upper landing, with their backs to me, murmuring.

'What's happening?' I asked. Everybody fell silent as I
joined them.

'Hello, Tim,' said Graham. Normally, he was irritatingly
chirpy in the mornings, but today he seemed just as subdued as
everyone else. There were strained smiles from Sally and Juliet,
and unreadable looks from Neil and Seb, and, especially, Polly.

'What's going on?'

'We've, er . . .' Graham scratched the back of his neck.
'We've had some contact, I think.'

'Contact? How?'

'Just show him,' said Seb.

'Show me what?'

Neil pointed at the wall. The dark green wallpaper had
been torn away, and some kind of ancient yellow paper under
that, revealing the bare plaster beneath.

Written on the plaster in sloping loops of pencil were the
words

NICE GIRL

And, underneath that,

BITCH WHORE

'Oh my God.' I suddenly felt a sensation of falling, as if
from a great height. I stumbled away from the edge of the
stairs and sat down on the carpet. *That exact spot—*

Graham squatted next to me.

'I know, Tim. We've all seen it. But – and I hate to do this –
I have to ask you the same question I've asked everyone el—'

'Did *you* write this?' said Polly. Her arms were folded.

'What? No! Why on earth would I write something like that?'

'I don't know.' Polly stood over me now, her gaze unwa-
vering. 'You tell me.'

'I didn't write it!'

'You seem very upset by it.'

I got to my feet. 'Wait there.' On rubbery legs I ran to my room, and returned with the dream journal.

I virtually threw it at Polly, who read the account of my dream with a tight-lipped expression.

'And this is from this morning?'

'It is.' I must have looked more spooked than I thought, as I saw Polly's anger give way to puzzlement. 'That's why I was so long getting up this morning. I was writing that.'

'What does it say?' said Neil. 'What did you dream?'

I read out my account.

'The figure in your dream . . .' Graham said. 'He touched the wall, yes? Does that correlate to where the wallpaper's damaged here?'

'I can't be sure,' I said. 'I think so.'

'A portent,' said Graham, bending over to peer at the wall. I noticed for the first time he had his camera around his neck; presumably he'd already taken plenty of shots of the writing. 'A dream-omen. This is exactly what I was hoping to see.'

'Oh, great,' said Polly. 'Bully for you! You're not the one being singled out for abuse.' She looked at me for a long moment. I looked at the floor. Graham sniffed and wound his camera on.

'Well, I wouldn't take this personally, any of you ladies. Mr Salt wasn't exactly a fan of the fair sex during his lifetime. However, even despite the content of the message, I think we can all see how significant this is.'

'Yeah,' Seb grunted blearily, lighting up a cigarette. 'We made a ghost swear.'

Graham ignored him. 'Tobias Salt has made contact with us. He's spoken to us via planchette, but now he's reached out from our minds, into the physical world. He's not just knocking chairs over or letting us write things for him. He wrote something himself, on a wall.'

'Like at Borley,' I said.

'Yes!' said Graham, his eyes sparkling. 'Like the poltergeist at Borley. The link between us and him is growing in strength.'

'Did you find the pencil?' I asked.

Sally smiled. 'That was the first thing I thought of. No. And we haven't found the torn wallpaper either.'

'We may not ever find it,' said Graham. He looked round him, and his smile faded as he saw the frightened faces of his volunteers, his troops.

'Come on, everyone!' he said. 'This is a success!'

'What is it an omen for?' said Neil.

'I'm sorry?'

'You said it was an omen. What for?'

'I don't know,' said Graham. 'Something that hasn't happened yet, obviously. Traditionally, some piece of bad luck or misfortune.'

'Great,' said Polly.

'Affecting all of us?' said Juliet.

Graham shrugged.

Downstairs, the telephone rang.

We exchanged glances, no one daring to say anything.

Eventually, Sally turned and descended the staircase, with an almost stately slowness, as the sharp ring of the telephone drilled through the hollow rooms and heavy frame of the house.

'This is stupid,' said Neil. 'About the omen. It's not rational.'

'I agree,' said Graham.

'Something bad, for one of us. Something bad for all of us. Who knows?' said Polly. There was a note of unease in her voice.

Sally returned, climbing the stairs with the same solemn, almost ceremonial pace with which she had descended.

'Tim,' she said hoarsely. 'It's for you.'

I picked up the mustard-coloured phone receiver from the hall table as carefully as if it were booby-trapped.

'Hello?'

'Hi, Tim.'

'Dad?' He sounded exhausted, washed out. 'What's wrong?'

'You need to come home. As soon as you can.'

'What is it, Dad? What's wrong?'

'Just get here as soon as you can, OK?'

'Tell me what's wrong!'

Down the line, I heard a deep sigh. I knew my dad, and I knew what he was doing. He was gathering the strength to admit something to himself, to speak it out loud, to make it real.

'It's your mum, Tim. She's had a stroke. She's in St John's Infirmary, she's unconscious. I'm with her right now.'

I said nothing. I did not move. I just stared, at a patch of the black wooden floor, where it met the skirting board. There was a knot in the plank, which projected a little way out of the wood. I stared at it for a long time. Consciousness is a funny thing, I thought. The knot had been there for as long as the house had stood, unnoticed by everyone who walked down that hallway. And now it was all I could see, linked irrevocably and for ever in my mind with this moment of fear and disaster.

My dad's voice burbled from the receiver as I put the phone back in its cradle. The coolness of the wall against my back, and the tense silence of the house, was broken, eventually, by the sound of many feet clumping heavily down the stairs.

*

Twenty-five minutes later, I was in the passenger seat of Seb's red Triumph Stag as the car ate up the winding country road. As I had imagined, Seb was a terrible driver, and under normal circumstances, I would have been terrified. As it was, I felt nothing. Seb steered with one hand, throwing the car round each bend with an insouciance that was as forced as it was barely controlled. Occasionally he would look sideways at me – perhaps to see whether I was all right, perhaps to determine whether I was scared, or maybe just to see if I was impressed. I stared ahead.

It dawned on me long before we pulled into the station that Seb lacked the emotional reach to speak to me about what was happening, that he was probably dreading the moment of packing me off onto the train. As is so often the case with emotional trauma and the English, I found myself more worried with how Seb felt about this minor discomfort than I did about the fact my mother was gravely ill.

At the station, Seb took my rucksack out of the Stag's boot and handed it to me with awkward solemnity, as if I had disgraced the family name and was off to join the Foreign Legion.

'You like the car?' he asked, clearly unable to help himself.

'It's amazing,' I said indifferently, looking at it properly for the first time. It was new and shiny, but a series of thin, ugly scratches ran along the bodywork, filled with brown rust like clotted blood.

'Oh, *that*,' said Seb. 'Some bastard keyed it a while back when I parked at school. Jealous, I expect.'

I nodded, and wondered if it was Neil.

'Good luck,' Seb said, smiling weakly. 'And hey.' He suddenly looked very serious. 'Look after your old man, hmm?'

'He's not the one who's sick.'

'No,' said Seb. The tone of his voice changed. 'But he has to live with somebody who is. Trust me, it can wear someone down. Much more than they let on.'

'You haven't met my dad,' I said. 'I'm sure he's fine.'

'Yeah, I'm sure he *looks* fine, from the outside. I thought my dad was fine, too, when Mum had her . . . thing. I really did think he was doing OK.' His voice trailed off; he was looking through me now. I saw that his eyes were momentarily dark with some unasked-for recollection. And then, realising how serious he was being, he snorted a half-laugh.

'Anyway, look, go easy on the old bugger.' He punched me on the shoulder. Even through my donkey jacket, it hurt.

We smiled at each other for an awkward second. I half expected Seb to salute. A couple of minutes later, as I sat down on a bench on the empty platform, I heard the roar of the Stag's engine receding into the sparkling summer country-side. I imagined the car's incredible noise was tinged with something close to relief.

Twenty minutes' wait for the train. An adult would have spent their time collecting their thoughts, steeling themselves for what lay ahead, but I was seventeen. I was concerned for my mum – of course I was, I loved Mum very much – but along-side this was an impatience, a wonderment at what all the fuss was about. She wasn't dead, part of me thought, so what was the problem? And this was perfectly normal. What child or young person with two healthy parents – parents who've always been there – can possibly imagine the world without them? She wasn't dead. She was unconscious, yes, but she would recover, wouldn't she? Mum would be all right, surely?

And in the meantime, my resentment at being plucked away from the first thing since Abi's disappearance that had any meaning to me grew, until the gathering summer heat and the wait for the train grew intolerable. I took my jacket off, stuffed it angrily into my rucksack.

The train came. I sat by the window, staring out at the Suffolk countryside, watching the flat fields blur by like a dream. I was so wrapped up in my own thoughts, I barely noticed London creep up at the windows, street by street. The train pulled in at Liverpool Street Station.

By degrees – a tube, another train, and another bus later – I found myself back in the world I knew – the infinite suburb, stretching out forever, thwarting escape in all directions, the place where I had grown up. I had only been away five days, but I felt as if I had travelled, inwardly, had been both encouraged and forced to consider new perspectives. It felt frustrating to be back home again, surrounded by the things one knew to the point of mania.

There was the newspaper kiosk by the bus station, which always smelled of tobacco and peppermints. There was the tree by the short cut, on the trunk of which someone had painted the letters *I.R.A.*, complete with careful full stops. Everything from street signs to house names was overfamiliar, worn out, tired. I crossed a road and ducked into the short cut, plimsolls crunching on the gravel path. I thought of Abi again, and then, intensely sweet and painful, the full glory of our joint efforts to transform this crushing everyday into something magical, to find goblins in the park and clay pipes in the garden, ghosts in the attic and witchery behind the lace curtains of withdrawn neighbours. The alchemy of our imaginations. I had been so adrift without it. The privets were choked with litter; the only incantations written on the concrete walls were the names of football teams and bands and doomed couples. I could not hold back the banality of this world on my own.

Angrily, I squashed the tears away at the corners of my eyes, choked down my sadness and walked on. The short cut became an entryway, which became a street. Soon, I found another bus stop, and waited.

I looked at my watch. Just under three hours ago, I had been at Yarlings.

35

St John's Infirmary was a Victorian building with recent bits grafted on, like a negative of the building I had just come from. The original hospital was a municipal thing of red brick, with no distinctive personality of its own, that could just as easily have been a town hall or a hotel or swimming baths. Growing out of this were several brutalist blocks of concrete and glass, housing the newer departments. I read signs for X-Ray, Outpatients, Intensive Care. Where would Mum be? At a busy central desk, an elderly receptionist gave me convoluted directions, and I wandered off in the direction she had indicated. Was this the same day? Woken by one nightmare, finding myself in another. I had not even had time to ponder the mystery of the writing on the landing wall, a problem that now seemed to belong to an entirely different world, with entirely different rules.

Halfway along one of the endless corridors of green paint and grey tile, I bumped into what was left of Dad.

He looked thinner and sicker and older than I had ever seen him look, but something more fundamental than lack of food or sleep had taken its toll. All sense of purpose seemed to have left him.

'Tim!' he said, smiling. He gave me a hug, clinging onto me. I had to peel away from him.

'Dad,' I said.

There was a pause. He just stared at me.

'How is Mum?' I asked.

'Still unconscious,' said Dad. He looked overwhelmed by the statement, and immediately began to sound overly humorous and jokey. 'Do you want to see her? I'm sure she'll want to see you!'

'Yes,' I said. 'Have the doctors said anything?'

'No, they just said we should let her rest. I was just going to get a tin of pop and a sandwich. Can I get you anything?'

'I'm fine, Dad.'

'Right you are. She's in bed number nine. The head nurse is Sue, she seems to be top dog here.' He was behaving in a way that was so normal it was eerie. I hadn't heard him say things like *right you are* and *top dog* and act this chipper since before Abi vanished. Why would he pick now to pretend his hardest that everything was OK? Right at the moment when it absolutely wasn't? I heard him whistle as he walked off down the corridor, something jaunty and incongruous. I pushed open the door of the ward.

Twelve identical beds, in two rows of six. Two of the beds had pale blue curtains drawn around them. All of the beds were occupied; I saw various sleeping women, all much older than Mum. I stood for a couple of seconds, unsure how to proceed, until a tall, toothy woman in a starched nurse's uniform tapped me on the shoulder.

'Are you Timothy Smith?'

'I am.'

'Your mother's through here. She's still unconscious, I'm afraid.'

'Is she OK? Will she be OK?'

The nurse, presumably Sue, didn't look at me. 'The signs are good she'll recover, but she might have lost some brain function.'

'What does that mean? How much brain function?'

The shrug again. 'We don't have any way of knowing at the moment, I'm afraid. We won't know until she wakes up.' Nurse Sue's sensible shoes clack-clacked on the parquet floor, until she eventually stopped at one of the two beds that had a blue curtain wrapped around it. She parted the curtain enough for me to pass through.

Mum's face was pale yellow and clammy-looking, a wax-work. She seemed both aloof and terribly vulnerable, as if sleep were an act of defiance, but one that was costing all the resources her enfeebled body could summon. As I stared at her, her neck twitched convulsively and her back arched to lift her head from the pillow. When she had expended all her energy, she sank back into the pillows that Sue had taken the opportunity to plump up for her. She looked unlike any memory I had of her, as if a different person now inhabited her frail body.

I sank down into an orange plastic chair. I didn't want to look at Mum. Turning away, I saw the chart at the head of her bed, bulldog-clipped to the grey metal bedstead.

'That isn't her name,' I said.

'I'm sorry?' said Sue. She was checking the drip that ran into Mum's hand.

'Mrs Alice Louise Tyler. That's not her name. Her name is Alice Smith.'

'Yes, there was some confusion over that. Your father authorised it, though. He said that given the separation, it was probably for the best, from a legal standpoint.'

'The . . . separation?'

I saw alarm in her eyes. 'Er, I believe that's what was discussed. I wasn't here when your mother was admitted.' Nurse Sue glanced nervously at me, and returned to adjusting the catheter.

The curtain screamed along the rail, and Dad was back, grinning an embarrassed grin.

'Hey,' he said. 'What did I miss?'

'Dad,' I said. 'Are you and Mum separated?'

'Call me if you need anything,' said Nurse Sue, clearly well practised at extricating herself from awkward conversations. She drew the curtain behind her as she left, either to screen the ward from us, or, more likely, us from the ward.

'Dad?'

He half-looked at the floor.

'What does that mean? Are you still living together?'

'Well, of course we are. Where would she go?'

'So what does it mean?'

He sighed heavily. His clothes hung off him. He looked like he wanted desperately to just lie down.

'It means that we're still living in the same house, but not as man and wife.'

'I'm no clearer on what that means.' I knew I should cut him some slack, but I felt like being ruthless.

Dad sighed again. He looked down at Mum, lost in unconsciousness. It seemed very lonely for her, and I suddenly understood where she was, and felt desolate.

'We're not speaking. We're sleeping in separate rooms.'

'OK.'

'We were also talking about a divorce,' he said quietly.

'Oh.' I felt a panicked jolt all over my body. My parents simply weren't the kind of people who got divorced, and I had never considered it as a possibility. It shaped the immediate future into something much more confusing.

What will happen to me? I wanted to ask.

'How seriously were you discussing this?' I asked.

Dad shrugged helplessly. 'Pretty seriously, Tim.'

What will happen to me?

'Don't you love each other any more?' I asked.

Dad smiled a joyless smile. 'It's not as simple as that, Tim. You haven't been around much the last few months. It's become . . . difficult to live with your mother. She does the same thing every day. She just sits and smokes.'

'She's always smoked.'

'Not like this, Tim. You've seen her. It's all she does. She doesn't leave the room if she can help it, let alone the house. She's like a zombie.'

'But she's just . . .' I wanted to say *grieving*, but found that the word encompassed more than I was willing to admit. 'She's been through a lot.'

'We've all been through a lot, Tim. All of us.' He motioned towards Mum. 'Let's just get through this first, hmm?'

His calmness was infuriating. I felt rage surge through me.

'Yeah, well, you don't seem too affected by it all. How's the redecorating going? Have you managed to wallpaper the spare room yet? Has it plugged the gap where Abi was?'

He looked at me with an expression I had never seen him wear before – one of pure, cold anger – and I fell silent. I had gone too far. I was very conscious of the fact that we were standing arguing over Mum's motionless body.

'Go home,' he said, quietly. 'We'll talk about this later.'

My voice, when I spoke, sounded cowardly and overly conciliatory. 'OK.'

The curtain screamed aside, and I went.

I was afraid of going home, much more scared than I had been
of spending time at Yarlings. Yarlings had been, when all was
said and done, an adventure to me, an escape, and our family
home, characterised even more than ever now by absence,
was the thing I had longed to escape from. I wished, as I put
my key in the lock, that there was somewhere – anywhere –
else to go. Although it was summer, the house felt chilly, the
air in the hallway unmoving and stale.

In the five days I'd been away, Dad's mania for redecorating
seemed to have subsided, and very little had changed in the
house, as far as I could see, although the living room was obviously the next room he had his sights on, as there were small
test squares of paint on the wall. I turned the television on and
sank down on the sofa. *Nationwide* was on; they were interviewing a man who was growing vegetables in an old car, a project
that seemed to cause both the interviewer and the man doing it
almost dangerous levels of hilarity. I turned it off, although the
absence of chatter made the house seem even more depressing.
It was hard to believe it was summer; hard to believe it wasn't
even dusk yet. Had the house always been this dark?

Although – or perhaps because – Dad and I had so much of
urgent importance to talk about, we barely talked at all when
he got home. Rather, he slunk back into the house like an
exhausted shadow, sitting down on the sofa next to me as if it
were the last thing he ever intended to do.

'Are you hungry?' I asked. 'Shall I make tea?'

'That would be nice, Tim,' Dad said evenly, as if reading
from a script. 'Thank you.'

It took me about half an hour to make beans on toast, toasting the white bread under the grill and heating the beans up in the large aluminium pan my mother had, once upon a time, used to make soup. I set the table for two, and we both ate in silence. Halfway through dinner, I realised that this was the first time any members of our family had eaten together, at the table, since Abi had disappeared.

Dad trudged off to bed early, ascending the stairs with the same exhausted finality with which he'd come home. Soon I crept upstairs too.

My room was cramped, cupboard-like, even smaller than I remembered it being. Even my room at Yarlings was large, compared to this. I wondered what everyone at Yarlings was doing. I wondered, especially, what Sally was doing, and whether she was thinking about me.

36

I could hear clattering downstairs; distracted, without focus, rattling the cutlery and slamming cupboard doors. Dad was evidently awake. I pulled my clothes on, splashed cold water on my face and headed downstairs.

'Hot water's on, if you want a bath,' said Dad, without looking at me. 'Although tell me if you don't because I don't want to heat it up for nothing.'

I liked that he was at least attempting to look after me. 'I'll have a bath, Dad.'

'I made tea.' He gestured towards a mug on the kitchen counter.

'Thank you.' I took a sip of tea. It was cold. 'Are you going to see Mum today?'

He looked at me with a hint of derision and, for a second, he was very much his old self. 'What did you think I was going to do? Climb Everest? Are you coming with me?'

I nodded, delighted and saddened by this little flash of business as usual, and sipped more of my cold tea.

Mum's condition, unsurprisingly, had not changed. In fact, the condition of all of the patients on her ward seemed to be immune to change of any kind. The very elderly ones lay with their eyes closed, as if cocooned, and the younger ones – although, apart from Mum, they were all at least sixty – occasionally writhed and yowled, tormented by toxic dreams.

Mum looked calm and peaceful. I could almost believe she was merely asleep. The ward was oppressively hot, and all the windows were closed. Neither Dad nor I felt it was our place to open them, so we simply sat either side of her, sweating, each unsure of what to say or do. There was no shortage of things in immediate need of discussion, but no way either one of us was going to deliberately address any of them. And so we sat.

The woman in the bed next to Mum's muttered something, and I saw her face stretch and almost elongate in the throes of a noiseless scream. I winced.

'Can't they put Mum in a room on her own?'

'I asked them that. They don't have enough beds. That's why she's here, with the older ones who've gone doolally.'

The woman next to Mum bared her teeth for a second, and then opened her eyes. She saw me and smiled a lascivious, hungry smile, and then buried her face in the pillow.

I thought of my dream of the previous morning, of the furious, malign cloud at the top of the staircase in Yarlings. And then, waking to discover the message. What had it said? So much had happened and there had been so little time to process it. NICE GIRL, it had said. BITCH WHORE. *Nice girl*. The phrase that had passed between Polly and me before she kissed me.

The woman in the bed next to Mum's suddenly sat up and laughed a long, loud, filthy laugh, that seemed to hang longer than was natural in the feverish air of the ward.

'Where are you going?' said Dad. I realised I was on my feet.

'Get some fresh air,' I said.

I had noticed the phone on the way in; a wall-mounted payphone covered by a transparent dome of smoky brown plastic. I put all the change I had into the slot, and dialled Yarlings.

'Hello?'

'Sally?' *Thank God. Thank God.* 'It's Tim.'

'Oh Lord, how are you? We're all worried about you. Is your mum OK?'

'She's still unconscious,' I said. 'They expect her to wake up soon, but there's no telling when, exactly. How is everything there?'

'Good! We just had the ol' usual daily séance.'

'Oh.' I was upset. 'You had one without me?'

'Yes. We discussed suspending the experiment, but Graham thought we'd lose momentum.'

I was suddenly terribly afraid I was no longer required at Yarlings. 'You still want me to come back, right?'

'Of course! It's not the same without you. Tobias Salt was in a very bad mood, very sluggish and angry. I think he misses you, Tim.'

'Me? Good God.'

'We *all* miss you, Tim,' she said, and my heartbeat faltered a little.

'Sally, there's something I have to tell you.'

'Oh? Sounds serious!'

'After we'd been to Rollright, and you went to bed, and Polly and I stayed up talking, she . . . she was asking me about you and how I felt about you, and' – I took a deep breath – 'she kissed me. It didn't mean anything, and it took me by surprise, so I didn't stop it as soon as I should, but . . . I just wanted to tell you.'

To my immense relief, she laughed. 'Oh Tim! I'd have thought you had enough to worry about without focusing on a little thing like *that*—'

'It's not little,' I said. 'To me. I really like you, Sally, and I don't want you thinking—'

'Poor, sweet Tim.' There was still laughter in her voice. 'Please don't worry about it. Especially given your current circumstance, hmm? Just make sure your mum is OK and come back to us when you can. Just let us know when.'

Dad asked me if I wanted to go to the high street and pick up some paintbrushes, but I politely declined. Apart from the world-class tedium of this mission, there was always a chance I might run into Tony Finch, or, worse still, Janice Tupp, if I hung around for too long. I elected to go home.

The house was cool and dark. I sat for a long while on the sofa, running the events of the last few days over and over in my mind. It had been good to talk to Sally; to confirm that I was still in her thoughts, still part of events at the house. I wanted, of course, to go back to Yarlings as soon as possible, but it seemed indecent to leave so soon, with Mum still trapped between sleep and wakefulness.

There was a large brown envelope, stuffed with papers, on the coffee table. I gasped as I emptied it and saw Abi's face staring back at me, the portrait I had taken the day we faked our ghost photo. The envelope was full of clippings from various newspapers, both national and local, about Abi's disappearance. Some of these were familiar to the point of nausea, as I had read and re-read them incessantly in the days after Abi vanished, whilst others – more recent – were new to me. I read one of the newer pieces, where my portrait of Abi was joined by pictures of two other girls roughly her age who had disappeared in Cambridge a few months later. The Mr S sketch was reproduced too, alongside a description from someone who'd seen a man with dark eyes and long black hair hanging around a school prior to the disappearance of one of the girls. The witness described him as tall, and possibly of no fixed abode. Again, the van was mentioned. And there, again, was nothing but speculation, and more questions than answers, and nothing helpful or concrete.

I carefully replaced all the clippings in the envelope. Who had collected these? It was the kind of thing Dad did with subjects less tragic and personal, but as far as I could tell, his strategy for dealing with Abi's disappearance so far had been one of resolute denial and avoidance. Mum, however, had dwelt on every detail, but the idea she'd commit to anything this organised, and so close to the thing that was devouring her, didn't seem plausible either.

The local paper, the *Courier*, sat on the table. I picked it up and idly scanned the front page. An inquest was taking place after a fire in a local pub, with an unsubtle editorial insinuation that it had been an insurance job. A local builder's merchant had been acquitted of accepting stolen goods.

I turned the page.

LOCAL GIRL'S DEATH RULED 'MISADVENTURE'

Police have ruled out foul play after a local girl was found to have died of a drugs overdose. An ambulance was called to an address in Laughton Gardens, where the young woman, Janice Tupp, was living with her boyfriend, Kevin Masters.

'Jesus Christ!'

The sound of my own voice startled me in the empty house. No, this couldn't be, surely? I had seen her just last week.

Masters called 999 after Tupp, 17, fell unconscious and became unresponsive. Masters told ambulance staff that she was addicted to heroin, and had relapsed after a recent attempt to kick the drug. Miss Tupp's mother is said to be 'distraught', and has asked for privacy at this difficult time.

I re-read the short article twice, then folded the newspaper with excessive care and replaced it on the coffee table. Then I simply sat, staring into the reflection of the living room in the grey-green of the dead television screen.

Once, my sister and I had played a trick on Janice Tupp. And Janice had turned the tables, visiting on us the same disturbed and haunted feeling we had no doubt produced in her. And now, a few years and a lifetime later, out of the three of us who had gathered that day, only I was still definitely alive.

Then I was on the darkened stairway, with no recollection of how I got there, heading upstairs. I had to see the attic. I had to convince myself – the only remaining witness – that this event had happened at all.

Dad had repainted the upper landing a month or so ago, in a jaundiced yellow that made the space seem somehow smaller, but the wooden ladder up to the attic had not been touched. I turned the light on and climbed. I thought for a horrible second that Dad might have redecorated up there too.

As soon as I saw the attic, relief flooded through me. It was, more or less, exactly as Abi and I had left it. There were the bookcases, filled to bursting with Pan Anthologies of

Horror and Fontana Books of Ghost Stories and books on English Folklore; there were the two armchairs facing each other, with the small table in between. And there, too, was the doll's house on top of the chest, with a fracture running down its front, no doubt still harbouring its horrible little tenants. There were the bits of taxidermy, the shells and skulls and horns we'd found on innumerable country walks. I ran my hand over the back of the armchair Abi had always sat in, and I saw the dark brown wall, the wall on which we had chalked our towering entity, bringing him into existence through the medium of chalk dust that billowed and blurred like smoke, to change the course of all of our lives. I shuddered, and felt a chill.

The next afternoon, although Dad cheerily asked me if I wanted to come along to the hospital to see Mum again, I simply couldn't face it. The idea of being trapped in the boiling ward, between the voluntary and involuntary silences of both parents, made me feel almost ill. Mum had been cut off from me, first by grief, and then much more dramatically by illness, but the more I thought about it, the more Dad had always been cut off from both of his children, long before Abi disappeared. He would never ask me what was bothering me, and if I told him, he would not be interested. My distress at hearing of Janice's sad, squalid fate was just another of the many important things in my life he would never know anything about.

I stayed at home. It occurred to me to ring Yarlings, but I had nothing new to say, and the chances of Sally answering the phone again were slim. Eventually, the emptiness of the house grew oppressive; I fidgeted and thought. I needed something to occupy me. What would be the best use of my time? It had been a long while since I had asked myself that question.

In the attic, I pulled out several books from mine and Abi's library. If I couldn't be at Yarlings, I could at least attempt to discover something useful at home. I settled into my armchair – I wouldn't have dared sit in Abi's – and started to read.

The haunting at Yarlings seemed to have some points in common with other famous hauntings. The loud crash we had heard had some precedent in the haunting of Hinton Ampner, as described by Sacheverell Sitwell, Elliott O'Donnell and others; but the case it most closely resembled was still that of Borley Rectory. I read again Harry Price's transcripts of the séances, where it seemed some discarnate thing was growing in strength, making itself known.

It was early evening when I awoke. The attic was silent, as was the house, which told me that, although I must have drifted into sleep, Dad wasn't home yet. I stretched and craned my neck. I headed back down the ladder. Halfway down, I froze.

I found myself staring into a room I'd never seen before.

It was where Abi's room had been, but it was not Abi's room. I could have sworn the door had been closed when I went up to the attic.

I switched the light on and walked inside, utterly unable to decipher what I was seeing. What was formerly Abi's room – with all of Abi's things, exactly as she had left them on the day she disappeared – was now empty of all furnishings. White wallpaper covered the places where the posters and pages of magazines and Abi's own drawings had been. Her bed and desk had disappeared, replaced by a single bed and a bedside table with a sorry-looking potted plant on it.

I must have descended the stairs at some point. I must have gone into the living room and sat on the sofa for a long time, because that's where I was when I heard Dad's key in the front door. He padded down the hallway to where I sat.

'What are you sitting here in the dark for?' He flicked the overhead light on. Something about my body language made him pause for a second. I glared up at him.

'What is it?' he began to say.

'Abi's room,' I said, over this question.

A strained silence fell.

'Did you hear me? What do you have to say about it?'

'I don't have anything to say about it.' He sounded weary, a weariness with no discernible limits.

'You have . . . nothing to say?' I spat, hunching forward on the sofa.

'Tim, it's been a long day, and I'm tired. Just give it a rest, yeah?'

'What have you done with all of her things?'

He sighed and turned away, as if the conversation bored him.

'I *said*,' getting to my feet now, 'what have you done with her things?'

'What I should have done ages ago,' he muttered, looking away.

'I beg your pardon?'

'I said, what I should have done ages ago! I binned the bloody lot!'

'What?' I bellowed. 'Why would you do that?'

'Because she's not coming back, Tim!' Dad shouted back. 'She's dead! She's lying dead in a bloody ditch somewhere, or worse, and the sooner we all move on—'

My first blow was a good one, and it caught him unprepared. He fell backwards, hard, against the wall, and I saw his face look shocked and then angry before I landed a second. He bent double, and I was unsure what to do next when he straightened up, and, with a furious, animal roar, grabbed me by the shoulders and hair and threw me out into the hallway. I went sprawling on the rug.

'She's *dead*!' he screamed, as if scalded. His fists came down on me, flailing, uncoordinated, relentless. I tried to crawl away, but he picked me up and hurled me against the wall, pinning me there with a forearm. His eyes contained nothing I recognised.

'What did you do with her things?' I sobbed, through the pain in my stomach and ribs.

'What?' he said scornfully, as if this were the last thing anybody could possibly be concerned with at this point. *'What?'*

'Her things! What—' My breath left me and I had to pause. His forearm still pinned me to the wall. *'What – did you do – with her things?'*

The pressure of his arm on my neck subsided, and I felt the strength drain from him. 'I threw it all out.' He looked away as he said it.

I threw his arm off me in disgust.

'Tim,' he started to say, behind me. 'Tim—'

I shook my head sadly. My rucksack was in the hallway and I scooped it up as I left.

'Tim, please. I'm sorry. There's no excuse for what I just did. I've been under a lot of stress lately, and your mother— Tim. Please—'

Evening had become night. The first stars were twinkling. The street was very quiet, as if it had been listening.

I walked down the sloping pathway to the gate, when an idea struck me. Returning to the house, I ducked into the side passageway where the bins were.

They were all empty, apart from one, half-filled with kitchen waste, chicken skin, potato peelings and newspapers.

I was about to leave when I spied something – a flash of bright blue – stuck in the filth at the bottom of the bin.

Of all the things that could have survived.

It was face down. Open, on one page, as if tucked there deliberately.

This was my one chance, I realised, my one opportunity to know. I rolled my sleeve up, and, with infinite care, reached into the cold slimy scraps, taking care to keep the place in the book it had fallen open on. I dragged it out, and laid it carefully on the concrete, revealing the message that was uppermost, the page that luck and circumstance had chosen to show me from our Book of Fates. And there, in Abi's handwriting, the words, the only words there could ever be, and what other words did I expect?

THERE IS NOTHING

I picked up the book and something fluttered out. Two dead eyes stared up at me from a formless face that looked like smoke, but only I knew was really chalk. I placed the photo inside the book and closed it with care. Abi and I had both signed our names on the front; I wept a little. Several feet away, through the wall, was Dad, collecting himself and reshaping what had just happened into something less jagged, something he was less to blame for, unaware of how much he had harmed me. I was painfully aware, too, of how much I was now responsible for his wellbeing, and how the right thing to do would be to stay, to apologise, to forgive, to embrace, to see him through this period and hope and pray that Mum would wake up. But the truth was, in that moment, I despised them both.

I began walking.

IV

37

I called Yarlings from a phone box at the station. The mouth-piece of the receiver smelled of stale cigarette smoke and Wrigley's chewing gum. The dial tone sounded for what felt like minutes: I imagined that everyone was at the other end of the house, arguing about who got up to answer the telephone. Eventually, I heard Neil's lugubrious voice.

'Hello?'

'Hi, Neil?'

'Tim? How's your mum?'

'She's fine, thanks. Well, I mean, not fine as such. She's still unconscious.'

'I'm sorry to hear that,' Neil said indifferently.

'The truth is,' I said, preparing to lie, 'I'm pretty useless here, to be honest with you. Dad's got things under control and I'm just getting in his way.'

'Oh?' Neil sounded surprised.

'Yeah, Mum's stable and unlikely to change much at the moment so . . . look, I know it's getting late, but is there any possibility someone could pick me up from the station tonight? The last train gets in at your end at about eleven-fifteen. Would that be OK?'

'Well,' said Neil, 'I can't drive, so it won't be me meeting you.'

Somewhere in the phone system, the pips sounded. I had already put the last of my change into the slot.

'But do you think someone will be able to meet me?'

'Yeah, I'm sure one of the others will be able to pick you up.'

'Thanks, Neil. Eleven-fifteen, yes?'

'Yes. Someone'll be there.'

Relief flooded through me. 'And how have things been at the house?'

'Ah. Now you're asking. There's been—'

The call ended.

Two hours later, with the moon rising on a warm English summer night, I sat with my cupped hands to the window of the train and stared out at the dark blur of fields and farms and towns. Eventually, I stood waiting by the door of the train, irrationally terrified that I would miss my stop and end up wandering the dark, unfamiliar countryside alone. What could be worse than that?

I was the only person to disembark at the tiny station. In the ticket hall, next to the dead fireplace, was Sally. She smiled a radiant smile; she wore a large patterned coat lined with fake fur, and a pair of knee-length orange boots. She looked far too exotic and vibrant for the drab little station, like a hoopoe in a suburban garden. She hugged me and I buried my face in her hair, which smelled of the sunshine at the Rollright Stones. I could have cried with relief. The past was traumatic, the future uncertain, but right now, there was this.

'How is everything?' she asked.

'Fine, now.' I felt bold and light-headed, able to say things like this.

'How is your mother?'

'The doctors expect her to make a full recovery. We just have to wait.' I said this less as a conscious lie and more as a way of terminating the conversation as quickly as possible. 'How has everything been at the house?'

Sally smiled. 'Interesting. It's been interesting.'

'What do you mean? Did something happen at the séances?' The only other person in the waiting room, an elderly man, looked up briefly from his newspaper, but said nothing.

'Not as such,' said Sally, lowering her voice. 'In fact, the last few sessions have been quite garbled. But it turns out that someone made his presence felt in . . . other ways.'

'Really? How?'

'I'll tell you all about it on the way. Better still, if you wait ten minutes, the others can tell you.'

Sally eased the car round the U-shaped driveway, and I saw that there were lights on all over the house. Yarlings seemed more solid than I recalled, more purposeful, somehow bolder. I was reminded of Sally's painting, where she had made the house so concrete a presence it seemed to oppress its surroundings, melting them into vapour. If, once, Yarlings had felt to me half-dreamed, half-imagined, then now it was fully present, fully and undeniably *here*. The surrounding trees, still as photographs in the windless night, seemed to shrink back from the house, as if they were afraid to touch it.

I knew it was dangerous to view this as a homecoming, but I was unable to stop myself – the sweet cold smell of an English summer night, the distant cry of a barn owl, the beaten gold three-quarter moon – I almost felt these things were my birthright. My fingers touched the jagged wall as Sally fumbled for the keys; I worked my fingers into the space between two stones, felt the rough mortar. I desperately wanted to feel the moment, to experience the house, the evening, Sally – all of it. To be part of the world, not distant from it. At that moment, the need to be present – to exist, and matter, somewhere – felt almost physical.

Everyone except for Graham was in the Great Hall. Seb, Juliet and Polly sat in armchairs in front of the lifeless fireplace, playing cards. Neil sat some small distance away, reading, and was the first to look up when I entered.

'Welcome back,' he said, returning to his book. 'Couldn't stay away, hmm?'

'Tim!' said Juliet, rising to greet me.

'You don't hang about, do you?' said Seb. 'It's only been two days.'

'It's good to see you!' said Polly, with a huge smile. 'How is your mother?'

The lie had become my truth, now, and it was easy repeating to them what I had told Sally.

'Well, we're very glad you came back,' said Sally, and smiled at me.

'What's been happening here?' I said. 'I understand Tobias has been active?'

'Very much so,' said Neil. 'We heard footsteps.'

'Really?' I tried and failed to keep the disappointment out of my voice.

'Oh yes,' said Polly. 'All the way along the upper landing, thud, thud, thud, then they stopped – as if something caught his eye, and he wanted a better look. Then they started again.'

The hairs on the back of my neck stood up. 'Wow.'

'It was really far out,' said Seb. 'Great stuff!'

Juliet tutted and shook her head. 'It was *horrible,* you mean.'

'What?' said Seb. 'Oh, come on. After hours of cryptic

messages, it's quite a relief to hear him be unambiguous for once.'

'It was that good?' I said, before I could stop myself.

'It was great!' said Seb, grinning. 'Heavy footsteps, like hobnail boots. Proper haunted house stuff! Personally, I was disappointed the old sod didn't rattle any chains, but you can't have everything.'

I was annoyed. Yes, I had seen Mum, but she hadn't seen me. It had been a matter of total indifference to her whether I had been there or not. And Dad had been around only to be unreasonable. And now I had missed the most impressive manifestation produced so far.

'What did Graham make of it?'

'He wasn't here. He was in his study.'

'And you're sure it wasn't him?' I said, before I could stop myself.

'Tim!' said Sally, somewhat aghast.

'I have to ask,' I said. 'It's hardly scientific if you're not all accounted for.'

'He was definitely in his study,' said Neil. 'Came running in through that door when he heard the commotion.' He paused. 'Although now you mention it, he could have come down through the back stairway after producing the footsteps.'

'Graham wouldn't do that!' said Sally, hotly. 'He's as excited as any of us by all this!'

'It's all right,' said Neil, alarmed. 'I didn't say he'd done anything.'

'You certainly implied it.' Sally seemed extremely upset. She shot me a hostile look and I felt sick. 'And Tim, you weren't even here. Graham wouldn't do anything of the kind.'

'What wouldn't I do?' said Graham. He had performed his usual trick of coming in without anybody hearing. I had a very strong mental image of him creeping towards us as we argued, enjoying our discord, drinking it in.

'Neil thinks you may have faked the footsteps we heard,' Sally said bitterly.

'Why would I do that?' said Graham. He seemed genuinely baffled by the question.

'We have to consider all the options,' Neil said grumpily. 'It was Tim who started it.'

Graham turned to look at me, as if noticing me for the first time. 'Hello, Tim! You're back early! How is your mother?'

I repeated the same explanation, mechanically, like a recording.

'Well, it's jolly nice to have you back. Even if you are, once more, casting doubt on what happened here.'

'No!' I said quickly. 'I was just curious, that's all. And I'm sorry if my absence from the séances held you up in any way.'

'Well, the séances certainly felt somewhat reduced with only six of us. I'd like to try again as soon as possible, really,' said Graham. 'Now that we're back to a full complement of volunteers.'

'I'd like that,' I said.

'Well then,' said Graham. 'No time like the present.'

I stared at him as if he had just sprouted antlers.

'What, *now*?'

38

And so, once more, we took our places around the table in
Tobias's room. This would be the first session we had conducted at night, and I wondered if that changed anything.
Graham started the tape recorder, the red rectangular light
burning as the spools turned at their own leisurely speed,
sampling time itself. The electromagnetic field detector and
the voltmeter signalled that they were awake by trembling
their needles in unison, and then settling back to zero. This
time, at Graham's almost defiant insistence, the electric lights
stayed on. No candles with leaping, guttering flames, no pools
of dark shadow, no place whatsoever for misunderstanding
or suspicion to gather and multiply. The room was a cube of
light, set in miles of pitch-black countryside.

'Who's going to conduct the session?' I asked.

Involuntarily, everyone looked to Sally.

'I really don't want to,' she said. 'Please.'

'All right then,' said Graham. 'Anyone else?'

No one said anything. No one moved. Certainly, no one
volunteered.

'I'll do it,' said Juliet eventually.

'Jules, are you sure?' said Seb. There was a concerned,

protective note in his voice I hadn't heard before. It was almost sweet.

'Yes,' said Juliet, very definitely. 'On the condition that, next time, someone else does it.'

'Of course,' said Graham. 'In that case, shall we begin?'

We each placed our fingertips on the planchette, making a circuit in our imaginations if nowhere else.

Juliet nodded. 'Right then!' With her free hand, she scraped her hair back behind her ears. 'Let's see how this goes, shall we?' Her voice was nervous. She glanced up at the tape recorder and took a couple of deep breaths. When she spoke again, her voice was calmer, more grown-up. 'So – the usual crew are all here, seated around the table—' She broke off, and looked from Graham to Sally. 'Do I have to say everyone's name?'

Graham shook his head. 'It's fine.' He cleared his throat and spoke over our heads, in the direction of the quietly whirring tape recorder. 'This is Graham Shaw. Everyone from the last session is present, with the addition of Tim Smith, who's returned to the group. Juliet Fields-Ray will be conducting today's séance and acting as operator.' He gave a nod in Juliet's direction.

'OK!' said Juliet. She took another deep breath and closed her eyes. After a couple of seconds, she opened them again and spoke.

'Mr Salt,' she said. 'Are you there? Speak to us if you are.'

Immediately, the planchette trembled, and the pencil scratched across the table.

'Oh, Jesus,' she breathed.

'It's OK,' said Sally, tenderly. 'It's OK, Jules. Just let it come.'

Under our fingers, the planchette danced. A series of loops and curls, not quite letters. Unexpectedly, Juliet uttered a small moan that was almost sexual.

LLLLLLLLLLLLLL went the loops, as if resolving into language.

'Mr Salt?' said Juliet. 'Is that you?'

all

Juliet glanced up at me, unsure, then addressed the pointer again. 'Could you speak to us?'

Leave

'You want us to leave?'

Yes

No

'You want us to stay?'

NO

Who

Who is there

Juliet leaned forward to address the planchette, as if it were a microphone. 'Just the seven of us, Mr Salt. You've met all of us before.'

NO

EIGHT

I looked nervously about the room, at everyone else. For a split second, I again considered the thought I had promised myself I wouldn't think, that Mr Henshaw had explicitly warned against. To push it aside, I forced myself to picture our notebook, signed by both of us, lying open on the words *THERE IS NOTHING.* But if that were true, how could any-one return to inform me of that fact?

'Who else is here, Tobias?'

Not here

Gone

'They have gone?'

Yes

Juliet frowned. 'Who has gone?'

You Know

'Who?'

LUCY

Juliet gasped as if slapped.

LUKE

LUCY

Juliet raised a hand to her face and emitted a loud and violent sob.

'What is it, Jules?' said Seb. Momentarily, his eyes sparkled with something I thought might be fear.

LUCY

LUKE

Juliet bit a knuckle. The colour had drained from her face. Seb's frustration bordered on rage. 'Jules, what is it? Do you know these people?'

Juliet merely sobbed once more.

Oh YES

ALL GONE

'No!' said Juliet. 'Why – why would you—'

'Shall we stop this?' said Neil. 'Let's stop this.'

'It doesn't make sense,' said Graham. 'Mr Salt, did you mean lucky? Is that what you meant?'

GONE NOW

NO MATTER

ALL GON

'*NO!*' Juliet shouted. There were tears running down her face, but her voice was angry and defiant. '*NO!*' She leapt to her feet, her chair tumbling over behind her, flung the door open, and ran.

Seb got to his feet and started after her. Neil grabbed his arm and pulled him back, and Seb was, for a second, unable to process the idea that Neil might lay a hand on him. He recovered, and shoved Neil roughly aside. Neil lost his balance and sprawled on the floor. Seb headed after Juliet, the stairs thundering as he ran up them.

Graham signalled for Sally to stop recording.

'What just happened?' said Polly. 'What was that?'

Neil picked himself up. His face was drawn and pale.

'Neil?'

'I – don't know!' said Neil. His glasses had come off and he patted the carpet until he found them. 'It tried to needle Jules, though. Very – deliberately.'

'Who's Lucy?' I asked. 'Who's Luke, for that matter? Are they people she knows?'

'How should I know?' Neil said caustically, as if I had been the one who had shoved him to the floor.

'You know her better than we do,' I said. 'Do you recognise those names? Has Juliet ever talked to you about those people?'

But Neil simply shrugged. 'No. I don't know anybody by either of those names.'

Polly looked down at the paper, filled with inexplicable writings in a hand that wasn't any of ours. I looked too. Hard, definite marks, forming block capitals that made words that shouted and taunted. With their perfectly plumb lines and sharp corners, the neat letters gave a strange impression of great strength, barely controlled. Her lips pursed in thought.

'Well, Juliet certainly knew who they were.'

'What the *hell* was that?' said Seb, crashing back into the room. 'What did you do to her?'

'Is she OK?' asked Sally.

'No. She's more upset than I've ever seen her. Who the blazes are Lucy and Luke? Were you *trying* to upset her?'

'We didn't do anything!' said Sally, her voice strained.

'Juliet briefly became a conduit,' said Graham. 'She was merely the instrument by which—'

'Yeah, I know how it's meant to work, *Graham*,' said Seb venomously. Graham's teeth clamped down on his pipe with an audible click, but he said nothing.

'And you,' Seb said, turning to Neil. 'Don't you *ever* put your hand on me again.'

'I don't think there's anything to be gained by—'

'Oh, shut up, Awful. I'm tired of you, moping around, shadowing me and Jules. You think I don't know what a pathetic little crush you have on her?'

Neil flinched a little, but said nothing.

'Oh, you honestly think I didn't know? That I hadn't noticed?'

Neil, reddening, looked at the table.

'It's pathetic, Audle. You're pathetic. With your sneering and your damp handshakes and your bogus intellectual superiority.'

'Seb—' said Graham.

'You know what, Audle? Juliet *tolerates* you. You amuse her. Like a pet. Like a lame old dog, one that you can't quite bring yourself to have put down. Think about that next time you leap in to defend her, you weird toad.'

'Seb,' said Graham. 'That's enough.'

'*You don't know,*' Neil said quietly.

'Oh, what was that?' bellowed Seb. 'You think you know Jules better than me, is that it? Just because you've been moping around after her for years?'

Neil looked up at Seb. I saw defiance in his large, wet eyes.

'You really don't know her at all,' he said.

Seb glared at him for a second, and I thought he might lash out and strike Neil. I had no doubt that Seb could obliterate

Neil if he so desired. Instead, however, Seb simply threw up his hands, made a half-shout of frustration and left the room.

In the silence, the ticking of the clock was suddenly very loud. I counted a dozen ticks before Graham got up out of his seat, slapping his hands on his thighs.

'Well now,' he said. 'I think we should probably call that a night.'

Once again, I found myself in the single bed in my room, staring up into darkness. I suppose I should have been worried about my mother, between life and death, and my father, trapped in his own purgatory, with no map to orient him, but I wasn't. I was most afraid that Juliet's distress and the growing animosity between Seb and Neil meant that the ghost hunt at Yarlings was at an end. It was still the best thing in my life; an escape. I needed it. At least for a while longer.

It was very late by that point, or very early, but still sleep did not come.

After a while, I wandered out into the emptiness of the long corridor, where the starlight fell through the leaded windows in ingots of dull silver. I was aware that the only mind there was my own, alone, forever alone, utterly unable to understand or really communicate with other minds, other souls, even those closest to me. Maybe I was the ghost, I thought. Maybe we were the ghosts, trapped in this house, deluding ourselves that we left from time to time, engaged in some meaningless quest that would occupy us for all eternity.

At the end of the corridor, I was surprised, although not greatly, to see Abi. She was calm. She appeared to be talking, but I couldn't hear what she was saying. She carried something in her hands that glimmered and shone, but I couldn't see what it was.

39

'That's about it,' I said. I was careful to remove any mention of Abi from the dream. I didn't want to talk about her at Yarlings, where I could still pretend I belonged to a version of history where my recent past hadn't happened. I could lose sight of it all here, pretend that back home there was normality to return to.

On the other side of the breakfast table, Polly's eyes narrowed. 'So – just a weird bright light?'

'That was all that was there,' I said.

'Hmmm. It's funny, because *I* had a strange dream last night too,' said Polly. 'About *you*.'

'Really?' I looked at her but didn't stop digging around in a jar of marmalade with a knife as I listened. 'Do tell.'

'Well, it was you, but it *wasn't* you. You were thinner and wearing different clothes. And you were –different. It's hard to explain. You had two other people with you, but I couldn't see either of them clearly. But you were definitely here, in this house. And that's the weird thing.'

'What?' I said, through a mouthful of marmalade and toast.

'The house . . . wasn't the house. I mean, it was, but it was totally different. It was blue and yellow, all the way through, painted to look . . . I don't know, like a ship or something, but it hadn't worked. Like putting clown's make-up on a seriously ill person.' She caught sight of my expression and smiled, pulling her long sleeves over her hands. 'I know it sounds daft. But it felt real.'

'So did mine,' I said.

'What do you think will happen today?' she asked. 'I mean, after last night?'

'I don't know,' I said. 'But my guess is that Graham will be forced to shut it all down.'

'You really think so?'

'You saw how Seb was with Neil last night. They could barely be civil to each other beforehand; it seems very unlikely they'll be able to even manage that now. That, and Juliet reacting so violently.'

'So we'll be going home today?'

I nodded. It was depressing hearing someone else say it. I would have to crawl home, to face Dad, and apologise for what he would no doubt call 'over-reacting' to something I found unforgivable. Then he would, of course, apologise to me, and I would hate him even more. And then at some point we would go and see Mum and she would be much as she was the last time. It was as bleak a prospect as I could imagine.

'Wow,' said Polly. 'It will really be an end to it, then.'

'You sound genuinely sad.'

'Yes,' Polly said. 'It's just . . . I thought we might get some answers, that's all. I think something's definitely happening here. Something we can't see in full, yet. I just want to see it through.'

I nodded. 'I know exactly what you mean.'

Polly gave me a serious look. 'Tim. Do you want to see me again? After today?'

'What do you mean?'

'Well, if this truly is the end, we'll never see each other again, unless we make the effort.'

I looked at her. My face must have displayed enough confusion that she felt the need to clarify. 'And I *do* want to see you again, Tim. I *do* want to make the effort.'

'Right,' I said, in a deadpan tone.

'Oh, right, I was forgetting. *Sally*.' Polly spoke the name in a childish, sing-song voice. 'You like *Sally*.'

I didn't speak, but the embarrassed silence I returned was answer enough.

'Oh God,' said Polly. 'Poor Tim.'

'What do you mean?'

'Poor Tim. Be careful there, won't you?'

'What do you mean?'

'If you can't see it, I can't help you. But be careful.'

At the time, I assumed this was the kind of wily, cryptic statement a woman who had been spurned could be expected to throw back at the object of her affection. A pre-emptive curse to sour the prospect of any possible rival, or to sound like a bell in the mind years later, if any possible romance went awry, so that the object of that affection would then say, *Ah, but she tried to warn me, that one. The one that got away. That good and true one.*

Now I can see that this was vanity and stupidity, and that Polly really was trying to warn me. And that I should have listened.

Inevitably, Sally clattered in soon after, with Graham. They both carried binders full of notes – their own individual record of events at Yarlings. At the sight of Sally, I blushed a little.

'Morning, you two!' Sally said cheerfully. 'Is there toast? Gosh, I'm *famished*!'

Polly shot me a bemused glance across the table as if to say, *This? This is what you want? The secret love child of Aleister Crowley and Enid Blyton?*, but I ignored her and smiled up at Sally.

'Well, I must say, you two seem very chipper, for two researchers whose pet project has come to a premature end.'

'I'm sorry?' said Graham, pouring himself a cup of tea. 'Whatever do you mean, Tim?'

'I mean after last night. We can hardly go on as we were, not with Seb and Neil . . . the way they are. With each other.'

Graham grinned, sitting himself down next to me. His eyes all but twinkled. 'Oh Tim, honestly. That was yesterday. I promise you, it's all fixed this morning. Water under the bridge. Are there any cornflakes left?'

'Fixed?' said Polly. 'How? They were ready to murder each other yesterday! How can they possibly be—'

Seb and Neil trooped into the room.

'Morning,' said Seb, and coughed furiously.

Polly squinted at them both quizzically. 'How are you two doing?'

'Don't worry,' said Seb. 'We've all had words. And whilst Awfu— Neil and I are hardly going to be best pals, we've agreed to put our differences aside, for Juliet's sake. Then, we'll take a view on things.'

'How is Juliet?' asked Polly. 'Can we bring her anything?'

'She's sleeping,' said Seb. 'She just wants to be alone to rest. That session yesterday really upset her, for some reason. Of course, Neil thinks he knows why, but he won't tell me. Which leads me to think he doesn't.'

'Think what you like,' said Neil. He seemed less intimidated by Seb today, more like the relaxed version of himself who had emerged at Rollright.

'Now then, you two,' said Graham. 'Pack it in. Before it even starts.'

'Anyway,' said Neil, sitting down, 'Juliet made it clear that she could tolerate being here if Sebastian and I were civil to each other. She wants to see the experiment through. She really does.'

Seb sat down too, at the opposite end of the table. 'She just needs a while to rest.' It was as if they were competing to bring us the most urgent update on Juliet's wellbeing. 'A day or so without doing a séance.'

Graham frowned at this, as if it were a supremely unreasonable request.

'Well now, Seb, I understand that she's distressed, but I would prefer it if we were all present this afternoon—'

'No dice, old man,' said Seb, with a brisk, cold smile. He suddenly looked very grown-up. 'Maybe tomorrow, but for the time being, let's just leave her alone, hmm?'

And then the discussion was over, save for the frustrated click of Graham's teeth on the stem of his pipe.

We spent our unexpected afternoon off reading, or simply doing nothing. At some point, I decided that the incessant fug of cigarette smoke inside the house was too choking, too unpleasant, and too reminiscent of Mum to tolerate, and went for a walk. At the rear of the house was a brick pathway that wound through an overgrown herb garden, bordered by a sparse yew hedge. I slumped down on a low wall that was barely keeping back a huge crowd of purple sage. It was another hot day. The bricks drank up the sunlight hungrily and were warm to the touch.

I looked up to see a face. A smiling face, poking through the hedge.

'Hello, Polly.'

'I'm not Polly!' she said, in a funny, nasal voice. 'I'm Jack-in-the-Green!'

'Right.' I smiled. 'Are you just here to act like a loony, or did you want something?'

'A bit of both, I think.' She stood up and walked round the hedge to where I was. 'And what are you doing, Tim?'

'Thinking,' I said.

'Hmm. Is that what that looks like? Are you thinking about Sally, are you, Tim? Sally, free and easy?'

'That seems unpleasant.'.

'I was referring to the song – oh, never mind. Look, whilst you're here, and the others aren't, I wanted to ask you something.'

I shrugged. 'Go ahead.'

'Timothy, do you think this house is haunted?'

'I think we've seen evidence of that, certainly.'

'Did it ever cross your mind that haunted houses aren't haunted unless there are people in them?'

'You think it's all fake?'

'No.' Her earlier frivolousness fell away and she looked sad and serious. 'That's not what I mean.'

'Then – what?'

'I have a suspicion, Tim. But I need to see more before I can say anything for certain.'

That evening, I called Dad.

The phone rang for a long while before he picked it up; I presumed he was disentangling himself from some very involved DIY project.

'Hello?'

'Hi, Dad.'

'Tim,' he said warily.

'Dad, I just needed to—'

'Is this about all that stuff in the papers?'

'What stuff?'

'They've been trying to connect Abi's disappearance to a couple of similar cases around the same time in Cambridgeshire. That's where you are, isn't it?'

I felt the anger coming. Why did he never pay attention? 'No, Dad. I'm in Suffolk, remember? One county along.'

'Oh.' He seemed disappointed. 'Anyway, it struck me as a load of noise about nothing.'

'How's Mum?' I asked.

'No change,' said Dad. 'I'll call you if there is. When there is.'

There was a long pause. I realised he wasn't going to bring our fight up, and if I didn't mention it now, it would be lost to history, never talked of again.

'Dad,' I began. 'I'm sorry. About yesterday. I'm really sorry.'

'Oh.' He sounded distracted, as if recalling something of no consequence, from many years ago. I persisted.

'I shouldn't have – done what I did. But you had no right to do – what you did.' I was aware that I wasn't using specifics of any kind. I took a deep breath. 'Destroying Abi's room, I mean.'

'I can't talk about this now,' said Dad.

'If we don't talk about it now, we'll never talk about it, Dad.' *I need you,* I wanted to say. *I need help. Guidance. Sympathy. Anything. Help me. Please.*

'Well, look, Tim, I have to go. I have to clamp some wood-work I've just glued.'

'Dad—'

'Goodbye, Tim. I'll see you when you get home.'

40

The next day, Graham decided enough was enough, and even if Juliet was not feeling up to it, Seb and Neil had a duty to participate. They had, after all, agreed to come to Yarlings for one purpose only. The experiment, Graham informed us crisply over breakfast, would resume. And so, at midday, we trooped into Tobias's Room, and took our now-familiar places around the table, leaving Juliet's chair empty.

Graham lit the candles, turned off the light, and closed the curtains, almost defiantly, as if to say that any suspicions of trickery anyone might still be entertaining were by this point surely unfounded. 'Tuesday, the eleventh of June, 1974,' said Graham, '12:01 p.m. Present are myself, Graham Shaw, Sally, Polly, Tim, Sebastian and Neil.'

'And Juliet,' said a voice from the door.

'Jules!' said Polly. Juliet smiled a slightly bruised smile. There were dark circles under her eyes, and her skin was pale.

'Juliet, are you sure you're OK to be back with us today?'

She nodded. Graham raised his eyebrows and pointed to his mouth, indicating that she should voice this consent for the tape recorder.

'Yes,' she said, defiantly, staring into the red light of the tape recorder as if it were a sceptical observer. 'I'm here, aren't I?'

'That's the spirit!' said Graham. 'But are you absolutely sure?'

'I feel I'll be better able to control the experience, if the experience is happening to me,' Juliet said carefully. 'Rather than running away from it.' I sensed that this was something she'd given a lot of thought to over the last day or so.

'Very well,' said Graham. 'If you're certain.'

Seb touched her arm as she sat down. 'Jules – you really don't have to—'

Gently but firmly, she pushed his hand away. 'Shh. I want to.'

'All right then,' said Graham, in a voice that suggested he wanted to get things underway before she changed her mind. 'I state for the record that also present today is Juliet Fields-Ray, which gives us a full complement of participants. Time is currently 12:04. Hands to the pump, everyone.'

The pencil stood in the middle of the blank sheet of paper, a single point in a white void of potential. Juliet was last to place her fingertip on the pointer.

'I will be operator today,' Graham said solemnly. 'I don't imagine I'll exactly be trampled in the rush for volunteers.'

'Oh no. I'll do it,' said Polly briskly.

Graham's brow furrowed. 'Are you absolutely certain?'

Polly smiled. 'What? Given the way two of the previous ones have ended? With whoever conducts it bursting into tears? I'd be mad not to.' Seb snorted at this, but Graham simply nodded.

'Very well. Today's operator will be Polly Rook.'

'OK.' Polly took a deep breath. 'Are you there?' she said, without hesitation.

Immediately, the pencil quivered.

'Mr Salt,' Polly said. 'Is that you?'

YES

'Er – hello?' Polly said cheerfully, as if this were a blind date.

The pencil trembled but didn't move.

'Is there anything you particularly wish to tell us? Perhaps you want us to say prayers for your soul, so that you might leave this house?'

At this suggestion the pencil slashed violently across the page. Words began to appear under our hands, in stark block capitals.

NO PRAYR

Polly looked puzzled. 'And why not?'

WHAT GOOD

'It might help you to move on?' said Polly. 'Prevent your soul from being bound to this house—'

Again, a series of jagged, angry scratches filled the paper. 'Slow down,' murmured Polly, her eyes darting back and forth. 'Too fast.' Sally removed the sheet of paper from under the pencil and replaced it with a fresh one.

'Unless, of course, that's *not* why you're here?' said Polly.

'I'm sorry, Polly,' said Graham. 'Where is this going?'

Polly shook the hair away from her face as she addressed Graham directly. 'I just thought it would be helpful if we asked Mr Salt a few more direct questions, rather than just make assumptions. I'm sure we can all see the value in that.'

'Yes,' said Graham uncomfortably. 'But—'

'Mr Salt?' said Polly. 'What are you?'

The planchette juddered, as if stunned. And then began to write, calmly and distinctly, across the page

I AM NOT THE

315

HOUSE
'Well, we know that——' Seb began.
GRAETER
GRATAER THAN THE TRIANGLES
GREATER THAN THE WOUNDED BOY
GREATER THAN THE ENTWINED LIARS
GREATER THAN THE UNLUCKY ONE
Polly glanced around her in consternation. 'What are you talking about, Mr Salt? We don't understand.'
ALL OF YOU
'Us? What about us?'
I WILL
ALL OF YOU
RUIN
A tangible crackle of fear ran through our circle. 'What – what do you mean by that?'
ALWAYS WAITING
IN THE PAST
IN THE NOT
WAITING
TWO HALVES
SILT STREAM
THER
BARE
AS A WINTER TREE
'We don't understand, Mr Salt,' said Graham. 'Tell us more.'
THER LIES
TIME
IT IS TIME
'Time for what? What are you telling us?'
RED BLUE

ALMOST DOEN
CANOT LIVE
CANOT DIE

I gasped. Abi's poem, her invocation, the one she had written to summon up our chalk ghost, to animate it. Hadn't she written something like that?

SO COLLD
SO WET
AMONG THE WEEDS
CANT HIDE FROM HIM
FUNNY FACE

'Jesus!' said Polly.

'What does that mean?' I asked.

'How can he know that?' Polly wondered aloud, her voice barely a whisper.

'What do you mean?' I said.

I KNO
ALL OF YOU
I KNOW

'What are you telling us?' Graham asked insistently.

THE END
OF WH

'Of who?'

WHO YOU WERE

Then, incised very firmly and definitely into the paper:

T S P N J

'Gibberish,' said Seb, shaking his head.

TSPNJ

'No,' I said. 'Look. They're – initials. It's *us*. Well, some of us.'

I thought again of Sally's theory that Mr Salt was a gestalt, a creature composed of all of us. Our distilled essence. If this were the case, might this be its way of telling us so? Part of me accepted this as plausible; another part was amazed and horrified by the things I was now willing to consider after a week at Yarlings. I glanced at Sally but she did not look up from the trembling planchette.

'Us? What about us?' urged Graham. 'Tell us!'

ITS HERE

'What's here?'

BEGIN THE END

IT IS

TIM

My blood ran cold. 'Me?'

TIME

IT IS TIME

'Time for what?' Graham said urgently.

ANS

ANSW

'Answer,' said Graham. 'Answer what?'

ANSER THE

'Answer *what*?'

ANSWER THE

CALL

'What call?' said Graham.

From its hook in the distant hallway, the telephone began to ring; crisp, clear and indifferent.

We listened to it ring for a full minute, before Graham stood, inhaled deeply and left the room.

Lit by the candles, our faces were masks of worry and concern, suspended in space. Everyone's eyes glittered with apprehension, pupils large. I could hear Juliet's breathing, shallow and quick.

'That,' said Seb, ever the pragmatist, 'was *freaky*.'

'It certainly was,' Polly said quietly. I thought I glimpsed a tear on her cheek, but she rubbed her face with her sleeve before I could be sure.

'He likes the old phone, doesn't he?' said Seb.

'Graham did tell us Mr Salt's manifestations are supposed to be associated with the ringing of bells,' Polly said acidly. 'I suppose it doesn't matter which bells.'

'How are you, Juliet?' Neil asked. He reached out to touch her arm. 'Are you OK?'

Juliet nodded slowly. 'It's intense when it happens and it's intense when it stops happening, isn't it? Good God, listen to me.' She laughed a little. 'Who do you think the phone was for?'

'Graham,' I said. 'It must be. He wouldn't be gone this long otherwise.'

'Are we still recording?' said Neil. 'Shall I turn it off?' Sally nodded, and Neil got up and pressed STOP.

Graham returned.

'Is everything OK?' Sally asked.

'Absolutely fine,' said Graham. 'It was the Institute, that's all. They were calling to remind me that I'm due to give a presentation to them tomorrow afternoon.'

'So it was something you already knew?' said Polly. 'Thank God. We all expected the worst, after – after that.' She gestured towards the page of scrawl.

'You're going away tomorrow?' Neil asked.

'Yes,' said Graham. 'I'm sorry I forgot to tell everyone, but it seemed so minor. I'll be back before you know it.'

'What's the presentation about?' I asked.

'My work here, of course. Methods. Results. A broad outline of what I've been up to, basically. I mean, thank goodness I now have something to show them.'

'You're not worried they're going to cut your funding, or shut the whole thing down?' said Polly.

'What?' Graham looked genuinely shocked. 'Why ever would they?'

'*Begin the end.*' Polly tapped the sheet of paper in front of us. 'That's what Mr Salt said, shortly before he told us to answer the phone.'

'Ah,' Graham smiled. 'I see what you mean. Well, given that Mr Salt's communications are themselves a tangible result, I can't say I'm too worried about it. I hardly think they're likely to shut this down when they see the kind of results we've been getting.'

Graham smiled down at the planchette. 'Sorry, Tobias, old chap! Nice try. Looks like we'll be bothering you for a little while longer!'

41

The next day was hot and sticky. Even before ten, the house had become stuffy and the atmosphere oppressive; by eleven-fifteen, we had all separately converged on the front lawn and were lounging on the dry grass, reading, or simply basking in the sunshine. Graham did not join us; presumably he was either packing or preparing his notes.

'It's supposed to rain later,' said Polly, staring up at the cloudless sky. 'Has Graham gone yet?'

'Not quite,' said Neil. 'He's still fussing over his files and things.'

'Well now.' Seb was shirtless again, lying on his back with his sunglasses on, smoking. 'If Graybags is off until late evening, shall we make hay while the sun shines? By which I mean – pool our cash and buy some booze?'

'From the village?'

'Where else? You don't mind going, do you, Timbo? You said they sold wine in the shop. Failing that, you could try and bribe the yokels in the pub?'

It seemed a daring plan, but a not unfeasible one. 'OK,' I said. 'But Graham's not out all night. He'll be back by ten at the latest, he said so himself.'

'Well, we'll have to start early, then, won't we? And be in bed by the time he comes back. Who's in?'

Juliet shrugged. 'It's been a long week, hasn't it?'

'Marvellous. Who else?'

'I'm in,' said Neil immediately. 'I could do with a drink.'

'Really? Well now. There may be hope for you yet, Awful.'

'Don't call me—'

'Yeah, yeah. Who else? Polly?'

She nodded. 'We need this, don't we? It'd be a waste not to.'

'Smashing.'

A shadow fell across my face, and I looked up to see Sally.

'What's smashing?' she said.

Everyone was silent.

'What's smashing?' she repeated, sitting down.

'The results of yesterday's session,' said Seb, propping himself up on his elbows. 'We were all . . . really impressed by them.'

I sighed. There was, to me, no point in doing this if we excluded Sally. 'As Graham's going away, we're going to pool our money and buy some wine.'

'Smith!' barked Seb. 'You . . . traitor!'

'And then,' I continued, 'we're going to get pleasantly intoxicated, and shortly before Graham gets back, we're all retreating to our respective rooms so he won't know. And, unless we're in a really terrible state tomorrow morning, he never *will* know.'

I looked directly at her, into her blue-green eyes, her red hair haloed with sunlight. 'Would you like to join us?'

For a second, the day held its breath as Sally looked at me, her expression unchanging. And then, her freckled face broke out into a wide smile.

'What a fantastic idea!'

*

At roughly midday, we all lined up at the front of the house to see Graham off, as if he were an Elizabethan explorer undertaking a voyage by galleon to the Americas, rather than a man about to drive to Central London, and scheduled to return later the same day.

'Goodbye, Sal,' Graham said, hugging Sally. 'Look after these reprobates, will you? I'll be back before you know it!'

'Don't worry,' said Sally. 'We'll be fine!'

'Better than fine,' said Seb, cheerily. 'Drive safely!'

'I will,' said Graham. 'Be good.' His ancient Vauxhall crunched down the gravel driveway. At the gates, he wound down his window and gave us a small wave, before dropping out of sight. The engine puttered through the avenue of trees where the B-road ran.

'Off he goes . . . And . . . He's gone. Right, you. Go and get us alcohol.'

'What, *now?* It's not even—'

Seb grinned. 'No time like the present. Besides, it's the countryside. The locals are bored. Trust me, if I lived here I'd start drinking at dawn.'

The day grew even warmer as I trod the winding pathway through the woods, the sunlight slanting through the oak and birch, the sandy soil sparkling like a cache of diamonds.

The village stretched along the single road that ran its length; you could almost see through the place and out the other side. There was the clutch of houses whispering in conspiracy; there was the small triangular lawn where the road branched off. Small details – the colours and names of houses, the concrete garden gnomes – returned to me from my first visit here. The good weather had brought people out, and the village wore an almost holiday air. The villagers – all old, as far as I could tell, although at seventeen my concept of 'old' began somewhere around thirty– smiled benignly at me, or tilted their heads in acknowledgement as I passed.

In the tiny shop, I filled a wire basket with various genuine supplies – Sally had given me a list – cheese, bread, apples and milk. Underneath these, I hid five bottles of red wine, selected according to price and alcohol content, an approach a million miles away from my original idea of impressing Sally with my refined good taste. My thinking was that the woman behind the counter would ring up the non-alcoholic items first, and so, even if she doubted my age, wouldn't want to cancel the transaction and start all over again, and might just turn a blind eye to the wine.

At the till, the woman gave me a perfunctory smile without making eye contact, and began to ring up the items at the top of the basket. The cheese. The bread. The milk. The apples thudded into the metal bowl of the scale to be weighed. We could now both see the five identical bottles lining the bottom of the basket. The till lady expertly transferred the apples into a paper bag, spinning it by its corners to twist it shut. My heart pounded.

She looked at the bottles, then at me.

'I shouldn't be selling you this,' she said.

'Wh-why?' I stammered.

She nodded at the wall to her right, where a clock read 11:55.

'It's before one.' She looked at my clearly terrified expression and her face darkened. 'Licensing laws.'

'Oh.' I had not expected this. Should I wait? Come back? Go and look at the fourteenth-century rood screen for an hour?

The till lady's large face broke into a laugh. She had been pulling my leg. 'I won't tell if you won't!' she said cheerily, and rang the first bottle up.

*

The high street was just as I had left it, and the sun was still shining. I was still unable to process that I had just walked away with five bottles of red wine, at noon on a Wednesday. For it to be that easy seemed to speak of a colossal administrative error somewhere in the universe. I was still wondering when the inevitable correction would occur, and what form it would take, when I heard a voice calling after me.

'Hey! Hey, you there!'

I stopped dead. I felt curiously relieved that the whole ordeal was over.

'Hey!'

Yet the voice was not that of the till lady. It was too educated, too layered, too rich. I turned around.

The woman from the bookshop. Hattie Wells. She was wearing a pencil skirt, pinstriped blouse and blue suit jacket. Her large glasses, with their pink transparent frames, sat on top of her head. She smiled, although she looked flustered.

'It's Tim, isn't it? I saw you from the shop.'

'It is.' I smiled weakly. 'It's Hattie, isn't it?'

'It is. You're still up at Yarlings, then?'

'I am.'

'Excellent. I tried telephoning a couple of times, but no one answered. Do you have a minute?'

Hattie Wells's bookshop was even less like a commercial premises – and more like the parlour of a mad aunt – than I recalled. Precarious stacks of randomly-ordered books stretched up to the ceiling, beyond all reason, past the spider-plants and the ornaments and the carriage clock. The French bulldog looked up at me vaguely as the doorbell clanged, then returned to resting her chin on her tartan blanket. Hattie Wells made a great show of clearing a pile of papers and a squeaky dog bone from a chair, and motioned for me to sit. I played with the handles of the plastic shopping bags, and wondered what this was about. Hattie Wells settled into her chair behind the desk, steepled her fingers and stared at me.

'So,' she said at length. 'Tobias Salt.'

'What about him?'

She frowned down at the Xeroxed pages Graham had given me, then stabbed her right forefinger into the dead centre of the page and pushed it towards me.

'This document,' she said, 'is nonsense.'

'I'm sorry?'

'There never was anyone called Tobias Salt, and if there ever was, he certainly never lived up at Yarlings.'

'No. You must be mistaken?' But I knew already that Hattie Wells belonged to that class of Englishwomen who didn't make mistakes. She shook her head.

'I'm afraid not. The story was so fantastical, so grotesque, that I was at a loss to account for why I hadn't heard it before. So I visited the town hall, the local history archive, delved into the parish records, and so on and so forth.'

She looked directly into my eyes. 'Yarlings was built in 1605. That's about the only detail in this entire document that's true. It was built by a man named Geoffrey Swinn, of the Swinn family. However, the house was owned by him and his descendants for the next two hundred or so years.'

'That's not possible.'

Hattie Wells carried on speaking, as if she hadn't heard me. 'During that time, Yarlings suffers the dramatic and sudden subsidence which ultimately destroys the north wing. The house was empty for years after the last living Swinn, Rebecca, dies. The place is then bought by a Reverend Mountford in the late 1840s, and it's Mountford who rebuilds the north wing in the reliably awful Gothic Revival style. Mountford tries to make the place into a campaign headquarters for his pet cause, the temperance movement, but his health is failing, and he dies in 1855. After that, it's bought by the Collmere family, successive generations of whom live there until about five or six years ago. After that, they relocate to London, and rent the place out, sporadically.'

'But . . .' I grasped for something to hold onto as the floor collapsed under me. 'I mean, you're sure you've got the right Yarlings? There might be other houses in the county with that name?'

'Oh, I'm sure there are a couple. But none larger than a cottage. It's also highly unlikely that there would be two houses with the same singular blend of Jacobean and Victorian architecture.'

'But what about the marks? On the fireplace? I've seen them!' I had run my fingers into the grooves.

With a pen, Hattie Wells flipped open an old volume on her desk, and I saw a line-drawing of a stone hearth with a wooden lintel, not dissimilar to the one in the Great Hall. There was a design carved into the beam. It was a close cousin of the symbol at Yarlings, though perhaps not as ominous-looking, and this time with a date: *1536*.

'They're common all over Suffolk, Norfolk and Essex – all over the country, to some degree. The hearth was the heart of the home, and it's logical that people would carve good luck symbols there to protect their household. The carving at Yarlings is likely no more than that.'

I stared at the open book, as if I would somehow find an answer there beyond the obvious. A last, desperate thought struck me.

'What about the portrait?'

Hattie Wells looked down at the front page of *The True History of Tobias Salt*. 'I've no idea who that is,' she said. 'But I expect, given time, I could find out.'

'So what does this mean?' I asked, superfluously.

'It means that this' – Hattie Wells prodded the document with her pen, as if it were toxic – 'is balderdash from start to finish. There's a sprinkling of factual detail, but no more than window dressing.'

'It's . . . lies?'

'Yes. Not very sophisticated lies, at that. Who gave this to you, again?'

'The – someone I know.'

'Well.' Hattie Wells sat back and folded her arms. 'I'd say he was playing a prank on you. Trying to scare you. Has there been any supposedly ghostly activity since you came to the house?'

I met her gaze with all of my concentration.

'None whatsoever,' I said.

She held my gaze for a second, and then looked away. I exhaled inwardly with the effort.

'Well,' she said again. She gave no indication as to whether she believed me or not. 'In my experience, people often do strange things, for unfathomable reasons. I'm sure your friend has very good motives for fabricating an entirely bogus history for the house, and I'm sure those reasons will become evident in due course.'

'There's no chance you could be wrong?' I said, before I could consider the wisdom of such a question.

Hattie Wells regarded my insolence icily over the top of her bifocals.

'None whatsoever.'

'Right,' I said, getting up to leave. I took the Xeroxed pages, folded them up and put them in my pocket. The wine bottles clanked as I picked the shopping bags up. Hattie Wells glanced at me, but said nothing.

'Thank you,' I said. 'That's . . . hugely helpful.'

'You're welcome,' she said, not looking up. 'I'll admit it was disappointing to disprove such a fantastic tale, but it did *sound* too good to be true.'

'Of course. Thanks again,' I said, for want of anything better to say.

I made my way to the door. Hattie Wells smiled briefly at me, but she was already picking up another book, becoming involved with another text, luxuriating in her private library, where she'd almost certainly not sold a book in a long time, and I was fading from sight.

The walk from the house to the village through the summer splendour of the countryside had been, to my mind, quasi-magical; however, I barely noticed the walk from the village back to the house at all. My mind raced with conflicting explanations and thoughts. Most pressing were two huge, unavoidable questions: *Why would anybody do this?* and *Will I tell the others?*

To the first question, I had no easy answers. Graham did not seem like the kind of person who was even capable of a practical joke, so that could be ruled out. Had he been misinformed? This also seemed unlikely. Graham's methods may not have been exactly scientific, but they were thorough, and it didn't seem probable that he'd fail to check the provenance of the house so spectacularly. Which left the distinct possibility that Graham had made it all up, as something to do with our experiment. And if that was the case, did Sally know? Was she aware that the entire Tobias Salt story was fiction?

The second question was easier to answer. I rounded the last stretch of the woodland path and saw Yarlings, as if for the first time; the ancestral home of the Swinn family, partially rebuilt in the mid-1800s by a teetotal clergyman. A place with no violent, spectral or occult associations whatsoever, no history of being haunted in any way.

Until now.

'What's the matter, old chum? You look like you've seen a ghost!' Seb snorted with laughter at this comment, clapping me on the shoulder. He had been standing in front of the house, smoking. He either saw the outline of the bottles in the shopping bags or heard them clash together as I walked; either way, his face lit up.

'Mission accomplished?'

'Oh yes,' I said.

'How many?'

'Five.'

'FIVE! Good work, Smith. I'll see you make sergeant for this. Is it too early to start now?' He glanced at his watch. 'Bloody hell, actually, it probably is. It's only one o'clock.'

One o'clock, I thought. Was that all?

I headed inside.

42

There was, I decided, only one person I could speak to. After putting the wine in the kitchen, I padded down the corridor and rapped lightly on Polly's door.

'Polly?'

'Come in. It's not locked. Oh, hi Tim!' She was doing some sort of embroidery, and put it carefully aside as she stood up to greet me. Polly's room was in the Victorian wing of the house, about twice the size of mine, with a view onto the small rear lawn and the woods beyond. As well as a wardrobe, there was a writing desk, on which sat some hardback books, a hairbrush, a transistor radio. There was also a large grandfather clock with a loud, stately tick. She saw me looking at it, and smiled brightly. 'Don't worry, you get used to it after a while. In fact, I don't know how I'm going to get to sleep without it when we go home.' She blinked as she got a proper look at my face. 'Good God, Tim, what's wrong? You look terrible!'

I told her. About Hattie Wells, about Tobias Salt, about the Swinn family and the Reverend Mountford, and the entire history of the house, a history in no way supernatural or ghostly. Her eyes grew wider as she listened. When I finished speaking, she was silent for a long while.

'You're sure about all this?'

I nodded.

'And you think this woman is trustworthy? Graham implied the locals were very – protective – about this story.'

'She doesn't seem the kind of person who's even capable of lying, let alone one who has any interest in doing so. As I say, she's a local history buff, and the Tobias Salt story was catnip to her. She couldn't wait to investigate him.'

We both fell silent for a while, thinking.

'So we've been lied to,' said Polly. 'I mean, I suspected we weren't being told the whole truth, but this is way beyond anything I imagined.'

'But why?' I said. 'There are thousands of places in Britain that are genuinely haunted, with real tales every bit as grim and bloody as Tobias Salt's fake one. Why not pick one of those, if you want to contact a ghost?'

'We have to conclude,' said Polly carefully, with the air of someone picking their way through a maze, 'that, as far as the experiment we're involved in goes, that is not its purpose.'

'What, then? It makes no sense!'

'Not at the moment. We need more information.'

'Unless you're prepared to break into Graham's study,' I said, 'we're unlikely to get any.'

Polly was quiet again for a while, and then she smiled. 'Oh, I don't know.' Her smile grew broader. 'I think I know a way we can find out more. But you're not going to like it.'

At seven o'clock precisely, we began drinking. Seb counted down the seconds on his watch from ten, and as the chimes of the grandfather clock in Polly's room reverberated through the house, he cheered, opened the first bottle and started pouring us all a glass.

I had never drunk red wine – or wine of any kind – before. Dad said that wine was something that only old ladies and Spaniards drank, and refused to have it in the house. What was wine like? I took the glass Seb had poured for me, and was about to take a huge slug, as if it were Tizer, when Sally gently put her hand on mine to stop me.

'I know it's hardly a vintage, Tim, but you have to take your time with it. Sip!'

'Yeah, Comprehensive,' Seb sniffed, pouring a glass for Neil. 'You're not in borstal now. Right. Is that everyone?'

'It is,' said Polly. 'Unless you want to pour a glass for Mr Salt?' She stared at Sally, but Sally didn't notice either the comment or the stare.

'Well, in that case, I propose a toast,' said Seb. 'To Tim. The one who risked death and dishonour by going to the village and procuring us booze. *And* you brought that bottle of whisky.'

'Whisky?' said Sally.

'A small bottle,' I said, hastily. 'We didn't even finish it.'

Seb ignored her. 'Here's to Tim!'

'Tim,' everyone said. I smiled and took a sip. Wine, it turned out, was to fruit juice – which I was expecting it to taste like – as chess was to noughts and crosses. Wine tasted *deep* – stratified, slightly spoiled, like rotten fruit, but exhilarating, like spring water. It didn't reveal itself all at once, and the taste of it seemed to change even as you were drinking it. It was difficult to enjoy and yet impossible to dislike. I took another sip.

'To me,' I said.

Strangely, the early part of what was to be our last night at Yarlings was probably the best time we ever had there.

Everyone was relaxed, and the wine made the conversation pleasantly confessional, as we compared our young lives thus far, and the things we'd got up to. As far as alcohol went, it turned out that whilst I was not the most experienced, as I had suspected, neither was I the least, as I had feared. Neil had hardly ever drunk at all, and had very little interest in it; Polly swore that that night constituted the most wine she'd ever had, and that she'd have to be careful.

The conversation turned to love and sex and all matters related, and in this none of us could compete with Seb and Juliet, who were, almost proudly, sexually active. Neil, I suspected, had never so much as kissed a girl, and nothing he said on the matter disproved this; Polly had had one boyfriend at her school, who she called 'a total idiot', and said they didn't even speak any more. Sally was coy on the subject, saying she'd recently met someone she liked very much, but they were taking things slowly. The blood in my body seemed to glow warmly after she said this.

We moved on to miscellaneous wild exploits we'd undertaken, and I found – to my surprise – that I was easily the most accomplished of all present in this area. My apprenticeship in hooliganism under Tony Finch had given me a wealth of stories of adventures hilarious, dangerous and pointless, and sometimes all three, and the first rush of wine my system had ever had evaporated my inhibitions and made me quite the raconteur. The story of Tony Finch and me starting a blaze in our factory, which we then had to control and put out, proved to be the pièce de résistance, and I was surprised at how such an unpleasant and troubling memory could become such a good story.

I expected Polly to subtly and slyly move the conversation around to events at Yarlings, but, after a couple of hours, when an appropriate lull arose in the chatter, she simply turned to Sally and addressed her directly.

'Sally, why is Graham organising fake séances?'

Everyone fell silent, apart from Seb, who burst out laughing. Sally looked as if she'd been slapped.

'I *beg* your pardon?'

'Oh, come on. Enough is enough. Whatever's happening here, we know we're not being told the truth.'

'I don't know what you mean,' said Sally. Her tone was unsure.

'This "experiment" we're all here to do. I'm no clearer on its purpose now than I was at the start.'

'Its purpose is simple,' Sally said guilelessly. 'To make contact with the ghost of a man who once inhabited this house—'

'Ah, but that's just it,' said Polly. 'We only have your word there ever *was* a Tobias Salt.'

Sally looked stunned. Polly smiled sardonically and carried on. 'We haven't been able to find any mention of him anywhere. You'd think that such a dramatic story would be more widely known.'

'Graham explained that!' said Sally. I felt terrible for her. I wanted Polly to go easy on her, but she kept talking.

'Yes, he did, didn't he? He said he'd found the story of Tobias Salt in the parish records. Very convenient. Only, I checked the parish records, Sally.'

'How?' Sally looked as if she might cry. I desperately wanted to put my hand on her shoulder, but I didn't dare. And Polly pushed on, just as relentlessly as Hattie Wells had.

'Never mind *how*, Sally. I checked them.'

'And?'

'Nobody by the name of Tobias Salt ever lived here, Sally. Not ever.'

'Wow,' said Seb, round a belch. 'And I was afraid the evening might be dull.'

'The records could be wrong, though, surely?' Neil said.

'Not that wrong,' said Juliet. 'Sally, what's going on?'

'Tobias Salt is real,' Sally insisted. 'I don't know what the parish records say, or any other records for that matter. But Tobias Salt is *real*.'

'Because he's contacting us at the séances?' said Neil. 'That doesn't follow.'

Sally fell silent.

'If there's no ghost,' said Neil, 'then why are we here?'

'Why indeed?' said Polly. 'My guess is that the experiment is actually on us, to gauge our levels of fear, or the degree to which we'll convince ourselves there's a real ghost in this house.'

Sally shook her head slowly. 'No. That's not it.'

'What, then?'

'Yeah,' said Seb. 'We have a right to know what's going on here. Especially if it's all rubbish.'

'Tobias Salt is real,' Sally repeated, not looking at any of us.

'Well then,' said Polly, smiling. 'Prove it!'

'How?'

Polly smiled, again.

Tobias's room was always palpably colder than the rest of the house, with a heavy, damp chill that came straight from the fens. Dark clouds had already begun to clot in the evening sky where the daylight died; it looked as if the hot day would end in thunder. The first few raindrops already streaked the window panes. Neil drew the curtains on the dreary dusk and turned the tape recorder on. The useless electromagnetic field detector was also activated, the needles flickering their usual vapid hello.

We took our places around the table, moving Graham's empty chair against the wall. No candles were lit, and Polly insisted the lights be kept on. Sally's voice, for the benefit of the tape recorder, began the ritual.

'Evening of Wednesday, the twelfth of June. Special session convened to answer various – doubts – expressed by the participants, over the validity of phenomena experienced thus far. Present: Tim Smith, Sebastian Stourton, Neil Audle, Polly Rook and Juliet Fields-Ray. And myself.'

'Are we absolutely sure we want to do this?' Juliet asked.

'Yes,' said Neil, very definitely. 'If we're being tricked or conned, I want to know how.' To my surprise, Seb nodded in agreement.

Sally continued. 'Session will be conducted via planchette as before, with everybody—'

'No.' Polly put her hand on Sally's. 'If we just do what we've been doing all along, that will prove nothing.'

'So what do you propose?'

Polly spoke clearly for the benefit of the tape recorder. 'OK, so for this session, the planchette will be used, but just by you, Sally. Is that OK?'

'No!' Her discomfort and reluctance were very real. Again, I wanted to put my arm round her, protect her.

'Sally.' Polly clasped Sally's hands 'It's the only way you can convince us, now, that something real is taking place here.'

Sally bit her lip. 'I'd really rather not.'

'That way, we'll see whether you're manufacturing phenomena, or if they're –you know. Real.'

'Can't we wait until Graham returns?'

Polly shook her head. 'We have to do this now.'

Sally nodded. With quiet ceremony, she placed her hands on the planchette.

'All right.' She smiled a small, tight-lipped smile and closed her eyes. After a couple of seconds, she opened them again, and addressed the planchette at her fingertips.

'Mr Salt? Are you there?'

The planchette didn't move.

'Mr Salt,' said Polly. 'Are you with us?'

Nothing.

'He's not normally this shy, is he?' muttered Seb.

'Mr Salt?'

Again, the planchette remained resolutely still.

A minute or so passed. The minute felt very long to me. God only knew how long it felt for Sally. I was on the verge of calling a halt on the whole thing, when Polly spoke.

'I don't think—' she said.

And then, under Sally's hands, the planchette jerked violently to the right. Sally gasped.

'Stop that!' said Juliet, alarmed.

'I'm not doing anything.' Sally spoke through gritted teeth.

'Mr Salt?' Polly said carefully. 'Is that you?'

The swooping movement of the planchette was confident, bold, almost triumphant.

YES

I AM HERE

IAM

THROUGH

'What do you mean, through?' Polly asked. We watched in silent wonder as the planchette moved jerkily across the page. Sally stared at her fingertips.

HERE

FULY

'A full manifestation?' I said. 'Is that what you're saying?'

OH YES

GLORIOS

ADVENTUM GLORIAE

IN SPITE

'All right,' Juliet said. 'I think we've seen enough. You can stop this.'

'No,' Sally said, terror in her voice now. *'I can't.'* Under her whitened fingertips, the planchette ground out more words.

A KNIGT MOVE

AL YOUR HISTORYS

UNDON

I AM THE HERE NOW

The lights, incredibly, flickered and lowered, then returned to full power.

'Jesus!' Seb gasped. In that moment, I felt terror. This was different to any other session we had had. The atmosphere felt charged, all at once, pregnant with seething, malign possibility. I remembered the day after Abi had vanished, when I had imagined I had sensed – something – observing me in the empty attic. No – it had been more than mere observation. It had been . . . what? Scrutinising? *Evaluating?* Sally stared down at her hands on the planchette as if she were holding a venomous snake.

'Have you spoken to us before?' asked Polly.

OH

YES

'When?'

I WAS NOT

NOW AM

Again, I thought of the invocation Abi had written, so very long ago. *I don't exist,* she had written. *Yet here I am.* Maybe there was a chance, I thought. Maybe there was the merest, slightest chance, and I had to take it.

'Abi?' I asked, before I could stop myself. The juddering planchette replied with almost indecent haste.

NO
BUT NOW
ALWAYS
ALWAYS WITH YOU
HERE

'Can we stop now?' said Juliet, her voice breaking a little. 'Please?'

'What, then?' I said. 'Show us. Show us what you are.'

NEVER

'Tell us, Mr Salt,' said Polly, her face white. 'Tell us what you are.'

OH NO
FUNNY FACE
SWEET FUNNY FACE

'Jesus!' gasped Polly, with genuine anger. 'Stop that! Stop saying that!'

Juliet stared at Polly, wide-eyed. 'What does that mean? Does that mean something to you? Like the other day, when—'

Polly said nothing. She looked sick. The planchette skittered across the paper like a horseshoe crab, trailing gibberish.

'Is this enough?' Sally cried bitterly. 'Is this enough? Please!'

The carriage clock on the mantel jumped and rattled.

'Bloody hellfire,' said Seb. 'Did you see that?'

Above us, along the length of the corridor that connected all the bedrooms, we heard something sprint, madly, as a toddler might. We all looked up at the ceiling. When we looked down again, Sally's head was drooping and her whole body sagged as if hypnotised. She was muttering something to herself. Seb, seated next to her, glanced urgently at us, silently asking, *What shall I do? Shall I touch her? What shall I do?*

Sally's head lolled upright. Her fingertips whitened on the planchette, and, with a fierce energy, it shot across the board, slashing words into being.

TIME NOW TIM AND AGAIN TO SHOW YOU ITS TIME

RIP AND RENDE MAKE KNOWNE WHAT BARELY IS AT ALL

THEN OUT TO OUTSIDE STOPTO STOP IN FEAR

WHER A WINDEMILL CHOPS THE SKY SINCE TIME BORROWED

AND BLOODIE HANDS

MISLEADE

MISLEADE

'Slow down,' said Polly. 'We don't understand.'

The planchette see-sawed back and forth. Sally let out a low moan of distress.

'Enough,' I said. Sally moaned again. The planchette scampered across the paper, malicious and gleeful. I wanted to tear Sally's hands away from it, but in that moment, I discovered, I was afraid to touch them.

HAHAH AHAAH HAHAHA

AND OUTE TO OUTE TO WHER STRIPPED BARE AS A TREE IN WYNTER

YOU WIL I WILL

SHOW YOU

RUIN

BUT FIRST

FIRST—

The planchette slashed a long, deliberate dash along the page. Then, in large, precise letters, like a threat:

BUSYNESS

And then the lights fizzed and went out entirely, and we were in the dark.

I heard the others exclaim and shout, heard chairs move and scrape, heard a crash as one fell over.

'Sally!' I shouted.

'Shush!' said Polly loudly. *'Listen!'*

Outside, in the long corridor that ran through the ground floor, there were footsteps. Heavy, creaking steps, pacing without hurry but with definite and deliberate intent.

Someone – Seb, I think – found the door and opened it. Meagre twilight flooded in, and we all made our way gratefully towards it. I heard the hallway light switch click repeatedly.

'Electricity's gone,' said Seb. 'Shit!'

'What's that?' said Juliet.

'What – oh God!'

A fluttering luminescence dancing through the blue twilight, coming from the corridor, moving with something that could only be described as purpose. Silently, we stared ahead of us as the light danced and intensified. Then – a torch beam, shining at us, as we threw arms and fingers up to shield our stinging eyes. And behind the torch, a voice.

'What on *earth* is going on?' said Graham.

43

'Graham,' sobbed Sally. *'Graham!'*

'What's happening?' Graham sounded almost angry. 'Why is the electricity off?'

Sally practically fell into his arms as she burst out crying. 'He's here! Oh, God help us, he's here. We brought him here. He made the lights go out and he— he—'

'We heard – something – running around upstairs,' said Polly. She looked over at me. Her face was chalk-white.

'Good God,' said Graham, transferring his torch to his right hand, the better to put an awkward arm around Sally's shoulders. 'I heard that too. I thought it was one of you.'

'Wait, why didn't we hear you come in?' said Neil. 'Or see you, for that matter? Your headlights would cut across the entire front lawn.'

'I turned them off,' said Graham. 'I saw all the lights were off, apart from a glimmer of light in this room, and surmised you had initiated a session. I didn't want to interrupt things, so I cut my headlights and drove in slowly.'

'Hmmm,' said Neil.

'You're not seriously suggesting I did all this? That I shut off the electricity? You're not really suggesting that? At this point?' Graham shook his head gravely. 'Whatever you heard or saw here wasn't me. I came in, heard you in Tobias's room, heard the footsteps, and then the lights went out. Now I'm going to find the fuse box and get the lights back on. You lot stay here.'

Far above us, the roof thrummed under what was now a heavy rainstorm. Sally sank down limply to the floor of the darkened hallway, and I sat next to her, putting my arm round her. I was annoyed with myself that I hadn't thought to comfort her sooner; that it had fallen to Graham, of all people, to have the presence of mind to wonder how she might feel in all of this.

Further along the corridor, a small flame appeared as Seb flicked open his Zippo lighter. I could discern Polly, Neil and Juliet hovering uncertainly nearby. There was barely any light to see by, but I got the impression that Sally was staring – at everyone else, or the wall, or just the darkness – and thinking.

'I'm – sorry,' I said eventually. 'That seemed – unnecessary.' I couldn't think what else to say.

'He's here,' said Sally quietly, not looking at me. 'He's *here*.'

A clatter of angry footsteps headed towards us out of the darkness. I saw the torch beam flash in agitation.

'Which one of you did this? Was it you, Tim?' I had seen Graham irate before, and I had seen him irked and upset. But I had never seen him enraged. And here he was, absolutely apoplectic, so much so that I felt even his useless electromagnetic field detector might have picked up on it. He looked, by the light of the torch, almost like a different person.

'What?' I said. 'What did I do?'

'*You know damn well!*' shouted Graham.

'Did what?' I said. 'What are you talking about?'

'Come and see,' Graham said. 'If you really had nothing to do with it. Follow me.'

In a crocodile, like children on a school trip, we followed the flickering light of Graham's torch through the corridor. Graham stopped outside his study and held the torch up.

The door was broken, sagging inwards from the middle. A crack ran down the dark woodwork, exposing the yellow wood beneath. It ran from the top all the way down to the lock mechanism, which had erupted from the wood.

Beyond the smashed door, the room was chaotic. Folders and paperwork had been torn apart, shaken, thrown. A heavy typewriter lay face down on the floor, like a gigantic beetle. The desk it had sat on had been upended and thrust against the wall. The shelves had been cleared, as if someone had reached an arm into them and swept all the books and papers out in fury.

'You see?' said Graham. 'This is terrible, wanton destruction. The fuse box has been smashed too.'

'What, so we're stuck in the dark?' said Juliet.

Graham nodded gravely. 'For the time being, yes.'

'Wow.' Seb pushed the broken door thoughtfully. 'Splintered like matchwood. Someone really went at this.'

'Who?' I said.

'I think we know,' said Sally quietly.

We all turned to look at her.

'We've had writing on the walls. How is this any different?'

'No,' said Neil firmly, shaking his head. 'No!'

'Look,' said Polly. 'On the shelf there.'

We looked.

'Those folders are the only things left untouched,' she said. 'T, S, P, N, J. Our initials. Good God. From the séance yesterday.'

We stared for a long, cold moment at the files on the shelf.

'Why do you have files on all of us?' said Juliet quietly.

'Graham and I had to research you all for suitability,' said Sally. 'The experiment is almost over, and then we'll be able to tell you everything about what we're doing here. And we will, I promise.'

'Who's the other P?' said Polly.

'What do you mean?' said Seb, peering at the shelves. 'Oh, yeah.'

I saw it too. Set slightly aside from the others was another folder, marked with the letter 'P'.

'Please!' said Graham. 'It's unfortunate that this has happened, but I don't want it to compromise all we've achieved here. Please tell me you'll just leave this room and its contents alone, until the weekend, when the experiment is done.'

One by one, we agreed.

'Thank you,' said Graham. 'Now, first things first, we need to get the lights back on, then we can have a proper, adult conversation about where we are here. Sally, come and help.'

Seb, Juliet, Neil, Polly and I fumbled our way to the Great Hall, and across its moonlit vastness, to sink down into the three-piece suite gathered loosely in front of the fireplace. Seb fetched the candles from Tobias's room and set them along the hearth. We sat in silence for a couple of minutes, listening to the worsening rain outside hurl itself against the window panes.

'What now?' I said.

'I have no idea,' said Neil.

'I do,' said Seb cheerfully. 'Tim, is there any of your whisky left?'

'A little bit, yeah.' There was about a third of a bottle left from my first evening here.

'Super. And where would that be?'

'In my wardrobe,' I said. 'Under my rucksack.'

'Marvellous. As recent events have sobered me right up, I'm going to spend the rest of the night getting as drunk as circumstances will allow. I'll settle up for the grog tomorrow.'

'Don't you want to wait for Graham?' said Neil. Seb demonstrated what he thought of this suggestion by ignoring it completely. He patted me on the shoulder as he left.

'Thanks a million, old man. Right. I'll see you lot tomorrow.'

He clattered up the stairs.

'Wait for me!' said Juliet. 'I'm not going up there alone. Not after all that. Night, all!' Her footsteps, too, rang out on the main stairwell and subsided into silence.

'Much as I hate to admit it, I think Seb has the right idea,' said Neil. 'Not much to be gained by sitting here in the dark. It makes more sense to talk about all of this in the morning, when Graham's calmed down.'

'Goodnight, Neil,' said Polly. As soon as Neil's footsteps faded, she turned to me. 'Right. You and I need to talk.'

'We do,' I said. 'I think—'

'Shh,' she said, putting a finger to her lips. 'Not here. Come on. We'll go to my room.'

We padded up the stairs. When Polly glanced back to make sure I was following, I saw a glimmer of thoughtful worry in her eyes. The noise of the rain outside was much louder in Polly's room, and I could hear distant thunder.

There was a mirror propped up on a chair, along with some make-up, and Polly cleared this away and gestured for me to sit. As well as the candles we'd brought up, she lit two more candles, which stood in saucers on the mantelpiece. She then closed the door behind us. The ticking of the grandfather clock was a measured, calming pulse over the chaos of the rain outside. Polly sat cross-legged on her bed and looked at me with intense concentration.

'OK. First things first. Do you think Sally and Graham faked all that?'

I shook my head.

'Me neither. That leaves us with two possibilities. One – Sally's bonkers and doesn't know it, and that stuff at the séance was as much of a surprise to her as it was to us, or—'

'There is something here,' I whispered.

'There is something here,' she said gravely.

We both sat, deep in thought.

'Let's look at it a different way,' said Polly at last.

'How?'

'Well, if Tobias Salt never existed, what are we dealing with here?' She continued before I could answer. 'Let's say it's a mass of data, waiting for a correct interpretation. Let's consider this thing as if it's real. Not a con trick or down to subconscious effect or any other bloody thing. Let's say it's real. What do we know about it? Based on what we've seen?'

'It's . . . I don't know. It's intelligent?'

'Yes. It's clever. Good. And what kind of intelligence would you say it was? Based solely on the messages we've received?'

The answer was depressingly plain. 'A malevolent one. Possibly even a violent one, considering what it did to Graham's study.'

Polly blinked, looked up at me. 'You really think that was our ghost?'

'You don't?'

She shrugged. 'We all left the room whilst we were drinking at some point, to smoke or go to the loo or whatnot. Any one of us could have slipped away to the other end of the house for five minutes.'

I considered this. Polly saw my doubtful expression and shook her head. 'Never mind. What else do we know?'

I couldn't think of anything.

'*I'll* tell you,' Polly said angrily. 'He *knows* things.'

'What kind of things?'

'During the last sessions, it wrote the words SWEET FUNNY FACE, remember? That was . . . that was for me. Never mind how, but it relates to something personal to me, something unpleasant. I think it did the same thing to Juliet too, and that's why she was so upset.'

Polly's eyes were wide. 'And it did it to you too, didn't it, Tim? You said a name in there, Abi, was it?'

I felt a slow, cold fear congeal over my skin. A terrible half-formed possibility, becoming more tangible in my mind.

'The question is, *how did it know those things?*'

'Mind-reading?' I said, but it sounded desperate, even to me. Somewhere, I heard Abi's voice talk of Ockham's Razor.

She exhaled. 'You know that quote from Haldane? "*My own suspicion is that the universe is not only queerer than we suppose, but queerer than we can suppose*"?'

I smiled. 'Yes, I've heard that.'

'Well, if this is an intelligent force, maybe it's entirely different to us, more different than we can ever know. Maybe it's *unknowably* different.'

'Meaning?'

'Maybe our poltergeist knows more than we do. About ourselves. Maybe, to him, our lives are laid out like pages in a book. We have to experience the story page by page, in order, but he'd be able to skip to any place he pleased. Imagine the nasty tricks he'd be able to play on us then!'

I found myself thinking about chess pieces – pawns, which must move one plodding space forward at a time; and knights, which can swoop in backwards, forwards and sideways to check other pieces, or remove them from the game altogether. 'All right, if we're getting into the realms of wild speculation—'

'That's what we're here for, Tim.'

'How do you think it found us? Why choose us to make contact with?'

She smiled. 'We're the only ones looking for it.'

'What do you mean?'

She shrugged again. 'Just a half-formed suspicion. But maybe human consciousness is part of it. Maybe it can't exist here without someone bringing it into being in some way.'

'We're . . . imagining it into existence? We've invented it, so it exists?'

'Or we allowed it in.' Polly smiled. 'Wild speculation, Tim.'

'The phrases it used, the ones you say were calculated to upset us – couldn't it all just be a coincidence?' I said.

Again, Polly shrugged. 'And where do coincidences happen, Tim?'

'I don't follow.'

She touched a fingertip to my forehead. 'The same place you feel sorrow, and pain, and rage. And fear. The only place that's real, to you. Maybe we've been giving reality to it. To something that shouldn't exist.'

And in my mind I saw very clearly, then, the illustration of 'Mister S' that had accompanied every single report of Abi's disappearance, eyes burning out of a featureless face. Had something made that face, or chosen it? And then, I heard Janice's voice, telling of the broken house, with the broken people in it. I was suddenly very afraid.

'Tim,' said Polly. 'What is it?'

I wanted to tell her everything. About Abi. About our ghost, and Janice Tupp. About Abi's disappearance, and Janice's death. About Mister S, and first hearing the words 'Mr Salt', and my horror now at that small and terrible coincidence.

And the thought that I alone could attach that meaning to those words, a horrible, pointed, taunting meaning, taking the name of my sister's uncaught killer, utilising it. And how my mind was the only place in the universe such a connection could possibly be made.

I imagined something cruel and callous, in ways no human could be. Something that delighted in misery, in connecting things in our lives that invite madness. Tormenting us, like a child holding a magnifying glass over an ant's nest – not to see what we do, but simply because it can, because such things amuse it. To twist events and influence lives to bring pain and distress, because pain and distress are joyful to it.

I heard my own breathing. It seemed very loud, even louder than the rain. Polly looked up at me, her eyes bright with concern.

'Nothing,' I said eventually. 'It's nothing.'

From the corridor outside, we heard shouts.

44

Neil was, at first, barely recognisable. Even by the dim candlelight, I could see that his nose was bleeding freely and his forehead was cut; one of his eyes was bloodshot and already starting to close. Yet even these things were incidental. The change in him was a more fundamental one. The detached, wry observer had fled, and been replaced by a creature of anger and fear, both of equal strength.

'Get off me!' he sobbed, but his teeth were bared in a snarl.

'What the hell's going on?' said Polly. 'Seb, stop it!'

Neil thudded into the gallery wall and slid along it in retreat, but Seb was on him, punching him again and again, all expert blows, all to the head and face. Neil whined, and Seb grabbed him by the throat.

'Jesus, Seb!' I said. 'Let go of him! What's got into you?'

'Ask *him*!' roared Seb. 'He knows what he's done!'

'I've done NOTHING!' howled Neil. 'Get off me!'

'Really, Audle? Nothing?' Seb held up two crumpled sheets of paper, covered in neat, precise handwriting. 'You did *nothing*, did you?'

'Please!' begged Neil 'I don't know what you're talking about.'

'Really, seriously,' said Polly. 'Get off him, Seb. You're hurting him.'

Seb growled in frustration and smoothed out the pages with one hand whilst pinning Neil to the wall by his collar with the other. He read from the pages, with barely contained fury. *'Neil told me of his connection to Juliet, and that they had been friends for years, long before she met Sebastian. He said they shared everything, including many secrets that Sebastian was unaware of.'*

'So?' said Neil. 'That can't be a surprise! Jules is my friend.'

'Don't say her name,' Seb said murderously. 'Don't you *fucking dare!*'

I saw Polly flinch, as I'm sure I did. That word had power, back then. It was seldom used. If it was heard on television, even late at night, there would be complaints. If you saw it in a book, you'd stare at the word for a while, unable to believe it had been typeset and printed somewhere. Back then, that word could silence a room, or draw a sharp intake of breath, as if one had been punched. It indicated, very clearly, that a situation was not normal.

'What is that?' I asked, looking at the crumpled sheets of foolscap in Seb's hand. 'Is that from Graham's study? How did you get hold of it?'

'Someone shoved it under my door,' said Seb. 'Nothing else, just these two pages from Neil's file. I *knew* she'd gone away with someone that weekend, Audle. I bloody *knew*. I just would never in a million years have guessed it would be with *you*.'

'It wasn't what you think,' said Neil. 'It wasn't anything!'

Seb read from the pages again. *'Sebastian is entirely unaware that Neil and Juliet spent a weekend together, nor why, although if he were forced to think about it, the answer would be obvious.'*

'Wait,' said Polly. 'You say somebody shoved these pages under your door?' She shot me a concerned look.

'It's not—' Neil began.

Seb punched him in the stomach, hard. Neil issued an awful gasp of shock and pain and crumpled to the floor. Polly grabbed Seb's arm and pulled at him; this simple action made me remember that I also was not just a spectator, but could act. I grabbed Seb's other arm as he wrestled with Polly.

'Easy,' I said. 'Come on. We can talk about this.'

'I don't want to talk about it!' said Seb.

'It – was – not—' wheezed Neil from the floor.

Seb kicked Neil in the stomach.

'You – don't – know,' gasped Neil. Seb kicked him again.

'For God's sake!' said Polly, wrenching Seb's face around so that he was looking directly at her. 'Stop hurting him!'

'What is the meaning of this?' said Graham, from the stairwell. Behind him, Sally stared open-mouthed in horror.

'Seb's lost his mind,' said Polly. 'He attacked Neil, and—'

'Stay out of it,' Seb hissed. 'It's none of your business.' He pushed against me and I almost fell over.

'Are those . . . my notes?' said Graham, as if that were the most pressing thing to notice about this situation.

'What's got into him?' shouted Sally. 'Neil, are you all right?'

'I've – done – nothing wrong!' said Neil, scraping himself up into a sitting position. He seemed to have regained control of himself. His face had lost the furious, animalistic cast it had assumed earlier.

'Shut up, Audle. Just *shut up.*'

'Those *are* my notes,' said Graham quietly. 'How did he get hold of my notes?'

Neil looked up at Seb with defiance, meeting his gaze head on. Sometime later, I would wonder at just how brave and extraordinary this small gesture was.

'You're an idiot, Seb. A clumsy, loud-mouthed idiot, who damages everything around him, without even noticing.'

Under my hands, I felt every muscle in Seb's enormous frame tense. I was familiar with this kind of explosive anger, and I knew what was coming. Seb inhaled slowly and carefully, making a series of noises that were not words.

I believe he might even have killed Neil then, either accidentally or on purpose, or simply without thought of any kind. Behind him, however, a door opened.

'Christ!' Juliet looked pale and sick. She had clearly been asleep. 'Seb, leave Neil alone.'

Seb lurched and swayed, wracked by indecision.

'*Seb!*' barked Juliet. At the sound of her voice, I felt all resolve leave him.

'Explain to me,' she said crisply, 'why you're hurting Neil?'

'You tell me,' said Seb, although there was doubt in his voice now. 'You're the one who spent a dirty weekend with him, behind my back.'

Juliet sighed wearily.

'Was it worth it, Jules? Was *he* worth it? Bloody *Neil*, of all people?'

'Oh, shut up, Seb,' said Juliet. 'Stop being an idiot. As if anything like that would happen between us. Neil is my friend. You've never quite got that, have you? He's my *friend.*'

'Then why did you sneak off with him, without telling me?'

'Does it matter?'

'Of course it matters.'

Juliet's face became taut.

'Come here,' she said. 'The rest of you, please give us some peace.'

Seb lumbered dumbly over to Juliet and she took his hand, leading him into their room. She paused for a second to address us.

'Please look after Neil.' She slammed the door.

Slowly, carefully, Polly and I picked Neil up from the floor and slung his arms over our shoulders. Down the stairs we went, with Graham and Sally in tow, Neil between us, sagging and stumbling on legs made useless with shock and sour adrenalin.

Down we went, each one of us noticing, and reading, the words freshly scrawled on the wall, but not one of us acknowledging them or passing comment. Words which danced merrily in the flickering candlelight as we went by:

HAHAH AHAAH HAHAHA

45

Time was running out, and the walls of Yarlings seemed closer, the corridors narrower and smaller than they ever had before. Our time here was up, although we couldn't know it, and these were to be the last hours we spent there. Polly and I led Neil down the long corridor to the kitchen, with Graham and Sally following.

'Can't we try and get the lights on?' Polly asked.

'The fuse box is completely smashed,' said Graham. 'Whoever destroyed it was very thorough.' Again, he glanced at me.

'I don't think my nose is broken,' said Neil, in a detached way, as if this information didn't have any direct bearing on him.

'I have to check something,' Graham said thoughtfully. 'Sally, could you come with me?' She nodded, and they disappeared in the direction of Graham's study.

'I don't think my nose is broken,' Neil said again, as we steered him down the corridor. He lurched as if the house were an ocean liner in rough seas. 'It's just bleeding a lot.'

We sat him down at the kitchen table. Polly brought him a glass of water, and he took it with trembling hands.

'I didn't do anything wrong,' he said. He touched his nose experimentally. 'Ow!'

'Just leave it,' I said.

'I don't think it's broken or anything,' he said again. 'It's just bleeding a lot.'

'You just said that.'

'He's in shock,' said Polly. 'I mean, I think we all are, a bit. Drink your water, Neil darling.'

'I did nothing wrong,' said Neil. 'Excuse me.'

He got up, walked over to the sink and casually vomited into it.

'Oh Lord,' said Polly.

'God, it's *purple*,' said Neil, peering into the sink. 'Oh yes. We drank wine, didn't we?' He sat down and prodded his nose again.

'I did nothing wrong, you know.'

Polly smiled. 'We know that, Neil.'

'Actually,' he said, raising an index finger, 'I *did* do something wrong. I keyed Seb's stupid car, that time. But only because I was angry with him. Wanted to see how *he'd* like it if something he really cared about got damaged, thoughtlessly.' He stared intently into the grain of the wooden table as if trying to see his fate in the pattern.

'He didn't understand. I was the only one who could help her. The only one she could talk to. Do *you* understand?'

'We don't, Neil. I'm sorry.'

'Ah well.' He looked up at the ceiling. 'Doesn't matter. That weekend, I was the only one who could help. The only one she could turn to. Everyone else would have blamed her.'

'Neil, we don't—'

'And she couldn't have told Seb because he wouldn't have let her.'

He exhaled heavily. I wondered if he had forgotten we were there.

'So she came to me. She always comes to me.'

He prodded his finger on the tabletop, as if establishing a fixed point in a world of shifting variables. 'She will *always* come to me.'

I was heading back upstairs when I heard the sob. Just one, but agonised. I stood in the darkened stairwell, unmoving, trying to detect the source of the sound. As the shadows of numerous candles flickered, it felt as if the noise were coming from all directions, as if the house itself were weeping. And then there came a pause, and the gasps of someone trying to keep the noise under control, and then the unmistakeable click and fizz of a Zippo lighter, and I knew who it was. At the half-open door of Seb and Juliet's room, I paused, in an agony of indecision about whether to knock or simply to go in, but he must have seen or sensed me anyway.

'Piss off, Comprehensive,' said Seb. He sounded wounded and tired.

I opened the door. He was alone.

'Are you OK?'

Only one candle burned on a bedside table, but I could see that his eyes were bloodshot.

'No, I am not OK.'

'I'm sure that whatever it is, it's not as bad as all that.'

'Ha!' He took a long, thoughtful drag on his cigarette. 'It's not fine, Tim. And it's never going to be fine. Still, it's my own bloody fault.'

'What is?'

'Do you know what a mortal sin is, Tim?'

'I'm not sure I do.'

'Well, God knows I do.'

His eyes sparkled wetly, and his face contorted. He looked away from me.

'Seb—'

'That weekend she spent away with Neil. He was right. It wasn't – what I thought it was.'

He bit a knuckle, hard.

'I mean, I didn't really think it was, not really. But what else could it have been? I couldn't think. Well, now I know.'

And then he sobbed again, his head in his hands.

'Seb,' I said. 'Seb—'

He looked up, wiped his eyes roughly and breathed in. 'I'm leaving.'

'Don't be daft,' I said. 'Have you seen the weather outside?'

'Doesn't matter,' he sniffed. 'I can't stay here.'

'What about Juliet?'

'What about her?'

'What's she going to do?'

'Not my problem.' He got to his feet. 'Not now.' The deep inhalation again. He was transforming before my eyes. Something was closing down inside him, here and now, for the rest of his life. He was choking down his vulnerabilities, consciously changing into a different, perhaps reduced, person.

He wiped a tear away slowly, as if the action were already entirely alien to him, looking in puzzlement at the wetness on his fingertips. He was already forgetting what it was like to feel like this, to let things get the better of him. I knew in that moment that he would never speak about this again, and part of him would now for ever be unknown, to himself and the rest of the world.

*

The Great Hall was briefly illuminated by a thin sliver of moon, cutting through the rainclouds. Several black shapes moved against the dresser, and I saw that they were Sally and Juliet, hunting for candles and matches. Neil sat nearby, in an armchair. Both he and Juliet froze when they saw Seb. Sally, oblivious, continued searching, until, triumphantly, she held some candles and a box of matches aloft.

'I told you there were—' She stopped abruptly as she saw Seb. 'Oh.'

'Seb,' said Juliet.

'Don't talk to me. I just want to get my keys and leave.'

'At least let me explain.'

'Let her explain,' said Neil.

'You,' said Seb icily, 'can shut up.'

'Neil, please,' said Juliet. 'Seb, listen—'

'No.' Seb cut her off. 'I'm leaving. Just give me my keys.'

'At least stay until we get the power back on!' Juliet pleaded.

'I told you earlier,' said Graham, appearing out of nowhere, as usual. 'The fuse box is all smashed up. Like my study. It's nothing I can fix. The power's not coming back until we get an electrician up here.'

'But who would smash it up like that?' said Sally.

'*You,*' said Polly. She marched into the Great Hall, a candle held aloft. Her voice was cold with fury. '*You!*'

She rounded on Graham.

'Polly, what's happening? What are you doing?'

'You! You . . . *shit*!'

'What are you talking about?' Graham's voice was a strangled croak.

Polly held up something so that Graham could see it, so that all of us could see it. It was the folder from Graham's study, the one marked *P*. Even in the dim light, I saw Graham's alarm and shock.

'I told you *explicitly* not to—'

'This *thing*,' said Polly. 'All the details of your little experiment here. I was wondering why you hadn't wanted to share it with us.'

'Polly, please. Give that to me.'

'No, really,' I said. 'We'd all like to hear it.'

'Yes,' said Seb. 'I believe we would.'

Polly opened the file and brought her candle close to the pages.

'Initial proposal, submitted January, 1973. The experiment – to produce PK phenomena and other effects associated with ghosts – has already been successfully attempted by a group in Canada, during the so-called "Philip sessions", where a discarnate entity appeared to manifest itself to the sitters, despite them knowing that Philip's back-story was entirely bogus and had, in fact, been made up by the researchers themselves. In essence, the group "made a ghost".

'The sitters in that group were all level-headed adult individuals. It is my contention, therefore, that the experiment can be replicated – and to far greater effect – by a specially selected group, all of whom suffer from some form of emotional disturbance, or whose lives are marked by trauma, tragedy, secretive behaviour, or emotional issues relating to control or anger.

'Furthermore, I propose the participants be adolescents, hand-picked by myself and my co-researcher, as teenagers are frequently the epicentre of poltergeist activity. If one disturbed teenager can produce violent PK effects, then a group of similar individuals should be able to produce much more dramatic instances of observable paranormal phenomena. They should also be kept ignorant of the fabricated history of the entity.

'The ideal location for this experiment would be a house with no history of paranormal manifestation, but which nonetheless appears objectively foreboding in aspect, and ideally should be of considerable age.

Research proposal signed Graham K. Shaw, 23 January 1973.'

For a few moments, the only sound was the rain, battering the window panes, and the distant growl of thunder.

'You chose us,' said Juliet carefully, 'because we were *broken?*'

'That's – not fair,' said Graham.

'It sounds exactly like what happened,' said Seb, without a hint of friendliness.

'So, those files on us,' said Juliet. 'You chose us because you . . . *knew* things about us?'

'That wasn't the only criterion!' said Graham. 'You're all also highly intelligent, you have above average exam grades . . .' His voice trailed away pathetically in the darkness.

'Did you know about me?' said Juliet. 'About what I . . . did?'

'No! I promise. Not at first. I just knew that the three of you were emotionally . . . linked. In a complex way. And there were anger issues. As has been manifestly proved.'

'And you knew about Abi,' I said.

'Sorry, Abi?' said Graham.

'My sister!' I howled furiously.

'And . . . Stephen?' said Polly. 'You knew about Stephen? About what he did?'

Graham looked at the floor.

'So anything paranormal here was just . . .' For once, Neil fumbled for the right words. 'Just . . . us working ourselves up into a state?'

'No!' said Sally. 'That's just it. The very first session, with the knocking, and the voice on the tape . . . those were . . . real.'

'Delusions,' said Neil. 'We were tricking ourselves.'

'No.' Sally shook her head. 'That's just it. That's the whole point.'

'So you didn't fake anything that went on here?'

Sally took a deep breath. 'The crash upstairs. The first session after Tim came back—'.

'I knew it!' said Neil triumphantly.

'It was just to get started!' said Sally. 'Once you believed things were possible, they *became* possible! The chairs tipping over afterward – that wasn't us!'

'What about the footsteps?' said Juliet. 'When Tim was away?'

'Ah. That . . . that was me,' Graham said sheepishly.

'The actual physical manifestations?' I asked. 'The writing on the walls? Who did that?'

No one spoke.

'And my study door?' said Graham. 'Who smashed that in?'

No one spoke.

'What about the fuse box?'

Nobody.

'Putting those bloody pages under our door?' said Seb.

Nobody spoke.

Upstairs, a crash, as if a heavy piece of furniture had fallen. We all looked at each other.

Upstairs, the sound of creaking, as if something heavy were testing the floorboards, one at a time.

'I can't stay here,' said Seb. 'I have to go.'

'Seb,' said Juliet, as he marched across the hallway. 'Seb, please! We have to talk!'

'No,' he said coldly. 'We don't.'

'Please, Seb!' She sobbed. 'After everything! You can't just leave!'

'You made that decision a long time ago,' said Seb. 'When you acted for both of us. I'm going now.'

'Where?'

'London. Back to Mum and Dad's.'

'Please!' She grabbed at him. Slowly and carefully, he removed her hands and kept walking. She followed him out into the corridor. I heard the enormous front door open and close, and, presently, the sound of a car engine. White headlights flared across the front windows, and I heard Seb's Stag circle the gravel approach, and accelerate angrily along the B-road. The sound of the Stag's engine was swallowed up by the storm.

'He left,' Juliet breathed. 'He's gone.' She stared at the front door as if it would re-open at any minute.

'I know, Juliet,' I said. 'I'm sorry.'

'I'm leaving too.'

'What? How?'

'I can call a cab to the station. There's still one more train to London. Neil will come with me.'

'Don't leave,' I said. 'At least wait until tomorrow.'

'I'm not staying in this house.'

'Just until morning,' I said. 'Things will seem better then, I promise.'

She smiled sadly. 'Tim, do you remember what Mr Salt said? During the session the other day, the one that upset me so much?'

'He said some names. Luke and . . . Lucy?'

'No,' she said, shaking her head. 'Luke. And then, Lucy. That's what it said. Luke. And *then* Lucy.'

'I don't follow.'

'That's what I would have called it,' she said. She suddenly looked much older than she was, like someone with a long lifetime behind her. She choked back a sob.

'Luke if it was a boy. Lucy if it was a girl. I never told anybody that. Not Seb, not Neil, not anybody. Not a living soul.'

We found our way back to the hall. Polly stood before Graham, her arms folded.

'I'm leaving too,' she said, when Juliet informed her of her decision. 'I'm done with all of this. With being lied to, being used as a guinea pig. It's gone far enough. You've lost control of this whole situation, and you don't even know how.'

'I can't stop you leaving,' Graham said coldly.

'No, you can't. You also can't stop me from writing to the people who've funded this misadventure either, the Psychical Institute or whatever they call themselves. I wonder how much they know about all this.'

Even by candlelight, I could see that Graham's face had paled. 'I would advise you not to do that, Polly. They'll only be interested in facts, not one person's interpretation of—'

Polly was gone, headed upstairs. I followed her.

'You're really going?'

Polly looked up momentarily from throwing her belongings into a suitcase. 'Of course I am!' She sighed heavily and gathered her woollen cardigan about her. There were no tears in her eyes when she looked at me, and her expression was calm and rational.

'Come with us, Tim. Please. Come back with Neil and Juliet and me. We can get the last London train and all go home together.'

'I'm sorry,' I said. 'I can't leave the others.'

'Oh Christ, Sally? I wouldn't worry about her, Tim. I think she'll be just fine.'

'Nonetheless.'

'But it will *hurt* you, Tim. Don't you understand? Whatever's in this house now, that's attached itself to us. It will take you somewhere you don't want to be.'

'I'm sorry,' I repeated. 'I'm staying.'

'Tim,' Polly's eyes were wide and earnest, 'this thing is *real*. And it will *hurt* you. Just like it hurt Juliet, and Seb, and Neil. And me, for that matter. Do you understand? It's been playing with us for days, sounding us out – getting to know us – and now it's grown strong. We've been strengthening it. Do you understand that?'

I folded my arms defensively.

'Well then,' she smiled sadly. 'Good luck.' Unconsciously, she pushed the sleeve of her cardigan up her left forearm. I glimpsed – briefly, in the candlelight – a thicket of lines, of scars, deep and red, like stripes of melted wax, before she pulled her sleeve down again.

'Er—' I remembered her earlier request to keep in touch after all this was over. 'Do you still want my address and phone number and stuff?'

She glanced over at me as she buckled her suitcase and smiled mirthlessly. 'Thanks, Tim, but I'm fine.'

Fifteen minutes later, Neil, Juliet and Polly were packed and ready to leave. They sat in the hallway in their outdoor coats and shoes, their luggage around them, like evacuees. No one was willing to talk. The storm outside had worsened, and the panes reverberated constantly with driving rain, which seemed to come at the windows in spiteful handfuls.

Graham stood in front of Neil and Juliet, wringing his hands. I was reminded of a supply teacher, one who couldn't control the pupils he had been left with.

'You're sure about this?' Graham said.

Juliet stared up at him.

'Absolutely,' she said.

'And you, Neil?'

Neil nodded immediately, as I knew he would. The panelling of the hallway was briefly franked by the rain-refracted headlights of a cab arriving outside. Juliet stood up. We all trooped out to the hallway, carrying various bags.

'It's horrible out there,' said Sally. 'Please stay. See how you feel in the morning.'

'Goodbye, Sally,' said Juliet. 'Goodbye, all of you.'

'Goodbye,' said Polly, and smiled briefly at me. 'Be careful.' I hugged Juliet and endured one of Neil's reptilian handshakes.

'You know this breaks the contractual terms of the experiment,' Graham said pompously.

'Goodbye, Graham,' Polly said curtly, then turned on her heel and marched out into the rain.

'Goodbye, everyone,' said Neil, before running after Juliet. As he always had. As he always would.

The tail lights of the car, glowing like embers in the filthy night, dropped onto the B-road, and were visible no more. I stared after them for a while, thinking, and then closed the heavy front door with a thud.

46

'What now?'

Back in his ruined study, Graham was still piecing together torn-up papers by candlelight, as if the whole endeavour might still at this point be put back together. I was beyond furious with him.

He looked up at me briefly, but said nothing.

'What happens now?'

Graham didn't look at me as he answered. 'You need to go to bed, Tim.'

'What?'

'We all do. It's been a long, trying day, and we all need to keep our focus up, if we're going to recover anything at all from this.'

'We're just going to pretend nothing's happened? The experiment's over, Graham! Everyone's gone!'

'On the contrary, Tim. Admittedly, there have been considerable setbacks—'

'Oh really? Like the fact that all your hand-picked victims have staged a mass walk-out?'

'If you're going to be childish, Tim, this isn't a conversation worth having.'

I could feel the rage coursing through me. I wondered how long it would be before I hit him. I took a couple of deep breaths, tried to calm myself.

'How can you—' I began.

And then, from somewhere deep inside the house, Sally was screaming.

We found her in Tobias's room. She was curled up, sobbing, her hands covering her face.

'Sally!'

'I saw it,' she said hoarsely, her eyes staring through us. 'I *saw* it!'

'Where?'

She pointed upwards.

'It was *walking*,' she gasped, her voice hoarse. 'Along the *wall*.'

'Which wall?'

'Walking and laughing. Singing. Humming. Like a lunatic. As if it were the most natural thing in the world. For as long as I watched it.'

She looked as if she might be sick. I put an awkward arm around her.

'*Saying my name*,' she whispered.

'We have to leave,' I said. 'Whatever point you were trying to prove about group delusion or gestalt therapy or whatever else, you can pick out of your surviving notes, Graham. We have to pack up and leave.'

'Tim's right,' Sally whimpered.

'We can't leave!' said Graham. There was something in his voice that was almost panic. 'Not now! Think of all the work we've done here! Work of real value! We can't stop now, not when we've reached the Apparition Phase. We have to go on!'

Sally's stare burned into him.

'My career rests on this,' said Graham, abstractedly. 'I can't go back.'

From upstairs, a fresh thud, like a heavy piece of furniture being moved. Sally moaned.

'I *won't*!' said Graham. He looked up defiantly at the source of the noise.

Thud.

'Graham!' yelled Sally, her voice close to breaking point. 'Please!'

Thud. Maybe something had come loose in the rain, I thought. Some giant tree branch, which was now banging mindlessly against the side of the house. Maybe.

Thud.

'I won't go!'

Thud. Like a great heartbeat now, regular and strong. Thud. Thud. Thud.

'GRAHAM!'

Graham took off his glasses and cleaned them, very slowly and deliberately.

'All right then,' he said at length. 'We'll go back to my place near the College for a day or two and regroup. I will talk to the fellows at the Institute, try and salvage something from this mess. You clear out your room, and Sally and I will clear out our rooms and the study.'

'The study?' Sally spat incredulously. 'That'll take ages! We need to leave now!'

'I'm not leaving without my findings,' said Graham. 'We have to salvage something.'

'You can come back for them. I'm not staying here a moment longer.'

'No, look, Sally—'

'YOU DIDN'T SEE IT!' shouted Sally. A reply died on Graham's lips.

'You didn't see it.'

Whatever I felt about leaving Yarlings, there was nothing but relief at abandoning my bleak little room. I had brought very little with me to the house, and it didn't take long to gather it all up and throw it into my rucksack. I was fiddling with the straps when I happened to glance up at the bed.

I froze.

There, on the pillow, as if placed there deliberately, I saw the awful face that was no-face, staring out of the photograph that Abi and I had taken, a lifetime ago. The photograph I had found with the notebook as I had fled home.

I supposed it was just about plausible that Seb had found it, that it had fallen out of the notebook whilst he was searching for the whisky in my bag earlier. It was just about plausible that he had thought it amusing to place such a thing on my pillow, to scare me. Just about.

The skin of my arm, goosebumped by a feeling I didn't want to examine too closely, felt both too hot and too cold as I reached for the picture.

I snatched it up and stuffed it into my bag.

Sally was too distressed to drive, and I couldn't, so the decision was taken to simply load everything into Graham's car, leaving Sally's in the driveway, to be collected later. After clearing out our rooms, Graham and I set about removing the heavy technical and recording equipment from Tobias Salt's room together, as Sally refused to go back in there. We exchanged only a few necessary words as we did this. Once the equipment was loaded into the boot, we bundled our own bags into the car. The rain continued, unrelenting. As Graham padlocked the front door, and Sally sat in the front passenger seat, staring straight ahead, I looked up at the dead black windows of Yarlings, and thought how empty and utterly devoid of life the place looked, almost as if it had been empty for years. The evening had begun – months ago, it seemed – with a group of happy young people drinking and laughing and sharing stories. And now, it was past midnight, and the place was abandoned. Graham jogged over to the car, and we both got in. Yarlings shimmered briefly in the silver light of the car's headlamps, then we turned away down the gravel drive and out onto the tree-lined road outside.

We passed through the village, but the place was so dark and the rain so heavy I could barely make out individual buildings, let alone see familiar landmarks like Hattie Wells's shop. Soon, all signs of human habitation dropped away and the fields opened up, vast and uniform, as the sky rumbled. We passed the station, closed for the night, the final local landmark I recognised. The car wound along the web of B-roads, as the roof thundered incessantly and the wipers squeaked across the windscreen.

'Sally,' I said, at length. She glanced back at me.

'Are you OK?'

She gave a small, barely perceptible nod.

Then silence fell again, for half an hour or so.

I got the strong impression that Graham was lost. He was increasingly hesitant when turning corners, and on two occasions almost committed to a right turn before thinking better of it and heading left. Whenever the headlights picked out a signpost, he would lean forward and squint at it, then sit back with a tangible air of defeat.

'Are we lost?' I said, after the fifth or sixth time that Graham had done this. Graham ignored me.

'I said—'

'I heard you, Tim. No, we're not lost.'

'You just don't know where we are. Well, at least you're consistent, Graham.'

Graham snorted. 'Tim, I know you're upset. But there's no need to take that tone.' The paternalistic, teacherly edge was back in his voice.

I didn't answer.

'Besides,' Graham added, 'it hasn't all been a waste of time. In fact, I'd very much like to ask you some questions about your experiences at Yarlings.'

'No thanks,' I said. 'In fact, after tomorrow morning, I doubt you'll ever see me again, Graham. Sorry.'

'Oh.' Graham sounded genuinely sad. 'Well, Sally and I will be very disappointed not to have your contribution.'

'Oh, Sally and I will see each other again,' I said. 'Won't we, Sally?'

Sally's head sank onto her chest. Graham snorted again. 'I think you'll find it very difficult to see Sally without seeing *me*, Tim.'

And then I saw. The thing that had been staring me in the face all along. Graham and Sally were together. They were a couple. Whatever had taken place between her and me was a diversion, a distraction, without meaning or weight. Sometimes, facts that are obvious have to scream at the top of their voice to be heard, to be noticed. Polly had seen it, a long time ago, and had tried to warn me.

'You're with . . . Graham?' I shouted. 'Bloody *Graham*?'

'Tim—' Sally began.

'But we – at Rollright, I mean – we—'

Graham turned to look at Sally. 'What?' He sounded exasperated more than anything. *'Again?'*

'What do you mean, *again*?' I gasped. 'Stop the car.'

'Now, Tim—' Graham began.

'Stop the fucking car,' I said.

Graham pulled over at the side of the road. The car was filled with a hot, tense silence, as if the storm were about to erupt in here too. The rain thundered over the roof and the bonnet, an inexorable noise that spoke not of intention or purpose, but just blind, dumb circumstance, human beings and their schemes and plans running up against this filthy rat-black night, and its endless downpour. The wipers continued to squeal and labour at the windscreen, the headlights beyond barely cutting through the rain, just showing pools of descending white sparks that fell and fell relentlessly.

I felt – or imagined I felt – Sally's mood, as she sat, her back to me, her shoulders clenched tight. I was furious at that moment, more angry than I think I have ever been, before or since.

'Tim,' she said, without turning to look at me. 'Please let me—'

'Shut up. Both of you.'

Graham turned round, an elbow hanging over the driver's seat. I wanted desperately to smash his face in.

'I know you're upset, Tim . . .'

That was all it took. Turning from him, I shoved the door handle downwards and kicked the door open, jumping out onto the grass verge of an empty country road.

'Tim!' shouted Graham. 'You can't get out here! It's the middle of absolutely bloody—'

I slammed the car door, and threw my rucksack over my shoulder. The rain was even heavier than I had anticipated, but I walked on. The car crawled alongside me for a short while. I heard Sally calling my name, appealing to me to get back in. I got the impression she was crying, but I didn't want to look at her, didn't want to look at either of them. The car continued to keep pace with me as I stumbled along the verge. The rain plastered my hair to my head, to my ears, ran down my back. I shoved my hands deep into my jacket and kept on walking.

Graham's voice, then, shouting. 'Stop being a bloody idiot and get back in the car!' He sounded furious, for once. *Good*, I thought.

'Go to hell, Graham,' I muttered into the downpour. Ahead of us, the headlights picked out something from the hedgerow. A wooden sign, blackened by mould. I saw the words PUBLIC FOOTPATH, the sign pointing into a much-overgrown gap in the hedge. From some distant, dry place, I watched myself slink away from the road and down the muddy pathway.

'Jesus Christ!' I heard Graham say. His voice sounded even more annoying when he was angry. I heard a car door open, and kept walking.

The overgrown hedge obscured a dark wooden stile, glistening in the rain. I felt Graham's hand on my shoulder but slapped it away and climbed the stile, taking care not to undermine the gravity of my departure by slipping and falling.

My eyes adjusted to reveal a muddy path curving away into blackness, between a dark pine wood and a field of waist-high wheat, almost ready for harvest. A wire fence, recently erected, delineated the border between the path and the pine trees. Without thinking, I set off, marching along the path. The mud squelched and oozed underfoot. Within seconds, my socks were wet.

'Tim!' shouted Graham, although his voice was growing fainter. He had not climbed the stile. 'Oh, bloody hell! TIM!'

Rather than anger, Graham's voice contained an exasperation I had heard many times in my short life, from youth leaders, supply teachers, school counsellors – the universal whine of the weak adult who has failed to control young people in his care, and blames them for the chaos he now finds himself surrounded by. I realised that I despised him. I hated both of them. I had a very clear mental image of me walking back and calmly bashing Graham's head in with a rock.

Instead, and with some effort, I forced myself to keep walking, although the darkness quickly became so total I had to feel my way along the wire fence with my right hand. I heard distant voices, but they became quieter and less important, until the booming sky and the seething rain covered them up. About a minute later, I heard the sound of a car engine, then that too melted away, and then there was only the restless sky and the endless rain.

They had left me. True, that was what I had wanted, but I had also wanted them to plunge after me, regardless of the night and the rain, to demonstrate that I was worth enough, to both of them and in the grand scheme of things, not to be left here in this godforsaken place.

It occurred to me for the first time that I was not of sound mind, and hadn't been for a long time. My decisions should not be respected, especially not this one. I should not have been allowed to walk away from the car. I should not have been allowed anywhere near Sally. I should not have been allowed anywhere near Yarlings, or Graham, and his experiment. Mr Henshaw had been right all along and had tried to make me see.

I stumbled off into the torrential rain.

47

The fence gave way to a trail that ran into the pine woods, where it was quickly swallowed by darkness. Wrapped up in my anger, I walked perhaps a hundred feet along the trail, the soft, damp carpet of needles beneath my feet. It was silent in the pines. Stupidly, I spun on the spot, turning back round to see that the trail had vanished, and then I no longer knew which direction was forward and which back. I picked a direction and kept walking. The pine trees closed over my head, obscuring even the frail light of the storm, but the spongy floor of the forest was even and I didn't stumble. I walked on, feeling my way from tree to tree in what I hoped was a straight line.

Overhead, the sky cracked. I almost fell over the half-buried spine of a drystone wall, glowing green-white in the scant light. My eyes were adjusting to the almost complete darkness.

Lightning ticked overhead, and some distance away I saw a line of brilliant white where the trees gave way to open ground. It was up a steep incline, and, with only the after-image of the treeline dancing in my vision to guide me, I tripped and cursed up the slope. The trees ended abruptly, and I found it difficult to shake the idea I had just risen from the depths of a dark sea, to finally break the surface. Where the forest stopped, a field of rapeseed sloped downwards. There was no hint of a path. The clouds flared with trapped charge once more and I saw that the field terminated in a hedge, or a fence.

Keeping to the treeline, I made my way along the upper edge of the field. The mud was thick, with the consistency of wet cement, and the soles of my shoes grew heavy and uneven. And still, I wasn't afraid. I believed that at the foot of the hill, there would be a village, or a road. A way out, of some kind. And if not this field, then the field afterward, or, at most, the field after that.

I stumbled downwards along the border of the field, where the rapeseed gave way to a thin line of grass. The mud was treacherous, and I almost lost my balance every few steps, reaching out to flail at thin air, but I remained on my feet. The rain, which seemed to have briefly thinned to almost nothing, now began to fall heavily again. I half-fell into the bottom edge of the field, which turned out to be a tall chain-link fence with concrete posts, over and through which brambles, haw-thorn and ivy grew. I couldn't see clearly through the fence, but what was beyond looked dark, and long, and straight. I assumed it was a road. The fence extended as far as I could make out in either direction; I would have to climb it.

I threw my knapsack over first, then put the toe of one shoe into one of the diamond-shaped gaps in the wire mesh. My shoe, greased with mud, slid out of the fence again almost immediately, and I had to pause to wipe as much mud off my shoes as I could before trying again. I scaled the fence slowly and cautiously, my legs twitching and wobbling unreliably after my slog through the field. I swung over the top and dropped down the other side, almost oblivious to what might be there.

The drop was further than I anticipated and one of my knees gave under me, driving itself painfully into the bed of stones that formed the floor of this place.

It was a railway cutting. Two sets of rails, side by side, curving away over the hard, glistening stones into black nothingness in either direction. Grabbing my knapsack, I retreated to the shadow of the fence I had just climbed, driving my back into it, and clutching my knee. The rain was a wall of water, and anything more than ten feet away from me was lost to sight. I got to my feet and picked my way carefully across the first set of tracks, my eyes and ears straining for any sign of a train. If one came, it would be here practically before I was aware of it; I would have to throw myself clear. And still I was calm. Still, I resisted seeing my situation for what it was.

I looked up, for the first time, at the opposite side of the tracks, and saw. A bank of dark purple brick, at least ten feet high, entirely smooth apart from a few tufts of weeds, with no hand- or foot-holds to be seen.

I began to walk quickly along the slick, dark sleepers, then broke into a jog. I was aware of a tenseness that seemed to thicken the very air. Far above, the sky rumbled and laughed.

Something made itself known, or I became aware of the noise of it; a whisper of a sound, at the very edge of the perceivable. Stupidly, I froze, cocked my head to listen. The sound grew, slowly but purposefully, and I listened and listened until the whooshing gathered and grew and the sound became unmistakeable.

And then, all reason left me. In blind panic, I ran along the tracks, suddenly and completely aware of the realness of the situation. The noise grew and grew, rattling around the cutting, multiplying, coming from all directions at once, with no way of knowing which was genuine. I ran like an animal, with no thoughts in my head, just the terror of the present moment.

At first I thought it was just shadow, but a second rain-soaked glance revealed it: an ancient iron ladder, set into a shallow vertical recess in the brick. Without thought, I leapt for it, grabbing the rusted metalwork, crushing myself into the dark space as, inches behind me, the blare and roar of a train flooded by. Noise and light, noise and light, and I pressed my face into the wet brick and gasped. The whooshing continued, so very close to my head, tugging at me, threatening to pull me from the ladder and churn me to pieces under the wheels. Noise and light, noise and light, and the final blast of a horn like the cry of some biblical monster.

And then silence, arriving instantly, as if a curtain had fallen, and it was impossible to believe the train had ever been there.

I forced my hands to uncurl, to loosen their grip on the iron rungs, and lifted my sodden shoes up rung by rung until I reached the ledge created by the top of the brick bank. The rain was, impossibly, coming down even harder now, and when I held my hands up to climb another chain-link fence, the raindrops bubbled over them like hot fat.

I hoisted my body to the top of the fence. I was aware I was sobbing. With no small effort, I forced myself to make the encounter with the train a distant thing, something that had occurred to someone else, to push away the nearness of it and concentrate on a this latest challenge. Sitting atop the fence, I looked down and saw a chaos of low-growing ivy covering the ground beyond, which I expected to be soft and spongy, but when I landed it was as hard as concrete, and a thrill of pain squirmed through the knee I had already injured clearing the first fence. Confused, my fingers sought the ground through the tendrils of ivy and found a slab of stone; in the darkness I made out a line of lead letters: *AKEN FROM US AGED 4*. I was in a graveyard.

This was almost comforting to me. If there was a graveyard, there might be a church, and if there were a church, there might be a village, even a telephone box. As my eyes became accustomed to the gloom, I saw the shadowy shapes of a mute crowd of crosses, pillars and obelisks gathered around me. Ahead, an ancient yew squatted, its extraordinarily ugly trunk twisted and split into two, and beyond that, my heart leapt to see the dark outline of a church. A gravel path, flooded now, wound through the bare earth under the yew, soaking my shoes afresh.

My excitement was short-lived. Rounding the corner, I saw that heavy barred gates had been drawn across the church porch and padlocked shut: a piece of hardboard with a hand-written notice stapled to it was tied to the bars, but rain had washed the words away.

The church was in a curious condition. The windows were boarded shut, but from each one rose a black scar which covered the flint walls and climbed to the roof; the roof itself was covered with a tarpaulin which hummed quietly with the incessant downpour. Did someone set fire to the church, in the not-too distant past? Did it accidentally burn? It hardly mattered. The church had been burned, and its roof was missing. The only prospect of shelter was the roofed lychgate at the entrance to the churchyard. I made my way over to it and sat down on the large slate slab that formed the threshold between the rest of the world and what was presumably holy ground. I didn't think I needed to rest, but the second I sat, my body shook and trembled with relief.

I sat for a while, no longer hearing the rain, staring up at the bluish flint skin of the church, the scars of smoke along its flanks giving it a factory-like air, as if it were a place that made or destroyed things by burning and smelting. Eventually, the cold seeped into my wet clothes, and I staggered to my feet once more. My head swam.

From the corner of my vision, I saw movement. Somewhere in the black, sodden wilderness of the graveyard, the weight of something shifted and tensed. An animal? Would any animal be out in this? I peered into the unclean darkness under the yew tree, but nothing could be seen. Had I seen anything? Nothing moved now. I turned my back on the graveyard and walked through the lychgate, into the rain.

Outside the walls of the graveyard, the overgrown road was little more than a cart track of sticky clay and gravel, the branches of the trees stretching above me like the arms of blind men, feeling their way across the pathway to find each other. About fifty yards from the church, the cart track turned sharply to the right, winding its way through some more woods and disappearing into blackness, but there was also a kissing gate, leading into another field.

I didn't want to take another footpath, but neither did I much fancy traipsing along this dismal cart track through yet more dark woods. *Make a decision*, I thought. The field beyond the gate looked like grazing land; rough terrain, but better lit than the woodland track, which vanished fairly quickly into absolute blackness.

I looked back along the cart track, the way I had come. And I saw.

A dark shape detached itself with careful slowness from the mouthful of darkness held by the lychgate.

There was someone standing by the lychgate, unmoving. Impossibly, someone else was out in this weather. I had been right – they had been watching me in the churchyard, and they were watching me now. I couldn't discern any detail at this distance, but I knew – as surely as I knew anything – that they were looking at me, scrutinising me. And still, they didn't move, staring right at me. The flesh on my arms prickled in waves.

Were they closer now? No. They didn't move. My mind immediately started to dissuade me of what my eyes had seen. Maybe there had been some unseen gatepost back there, some forgotten standing stone, tall, weather-roughened, marking the boundary of a long-vanished estate, or a grand house that was now just foundations. My vision swam as I stared at it, trying to work out what it was, where its outline began and ended. No, I had been tricked. The night and the rain and the awful surroundings and my near-death by speeding train had addled my senses, sharpening some, dulling others. And yet, the feeling that I was being watched was very strong, and remained strong. But all of that was just me, surely? I was manufacturing threats, reasons to keep walking, to keep going. The feeling of being assessed, as if someone were staring straight through me. I knew the feeling wasn't real, but I was equally unable to make it subside.

I glanced back to the kissing gate, then back to the woods, reviewing my options. I still had no idea which way to go next. I was tempted to cut across the field. Although the ground looked rough, grass would be easier to navigate than whatever had become of the track through the woods in this storm. I might even be able to see some landmarks from the brow of the hill. The field it was, then.

Idly, I turned back to glance at the road behind me. I swore in shock, startling myself with the sound of my own voice.

The dark shape had peeled away entirely from the lychgate. It was out in the cart track now, frozen, unmoving.

After a second or two, it moved, and there could be no doubt any more. Somebody was following me. I froze, staring stupidly at the figure. Who would be out on a night like this? Who could be here, in this place? A poacher, or a local lunatic, some barely tolerated village flasher or child molester or alcoholic. The echo of my spoken curse rang in my ears, proof that my shock was genuine, that this was really happening.

The figure advanced, calmly, towards me. I glanced to my left again, down the woodland track, assessing its viability as an escape route, then turned back to look at the figure. I gasped. It seemed to have covered half the distance between us, and yet it still moved with the same measured pace.

I stared and stared at the black figure, until finally my resolve broke and I ran, hurtling down the cart track into the dark woods. What was I doing? If it was a local, they would surely know the woods, the fields, the pathways and cut-throughs. I would not be able to hide from them, not on their home terrain. I stopped to glance back and saw, at the place where the road turned, where I had been frozen merely seconds before, the black figure, outlined in the pale storm-light like a dark monolith, the shape of a man. I got an impression of height, of awkward thinness, of purpose. I saw very clearly that its feet were turned inward.

And then I was running, as fast as I could, along the overgrown track, my heart hammering as the branches and briars clawed at me and the darkness thickened. I ran without thought or intention, faster than I ever thought possible, and I didn't stop until the branches of the trees cleared overhead and the woods fell back behind me. I stopped and turned, fear racing through me, howling for breath. The trees held the darkness like cobwebs as I stared defiantly back at them. My skin crawled again, and I slapped my forearms.

Wriggling and bursting out of the trees like a maggot from rotten flesh, the dark outline came, and I was running again. Terror swept through me in waves.

Ahead of me, a hillock-dotted field of waist-high grass, criss-crossed by fox paths. Something white and man-sized stood sentry-like to one side and I noticed as I fled past it that it was a rusting electric cooker. Soon afterwards, I stumbled around a pile of rotting wooden pallets, and bounced off the crumbling chassis of a car. I skirted the dead car and made for a line of oil drums. Crouching behind them, I could see that my tormentor still advanced, crashing noiselessly through the undergrowth in a straight line towards the piles of rubbish, towards me. I realised I was crying.

Deeper into the maze of paths and fox trails. The weeds were shoulder height now, and although parts of machinery and other debris lay waiting to trip me, terror sharpened my vision. The rain seemed to have subsided a little, and visibility was better. I ran as fast as I dared, terrified that I might twist an ankle, or stumble and fall, and that I might be forced to see, to understand, and what was currently only terrible suspicion might be forced to collapse into horrible reality.

A line of tall silver birch loomed up ahead, trunks bone-white against the darkness beyond. Instinctively, I made for them. I reached a line of ragged stones delineating the edge of the rubbish tip and clutched the papery trunk of the nearest tree. From behind it, I looked out into the haze of weeds that formed a sea between the islands of scrap.

And there it stood, silent and unmoving, staring back at me. It was still some distance away. It simply stood now, like a chess piece, and once again I was convinced that I was being looked at, stared at, assessed, with an intensity that was unbearable. The rain began to pick up again, but still the figure didn't move, although undoubtedly they saw me. Something told me they would go no further.

'What do you want?' I could almost mistake it for a stone pillar again.

Keeping my eyes on the figure, I retreated into the trees. I took one step back, then another.

And then the ground gave way beneath me, and I was falling.

I was plummeting, at speed, down a steep, tree-lined slope, flailing for a handhold. I bounced off my back and onto my front; then fell again, crashing backwards through a curtain of ivy and, for a terrifying second, was in free fall, before a bank of damp river sand broke my fall, knocking the breath from me.

I sat up. The palms of both hands were warm and raw and I knew they had sustained cuts, but the light down here was so bad I couldn't tell if what covered my hands was mud or blood. I wiped them on my jacket and sat up. Miraculously, I seemed to be unharmed. My trousers were torn at both knees and my upper lip tasted of blood, but there was no other damage. I had been incredibly lucky. If my head had hit a rock on the way down, I might easily have died. And who would have ever found me, down here? I shuddered and was quietly and politely sick on the ground, then looked at my surroundings.

I was on a broad, flat bank of dark sand and pebbles at the edge of a fast-flowing stream. Looking up I could see what I had fallen through: the stream had, over the years, carved out this hollow under the roots of an oak tree, and the ivy had grown over the network of exposed roots. It was this canopy I had fallen through. I saw again how lucky I had been, though luck is always relative. I got to my feet and looked up, squinting through the rain, staring up at the slope, expecting again to see that terrible shape peering silently over the lip of the precipice, and though I waited expectantly for minutes on end, I was alone.

Follow the stream. What else was there to do? My eyes had adjusted to the darkness now, and it proved relatively easy to follow the babbling line of silver as it snaked its way through the trees and roots, shadowed as it was by a miniature shoreline of black sand. The occasional car tyre or beer bottle stuck out of the glistening ooze, but even these last traces of the rubbish tip fell away, and then there was just me and the rain-swollen stream.

I reasoned that it would be virtually impossible for anybody to follow me down here, but nonetheless, I kept looking back, over my shoulder, where my tracks showed deep black in the mud. But there was nothing. No one followed me.

I staggered along the stream bed for half an hour or so. My legs were weak. I struggled on, looking in earnest now for a place where I might stop, and rest. The stream twisted and turned through rank weeds and rotting stumps, but eventually, mercifully, obliged. The floor of the valley carved by the stream widened and flattened, the shore became broader, and there were large, smooth stones I could sit on. I sank down onto one, gratefully.

My head bobbed onto my chest and when my neck jerked up again, the woods were much lighter. The air was blue, paling and whitening as night became day. I had been out all night. My teeth chattered and my wet clothes clung to me. I ran a hand through my damp hair, smoothing it back over my head. The little glade was quiet save for the sound of the stream, chattering over the rocks. Looking up, out of the gully, to the sky where the day was struggling to arrive, I saw a giant diagonal cross standing sentinel, and eventually recognised it as the sails of a windmill.

On hands and knees, I knelt at the water's edge and cupped my hands, drinking the numbingly cold liquid. It tasted fresh and earthy, not quite like anything I'd ever drunk before. I stood up.

Twenty feet or so away, tied to the trunk of a dead elder, was a scrap of cloth. It had been very deliberately tied there, very neatly, secured with a series of tight knots. Coming closer, I saw that it was, of all things, a tie. The light was weak, but I could make out the colours, blue and red, blue and red. I approached it with a sense of something important happening, and I was suddenly terrified I would miss it, fail to grasp its significance.

Some way away, hanging from a tree, a rotting green satchel turned and turned, as it had surely turned for a long time, hanging from the tree by a single frayed strap.

Over the small ridge where the elder grew lay another patch of dirty silt, which time and the stream had formed into a round island, almost circular, a miniature oxbow lake of black mud. The sand here was undisturbed, perfectly smooth. In the centre of this disc, trapped within, the bare remnants of a figure lay half-buried, as if frozen for ever in the act of burying itself. It was nothing but bones now, clad in the filthy remains of a white shirt and a grey skirt, but once, it had been a person. What had been the head lay on one side, empty eye sockets staring with burning black intensity at absolutely nothing, the bottom quarter of the face buried in the sand, the lower jaw at an impossible angle, gaping wide-open in an enormous, crooked laugh.

I became aware that somebody was laughing. Very loudly, but hollowly, without reason or purpose, as if the part of their brain that was supposed to find things funny was simply being stimulated with electric current, or merely jabbed with a pencil, so that everything was funny. I was scared by the laughter, somehow; it sounded so strange, no voice I recognised. The more scared I grew, the stronger the laughter became, getting louder and louder, each successive guffaw becoming less and less meaningful, but more and more powerful, until it filled all the space there was, both inside and outside my head, rolling across the sky and all the land, licking at the world I knew like flame and scouring it away, away, until there was nothing left.

Epilogue

There was no going back now.

When I first thumbed the postcode into Waze, sitting at a table in a Caffè Nero, nursing a flat white, I experienced a feeling of daring, of betting myself I wouldn't do something, only to prove to myself that I would. Some weirdness with postcodes or parish boundaries had occurred since then, and the string of letters and numbers that signified a destination was not familiar to me. Or maybe I had never known the postcode to begin with. Either way, we were leaving. There was no going back now.

In the passenger seat, Dad embarked on another spectacular series of coughs, and asked me to turn up Radio 4, as the news was coming up. I informed him that it was already loud enough, but his complaints became incessant, and I pushed the volume up so far the bodywork of the car shook. The CEO of a British tech startup that had developed a piece of software for predicting user purchases based on personal data was being interviewed about the news that his company had just been acquired by Google for something in the billions. The CEO sounded neither interested nor bored; merely present, as if the acquisition of many billions of pounds was not really a serious matter for serious people. The pips sounded at mid-day and the news began.

There was very little traffic on a Thursday lunchtime. The grey road shone dully, spotted with pools of oily rainwater where trapped rainbows curled like ferns. We passed a series of retail parks and business estates, huge corrugated metal hangars, silently shouting their names at the aluminium sky. *Sports Direct. Argos. Homebase. Amazon click and collect.* Above us, an enormous steel mast supported an advert for a new Hugo Boss fragrance. A man flanked by two identical women descended a glass staircase. The three figures laughed feral laughs in each other's faces, for-ever, and then the lights changed.

'Where are we?' asked Dad. I ignored him. It was a hard question to answer, anyway. Where were we? A crazy golf course by the slip road, with a Mayan theme. A vast pagoda that was a Chinese food wholesaler. A southern ranch-style BBQ diner. A burger restaurant with life-size fibreglass dinosaurs baring their teeth over empty plastic garden furniture. All blur-ring past at the side of a main road which was, and could only ever be, in suburban England. The sun flared coldly for a few seconds, like a bare bulb of low wattage, and the sky and the road were suddenly and spectacularly made of gleaming mer-cury. Then the thick clouds clotted and the vision was over.

'This bloke again,' said Dad, talking about a pundit the host was interviewing. 'All he ever does is these programmes where he says his opinion. I swear he just says the same thing over and over again.'

'You said this earlier,' I said.

'Did I?' Dad looked grumpily out of the window. After a few minutes, he offered again the only other thing he'd been saying since the journey began.

'Can we get something to eat?'

'When we get on the motorway,' I said. Do all children and parents eventually swap roles? Is that their fate? Ahead of us, a semi-circular block of newly built luxury flats loomed, six storeys of blue brick, with balconies of orange and yellow and green, with a Tesco Metro and three vacant shop premises set into the ground floor.

Dad snorted. 'Hang on, I know this place! I swear I used to come out here birdwatching when it was a marsh. Now look at it.'

I snorted too. 'There hasn't been a marsh round here since the 1800s. You're not that old.'

'It was *somewhere* round here. You used to get reed warblers. Kingfishers. All kinds of things. Now look at it.'

The lights were red, so I looked. RETAIL OPPORTUNITIES, a sign said. Another said SHOWROOM OPEN, and a third said LAST FEW UNITS: URBAN – FUNKY – STYLISH. It was virtually impossible to have an opinion about anything I was looking at, whether it was the small, overlit supermarket, or the empty, expensive block that housed it, or the cashpoint, or the complete lack of any people.

'It's a depressing part of town,' I said. 'But it's the way out to the motorway. It's not the Appian Way, Dad.'

He was silent. The lights turned to green.

'This is the price you pay for convenience.'

I looked over at him. He had nodded off.

We stopped at another Caffè Nero at a motorway services, to get a sandwich for Dad and more coffee for me.

'Weren't we just here?' said Dad, looking around him.

'No, Dad. That was on the way out of town. You've been asleep for an hour.'

'Hmm,' said Dad, as if this information was not to be trusted. He looked around, chewing the air. With the sudden unguarded openness of an infant, he placed his hand tenderly on mine.

'Where are we going, Tim?'

'I've told you,' I said. 'We're going to look at a place for you. It came highly recommended.'

'I don't mean that,' said Dad. 'I mean, how are we getting there?' His hand was thin and cold, and its grip was very strong.

'I don't—We're in the car? You remember?'

'I don't want to go through Cambridgeshire,' he said plainly.

'What? We're not anywhere near there, Dad.'

'I don't want to go there.'

'We're in Essex, on the A12. We're nowhere near the M11, which would be—'

Dad wasn't listening. 'Never going *there*,' he said carefully. His eyes were wet. 'Not since . . . you know.'

'Dad—'

'Not since they found her there.'

I looked down at the table.

'*Never*,' said Dad.

The car's bonnet devoured the dull grey miles. Dad maintained a brooding silence. I thought he might sleep again, but I was wrong. The weather brightened a little, and the sun warmed the black trees and brambles that lined the road.

'We still don't know,' said Dad, eventually.

'Don't know what?'

'We don't know who found her.'

'Dad—'

'The police get an anonymous call telling them where she is. That's all we know. Somebody calls up and tells them *exactly* where she is, and that person knows exactly *who* she is.'

'Dad,' I said. This was the rarest of his few conversational topics, but the one he was most dogged in refusing to let go of.

'It must have been him,' he said. 'It must have been whoever killed her.'

'We can't know that,' I said. 'It might just have been someone who . . . stumbled across her. Who didn't want to get involved.'

'Pff,' said Dad, as he always did. 'Not where she was. Not hidden like that. You'd have to know. Or be told about it. Or shown. Too much of a coincidence.'

'I don't think we'll ever know, Dad.'

'Do you think the police traced the call? If it's a local number, it might belong to whoever—'

'Dad!' I snapped. 'Can we not talk about this, please? It's – I find it too upsetting.'

He sighed and nodded. Waze told us to come off at the next junction. There were traffic lights at the empty roundabout, and we dutifully waited for them to change. The wind outside stirred last year's dead yellow grass; heads of teasel and thistle bobbed. A short way away, a sparrowhawk kept itself aloft with rapid, silent wingbeats, its attention fixed on something below.

I became aware that Dad was crying.

'My girl,' he said, sobbing gently. *'My little girl.'*

He turned his face away.

Of course, the village had changed.

The tiny shop where I had once bought five bottles of red wine was still a supermarket, but a brightly lit one now, with the branding of one of the larger chains. It had a cashpoint built into the front of it; a revolving plastic sign for the Lotto turned slowly in the faint breeze. And there, just beyond, was the row of small shops where Hattie Wells's bookshop had been. I slowed the car. All of the shopfronts had been refitted; the sagging latticework of the Victorian frontage was long gone. The refurbished units were uniform; it was impossible to say for certain which one had been Hattie's. One shop sold designer soaps and fragrances, two of the others were now small art galleries. In the window of the nearest one, a sculpture of an elongated hare, cast in bronze, sprinted forever along a long piece of driftwood.

And there, at long last, was the B-road lined with trees, and there, at the end of it, was a sign:

HAZELWOOD ELDERCARE
PRIVATE PREMIUM NURSING HOME

Under these words were various badges and medals of accreditation, which Dad peered at suspiciously as we turned the corner.

And there was the house. The dark woods that partially surrounded it had been cleared some way back, so that the house seemed much less cramped, less hemmed in. Similarly, the front lawn was well looked after and recently mowed; flower beds bordered the house, where hydrangeas and rose bushes grew. The basic mismatched shape of the place was unchanged, but the Victorian wing had been augmented and – incredibly – made even uglier, by the addition of a large first-floor extension, with enormous windows, overlooking the neat lawn. The surviving Victorian brickwork had also been professionally cleaned at some point, the bricks glowing a dull, vulgar red, jarring still further with the original features. The seventeenth-century wing, however, was exactly as it was the last time I had seen it, and I stared at it for a long time after we got out of the car.

I helped Dad along the gravel path towards the main entrance.

'I still don't see why we're here,' he said.

The wooden front doors of Yarlings – I could only ever think of it as Yarlings – had been replaced with clear glass ones, onto which a line drawing of the building and the logo of the parent company had been sandblasted. The area immediately inside the doors – where once had been a long, dark wood-panelled corridor, and a large central stairway – had been reconfigured in a way so dramatic and complete that it was, to me, an entirely new space. The walls were painted daffodil yellow and sky blue. Behind a desk sat a woman in her mid-twenties, wearing a white blouse with a green nylon skirt. A gold name-badge pinned to her blouse said KERI, and when she smiled up at me I saw she had a nasal piercing.

'Can I help you?'

'Yes, it's Mr Smith. I called earlier?'

'Smith, Smith – Smith!' she said, clicking a wireless mouse. 'Ah, yes, here you are. And it's . . . Frank?'

'Hello,' said Dad cheerfully. 'I can't live here.'

'Dad! You haven't even seen it yet!'

'I've seen enough, thanks.'

'I'm sorry!' I smiled a watery smile at the young woman. 'It's been a long journey.'

'No, it hasn't,' said Dad. 'Not especially.'

'Well, one of my colleagues will be along shortly to show you the facilities. Maybe you'll change your mind when you see what else we have here.'

*

A few minutes later, a young man dressed in an outfit that made him look like a futuristic medical orderly came and greeted us. His name-badge said ADAM. He walked us through a fire-door and down a corridor that had presumably once been the main one I remembered, that ran through the ground floor.

'I don't know how much you know about the facility?' Adam said cheerily.

'Quite enough, thanks,' said Dad. 'Having seen it.'

'Dad. Please.'

Dad sighed, but was quiet.

'All right then!' said Adam, as if the last few seconds hadn't happened. 'We've twenty-four private rooms here, all offering complete comfort, and the very best in end-of-life care. Most of the rooms have excellent views, especially now that the landscaping has finally been completed on the new gardens at the rear of the house.'

'There are gardens?' said Dad. 'Can I see them? I love a garden.'

'Of course,' said Adam. 'They were designed by an award-wining architect.'

'Fancy that,' said Dad caustically.

We reached the end of the corridor. Adam pushed open a pair of double doors, and we were in the Great Hall.

Smaller, of course, than I remembered, with all the dark wooden panelling now painted a lustrous white. Eight dining tables, with four chairs each, floated on a vast green carpet. The enormous fireplace, alone among everything else around it, was entirely unchanged.

I approached it, almost reverently, and ran my fingertips along the grooves of the circular design etched into it. I felt in that moment that the carving, the incomprehensible sigil, was the only fixed point in the whole universe, and if I focused on it long enough, Hazelwood House would fall away and there would be Yarlings, and everything it represented, and had come to represent, in my mind.

At a nearby table sat the only diner; a very old woman with one severely cataracted eye, quietly slurping soup.

'Impressive, isn't it?' said Adam. 'Good afternoon, Miss Wells.'

I stared at her in wonder. I hadn't recognised her. Old age had mummified her into something smaller and more cramped, hunched over so that her long hair threatened to dip into her soup. She gazed at me for a second with her good eye, then looked away with distaste.

'My books have been stolen,' she said. Her cataracted eye glowed with captive sunlight.

'We'll send someone to look for them, Miss Wells,' Adam said breezily. 'Don't you worry.'

'All my words in them,' muttered Hattie Wells, returning to her soup. 'My *word-hoard*. It's not right.'

'What do you think?' Adam asked us.

'*Somebody* took them,' said Hattie Wells. '*Somebody* knows.'

'I hate it,' said Dad, cheerily.

Adam smiled as if he hadn't heard. 'Well, come through to the lounge. You can talk about it a bit more there.'

Through another corridor, which I was certain was a new addition, and then through a doorway, and we were in the lounge. Although it was now filled with comfortable sofas and armchairs, and a coffee table with a fan of magazines spread out upon it, I knew exactly where we were. The lounge was Tobias Salt's room. There, by the mullioned windows, was where Graham's equipment had stood, and there, above a different fireplace, was where Sally's portrait of Salt had been pinned. Now, there was a nondescript painting in acrylics of a bland Suffolk landscape, under a grey sky. Dad ignored the room entirely and wandered over to the window, to gaze out longingly at the lawn.

'Give it a chance, Dad,' I found myself saying.

'I don't think so, Tim.'

'But you haven't seen all of it yet. You said you wanted to see the gardens.'

'And so I will, Tim. And then we'll go.'

'Dad—'

'Tim,' he said, turning around to look at me. 'I can't die here.'

Dad asked to see the gardens. Adam offered to accompany him, but Dad insisted that directions would be enough.

After Dad left, Adam was clearly keen to leave, but I knew I would never get the chance to ask again. And so, after a few well-placed banalities about the house, I went for the jugular.

'Any ghosts? You'd expect a place this size and age to be haunted.'

He looked at me and smiled. 'You've looked up this place online?'

Of course I had. There wasn't much, but a couple of dedicated paranormal researchers and bloggers had succeeded in digging up fragments of the story of Yarlings, and what had taken place there, although their accounts were sketchy and the stories contradictory.

'No,' I said. 'Why, what does it say?'

Adam smiled. 'Apparently, some kind of ghost-hunt took place here, in the seventies, when it was empty. Bunch of people stayed here and summoned up a demon or something.

So the story goes! Apparently, it all got out of hand and they fled. The north wing caught fire the night they left. The fire destroyed the front parts of the Victorian bit, which is why the extension with the spa is there today.'

I had not heard this last part before. *The front parts of the Victorian bit.* Graham's office.

'Personally,' Adam continued, 'I think it's a load of rubbish. I've been here since we opened, eighteen months ago, and you couldn't imagine anywhere less spooky if you tried. I think the ghost hunters – if they were even real – probably just scared themselves stupid and started believing any old thing.'

'Probably,' I said.

'Come on,' said Adam. 'I'll take you back to the dining hall. You can keep an eye on your dad from there.'

The new gardens, at the rear of the house, were impressive. A large area had been reclaimed from the woods, and around a central circular lawn of fresh turf ran a path of orange gravel, bordered by radial beds of cottage-garden shrubs and plants; purple and green sage, rosemary and lavender. From the windows of the Great Hall, I watched Dad walk the entire circle. Two tired-looking men sat, immobile as statues, on one of the benches.

Dad stopped to talk to them, and after a couple of seconds, I saw them all shake with unmistakeable mirth. Dad had made a joke, and they had all laughed. It was bewildering. What did dead men have to laugh about?

I thought of everything that had happened here, in the space that had been Yarlings. And I thought of everything that had happened since. Mum had clung on for another year or so, a whimpering shadow, prone to fits of shuddering and howling.

It had been almost a relief when she finally died. I had eventu-ally gone to university, been married, and divorced, and married, and divorced again. I had no children, but my first wife and I had endured two miscarriages. I had had several careers, in which I had failed entirely to make any kind of mark. I had been in and out of therapy, and, after the collapse of my first marriage, had briefly been sectioned. I lived in a house I disliked, somewhere I didn't care for. I was too much of an intellectual snob, too quick to judge someone for a mal-apropism or a misused word, to form any meaningful friendships, so I was mostly alone. If I had to characterise my life, the image that always sprang to mind was a slow descent, a narrowing of horizons and potential, missed chances and bad luck, funnelling downwards, always downwards, to the dissatisfactions of the present. It had been forty-two years since I was last in this house, when, despite the stain of tragedy, everything had seemed possible, and the world, and I, had seemed limitless.

To say I never saw anyone from Yarlings again would not be quite true; once, whilst channel-surfing late at night, I saw Polly. Her hair was streaked with silver and she wore glasses, but her bright, questioning eyes and sardonic smile were unchanged. The onscreen caption identified her as *'Dr Polly Kendrick, professor of psychology'*. The documentary she was part of was about the abuse of children and young adults.

'You,' said Hattie Wells brusquely, as I crossed the room. Something in her voice made me stop dead by her table. I wondered if she had been a headmistress, once.

'Who's your friend?'

'He's not my friend,' I said. 'He's my dad.'

'What? Oh no, not *him*. *He* went out to the garden. I meant the other—' She looked unsure. 'Sorry, when you came in earlier, you had someone else with you.'

'Adam? The orderly?'

'No. Not Adam.'

'Someone else?'

'Yes. A man.'

I said nothing.

'Tall. Thin.'

I said nothing.

Hattie Wells looked puzzled. 'Where did he go?'

'Not far,' I said. 'He never goes far.'

Acknowledgements

All books are written over many different times and places, and with the help of many, many people. This book is no different.

I'd like to thank the following people, who made sure, in various places and times, that this book got written. Joel Morris, Jason Hazeley and Marc Haynes for unquestioning support. Zoë Tomalin for friendship and critical reading. Jess Williams for endless help and cheerleading, Simon Skevington for music choices. Alice Shaell and Eileen Peters for coffee and feedback. Rebecca Asher for support. Louisa Heinrich for reading and clarifying. Bob Fischer, whose landmark June 2017 article in issue 354 of *The Fortean Times* convinced me there was life in the twitching corpse of '70s Hauntology yet. Tim Worthington for help with some of the stickier period details. Jim Sangster, Mark Evans, Carrie Quinlan, Neil Edmond, Alex Young, Tora Young, Si, Annie Bryson and Shaun McTernan, Justine Jordan, Jo Unwin, Ed Wilson, Carrie Plitt, Dan Bunyard, Arabella McGuigan, Gareth Tunley, Alice Lowe, Debbie Easton, Dr. Carol Meale, and Barbara and Howard Moss. Carla, and Mum.

To Alexander Cochran at Conville and Walsh for agreeing

to take this on, and to Jason Arthur at Heinemann for taking it on and not letting go. Also Kate McQuaid at Heinemann, and Sarah Bance who diligently proofed and Henry Petrides who designed the striking cover.

And an endless, endless debt of thanks to my amazing wife, Victoria Moss, and our baffling, deafening, brilliant daughter, Sophia Raie.

This book is respectfully dedicated to the memory of the one and only Paul Condon. Happy trails, fella.